A Winter's Tale

CARRIE ELKS

Piatkus
An imprint of
Little, Brown Book Group
Carmelite House
50 Victoria Embankment
London EC4Y 0DZ

An Hachette UK Company
www.hachette.co.uk

www.littlebrown.co.uk

PIATKUS

First published in Great Britain in 2017 by Piatkus

1 3 5 7 9 10 8 6 4 2

Copyright © 2017 Carrie Elks

A CIP catalogue record for this book
is available from the British Library.

ISBN 978-0-349-41557-4

Typeset in Caslon by M Rules
Printed and bound in Great Britain by
Clays Ltd, St Ives plc

Papers used by Piatkus are from well-managed forests
and other responsible sources.

1

I am not bound to please thee with my answers
— The Merchant of Venice

'Kitty Shakespeare,' he said, looking up at her, his lips curved into a smile. 'That's an unusual name. Where does it come from?' Drake Montgomery was the executive assistant to the famous movie producer, Everett Klein. He had her resumé balanced on his lap like a napkin on a diner. His long legs were crossed in front of him, his elbows casually balanced on the armrests of his chair. On one side he was flanked by a beautiful woman he'd introduced as Lola, giving no clue as to her job title or reason for being there. On the other was Mr Klein's other assistant, Sheryl. Older, with glasses that kept sliding down her nose, leading to a constant battle with her finger. She pushed them up, the glasses slid down. It was almost hypnotic to watch.

Taking a deep breath, Kitty looked around the room. Like all the others she'd been interviewed in, it was bland and impersonal. She'd long since given up hope that she'd be allowed into the producer's office, where no doubt the walls were plastered with movie posters and photographs of actors, and the shelves stacked with constantly dusted awards. A mere intern – no, not even an intern, more a wannabe – didn't merit entrance to the inner sanctum, and certainly not an introduction to the producer himself. Which in Everett Klein's case seemed like more of a blessing than anything else. One of the top producers in Hollywood, he had a reputation that struck terror into everybody that came into contact with him. He was larger than life, with a temper to match.

And of course, everybody wanted to work for him. Having an internship at Klein Productions would be like getting a star on the Hollywood Walk of Fame. According to her supervisor at UCLA, even God stopped talking whenever Everett Klein opened his mouth.

With every second that passed, she could feel her heart rate increasing. She hated interviews. Hated talking about herself at all. Every time she opened her mouth she could feel her face heating up until she resembled a ripe strawberry. No wonder she hadn't got an internship yet.

Drake lifted her resumé up to his eyes, frowning, as if it was the first time he'd read her details. Then he laid the paper back down on the table, folding his beautifully manicured hands on his lap. His eyes scanned her, taking her in. Was he staring at her bitten fingernails? She self-consciously shifted in her seat, trying to hide her hands beneath her as she kept the friendly smile on her lips. 'Kitty's the name my older sister gave me when I was born. She said I looked so cute all curled up in my cot, she thought I was a kitty cat. The name stuck.' She glanced up at him to see if he believed her. It was only a partial lie, after all. The truth was much less heartwarming.

Though according to family lore it was Lucy, the eldest of

her three sisters, who gave her the name, the rest was a fabrication. In reality their mother had walked back into the house from the hospital, carrying a newborn Kitty in her arms, and told Kitty's sisters she had a present for them.

'A baby?' Lucy had said, her distaste obvious. She already had two sisters – why on earth would she need another? 'I'd much rather have a KitKat.'

Yeah, Kitty wasn't planning on sharing that one with the perfectly coiffed Drake Montgomery.

'And you're British?' he asked, as if her clipped accent and place of birth on her resumé wasn't enough to give it away.

She could feel the tell-tale beads of sweat breaking out on her forehead. Why wouldn't her foot stop tapping? She really needed to focus. 'That's right. I was born in London. I moved here last year for a postgraduate course in Film Studies.' She could feel the self-consciousness washing over her again. She swallowed hard, though her mouth felt as dry as the desert. They were all so intense as they stared at her, she felt more like a specimen than an interviewee.

'And before that you worked with children?' He winced, showing his perfectly white teeth.

'I was a nanny for a few years, yes.' She nodded vigorously. Was she overcompensating? She was definitely on her way to hyperventilating. 'After I graduated with my bachelor's degree I wasn't sure what I wanted to do next, so I took a job with an American couple living in London.'

Unlike most of her fellow students at UCLA, she hadn't gone straight onto the course from her undergraduate studies. She hadn't been able to afford to, for a start. It had taken two years of vigorous saving to pay for her year over here.

'That must have been interesting.' Sheryl, the other

assistant, offered her the tiniest of smiles. 'I imagine it's a bit like looking after the acting talent.'

'Except children have less tantrums,' Lola joined in, her voice deadpan.

'Well, yes.' Drake cleared his throat, then hastily changed the subject, as though the possibility of children might be catching. 'What made you decide to move over here to study?'

Kitty grabbed the glass of water that Sheryl had kindly placed on the table in front of her, lifting it up to moisten her lips. She could feel her heart pounding in her chest as she tried to remember the words she'd rehearsed over and again in the mirror. How was it possible to explain the way that movies had saved her as a child? The way she'd immersed herself in the silver screen, found herself comforted by strangers pretending to be somebody else. The way she'd dreamed of having the kind of Hollywood family that only existed in fairy tales.

She swallowed down her mouthful of water, catching Drake's expectant gaze as she replaced the glass on the table. 'I've always wanted to make movies,' she said quietly. 'From the earliest age I was fascinated by films. Not just the stories, but how they're made.' She offered him the faintest of smiles. 'I want to transport people to another world, take their worries away for an hour or two. I want to inspire them and entertain them, and make them leave the movie theatre wanting more.'

It had sounded so much better when she said it in front of the mirror. For a start, her voice hadn't been wobbly. And she hadn't been wriggling in a hard plastic chair, either.

Lola checked her phone, then whispered rapidly in Drake's ear, her voice too low to make out her words. Drake's eyes grew wide. 'Tell them I'm busy,' he whispered back. He pulled his own phone out and looked at it, swallowing hard when he read

4

the screen. He flicked the button on the side that turned the volume on to mute. The girl shrugged, and tapped a message on her own phone without bothering to look up.

Kitty's hands started to tremble in her lap. How many interviews like this had she been on? She'd already lost count. The rejection letters were piling up on her desk in the Melrose apartment she shared with three other girls, and they were just from those who bothered replying. But this one felt even worse – they seemed to have forgotten she was even here. The bead of sweat that had been clinging to her hairline finally started rolling down her overheated face.

A buzzing noise cut through the loaded silence of the room. Drake checked his phone screen again, wincing when he saw the caller. 'Shit,' he whispered, clearly not wanting to be heard. 'Now she's calling me.'

Clearing his throat, he looked up at Kitty. 'I really need to take this,' he said, sliding his thumb across the screen, and lifting the phone to his ear. 'Drake Montgomery speaking.' He paused as he listened to the person on the other end. 'No, Mr Klein's on set today, he can't be disturbed. He left strict instructions not to forward any calls.' Another pause as he winced again. Clearly whoever was on the other end of the line wasn't happy with the brush-off. 'I understand, Mrs Klein, I really do. That must be awful. But I still can't patch you through.'

The shouting that resulted from his refusal echoed around the room. Drake pulled the receiver away from his ear, his face a picture of panic.

'Do you have any idea how hard it is to get a nanny around here?' the female voice screeched. 'I need Everett to pull in some favours. You get him on the phone right now, before I lose it, Drake. This is a life and death situation here.'

Lola let out a little snigger, and Drake looked at her, his eyes wide. 'Hold on, Mrs Klein, I'm just in a meeting. Let me take this call outside.' He stood up, and covered the mouthpiece. Kitty didn't dare meet his eye, she was too afraid she'd join in the giggles.

'I'm so sorry, I have to go, I think we have enough to make a decision, though,' Drake said, looking almost apologetic. 'Sheryl will show you out. Thank you for your time.' With that, he pulled the door closed behind him, leaving her staring open-mouthed at the two women left in the room.

A glance at her watch told her she'd been here for less than ten minutes. That had to be a new record. It was only a matter of time before the rejection letter arrived in her mailbox, and she added it to the stack she already had.

It was officially time to start panicking.

Even after living in Los Angeles for a year, she still hadn't got used to the temperate climate. As she left the shiny office building that housed Klein Productions, Kitty stepped onto the pavement, feeling the sun warming her skin as she walked towards the parking garage. It was early December, but the temperatures were still in the mid-sixties, warm enough to walk about the town without a jacket. She couldn't remember the last time it had rained. Over here, a bad day consisted of a couple of wispy clouds that occasionally obliterated the sun. No wonder everybody looked so healthy and tanned all the time. It was almost impossible not to.

In a desperate attempt to look festive, the shops and offices lining the street had decorated their windows, filling them with fake snow and tinsel, and trees that sparkled with hundreds of tiny lights. But even with the faux bonhomie it was almost impossible to feel Christmassy. For a moment she thought about London – of the wet streets, of the darkness that descended before four in the afternoon, of the roasted chestnut stands and the hot-chocolate sellers, all the sights and aromas that made the season feel right.

And none of them were here.

It was strange, really, that a city whose livelihood depended on selling the idea of the perfect American Christmas had to fake it for themselves.

Climbing into her small Fiat, she felt her phone buzzing in her pocket. She slid her keys into the ignition, leaving them dangling there, before lifting her mobile and checked the caller. *Cesca*.

There was something about seeing her sister's name that always made Kitty smile. As the youngest of four sisters, Kitty had always looked up to them, and even as adults she looked forward to speaking to them.

'Hello?'

'Kitty? How are things over there?' Cesca's voice was warm. 'It's pissing down here. I told Sam that next time he wants to film on location he needs to choose somewhere warm with a beach.'

'I thought he was over all that lifeguard stuff.' Sam Carlton – Cesca's boyfriend – was an Italian-American actor, best known for his role in *Summer Breeze* – a movie franchise about a sexy teenage heart-throb. He'd met Cesca the previous summer, when they'd both been staying at a villa in Italy. She'd spent hours on the telephone telling her sisters how arrogant he was, and how much she disliked him, when they'd all known she was falling for him. The rest was Hollywood history. He'd declared his love for Cesca on a TV chat show then flown into London to sweep her off her feet.

7

One of the best parts of living over here in LA had been when Cesca and Sam were in town. Sadly, their visits to the city of stars were all too rare these days.

'There's only so much of the tortured, rain-soaked character movies I can take. Give me Sam in a pair of red shorts and nothing else any day.'

'A million American girls would agree with you,' Kitty said, smiling. 'There was an outcry when he said he wouldn't be starring in any more *Summer Breeze* movies.'

'Yeah, well everybody's replaceable, even Sam. And don't tell him you said that thing about a million girls – his head is big enough already.' Cesca's voice lowered an octave. 'And how are you? Have you had any news about your internship yet?'

'I just left another interview,' Kitty told her. She leaned her head back on her seat, her legs stretching out until her feet hit the pedals.

'How did it go?'

'About as good as the others,' she said. 'Which means terrible. I got all sweaty and panicky again, and said the stupidest things. I even made up an idiotic story about Lucy calling me a cat.' It was time to face it, she was terrible at interviews. 'Every time they asked me a question, I felt like an actor who'd forgotten his lines.'

'Who was it with?' Cesca's tone was sympathetic. 'Maybe Sam can have a word for you?'

'It was for an internship with Everett Klein.'

'Oh. Yeah, I don't think Sam could say much to change that guy's mind. I've heard on the grapevine he's a bit of an arsehole.'

'So have I,' Kitty confessed. 'But to be honest, I didn't even meet him. It was his assistant who was supposed to interview me. But even he couldn't concentrate on me, he was too busy talking to some screaming woman on his phone.'

Cesca sighed, her soft breaths echoing down the line. 'Do you want me to talk to Sam about helping you with this? He must have connections, I bet he could help you find an internship in no time.'

'That's very kind of you, but no thank you.' Kitty closed her eyes, blocking out the shaft of sun that had found its way through the gaps in the concrete wall. It wouldn't feel right asking Sam for help. She didn't want to be known as the girl who only found a job thanks to her sister's boyfriend. 'I want to do this by myself.'

'There's no shame in asking for help,' Cesca said softly. 'I should know, I thought I could do everything on my own, and I just ended up digging my own hole.'

Cesca's problems were well known among the Shakespeare sisters. At the age of eighteen she'd written an amazing play, and won a contest to have it staged in the West End. What had followed was a spectacular fall from grace, leaving Cesca destitute and depressed, barely able to support herself.

Thank goodness she was on the mend now. During her time in Italy she hadn't only managed to fall in love with Sam, but she'd also written a new play.

'I'm not at rock bottom yet,' Kitty said lightly, though sometimes it felt as though she might be teetering on the edge. 'I'll keep practising – who knows, maybe I'll be able to get through one without breaking out in a sweat. But if things get worse, I'll let you know, OK?'

'OK.' Cesca sounded reluctant to agree. 'But seriously, think about the offer. Sometimes all you need is a little step up.'

'I'll think about it,' Kitty promised, knowing full well she wouldn't.

'And we'll see you for Christmas in London, won't we?' Cesca asked. 'Have you booked your tickets yet?'

Kitty rolled her bottom lip between her teeth, thinking about her negative bank balance. She really needed to find some extra hours at the restaurant she'd been working at. 'I haven't made any concrete plans,' she told her sister. 'I'll let you know when I do.'

There was a pause for a moment. Kitty could hear the pounding of the rain against the window wherever Cesca was. 'You do that,' Cesca finally said. 'Because you know that Lucy will be grilling us all about our plans on Sunday.'

As the eldest of the four Shakespeare sisters, Lucy had played the maternal role in their family since their mother's death when Kitty was only ten. She was the one who took care of them all, worried about them, and made sure they all video conferenced once a week.

'I might be working on Sunday,' Kitty said, trying to remember her rota that week.

'You can run but you can't hide,' Cesca warned her. 'If you don't dial in, you know she'll track you down.'

There were pros and cons to being the youngest of four sisters. Being constantly nagged was a definite con, even if their concern made her feel secretly warm inside.

After they ended their call, she started up the Fiat, driving in the direction of her small shared apartment in Melrose.

She needed to pause, regroup and work out how the hell she was going to find an internship. Her future depended on it, after all.

*

10

Her supervisor paused the video, turning in his black leather chair to look at her. 'This is great, Kitty, really imaginative. I love what you did with the effects in the second half.' He clicked on his mouse, dragging the cursor back across the screen to highlight what he meant. 'What was your budget for this one again?'

Pretty much non-existent. Thank goodness for struggling actors desperate for any kind of exposure. 'We did it on a shoe-string,' she told him. 'Does it show?'

He shrugged. 'A bit, I guess, but you've managed to achieve a lot out of very little. That's a skill in itself.' He scribbled something down on the printed assessment sheet in front of him. 'I noticed a couple of errors at around ten minutes in, and near the end the boom was in shot a few times, but apart from that you're doing great. If you do another run-through of edits, it should be ready to submit in January.'

She couldn't hide the grin that threatened to split her face in two. This short movie was part of her final assessment, and if it was good enough it should smooth her path to graduation.

'And how's the search for an internship going?' he asked her.

Kitty's smile faltered a little bit. She tried to stabilise it, the muscles in her cheeks complaining at the effort. 'I've had a few interviews, but nothing concrete yet.'

'You'll be fine. Even Kevin D'Ananzo has got a placement.'

That was supposed to be reassuring, Kitty guessed, but it was anything but. Even if he was bottom of the class, Kevin D'Ananzo's interview skills were obviously better than hers. It wasn't hard – a stuffed rabbit would probably have impressed Drake Montgomery more than she could.

Stuffing her laptop back into the leather case, she said goodbye to her supervisor and headed out across the campus

11

and to the Young Research Library. The sun was high in the pale blue sky, the light casting shadows on the concrete pavements as the rays were halted by the leafy green trees. The campus was quiet – most undergrads had already returned home for their winter break, and her mind filled the silence with worries, about her lack of internship, her showreel, the two assignments that were due in before she left for Christmas.

She had almost reached the steps to the library – a grey, concrete building that always looked more like a parking garage than a place of learning – when her phone started to buzz. She crouched down, rifling through her heavy leather bag, eventually locating her cell on the third ring.

'Hello?'

'Is that Kitty Shakespeare?' The female voice had a valley twang. For a moment Kitty held her breath, wondering if she was finally going to be offered an internship.

'That's me.' Ten out of ten for originality, Kitty. She was really going to knock them dead.

'My name's Mia Klein. I hear you're looking for a job.'

It felt a bit rude to say she had no idea who Mia Klein was. 'Um, yeah, that's right.' She frowned, trying to work out who it was. She'd been to so many production companies they were all blurring into one. Mia Klein ... hmm.

'That's wonderful. Can you start tomorrow?'

Kitty blinked in the bright sunlight. *Tomorrow?* 'I don't graduate until January,' she pointed out. What was the best way to politely ask who Mia was and what company she was calling from? 'I wasn't looking for a placement until after that.' She felt a little bit of excitement growing inside her. Had she finally managed to get an offer?

12

'Can you work part time?' Mia asked. 'I really need you as soon as possible. It's very important.'

'I guess,' Kitty said, still bent down on the concrete in front of the library. 'Though I work part time in a restaurant, and it's their busiest time of year. I'd need to work my notice.'

'You'll be fully compensated. If I give you an address can you come over tomorrow? Make sure you bring your ID and your references.'

'Will a reference from my college supervisor work?' Kitty asked. She didn't think the restaurant manager would give her anything if she walked out at short notice.

'I was hoping you'd be able to give me the details of your previous employers. The ones in London.'

Kitty frowned. 'But I was a nanny over there.'

'That's right.'

'They won't really be able to say if I'd make a good intern or not,' Kitty told her, still blinking away her confusion. 'My supervisor here at film school will be much better placed to say that.'

Mia laughed, a tinkling waterfall of a chuckle that made Kitty feel about two foot tall. 'Oh no, I'm not calling about an internship, I'm calling about a nanny position. I need somebody to look after Jonas, my son, over the holidays. His last nanny quit, and the new one can't start until January.'

'I'm sorry, did you say your name was Mia Klein?' It was beginning to make sense.

'Yes. My husband's assistant passed me your resumé. Drake Montgomery. I believe you met him.'

'Oh yes. I definitely met him.' He'd made a big impression, after all. Especially when he abandoned the interview halfway through.

'So can you make it tomorrow?' Mia asked. 'At about two.'

'Um.' Kitty looked up at the library, at the grey walls, the shiny windows, her crouched body reflected in the glass.

What was it her eldest sister always said? Never look a gift horse in the mouth. The only problem was, she wasn't sure if this offer would turn out to be a gift or a poisoned chalice. It wasn't an internship after all. Nowhere near. But it was an opportunity to prove herself, to get close to one of the top producers in the town.

She thought again of that pile of rejection letters, and of Kevin D'Ananzo, the student at the bottom of the class who'd still managed to achieve what she'd found so elusive.

'Sure, I'll be there,' she finally said, standing and picking her bag up. 'Just text me the address.'

2

Speak what we feel, not what we ought to say

– King Lear

'So your brother is back in town. How does that make you feel?'

Adam looked at his therapist for a moment, rubbing his bearded jaw with his hand. He felt like a blinding spotlight was shining on him every time the man asked him a question. How many more hours would he have to spend here, answering questions that made every muscle in his body tense up? It had been what, three months since his first appointment, which made it another month until he'd fulfilled his commitment. The one he'd made when the LAPD had agreed to only issue him with a caution.

Another month of inquisitions. He could do that, couldn't he?

He moved his hand around to the back of his neck, rubbing the itchy skin there. His hair was getting long – longer than he'd ever worn it before. 'I haven't seen him,' Adam admitted, pulling at the collar of his checked shirt. Even the mention of Everett made his skin crawl. 'So it doesn't make me feel anything at all.'

Martin – his therapist – stared at him for a moment, as though he could see through the bluster and the hair and the muscle Adam had cultivated as a shield. 'But he's here in West Virginia? He's staying with your parents, right?'

'Yeah.'

'And you still haven't seen him?' Martin frowned. 'Are you actively avoiding him?'

Adam stretched his long legs in front of him, noticing the dirt encrusted on his old, frayed jeans. It had been a while since he'd bought any new clothes. A while since he'd done much of anything, except whittle and sledge and pretend everything was OK. He was teetering on the edge between 'he'll get over it' and 'we need to talk about Adam'. He'd like to stay on the easier side if he could, even if that meant doing a little clothes shopping.

'It's a big house,' Adam pointed out. 'And I don't even live in it. I'm at least a ten-minute walk from the main building. I don't need to be going over there every day.'

'When did they arrive?'

'Three days ago.'

Martin raised a single eyebrow. Adam wanted to swallow the words back down. He knew way too much information for a man who was pretending not to care at all, and Martin knew it too.

'Has he tried to speak to you?' Martin asked, tapping his pen against his bottom lip. Over the past three months – and countless sessions – Adam had noticed Martin do this often.

'Not that I know of.' Adam couldn't work out if that was a half-truth or a lie. At the end of the day they were both the same thing – he of all people should know that. Lies were never white, they were dark and sharp and cut people like a knife.

'I really think it would be good for the two of you to meet again.' Martin's voice was earnest. He leaned forward, resting his elbows on his woollen trousers, the pen still grasped in his hand. 'You've not spoken to him for so long, you've built him up in your mind to be some kind of demon. If you talk to him, you'll realise he's as human as you or me.'

Adam shook his head. 'Not gonna happen.'

'You sound very sure about that. Why do you think that is?'

Adam shifted his head to the side, trying to work Martin out. If you looked at it from a distance, the two of them had a lot in common. They both made money by coaxing out the truth, especially from unwilling mouths. Or at least they did, until Adam had messed it all up. Now he got by on the remains of his savings and his trust fund – supplementing it with income from his handmade furniture when he felt like it.

'Because Everett's an asshole.'

The briefest flash of a smile curved on Martin's lips. 'According to you he's been an asshole for all your life, and yet you were willing to spend time with him before. I want you to think about what's different right now. What you're trying to avoid thinking about by avoiding your brother.'

'OK.'

There was a silence for a moment, and Adam waited for Martin to break it. Instead the therapist stared at him until the pause became uncomfortable, enough to make Adam shift in his seat, and rub the back of his neck once again.

Damn, he knew these techniques. He could have written them all. He'd used them on businessmen and world leaders and military personnel who tried to bluff their way through his documentaries. And yet when they were used on him, he felt as awkward as hell.

He wasn't going to fill the silence in.

He wasn't.

Goddamn it. 'I don't want to see him, because every time I do I want to rip his fucking head off.'

Martin nodded slowly, showing no elation at his technique having worked. 'OK. And do you think it's a valid reaction to seeing him?'

'Yes, I do.' Adam could feel the blood starting to rush through his veins, hot and thick. 'And I think I should listen to my instincts. Look what happened last time I confronted him.' And look where he ended up. Here, in therapy, having to explain himself.

'Do you recognise how your body reacts when we talk about Everett?' Martin asked. 'I want you to check in right now. Explain to me what's happening.'

Adam closed his eyes, breathing sharply in through his nostrils. He felt torn between wanting to engage, to see if this thing they were doing could really make him feel better, and resisting it, having a little fun until he pushed Martin too far.

Maybe that's why he'd been so good at his job. He found people fascinating, but he found their reactions irresistible. Some of his best experiences had come from coaxing stoic men into revealing their inner emotions. Strange how being on the other side of the fence didn't feel quite so satisfying.

Ah hell. What did he have to lose? 'My heart is pounding,' he said quietly, trying to tune in with his physiological reactions. 'And my pulse is racing, I can hear it rushing through my ears.'

'What about your hands?'

Adam opened his eyes and looked down to his sides, where

his hands were tightly rolled into fists. 'Yeah, I kind of want to punch something.'

'Do you recognise what you're experiencing?'

'Fight or flight,' Adam said softly. 'Except I really want to fight.'

'Now look around you. Breathe in a mouthful of air. Take everything in. Tell me what you see.'

Adam scanned the room, his eyes taking in the details that most people overlooked. The way one of the blind slats was at an awkward angle, as though somebody had tugged the cord too tightly that morning. A gap in the bookshelf – dust free – where something had been removed recently. Martin's car keys, slung on the table next to the door, alongside his wallet and a yellow piece of paper – was that a parking ticket? As though he'd arrived late and carelessly dropped them down, without thinking of the security risk.

'I see your office,' Adam said, taking in another mouthful of air. 'I see your desk, and your books, and the half-drunk mug of coffee on the table next to you.' He glanced to his right. 'And I see your window, with the broken blind. It's snowing outside, and the flakes are sticking to the glass, as if they're trying to claw their way into the room.'

'That's good.' Martin nodded encouragingly. 'Can you see any threats in here? Anything that should cause your body to react the way it did?'

Adam's eyes darted around the room once again. 'No.'

'So how would you classify your reaction?'

Adam's lips felt dry and sticky. He picked up the glass of water Martin always left for him on the table – next to a box of tissues in case of client tears – and swallowed a mouthful. 'I'm reacting to something that's not there.' He put the glass down and rubbed his eyes with the palm of his hands. Somewhere in the past ten minutes he'd allowed himself to engage in the therapy. It didn't feel quite as bad as he'd expected.

'It's there,' Martin told him. 'But it's not in the physical world. It's in your mind, or in your memories. It's like those guys who came back from Vietnam in the seventies: you're fighting a war that's long since over.'

'You think this is just a reaction to what happened in LA?'

Martin shook his head emphatically. 'No, that's too simplistic. There are a lot more layers to it than that. We have to peel them back one by one, until you start to recognise them for what they are.'

Adam was interested now. Enough to lean forward, a frown playing at his lips. 'And if I recognise them, what then? Does it magically make everything better? Will I fall at Everett's knees and forgive him everything?' His chest tightened at the thought.

'Again, that's too simplistic. The aim of our sessions has never been to make everything feel like a fairy tale. It's been to help you recognise what's happening to you, allow you to take control of your reactions. To stop something like LA from ever happening again.' Martin crossed his legs, one knee over the other. 'And soon we'll need to talk about what happened in Colombia.'

Within a second, Adam sat up straight, flinching as though somebody had hit him.

'Not right now,' Martin said, putting his hand up. 'But we have a few sessions left, and before we finish I'd like to explore what happened there.' He glanced at his watch. 'We're coming toward the end of our time. I'd like to give you a little homework before our next one.' He turned in his chair, pulling a small notebook from the table beside him. 'I want you to keep a diary every time you react like you did today. I want you to write down what you're feeling, where you are, and what you think triggered it. Then next time we can discuss what you've done.'

'Sure.' Adam took the blue book from Martin's hands.

'Are you going to do it?'

Adam couldn't hide the smirk that played on his lips. 'Probably not.'

Martin sighed, his frustration obvious. 'You know, this would be so much easier if you just met me halfway.'

Adam could feel his muscles relax, his spine loosening at this return to more familiar territory. 'But it wouldn't be as much fun, either.'

'Fun for who?' Martin murmured, in a voice that didn't invite a reply. 'OK, Adam, you're free to go. I'll see you at our next session.'

Adam lifted his hand in a goodbye wave. In the strangest way, he was looking forward to that.

When Adam stepped out of the tall office building on Main Street, the snow was still falling, forming a fresh blanket of white on the ground. It was the first winter storm for the valley – though in Cutler's Gap, where Adam lived in his cabin, they'd had snow for weeks.

He had a few jobs to do while he was here in the town – letters to mail out and some supplies to buy. Things he couldn't buy in Cutler's Gap, with their single convenience store and run-down old bar. Though he liked the isolation, the lack of amenities could sometimes be a pain in the ass.

All the shops were decorated for the season, their white

wooden windows framed with twinkling lights, to highlight the displays inside. The street was decorated, too – the lamp-posts were spiralled with red tinsel from the ground to the top, with lights strung between them. And in the centre square, next to the bandstand, was a huge Christmas tree, standing proudly with a large star affixed to the top.

It was all ready for the Christmas parade, due to take place the following week. It drew visitors from throughout the state, and sometimes beyond, people desperate to enjoy the old-fashioned Christmas they rarely saw anywhere except on their television screens. Adam could remember the parade from his younger years – the intense excitement they'd felt as the band started to play, the way the firemen would throw candy out of the truck, while all the kids gathered around with their hands cupped out. It was a relic from a more innocent time.

Ironic, really, that he'd tried to escape LA and the nostalgia for small-town Christmases, and somehow he was back in the real thing.

It was nearly five by the time he'd finished his errands and bought a coffee to go from the Blue Bear café. The sky was already darkening behind the layer of snow clouds, the sun having given up her fight against the encroaching grey. Adam balanced his Styrofoam cup on the roof of his dark red Chevy truck, and slid his keys into the lock, releasing the door. He threw his bags on the passenger seat and then slid inside, gingerly starting the engine up.

He'd had this truck for years. It had spent most of the last decade in his parents' garage, surrounded by sleeker, shinier models. But there was something about its familiarity, its solidness, which stopped him from upgrading. Plus it was reliable on the old mountain roads, like a Sherman tank on the slippery ice. That counted for something when a short drive could mean taking your life in your hands.

Of course, short was a relative term. In this case it meant little over an hour for him to ascend the mountains and drive back to Cutler's Gap. Everything was spread out in West Virginia – it wasn't unheard of for somebody to drive two or three hours for a fresh loaf of bread.

He pressed his foot on the gas, revving the engine up, then slid the gear into drive. It was time to go home. And as he pulled out of his parking space and into the main road, Adam realised that's exactly what his cabin in the woods had come to mean to him.

3

*This cold night will turn us all
to fools and madmen*

– King Lear

Kitty leaned forward, her nose only inches away from the windscreen as she switched the wipers on to top speed. This had seemed like such a good idea a few hours ago, as she stepped onto the aeroplane at LAX, and was directed by an over-fawning flight attendant to the first-class cabin.

Three hours of pure luxury. Now there was an experience she'd probably never have again.

Her drive from Washington Dulles Airport to West Virginia was more like third class. The four-wheel drive she'd been told would be waiting for her at the airport had turned out to be a compact Kia. It was still better than any car she'd ever owned, but apparently it hated snowy mountain roads. But then again, so did Kitty.

The snow was falling thick and fast, the flakes coating the windscreen no matter how fast she tried to wipe them. She kept her foot gingerly pressed on the accelerator as she tried to slow her breathing. There was no point in panicking; she'd only make things worse.

A glance at the GPS on the dashboard told her she was less than twenty minutes away from her destination. Or at least from the town nearby. Though Cutler's Gap appeared in the choices on the GPS menu, the address for Mountain's Reach – where the Klein family were staying – seemed completely elusive.

The Kleins had flown to West Virginia the previous week, to spend some time with Everett's elderly parents who had a house there. Though Mia had begged Kitty to leave school early and join them, she'd managed to stand her ground for once. That's how she'd ended up flying here alone, agreeing to hire a car and make her own way to join them in Mountain's Reach.

She hadn't anticipated it would be quite so bloody snowy though.

She was so deep in her thoughts that by the time she realised the GPS was telling her something, she'd totally missed what it said. She glanced down, frowning, trying to work out if she should stay on the road or take a left. When she pulled her gaze back to the road in front of her, it was already too late.

The deer came out of nowhere – a sudden flash of mid-brown fur against the white blanket of snow. She barely had time to pump the brakes before its body hit her bumper with a sickening crunch.

The car skidded to a halt, the engine turning ominously silent as the dashboard lights flickered off. She stared open-mouthed out of the windscreen, her eyes taking in the carnage ahead.

Dear God, she'd just killed Bambi.

Her hand shook as she reached for the car door. It took two attempts before she could finally grasp it with her fingers enough to pull the handle, releasing the lock and allowing the door to open.

An ice-cold wind forced its way through the gap, making her shiver even harder. She swung her feet down onto the tarmac and pulled her hopelessly inadequate coat tightly around her. As she made her way to the front of the car she could see the bonnet was crushed from the impact, and the headlights were shattered. It didn't look as though the car was going anywhere right now.

When she'd heard it was cold in West Virginia, she'd assumed it would be London cold. A few degrees above freezing, maybe a bit of misty rain. But this weather was horrendous. The air felt arctic, making easy work of her thin jeans, light jacket and suede loafers. The snow was already seeping into her shoes, turning the brown suede a dark muddy colour. Flakes clung to her blue jeans, dampening the fabric, making her skin protest at the icy sensation. She looked over at the deathly still deer, wondering if she should just climb back into the car and wait out the storm, but then she saw something that made her breath catch in her throat.

Her heart raced as she stared at the deer, waiting to see if the leg twitch was just a figment of her imagination. But then it moved again, a little harder this time, enough to make her realise the deer wasn't quite so dead after all.

She went back to the car, grabbing her phone from her bag. Surely somebody could help them. She searched through the contacts until she found Mia Klein's number, pressing the green phone icon to connect the call.

Nothing.

Not a ring tone, not a voicemail. Just a click and then silence. She pulled the phone from her ear and looked at the display. A single bar was flickering in and out, like a naughty child playing hide and seek. Just as she thought it might be there to stay, it disappeared altogether, replaced by *No Service*.

Wonderful.

She brushed the snow from her hair, her teeth chattering at the cold dampness on her face. She was starting to feel bone-cold now, the sort of frozen that couldn't be cured with a simple bath and a change of clothes. No, this would take hours of warming until she could feel her toes again, and until her skin didn't feel as though it was going through some kind of Captain Birdseye deep-freeze processing.

Sighing, she lifted her phone up, so the display was in front of her, and took a few steps away from the car. The side of the road was lined with snow-covered pines, their tall canopies preventing any reception. Maybe if she walked further along she'd hit a sweet spot. She made her way along the road, her eyes trained on the non-existent tiny bars, searching for some sign of life. Treading tentatively along the frozen surface, her muscles taut from trying to keep herself upright, Kitty rolled her eyes at her situation.

By the time she reached the body of the deer, her clothes were soaked through from the snow. She stood over the prone animal, looking at the blood spilling out onto the road. Her hand shot up to cover her mouth as she felt her stomach begin to heave.

The deer's front legs began to move, seeking purchase on the frosty ground, but the rest of its body remained still as a statue. Kitty dropped to her haunches, her eyes meeting the deer's warm-brown stare. It looked as scared as she felt, wide and unblinking, and the reflected fear brought her tears to the surface.

'I'm so sorry,' she whispered, stroking the deer's surprisingly rough fur. 'I didn't see you coming, I never meant to hurt you.'

The deer, of course, said nothing. It could only lie there and gaze with glassy eyes, while its front hooves made the occasional fruitless movement. Kitty watched it helplessly, rubbing her chin, wishing she knew what the hell she could do to help the poor beast.

Above her, the sky was darkening as the storm took hold. Kitty glanced up, then back at the deer. Not a single car had passed her since she'd come to a skidding halt ten minutes ago. When was the last time she'd even seen a house? She'd passed a small town around forty minutes ago, Hartville, or Harville or something? Since then the road had only been lined by snow-covered trees, with the occasional break in the forest for a gravel road that led to who knew where.

Who knew how long she would be stuck here?

Focus, Kitty. OK, so what would her sisters do if they were here? Lucy, her oldest sister, was easy. By this point she would have probably organised some kind of vet ambulance, had her car towed away, and set up an appeal for endangered deer. Juliet, the next eldest, was more of a romantic. She'd be too busy staring at the winter wildflowers and wondering if there were bears living in the forest.

Bears? Oh shit. Kitty bit her lip, trying to remember if there really were bears here. Did they hibernate in the winter? It would be just her luck to be eaten alive and never seen again.

Trying to distract herself, she thought about Cesca, not that much older than Kitty herself. Cesca would probably be as clueless as Kitty, if her description of arriving in Italy last summer was anything to go by. Thank goodness they'd had Lucy to look after them growing up, otherwise none of them would have survived.

A rustling noise came from the forest, the evergreen leaves shaking in the wind. It was just the wind, right? Kitty felt her spine stiffen, her body on high alert. There was no way she could run on this icy ground in her Steve Madden loafers.

She was just imagining all the grizzly ways a bear could kill a person when she heard the low rumble of an engine coming from behind her. A moment later, she could see the headlights, too, cresting over the hill, approaching her and the deer at a fair speed.

She stood up, waving her arms madly. 'Hey,' she yelled. 'Over here!'

It turned out to be a rusty old flatbed truck, dark red paint chipped and peeling from its bulky frame. The truck slowed down, coming to a halt beside her abandoned rental car, the driver turning off the engine and opening the door.

The skin on the back of her neck prickled up. What had seemed such a good idea a moment ago now seemed foolhardy. She was in the middle of a deserted mountain in West Virginia, with a busted car and a phone that wouldn't work. Now a stranger was climbing out of a beaten-up Chevy, and for all she knew he could be some kind of axe murderer, desperate for his next victim. Maybe a bear attack didn't sound so bad after all.

Her fears intensified as the driver climbed out of the truck. He – and, boy, it was definitely a he – was tall, well over six feet, with a thick beard and a dark-knit beanie pulled down tightly over his head. Between the hat, his thick coat and his sturdy jeans, his only exposed skin was between his hairline and his beard.

And those molten chocolate eyes that were taking her in.

Oh boy. In spite of her frozen body, she could feel the blood rush to her cheeks. Even though she could only see a small part of his face, she could tell he was attractive, with a strong, straight nose and high sculpted cheekbones. She wasn't sure whether her heart was pounding from fear or interest.

Glancing over at where Kitty was standing next to the deer, the man grabbed something from his truck, before turning around to face her once again.

He was carrying a rifle.

Yep, it was definitely fear.

Cradling the gun in his arms, he walked towards her. The closer he got, the more she realised just how tall and muscled he was. His proximity heightened Kitty's fear into some kind of hysteria.

'Don't shoot!' she screamed, throwing her hands up in the air. 'For God's sake don't kill me.'

Surprised, the stranger stopped walking. 'What the hell?'

His voice was low and rough, matching his determined demeanour. Kitty felt herself start to shake, her muscles quivering as she stared at the serial killer in front of her.

'I'm sorry.' She tried to make her voice as even as possible. Don't show them you're afraid. 'Please don't hurt me.'

The man stared at her for a moment before shaking his head. 'Do I look like I'm going to kill you?' An element of derision laced its way through his words. Immediately she felt her hackles rise.

'You're carrying a gun,' she pointed out.

'To put the deer out of its misery.' He gestured at the animal beside her, then shot her a scornful look. 'Unless it's dead already.'

'I . . . I thought it was,' Kitty said, her teeth starting to chatter, from a mixture of the cold and the shock. Not that the guy in front of her was helping any. He may have looked good, but contempt for her was pouring out of him. 'But its front legs are moving, see?'

The man came closer still, then crouched down next to the deer, placing his hand against its neck. 'Its pulse is weak,' he said, stroking the deer again. Then he lowered his lips, until he was speaking into the animal's ear. 'Don't worry, girl, you won't suffer.'

It was only when he loaded his rifle that Kitty realised his intentions. Her fear for her own safety vaporised, quickly replaced by indignation. Surely he wasn't really planning to pull the trigger?

'Don't kill it,' she shouted, about to launch herself in front of the deer. 'It's still alive, it just needs help.'

The man cocked his head and looked at her through narrowed eyes. 'She's dying,' he said sharply, stroking the doe, his hand pressed against her spine. 'The impact's broken her back. You need to move away so I can take care of her, it's the kindest thing to do.'

Kitty wanted to cry. Her relief at the deer being alive vanished, replaced by the knowledge that she was suffering from her injuries. Rising up to her feet, in her useless suede loafers, Kitty half stepped, half slid backwards, letting the husky man do what he needed to.

She couldn't watch him do it, though. She looked away, holding her hand over her mouth and steeling herself to hear the loud bang of the gunshot, waiting for the stranger to kill the poor animal. When the loud crash came, resonating through the trees, she let out a little scream before fighting tears, trying to ignore the loud sigh that came from the man.

'It's over,' he said, not bothering to hide the irritation in his voice. 'You can look now.'

When she turned around it wasn't the deer she looked at, but the tall stranger staring at her. Now he was close up, she could get a better look at him. He was younger than she'd first thought, maybe in his late twenties or early thirties, judging by the smoothness of the skin around his eyes.

There wasn't a wrinkle to be seen. Not that she was looking.

'Did you call out a recovery truck?' he asked gruffly.

Kitty shook her head. 'I couldn't get any reception.' She waved her phone at him as if to prove her point.

'Where are you headed?' he asked. If she didn't know any better, she'd have sworn he'd rolled his eyes.

'To a place near Cutler's Gap.'

The stranger inclined his head at the truck. 'Jump in, I'm headed that way myself.'

Kitty paused, trying to work out if that was a good idea. Seeing her hesitation, he sighed loudly. 'Listen, lady, it's been a long day and I just want to go home and drink a beer in front of my fire. You can get in the truck and I'll take you wherever you need to go, or you can stand right here in your wet clothes and pretty shoes and let yourself freeze to death. The choice is yours. Either way, I'm getting in and I'm driving home, and I won't be coming back.'

He slung the leather gun strap over his shoulder and bent down next to the deer, lifting its body with ease. Carrying it across the road, he laid it gently in the flatbed of his truck. He didn't look back at Kitty, but simply walked around to the front of the vehicle and pulled open the driver's side door, putting the rifle on the back seat. He was sitting down behind the wheel by the time she realised he really meant it. He was planning to start up the engine and leave without her.

Running in her stupid shoes, Kitty reached the truck as he turned the ignition. Breathless, she yanked the door open and climbed onto the worn-out seat beside him.

Without a word, he put his foot on the accelerator, slowly pulling away from the scene of the accident. His mouth was set in a grim line, his eyes narrowed and piercing.

Welcome to Cutler's Gap. Home of Dead Deer and Sexy Bearded Assholes.

4

Now is the winter of our discontent
— Richard III

Adam stared out of the windscreen, concentrating on the road ahead while trying to ignore the girl shivering quietly beside him. She was British — he'd guessed enough from her accent — but apart from that he had no idea how she'd ended up stranded on the mountain road. Or why she was heading for Cutler's Gap, for that matter. Glancing to his right, he caught sight of her soaking jeans clinging to her thighs, trying not to notice the way they were slim and lithe. The ridiculous brown suede shoes she'd been sliding all over the road in, cute yet completely inappropriate, were dripping water on the floor of his truck.

There weren't a whole lot of pretty girls in Cutler's Gap. Wasn't a whole lot of anything, really.

'What's your name?' he asked, to kill the silence as much as anything else.

'Kitty,' she replied. Her voice was hoarse and low, like a winter wind.

'What's your business in Cutler's Gap, Kitty?'

Adam glanced at her thighs again – he couldn't help himself. It had been a long time since he'd seen legs as shapely as hers. Jeez, he needed to get some control. The last thing he wanted was to show any interest in a vapid blonde. He'd met enough of those when he'd been in LA, and they'd all been the same: giggly, friendly and hardly a brain cell between them.

She must have noticed his scrutiny, wriggling in her seat to inch away from him.

To his satisfaction, she had no luck.

'I'm here for a job,' she finally replied.

Adam laughed, short and sharp. 'No offence, ma'am, but that's a crock of shit. There's no work in Cutler's Gap. None that I'm aware of, anyway.'

Kitty turned to look at him, lips thin with anger. 'Are you calling me a liar?'

The girl was pretty in that overly processed Californ-i-a kind of way. If it wasn't for her clipped accent he might have described her as All-American, but her streaked blonde hair and light tan obviously came from a bottle. Sitting there with her thin jacket and tight jeans, she was the kind of sexy little thing he used to have a thing for.

Now, of course, he knew better. He just needed to remind his body of that.

'No, ma'am, I'm not calling you a liar, I'm telling you there are no businesses here. No mines, no mills, only a few run-down houses and a convenience store, plus a bar that's seen better days.'

That was no exaggeration, either. One of the things Adam loved best about Cutler's Gap was the fact that nothing changed. No one came, no one went, and nobody wanted to know his business.

Well, almost nobody.

'I'm not coming to work in a mill,' Kitty said, her nose wrinkling with disdain. 'I'm a nanny, if you really want to know, and I'm here to take care of a kid.'

Adam said nothing, still staring ahead at the snow-covered road. Unlike Kitty's rental car, his truck was prepared for the winter, with snow chains on the tyres and an engine tuned for the conditions.

'I work for Everett Klein,' she continued. 'I'm sure you've heard of him. He's staying with his parents for the holidays, up in the mountains.'

'I've heard of him,' Adam mumbled, his stomach dropping at the mention of Everett's name. He hadn't realised they were flying a nanny in. That's what he got for avoiding his brother like the plague. As soon as Everett and his wife had arrived – in a huge black Escalade that was totally out of place in the mountains – Adam had holed up in his cabin down by the lake, deciding to wait their visit out. He'd had enough of them when he'd been in LA, and their presence in Cutler's Gap was making him furious. A good reason to keep away until they'd all left town.

He wasn't planning on changing his mind now, so when he reached the gates of the big house he pulled the truck to a stop and put the parking brake on. The sooner he got rid of this girl the better.

'You can get out here, the house is just around the bend,' Adam said sharply, pointing at the drive, recently cleared of snow. When Kitty hesitated, he leaned across her and pulled the passenger door open. 'Don't worry, the walk won't kill you.'

'But it's dark out there.' She stared at him for a moment before twisting around and climbing out of the truck. Before she slammed the door shut, she leaned towards him, anger flashing in her eyes. 'I'd like to thank you for your help,' she began, waving him off when he tried to reply. 'But I can't. Because even though you look like a gentleman, you're clearly anything but.'

With that she gave a huff and turned on her heel, walking determinedly along the driveway. Adam watched her go, his lips twitching when she stumbled. The way her taut calf muscles flexed beneath the clinging denim when she tried to stay upright didn't escape his notice.

They were just legs. Long, sexy legs. The kind of legs that could drive a man crazy.

For a moment he considered getting out and offering her some help, but then he remembered who she worked for and nixed that idea. She may have been pretty – but her boss was a bastard that Adam never wanted to see again. So he started up the truck and drove down the winding track that led to his ramshackle cabin, leaving all thoughts of the soaking wet blonde far behind him.

Kitty muttered angrily to herself for the entire walk up the driveway, still fuming over the bearded man and the way he'd treated her. OK, so at least he'd stopped to help, and he'd offered her a lift to the Kleins' house, but he didn't need to be so rude about it. As for not taking her right to the house in the dark, especially when he knew she was wearing these shoes, that was nothing but cruel.

Just as well she would never see his stupid face again, even if she'd liked what she'd seen. What a miserable, angry, handsome man he was. Why were the good-looking ones always such arseholes?

When she reached the stone steps that led to the porch-covered entrance, Kitty bent down and pulled her wet shoes off, the cold air whistling around her icy feet. Her bare soles pressed against the cold floor as she stood in front of the huge front door.

According to Mia Klein's breathless monologue a few days earlier, the house was over a hundred years old. Purchased by Everett's parents in the early 1950s, they'd lovingly restored the dilapidated colonial building, making it into a home for their growing family.

Now, though, it was just the two of them, along with the old woman who took care of the house. Mia had explained that the family took the trip east every Christmas, but this year their plans had been hampered by the older Mrs Klein's recent accident – she'd slipped on the icy steps and had broken her hip. That was why Kitty's presence was so necessary; Everett and Mia had a lot of meetings and events to attend in nearby Washington, DC, and usually his mother looked after Jonas for them. But that plan wouldn't work without her being able to walk.

Kitty hadn't asked whether the Kleins had thought about curtailing their social engagements as a result of the accident – it wasn't her business, after all, and this unfortunate incident might just turn into a good thing for her. She really couldn't afford to look a gift horse in the mouth.

No, her job wasn't to question. It was to look after Jonas so well that Everett Klein wouldn't think twice about giving her a great write-up. Or even an internship. Now that would be nice.

Wiggling her thawing toes, she reached up for the door-bell. Pressing it twice, she could hear the chimes reverberate through the hallway and beyond. A shadow cast across the door, and when it opened, a smiling lady was standing there.

'Miss Shakespeare? I'm Annie Drewer, the housekeeper.' Annie pulled the door wider, gesturing for Kitty to come in. 'I didn't hear your car.'

Kitty stepped across the threshold. The warm air hit her skin immediately, stripping away the frozen chill. She closed her eyes for a moment, savouring the heat.

'I had an accident,' she told the housekeeper, sliding her bag from her shoulder. 'The car's a write-off, I had to leave it. I need to call the rental company and arrange for it to be picked up.'

'Oh my dear, are you all right?' Annie pulled Kitty at arm's length, looking her up and down. 'It can get so dangerous out there in the winter.'

Her kind concern brought tears to Kitty's eyes. 'I killed a deer,' she said, her voice wobbling. 'Then some horrible man drove me here, but he made me walk up the driveway in these.' She pointed to the misshapen loafers still grasped in her left hand. 'And now I've remembered that all of my clothes and my other shoes are still in that stupid car and I've absolutely nothing to wear.' With that, Kitty started to cry. The tears were unexpected, surprising her as much as they surprised Annie. Kitty wasn't one to cry at just anything, but it wasn't often she killed a poor deer, then got it in the neck from an arrogant bastard.

The woman clicked her tongue, pulling Kitty close, rubbing her back in reassurance. 'There, there, let Annie make you a warm cup of coffee.' Putting her arm around Kitty's shoulders, the housekeeper led her down the long tiled hallway. 'There's a fire in the kitchen, you can take the chill off your bones there. Soon you'll be feeling as right as rain.'

'You're English.' Kitty's eyebrows lifted with surprise. Though Annie's accent was mellowed by years of living in West Virginia, she still couldn't disguise her roots.

'Born and bred,' Annie agreed as they walked into the kitchen. 'I came over for a year in 1970, met a boy and never went back.'

The kitchen was warm and spacious, the windows facing out to the blue-black skyline . Kitty stared out of the glass, looking at the floodlit lawn which led to a dark wooded area that faded to nothing. The house was built on the side of the mountain, where the land sloped down to Cutler's Gap. Following Kitty's gaze, Annie told her that there was a big lake in the foothills – a large expanse of water where the Klein children had all learned how to swim.

'I've arranged for your cases to be picked up,' Annie said, sliding a steaming mug of coffee in front of Kitty. 'And I've let the younger Mrs Klein know you're here. She and the rest of the family are at the hospital, visiting with Mary. She's the older Mrs Klein. She should be coming home soon.'

Kitty took a sip of the hot, bitter liquid. The heat radiated through her as soon as she swallowed, defrosting her from her stomach upwards.

'Is Jonas there, too?' Kitty asked.

Annie clicked her tongue again. 'Yes he is. I told them it's no place for a boy, especially one as rambunctious as that one, but after he fell into the lake the day before yesterday, the younger Mrs Klein won't let him out of her sight.'

'He fell in the lake?' Kitty repeated, alarmed. 'Was he alone?' A seven-year-old boy shouldn't be left alone near an ice-cold lake. The thought of him being anywhere near it made her shiver. It may have been a year since she'd been in charge of any children, but even Kitty knew you kept an extra-strong eye on them wherever there was water.

'Yes he was, and he would have frozen to death, too, if his uncle hadn't found him. Luckily for us he was sent home with nothing more than a flea in his ear, but I shudder to think what could have happened.'

The two women exchanged glances, and Kitty sensed that Annie could be an ally.

'Thank goodness for his uncle,' Kitty whispered, trying to ignore the panic fluttering in her stomach at the thought of Jonas diving into the lake. 'Is he staying here too?'

'Not a chance, not while Everett is here. He won't have anything to do with ...' Annie's voice trailed off as the front door slammed, and voices echoed in the hallway. A boy's high-pitched yell, and a woman's soft drawl, followed by two low-pitched masculine voices.

The new arrivals walked into the kitchen, still talking rapidly. Everett Klein came first, followed by an old man who could only be his father, both of them sharing a similarly shaped nose. A young boy followed him, his blond hair lightly covered in snow. He stared at Kitty, but held himself back as if he was shy. She smiled at him, trying to make herself seem as friendly as possible.

'Oh, Kitty, you're here.' Mia Klein swept into the room, brushing the snow off her shoulders. 'I was expecting you hours ago.'

'I had an accident—'

'Oh, I'm sorry to hear that.' She blinked a few times, as though snowflakes had stuck to her eyelashes. 'Jonas, this is Kitty, she's here to look after you.' Was that relief Kitty heard in her voice?

Jonas's eyes widened. Kitty stood and walked over to him,

41

squatting down to make herself his height. 'Hi, Jonas, how are you doing?'

'OK.' He gave her the briefest of smiles.

'I'm here for the next few weeks. We're going to have a lot of fun,' Kitty told him, feeling sorry for the poor kid. He looked so perplexed. Hadn't Mia even told him she was coming? 'Are you excited for Christmas?'

Jonas nodded without speaking.

She gave him the biggest smile. 'Me too. I've got lots of exciting things planned for us. I think we can make this the best Christmas ever.'

He looked a little happier at that, the wary expression leaving his face.

'As long as you can stop him from jumping in the lake again, we're all good.' Everett's deep voice filled the kitchen.

Jonas's eyes widened, as if he'd been caught with his hand in the cookie jar. 'It was an accident. I didn't mean to.'

Mia stepped forward, running her red-taloned fingers through her son's hair. 'Of course you didn't, darling, but you shouldn't have gone near the the lake without us.' Glancing up at Kitty, Mia gave her an appraising look. 'That's why Kitty's here. She'll keep an eye on you when we can't.'

Everett half coughed, half laughed. Kitty glanced up at him. He was staring at her with an appraising gaze, as though he was trying to work her out. Though it was on the tip of her tongue to ask him where he'd been when his son almost drowned, she bit the thought down. She wanted to impress the man, not enrage him.

'Can we still go to the Harville Christmas parade?' Jonas asked, his face lighting up. 'Oma usually takes me but she can't walk at all. Mom says she's gonna be laid up all Christmas.'

This time Kitty didn't bother looking at Mia for confirmation. Instead she cupped Jonas's frozen pink cheeks, her palms luxuriating in their chubbiness. He was a good-looking child – the perfect combination of his parents' genes, and his clothes were expensive and well made. Yet she couldn't help but feel sorry for this boy who had everything he could want except his parents' attention.

'Of course we can. I wouldn't miss it for the world.'

5

We came into the world like brother and brother
– The Comedy of Errors

There was a trick to running in the snow. It took a different kind of person to see an hour out in the frozen landscape as a challenge, rather than a warning to go back indoors and warm up. Adam pulled his trail-running shoes – waterproof to keep out the cold – over his thick woollen socks, and zipped his windproof jacket over the thermal layers he'd put on earlier. The storm had died down sometime in the night, the clouds disappearing as though they were just wisps of smoke. Now the sky was a brilliant blue, the sun reflecting on the freshly fallen snow, making the layer of white sparkle like diamonds.

He started slowly, following his usual trail through the forest that lay between his cabin and the big house, feeling the snow give softly beneath his feet with each stride. As a child he'd learned that snow took on different characteristics depending on the flakes and the weather that immediately followed. Powder was good, ice was bad.

His route was the same every day. Partly because he knew where the snow was at its easiest, and partly because he had the survivor's instinct that familiarity could mean rescue in an emergency – it was always those who went off-piste who ended up never being found. After he left the canopy of the evergreen trees he emerged into the clearing between the forest and the big house – what passed for a grassy lawn in the summer, once the snow had melted away. He carried on past the house, following the road for about half a mile, then looped back on himself, running along the perimeter of his parents' estate before passing the house once again.

Sometimes he'd stop for a coffee with Annie before finishing his run back to the cabin. Not today, though. Not when Everett and Mia were in the house, lording it up. Best to avoid those two altogether.

He was almost back at the forest when he saw the two figures ahead of him, running and laughing as they exchanged volleys of snowballs. He slowed down, veering left in an attempt not to come in contact with them. A moment later the two of them turned, spotting him in his high-vis gear, standing out like a sore thumb against the white landscape.

He recognised Jonas straight away. His nephew was a good kid, a friendly, outgoing boy who seemed to idol-worship Adam in spite of his gruffness. He was wearing a thick jacket and snow pants, with a woollen hat and scarf covering him up. For a moment, Adam remembered how he'd seen him plunge into the lake the other day, his tiny body breaking through the thinnest layer of snow-covered ice. Adam had panicked, and ran from his spot inside his cabin as fast as he could, reaching the water only thirty seconds after seeing the boy fall.

But thirty seconds was all it took in weather like this. It was a miracle the kid hadn't suffered any lasting damage.

It took a few moments more for Adam to work out who was with Jonas, maybe because she looked so different to the previous day. Gone were the sexy, tight jeans and the pitiful suede shoes, instead she was bundled up in an expensive snow-suit that cinched in at the waist, her long blonde hair flowing down her back. As she ran towards Jonas, holding a snowball aloft, her hair lifted up in the breeze, revealing her slender neck. She was laughing, though the smile froze on her face as she turned to look at Adam, dropping the snowball clutched in her gloved hand.

'Uncle Adam!' Jonas called out, his face open and warm. 'Want to join our snowball fight?'

His plan to pass them unnoticed had clearly failed. Adam stopped running for a moment, lifting his hat off to cool down.

The girl was still staring at him.

Her skin was pink from the cold, her lips a cherry red. She had one of those perfect noses – the sort that people paid a lot of money to plastic surgeons for – lifting slightly up as it came to a peak.

'Hey, Jonas.' He shot the kid a smile. 'Not now, maybe another time?'

The girl gave him a tentative smile, one that seemed to light up her whole face. Adam felt his muscles pull in an attempt to respond to it, his lips wanting to lift up into a smile of his own.

He dragged his gaze away from her, refusing to let his body respond. She'd driven him crazy yesterday, with her lack of awareness about the weather, her car, the deer. A typical city girl thinking that the mountains were just like suburbia but with a bit of snow and wildlife. The sort who came barrelling in, leaving a trail of devastation behind them.

He'd seen enough devastation to last him a lifetime. He definitely wasn't going to invite any more in.

Lifting his hand in the weakest of goodbyes, he began to run again, his eyes trained on the line of trees ahead of him. He could feel the skin prickle on the back of his neck, as though she was staring at his retreating body. And he knew what her expression would be, too. He'd seen it last night when he'd all but pushed her out of his truck and onto the driveway of the big house. What had she called him then? *Anything but a gentleman.* For some reason that description rankled. It wasn't as though he went through life trying to make girls cry. He was too busy just trying to get through the day.

By the time he reached his cabin Adam's body was covered with a sheen of perspiration. He pulled his T-shirt over his head, screwing the thin material into a ball and throwing it onto the mat beside his door.

He finished his morning routine with a hundred pull-ups on the porch frame, contracting his large, iron biceps to lift his body. Staring out across the water, he could see the big house on the side of the mountain, and the plume of smoke that spiralled out of the chimney. He wondered if *she* was still there, staring at the gap where he'd disappeared into the forest.

He was still thinking about the girl as he opened the door to his cabin, hearing the creak of the hinges as it swung inside. He jumped, seeing the annoyingly familiar frame of his brother lounging on Adam's easy chair, his ankles crossed and his feet resting on a hand-crafted wooden coffee table that Adam had made himself. Everett's smart, sleek business suit was a contrast to the roughness of the cabin's interior.

Stalking across the living room, Adam opened the cupboard

and grabbed a fresh towel before heading towards the bathroom. Pointedly ignoring his brother, he walked into the tiny cubicle and pulled off his sweaty clothes.

Everett was still sitting there when Adam emerged ten minutes later. He was still wet from the shower, a white towel wrapped around his slim hips. Refusing to acknowledge his intruder, Adam grabbed a bottle of water from his refrigerator, lifting it to his dry lips and gulping it down.

'How long are you planning to ignore me for?'

His brother's words reminded Adam of his therapist. He leaned on the kitchen worktop, the bottle still clasped in his hand. 'As long as it takes,' he said, meeting Everett's gaze.

'So that's it. We have a little falling-out and suddenly I'm not welcome here? What happened to family loyalty?'

Adam steepled his hands, in an unconscious mirror of his brother's stance. 'I was wondering the same thing myself. Have been since last September.'

Everett sighed, his chest rising and falling in an overexaggerated movement. 'Isn't that all over with? Mom told me your therapy was going well. I thought you would've dealt with it by now.'

Adam stared at his brother, trying to work out how they'd ended up like this. Though they'd been close once, growing up, there were few similarities between the brothers, either physically or in personality. Sometimes Adam found it hard to believe the two of them were related. But as boys they'd been inseparable, the older Everett making up stories and planning escapades, while the younger, stronger Adam would carry out their plans, adding his brawn to Everett's brains. Even at high school they'd made a good team – with only one academic year dividing them they were often together. When Everett's overactive mind got him into trouble, it was Adam's fists that would help him to find an escape route. They'd been a band of brothers, the Klein kids. Nobody messed with them, not if they had any sense.

As they became older, their lives naturally diverged. Everett had always been driven to succeed, forcing his way to the top of film school with sheer determination. Adam's journey through school had been more roundabout. He'd started off studying directing, and then became naturally attracted to the long-form of documentary making. With his nose for the truth, he'd found a way to coax the most reluctant interviewees to reveal more than they wanted to. Some said his good looks didn't hurt him, either. More than one female was an avid Adam Klein fan because of the way he looked on camera.

But this divide between them was more than two brothers growing up. It was a chasm, caused by the events of last summer, leaving Everett standing on one side of the hole and Adam on the other. Neither one of them appeared to be willing to bridge the gap. Instead they were waiting for the other to somehow jump across.

Not that it was ever going to happen.

'I'm going to therapy because the police insisted on it,' Adam reminded his brother. 'And we all know who called them in the first place.'

Everett looked wounded. If Adam didn't know him better, he'd have said it was genuine. 'We had no choice.'

Adam swallowed the last mouthful of water, throwing the empty plastic bottle into the recycling bin. It landed inside with a satisfying thud. 'There's always a choice.' Not that he was particularly bothered about busting his brother's balls over the phone call. That was the least of his misdemeanours.

'Can't we let bygones be bygones?' Everett asked him. 'It's almost Christmas. Mom's being released from the hospital. She deserves to have her family around her. All of us.' He spoke louder to emphasise the last part, as though Adam hadn't already gotten the point.

'You've spent too long working in the movies,' Adam pointed out. 'You're starting to believe in all that shit. Happily ever after and family reunions only happen on the screen. And you know why?' His hands were still fisted. He held them tightly by his side. Everett couldn't see them, they were obscured by the kitchen worktop, but if he could, he'd probably be pleased at the reaction he was getting. 'Because they're all fucking lies, every last one of them. They're like that Ray Bradbury story where those guys land on Mars and it looks just like home – some kind of Rockwellian idyll with Mom and Pop and mash for tea. But then as soon as it's night-time the masks melt, and the real aliens appear.'

'And you've spent too long investigating the bad guys. You're starting to see them everywhere, even when they're not there. I'm your brother, Adam, not your enemy. Why can't we just leave all that stuff behind?'

Adam grabbed a freshly laundered T-shirt from the basket beside him, pulling it over his head to cover his now-dry chest. Everett made it sound so easy, as though forgetting the past was like closing a door. Everett may have perfected the act of the good older brother, but Adam was older and wiser now.

He could smell bullshit from a hundred yards.

'I'll be civil to you for as long as you're here,' Adam said, keeping his voice low. 'But don't think it means anything because it doesn't. I'll do it for Mom and Dad, and I'll do it for Jonas.'

Everett nodded. Standing up, he brushed the creases from his trousers. 'I guess that's it then.'

It was as far as Adam was concerned. He wanted Everett out of his home – of the place that had somehow become his sanctuary. And the sooner the better.

Everett cleared the distance to Adam's front door, grabbing his snow jacket from the hook on the frame. 'By the way, this place is a shithole, I can't believe you live somewhere like this.'

Before Adam had a chance to reply his brother was gone, slamming the door shut behind him. The younger – and bigger – of the Klein brothers stood alone in the kitchen, his blood boiling.

As always, Everett had to have the last word.

6

Men in rage strike those that wish them best
— Othello

Her second night at Mountain's Reach was as restless as her first. After putting Jonas to bed, Kitty lay open-eyed on the uncomfortable twin bed, her mind a whirl of thoughts that refused to let her drift off to sleep. In spite of the weather outside, her attic room was hot and stuffy, with a strange odour that tickled her nose. She tossed and turned until dawn came creeping through the cracks in the curtains. The outside sill was still lined with glistening snow, like a frosted cake. The emerging sunlight bounced off the icicles formed on the roof, reflecting the brightness in through the window.

This was her first Christmas away from home, away from the family that she held dear. Even though they were scattered across the world, she usually spent the holidays with at least one, if not more, of her sisters. This year, Cesca and Sam would be celebrating in London along with Lucy and their father. She could picture the four of them pulling crackers and telling stories around the crackling fire, surrounded by the same old ornaments they'd always put up, and a tree festooned with decorations they'd made when they were schoolgirls.

An unexpected wave of homesickness washed over her, as she thought of her sisters. Of Lucy, the eldest and the bossiest, of Juliet, the beautiful one. Of Cesca, the creative genius, who was riding a new wave of success. And then there was Kitty – the youngest of the four. And she'd been looking up to her sisters for so long, that without them beside her, she wasn't always sure where she belonged.

A rap at her door made her sit up, pulling the sheets up to cover her pyjamas. 'Hello?' she called out.

The door cracked open to reveal Jonas. After they'd spent a day throwing snowballs and building snowmen, he'd thawed to her. By night-time, he was talking to her as though she was his new best friend, and when she read his bedtime story, he'd curled up against her like a cat.

Children were so easy when it came to relationships. It was a shame adults weren't quite so simple.

'Good morning, sunshine,' Kitty said, giving him a smile. 'Did you sleep well?'

'It was OK.' Jonas shrugged. 'But we should get up now. It's nearly eight o'clock, Dad's gone out to a meeting but he's left a list of instructions for you. He said on no account should I be allowed near the lake on my own, which is pretty damn unfair, if you ask me.'

'You really shouldn't swear,' Kitty chided him gently. 'There are so many better words to use.'

'But Dad swears all the time,' Jonas whined. 'And he never tells me off.'

Kitty bit down a smile. 'If you want to go sledging by the

53

lake, you'll need to stick with me,' she said. 'Otherwise we'll have to stay near the house.'

Twenty minutes later, after a spell in the shower followed by a rub down with a warm, fluffy towel, Kitty walked down to the kitchen. Jonas had propped himself up on the counter and was chattering away to Annie as she laid out the breakfast dishes. The smell of warm oatmeal filled the room, making Kitty's mouth water.

Her stomach gurgled loud enough for Jonas to stop talking,

'Wow,' he said, wide-eyed. 'That was intense.'

It didn't take much to impress a young boy, and bodily functions seemed at the top of Jonas's list. She'd have to remember that.

Annie clicked her tongue and filled a bowl full of porridge, passing it to Kitty with an outstretched hand. 'Maple syrup's over there, and there's organic slimline honey if you're trying to lose weight. Mrs Klein insists on it.'

'Mom pours it all over her breakfast and then doesn't eat it,' Jonas added cheerily. 'It drives Annie crazy.'

From the narrow-lipped look of disapproval on Annie's face, Kitty could see he was right.

'Maple syrup's just fine,' Kitty smiled, reaching for the sticky bottle. Though she wasn't overweight by any means, she was what an ex-boyfriend had called 'sturdy', a girl with hips made for childbirth and a body able to withstand famine. In his more charitable moments, he'd tell her she'd outlive them all in a state of national emergency. Not exactly high praise. And exactly the reason he was an *ex*-boyfriend.

After breakfast, she took Jonas up to clean his teeth and get dressed. Choosing a warm sweater and thick trousers, she wrapped him up like a mummy, ready to face the frozen air. It had snowed again in the night, and though the roads had been cleared, the icy blanket stubbornly remained on the lawn and flowerbeds leading down to the forest that twinkled beneath the wintry sun. Jonas ran ahead of her, pulling his sled, shouting back at her with instructions and urging her to keep up.

Kitty pulled at the absurd bright pink snowsuit Mia had let her borrow. If Playboy bunnies frolicked in the snow, this was exactly what they'd wear. She couldn't help but feel self-conscious in it.

Even if it was better than freezing in her thin jacket.

'It's just through here,' Jonas shouted, disappearing into the densely packed forest. 'There's a clearing that leads down to the lake, with hills and everything. You're gonna love it.'

The faintest of smiles crossed Kitty's lips. As a child she'd always hated the snow, watching with envy as her braver sisters careered down the hill. They'd balanced precariously on their sledges, trusting blindly that when they reached the bottom they would somehow come to a stop. Meanwhile, Kitty would stand on the side of the slope, shivering, and will the hours away until she could go home and get back to the warmth and the TV.

The West Virginia winter put London's in the shade, though. The weather here wasn't just bitter, it was ice-age cold, making the vapour in her breath freeze as soon as she exhaled, and whipping her skin like a woman scorned. Kitty was already counting the minutes until she could persuade Jonas back indoors, perhaps with the aid of hot chocolate and marshmallows.

She was so lost in her thoughts, it took her a moment to realise he had disappeared; his trail of footsteps in the snow petering out as he'd entered the shade of the woodland.

Bugger, bugger, bugger.

She didn't bother chiding herself for her muttered swearing, picking up speed to run into the forest in the direction Jonas had taken. Her chest tightened with panic, making her breathing loud and heavy, and her movements laboured. Eyes scanning from right to left, she looked for signs of the young boy, but came up with nothing but trees.

Where was he?

'Jonas!' Her shout disturbed what few birds remained in the forest, stubbornly staying north for winter despite the lure of sunnier climes. Wings flapped loudly, and disturbed snow cascaded down from the branches, falling at her feet in large white clumps.

'Jonas, I can't see you,' she called again. A cracking sound came from her left, and Kitty whipped her head round, but there was nothing there. Nothing she could see, anyway. Still the pounding of her heart continued, hammering against her ribcage in a rapid tattoo. How could he disappear so quickly . . . and what if he made it down to the lake?

Images of his tiny body flashed into her mind. His skin grey, his face expressionless as he floated in the frozen water. *Oh dear God, please let him be safe*, she prayed, clasping her hands together as she continued to search.

A minute later she came to a large clearing. The land was covered in snow that sparkled like diamonds in the sun. At the crest of the hill Jonas was standing, holding on tight to his sledge with one hand, using the other to wave madly at somebody down by the lake.

Beneath the thick woollen hat Kitty had insisted he wore, Jonas's cheeks were flushed, and a big grin was painted across his face. 'Uncle Adam!' he shouted, his voice loud enough to echo down the canyon. 'Over here, can you see me?'

Kitty followed Jonas's line of sight, spotting the form of a man down by the lake, a little over a hundred yards from where she stood. Bent over a pile of logs, he was holding an axe in his hands, stopping mid-swing as he heard Jonas's shout. When the man stood up he was wearing only a T-shirt, despite the frozen weather. Kitty swore she could see his muscles ripple, even though she knew from that distance it should be impossible. Maybe the man had a body like the Wall of China – visible even from space.

Was it getting warmer out here, or was she having a hot flush?

'Jonas, come here,' Kitty shouted. 'You can't sledge down there, you'll end up in the lake.' The hill was steep, ending at the edge of the expanse of water, and the thought of Jonas ending in the icy lake made her heart clench wildly.

From the corner of her eye, she saw Adam place the axe down and walk towards them. In spite of her warm snowsuit, she could feel herself start to shiver. She'd met this man exactly twice, and both times he'd looked at her as though she'd stamped on his favourite toy.

He cleared the distance between them and the cabin in less than a minute. Jonas was grinning at him, still holding the end of his sledge in his gloved hand. He looked delighted to see him.

Unlike Adam, who had a face like thunder. Kitty could only assume it was aimed directly at her.

'Uncle Adam, will you sled with me?'

Adam lifted Jonas's hat off and ruffled his hair. 'Maybe later. I want to have a quick chat with your nanny first. Can you give us a minute?'

Kitty's mouth felt dry. The thought of a quick chat was making her feel sick.

'Talking's boring.'

Adam smiled at Jonas, the humour not quite reaching his eyes. 'It sure is. So just stand there and don't move, OK? We'll be back soon.' He turned to Kitty, the smile disappearing from his lips. 'A word, please?'

He stalked past her, his feet kicking up snow as he walked. Kitty felt his arm brush against hers. She took a deep lungful of air, trying to ignore the way her heart was hammering against her chest. By the time she turned towards him, he was ten yards away. She walked over to join him.

'Hi,' she said, reaching her hand out. 'Maybe we can start this again? I'm Kitty, Jonas's nanny.'

'I know who you are,' Adam said, pointedly ignoring her hand. 'What the hell were you thinking, letting Jonas run toward the lake on his own? Did you hear what happened the other day? The kid nearly drowned, I had to fish him out before he sunk right under. What kind of nanny lets a child run into danger like that?'

His verbal onslaught felt like a slap to her already sensitive skin. She recoiled, taking a step back from him, needing the distance it gave. 'I took my eyes off him for a second,' she protested. 'As soon as I realised he was in the forest I ran after him. And look, he's fine, all right? He knows not to go sledding without me.' She pointed at Jonas, who was staring at them both with narrowed eyes. He wasn't silly, he must have known they were arguing.

'No, it's not all right,' Adam told her. 'It's far from fucking all right. A minute is all it takes for somebody to get hurt. He's just a kid, he needs looking after. And if you're too busy doing your lipstick, or talking with your friends on your phone to do it, maybe you should just leave.'

A surge of anger washed through her. 'I don't know who pissed in your cornflakes this morning, but you're being completely over the top. Yes, he ran off when he shouldn't have, and yes, I'll be having a word with him, but you're way out of line to be talking to me like this.'

He shook his head vehemently. 'I'm not the one out of line.'

'Yes you are. I've no idea what I've done to make you so angry, beside kill a deer by accident, but every time I've seen you, you've bitten my head off.' She stopped to take in a deep breath. He was still staring at her, those deep brown eyes narrowed to slits.

'Yeah, well just do your job and we'll all be OK. That kid gets neglected enough, he doesn't need to add you to the list of people who ignore him.'

She straightened her spine. 'I don't ignore him, and I never would. And I resent any suggestion otherwise. Now perhaps we can end this discussion and I'll go and give him the attention he deserves.' She folded her arms in front of her.

He looked at her for a moment longer, his gaze flickering from her face to her crossed arms, and then down to her cinched waist. She really hated this damn outfit. Finally he gave her a slight nod. 'OK.'

Letting out her mouthful of air, she turned on the heel of her snow boots and walked back to Jonas, ignoring Mr Angry-Yet-Beautiful as he stayed motionless behind her. Twisting her lips into a smile just for Jonas, she blinked back the furious tears that threatened to spill over if she let them.

'Come on, let's go sledding.'

7

This above all: to thine own self be true

– Hamlet

'How angry did you get?' Martin asked, crossing his legs, the movement making his grey pants crinkle up. 'On a scale of one to LA.'

Was that supposed to be a joke? Adam wasn't sure. Martin was always so deadpan, he couldn't tell the difference between a joke and a pointed remark.

'I got pretty angry. The kid nearly drowned in the lake, for Christ's sake. She was being negligent.'

'You said she was only a few seconds behind him.' Martin scribbled something down on his pad. 'Maybe you could have given her the benefit of the doubt. Why didn't you?'

Adam licked his lips, dry from the heated air. 'I guess I saw red. It only takes a minute for an accident to happen. She shouldn't take her eye off him for a second.' He leaned forward, his expression intense. 'If something had happened to him, I'd never forgive myself.'

Martin's lips twitched as he wrote on his pad again. Adam wondered if he'd ever get to see those notes. 'I notice how agitated you get when you talk about this girl, Kitty, is that right? What is it that triggers you?'

'She doesn't trigger me. She just aggravates me.'

This time Martin allowed a small smile to break out. 'OK, so what aggravates you about her?'

Adam leaned back on the easy chair. 'She nearly hurt my nephew.'

'But by your own account he was in more danger before Kitty arrived in Cutler's Gap. And I don't remember you getting so aggravated at your sister-in-law for letting Jonas run free around the lake. Did this Kitty say something that hit a nerve?'

Adam closed his eyes for a moment, remembering the events of the previous day. He couldn't get her hurt expression out of his head no matter how hard he'd tried. She'd tried to be friendly, even offered him her hand, and he'd pretty much chewed her out as soon as he opened his mouth.

He didn't normally react so badly to people. At least he didn't before LA.

'She reminded me of someone,' he finally mumbled.

'Who?'

'Lisa.'

Martin's expression had a touch of the hallelujahs to it. 'Lisa your ex-assistant. How does Kitty remind you of her?'

He hadn't thought of Lisa in weeks. Not that there had ever been much to think about. Their relationship had been casual at best, one born of proximity and necessity rather than desire and passion. She'd been his assistant when he'd travelled to Colombia, and had seen nearly everything that went down. Everything except the worst part.

'She's pretty,' he said, trying to work out where the similarities lay. 'And she has this friendly image she projects, as though she isn't really waiting for you to turn around and stab you in the back.'

'Are we talking about Lisa or Kitty?'

'Both.'

'Interesting, What makes you think Kitty's going to stab you in the back? Does she even know you?' Martin laid his pen down, too absorbed to write.

'Isn't that what all women do eventually?' If you let them, that is. 'And men, too. Let's not leave them out.'

'Do you really believe that?' Martin asked. 'Do you really think everybody's out to get you?'

Adam laughed – a short, humourless one. 'Are you asking me if I'm paranoid?'

Martin's smile was more authentic. 'That's a question only a paranoid person would ask.' He shrugged. 'Seriously, though. This girl, you've met her, what, twice? Unless she's some cunning spy sent in by your brother, maybe you should take her at face value.'

Adam stared at his therapist for a moment, considering his words. One good thing about Martin – he allowed the silences to work for as long as they needed to. Sometimes they were more important than the talking, he said. Adam ran his thumb along his jaw, feeling the stiff bristles beneath his touch, thinking about Kitty and his response to her.

From the first moment he saw her, alone on that wintry road, it had felt like a punch in the gut. He remembered the tears welling in her eyes just before he shot the deer, and the stoic way she'd held herself as he drove her home to Mountain's Reach. She was sensitive, but she wasn't afraid to give as good as she got. He half smiled, remembering the way she'd called him out on not being a gentleman when he dropped her off on the driveway. A sentiment she'd repeated when he called her out yesterday, and she asked him who pissed in his cornflakes.

As his mind wandered over their two encounters – not to mention the one where he did everything to avoid her when he was running in the snow – he came to a realisation. She hadn't done a single thing wrong, apart from be human. It was him who'd behaved like an asshole.

Damn it.

'I owe her an apology,' he said softly, more for himself than Martin.

'Kitty?' Martin clarified.

'Yeah.' Adam nodded. He'd let his anger for his brother, and maybe Lisa too, seep into his interactions with Jonas's nanny. Just seeing her with her pretty blonde hair and perfect body reminded him of everything he hated about LA. The perfection, the easy smiles, the pretending to be your friend when really they were trying to get one over you. The lies that pulled on fancy outfits and masqueraded as truth.

'I might be an asshole,' Adam continued, 'but I'm not afraid to say when I'm wrong. And this time I'm definitely wrong.' He felt sick as he remembered her hurt expression, and the way she kept glancing at him when he stomped back to the cabin. Even worse, he'd let Jonas witness them arguing.

'So what are you going to do about it?' Martin asked him.

There was only one thing to do, when you'd made a mistake. Something Adam wished his brother knew something about. You held your hands up, admitted to it, tried to make things better. 'I'm going to apologise to her,' he told Martin.

Martin's lips held the ghost of a smile. 'That sounds like a good place to end today's session.'

*

'He said he'd lost his keys, but the weird thing is I found them the next day in the tray next to the door,' Lucy said. 'I don't know what's wrong with him. He's always been a bit forgetful, but I swear he's getting worse.'

Kitty crossed her legs into lotus pose, moving the laptop on her mattress so she could see them all on the screen. Cesca and Lucy, Juliet and Poppy; her three sisters and her niece. They carried on talking as she watched them, taking each of them in. After the past few days she was missing them more than ever, a longing that tugged deep at her heart.

'Maybe we should take him to the doctor,' Cesca suggested.

'He'll never go.' That was Juliet.

'Sometimes you have to put your foot down,' Cesca said.

'Have you tried it with Dad?' Lucy asked, grimacing. 'You know what he's like.'

'And we know who inherited his stubbornness.' Juliet grinned at her sister. 'Look, let's get Christmas over with and then talk about it again? There's nothing we can do so close to the holidays anyway. The doctor's surgery will be full of colds and flus, and the last thing we want is for him to catch something.'

Though Kitty pretended to moan about their weekly Skype date, there was something reassuring about it, too. Reminding her she wasn't alone in the world, that whatever happened she'd always have them. Even if everybody in Mountain's Reach hated her.

OK, not everybody. Just one, very fine, body.

'Talking of Christmas, we need to agree a time to talk,' Lucy said, always the organiser. 'We'll be having lunch at about two our time, which I think is nine in the morning where you both are.'

'Hey, we'll be in the same time zone for once.' Juliet smiled across the screen at Kitty. 'If only they'd let you have the day off, you could come to ours for Christmas.'

There wasn't much chance of that, even if she'd managed to pin Mia and Everett down for long enough to ask. They both seemed to be constantly busy. She'd noticed them have a few heated, yet whispering, conversations, too. Something definitely wasn't right there. Right now, she was pretty much the only responsible adult around here, save for the housekeeper.

She could only make this call because Annie had agreed to look after Jonas for half an hour. The two of them were in the kitchen, baking cookies.

'That would have been nice,' Kitty said. Impossible, but nice.

'So what time do you think we should arrange the call for?' Lucy asked. 'Before or after your lunch?'

'We're having lunch with Thomas's family,' Juliet said, her pretty nose scrunching up at the mention of her in-laws. 'We're sitting down at three, so I can do any time before that.'

'I'm not sure when we're eating, I'll have to check,' Kitty said. Surely they'd let her take an hour to spend with her family?

'How's the nannying going?' Juliet asked her. 'Are you getting on OK with the boy?'

'He's lovely,' Kitty told her.

'What about his parents?' Juliet asked. 'Are they OK too?'

'I wouldn't know, I hardly see them. Even when his mum's here, she's always busy. It's like she doesn't know what to do with a child his age.' Kitty screwed her nose up. Juliet nodded in sympathy. Of all the sisters, she knew what it was like trying to look after a child.

'You've had no luck asking his dad about that internship then?' Cesca's voice was sympathetic.

'Chance would be a fine thing.' Kitty shrugged. 'He's hardly ever here, either.'

'Maybe you can pin him down over the turkey,' Cesca suggested. 'Use a few skewers so he can't wriggle away.'

'I don't think he likes me very much,' Kitty said, remembering the few times they'd spoken. 'I'm not sure any of the Kleins are my biggest fans, really.' Apart from Jonas, that was. His enthusiasm for Kitty had only grown.

'Why, who else have you upset?'

Kitty chewed at her thumbnail, remembering her encounter with Adam. 'Everett's brother seems to have it in for me. He shouts at me every time we meet.'

'That's horrible. I hope you've told him where to go.' Lucy looked angry. Things were always black and white in her world. 'I hate people like that.'

Kitty wasn't very fond of him either. 'I think I jinxed it from the start,' she said, filling them in on her collision with the deer. Her sisters' amusement only increased when she told them about her row with Adam by the lake.

'You really asked him who pissed in his cornflakes?' Cesca asked, trying to hide her grin. 'What did he say?'

'I can't remember,' Kitty admitted. 'But I'm sure it wasn't nice.'

'Seriously, you've got guts, girl.' Cesca lifted her hand up, as if to offer her sister a high five. 'You insulted the famous Adam Klein.'

Kitty felt the blood drain out of her face. 'What do you mean?'

'I mean, he might have been some help with the internship, but not if he's going to be an arse about it.'

'Adam Klein,' Kitty repeated, feeling her muscles weaken. 'I didn't realise . . .'

It was so obvious as soon as Cesca said it. Of course he was Adam Klein. OK, so he'd grown a beard and for some reason was shooting deer and cutting wood with an axe, but there was no doubt he was the documentary maker she'd studied in her graduate course.

The scourge of criminals everywhere, Adam Klein was famous for his documentaries investigating drug cartels and human traffickers. His documentaries were perfect examples of how film-making could make a difference in the world, and half Kitty's class had a crush on him.

And she'd asked him if his morning cereal contained piss.

Dear God.

'Are you OK?' Cesca asked her. 'You look a little pale.'

'It must be the screen,' Kitty said, her voice thin. 'Don't worry about me, I'm absolutely fine.'

Later that night, she sat at the end of Jonas's bed reading aloud from the book on her lap, imitating the voices to make him giggle. They were reading the first book in her favourite childhood series, and she was enjoying it as much as he was. It reminded her of her mother; the way the brilliant actress performed, rather than read, a book, making the stories come to life in young Kitty's head.

Another thing she missed about her mother. She'd been missing it since she was ten years old.

As she came to the end of the chapter, Kitty slid a bookmark in and closed it up. 'We can read some more tomorrow,' she told Jonas, anticipating his disappointment. 'It's time for bed now.' She leaned forward to hug him. 'Goodnight, sleep tight, don't let the bedbugs bite.'

'Can we go sledding again tomorrow, too?' Jonas asked, a yawn forcing his mouth open wide enough so she could see his tonsils.

'I can't, I have to drive to the airport to pick something up.'

'What do you need to pick up?' Jonas sat up, looking at her intently. Like any child, something out of the ordinary was enough to catch his interest.

'Nothing special, just something I left back in LA.' She smiled at him, being deliberately evasive. The fact was, Mia had texted to ask her to pick up Jonas's gifts. She'd had them shipped from LA at a huge cost.

'How can *something* catch a plane?' Jonas asked, his eyelids starting to droop. 'Surely someone would have to bring it on the plane with them?'

'Sometimes you can put things in the hold of the plane, they don't always need a passenger to carry them on for you. Now try and lie down, it's getting late.'

Jonas did as he was told, falling back onto the mattress. 'What's a hold?'

Kitty pulled the blankets over his slight body, tucking them firmly around him. 'It's like the trunk of a car, except it's in the belly of the plane. That's where they store all your cases when you fly. They also put parcels and packages in there, and even some animals sometimes.'

'And humans.'

She shook her head. 'No, sweetie, not humans. They travel on the seats.'

'Not always. Dead bodies go in holds.'

A shiver forced its way down her spine. 'Who told you that?'

Jonas's voice was thick. 'I heard it somewhere. Uncle Adam

68

nearly ended up in the hold, but in the end he wasn't shot, so he came back in the plane.'

'He did?' She opened her mouth to say something, then closed it again. What should she say to something like that? She was flummoxed.

He nodded, his eyes finally squeezed shut. 'Yeah, Dad said he was lucky.'

'Yes, he was.' She waited on the chair beside his bed until Jonas fell asleep, his blankets rising and falling with his regular breaths as he escaped into his dreams.

Leaving his bedroom, flicking the lamp out and the night-light on as she went, Kitty turned to check Jonas one more time before she pulled his door softly closed. Then she turned to walk down the hallway to the stairs, and smacked straight into a tall, hard body.

'Oh!' She stepped backwards. 'I'm sorry, I didn't see you there.' In the gloom of the hallway, it took her a moment to realise who it was.

'I was waiting for you,' Adam told her. He leaned his head to the side, looking down at her.

'You were?' She swallowed hard. 'Why?'

'Can we talk somewhere?'

'What about?' Her hackles rose on the back of her neck. She wanted to say something snarky, but this was Adam Klein.

Adam bloody Klein. She should be fangirling at his feet or something.

His face twisted, as though he was thinking something through. 'I guess here will do,' he said. 'I know Mia and Everett are out, I asked Annie. And my dad's visiting my mom in hospital, so nobody will interrupt us.'

She glanced back at Jonas's door. 'If we keep our voices down, maybe we won't wake the kid up either.'

For the first time since she'd met him, he unleashed a smile on her. And boy, was it glorious. One of those all-American, handsome grins that made you weak at the knees.

Or they did if you were into that kind of thing. Which Kitty wasn't. Not at all.

'I owe you an apology,' Adam said, reaching out to lean casually on the wall beside her. 'I said some things I shouldn't have, and I definitely said them in a way I shouldn't have. I'm sorry.'

Well this was unexpected. Kitty couldn't think of a single word to say in response. It was as though somebody had taken her brain and replaced it with a giant ball of cotton.

'So will you forgive me?' Adam prompted.

Kitty's eyes felt as wide as a ten-ton truck. 'OK?'

'Is that an "OK, I forgive you" or "OK, I'll say anything you want if you'll just leave me alone because you scare the shit out of me"?' Adam asked.

'Um, a bit of both, probably.'

He laughed, and it animated his whole face, crinkling the skin between his eyes, and causing his cheeks to rise up. He was horribly handsome. No, not horribly, just handsome. God only knew how much better he looked without the overgrown beard.

'I guess I'll take it, then.' He pushed himself off the wall, giving Kitty the space she didn't realise she needed. Her body sagged with relief. 'I really am sorry, I'm not normally such an asshole, at least I never used to be. I promise that next time I see you, I won't snap your head off. Goodnight, Kitty.'

There was going to be a next time? Oh boy. Kitty wasn't sure whether that thought excited or terrified her.

A bit of both, probably.

8

I desire to hear her speak again,
and feast upon her eyes?

– Measure for Measure

From his vantage point inside the treeline, Adam stopped to catch his breath as he watched Everett climb into the black sports utility vehicle, holding his phone to his ear as though it was some kind of body part. Waving absent-mindedly at his son who was standing beside Annie Drewer, Everett barely even looked at Jonas, too busy shouting orders into his mouthpiece to notice his son's expression of disappointment.

That's when Kitty came running out, coming to a stop where Jonas was standing, looking sad. Heading back towards the boy, she scooped him up into her arms, tickling his sides and blowing raspberries on his neck.

Adam found himself smiling when he heard his nephew's high-pitched giggles – his hysteria was just on the right side of humour. It teetered on the edge, threatening to become tearful, but the girl whispered in Jonas's ear, bringing another smile to his face.

The next moment she looked up, her eyes scanning the

treeline, and Adam found himself stepping back, as if to avoid her gaze. He couldn't help but stare at her sculpted cheeks and full lips, admiring the way her ice-blue eyes flashed. She sparkled like a jewel beneath the cold winter sun. He tried to swallow down the flash of desire that shot through his body. It was just the abstinence talking, after all.

'Are you ready, Kitty?' Everett shouted from the back seat of the Escalade, pulling his cell phone from his ear long enough to show his displeasure. 'We need to leave now. I've a plane to catch.'

Kitty ran to the car, a flustered expression on her face, while Everett shut the window, tinted glass obscuring his face.

The engine sparked to life, growling like a hungry lion, and Kitty pulled the car away slowly. Adam watched them turn the corner onto the main road, following their progress until they disappeared around the bend, the low hum slowly dissipating to nothing.

He was about to restart his run when he heard Annie's shout. 'You can come out now.'

Adam looked around, trying to work out who she was yelling at.

'You think I can't see you behind the trees, Adam? I can see you perfectly fine. You'll be pleased to hear that it's just me and Jonas, so you might as well come in and have a coffee.'

Running a hand through his hair, Adam stepped free of the forest and across the driveway, where Annie and Jonas were standing in the shelter of the porch. His nephew grinned wildly, delighted to see him, while Annie wrinkled her nose at his dishevelled appearance. A bead of perspiration ran down his forehead.

'You go and take a shower while I fill up the coffee pot.'

She fussed around him, the same way she did when he was about ten years old. Some things didn't change. 'I can't have you stinking out my kitchen.'

Adam smiled, pulling her into a hug that made her squeal.

'Get your hands off me, you dirty, sweaty boy.'

'What shall I put on after my shower? Or do you want me sitting in your kitchen in my birthday suit?' He raised his eyebrows at her, his voice teasing. Annie grabbed a dishcloth from beside the stove, attempting to swat him with it.

'It's nothing I haven't seen before, young man,' she grumbled. 'But there's plenty of clean clothes in the laundry room. Unless you've put weight on since you brought them over, of course, in which case maybe you should go back and finish your run.'

'Where is everybody anyway?' Adam asked. He knew that Annie would never swing a trap on him. If she said it was only she and Jonas, he believed her.

'Mrs Klein has gone to Fragrant Pines,' Annie told him, referring to an expensive spa near on sixty miles away. 'And Everett has been called back to LA.'

Adam swallowed, staring out of the window. 'Why's he taken the nanny with him?'

Annie tipped her head, staring at him strangely. 'Kitty?' she asked. 'Why do you want to know?'

'I don't,' he replied hastily. 'I was just making conversation.'

Annie narrowed her eyes. 'Whatever you say. I'll believe it if you do. And anyway, she's not heading back to LA, she's just dropping him off. You'll be pleased to know that after that, she's coming straight back here.'

Not wanting to get embroiled in *that* kind of conversation, he gave an enigmatic shrug then headed for the stairs. 'Guess that's my cue to take a shower,' he called back to her with a grin. 'Unless you want me to stand here gossiping like an old woman.'

The dishcloth whistled through the air, narrowly avoiding his head. Adam reached down to grab it, flicking it back easily, so it landed on the kitchen table. It all felt so normal, so real. Like he was a kid again, with little more than an assignment to mar his day.

For the first time in for ever, it was hard to wipe the smile from his face.

'Uncle Adam, why don't you like my dad?' Jonas leaned down to grab a handful of snow, patting it onto the abdomen of the giant snowman they were building. Spending alone-time with his nephew was a pleasure, and one Adam hadn't had much chance to indulge in since Everett and his family had arrived in Cutler's Gap. There was something about the innocence of Jonas that took his mind off things, stopped him from getting too lost in his own thoughts.

Adam wasn't so keen on the penetrating questions, though.

'I don't hate him, we just don't get on very well. He wanted me to do something I didn't want to do, and we ended up having a big argument.'

'Was that why you left California without saying good-bye?'

Adam frowned. 'Something like that.' He had no idea how much Jonas knew about that day in LA. Hopefully very little.

'I asked Dad where you'd gone and he wouldn't tell me, he just stomped off and went out to work. Mom told me to stop asking so many questions, and that I was upsetting him.'

'You don't ask too many questions,' Adam said, his voice

thick. 'You just ask the questions people are afraid to answer. The right kind of questions.'

Jonas looked surprised. 'I do?'

'Yes, you do. That doesn't mean I always want to answer them, though. Doesn't mean I will, either. But you shouldn't stop asking questions because they make people uncomfortable. That only means you're on the right track.'

Jonas took this as a green light for more. 'So why did you leave? Was it because I used to bother you all the time?'

Dropping onto his haunches, Adam pulled his nephew close. He yanked his glove off along with Jonas's hat, ruffling the boy's blond curls with his large, calloused hands. 'That wasn't why I left. The reason I had to go was because your dad and I had a big falling-out, the same way you do with some of your friends. We decided it would be better if I came back here.' Not quite the truth, but not a lie either.

From the look on Jonas's face he didn't understand. Not that Adam could blame him. In Jonas's world grudges were held for hours, not days or months. And in the schoolyard, resentments were held over some imagined slight that was soon forgotten.

Jonas opened his mouth to ask another question, then closed it again as a car swung into the driveway, its wheels crunching on the gravelled path. The old Ford came to a stop by the porch steps, and Francis Klein – Adam's dad – climbed out, pausing before he closed the door to rub his hands across the face.

'Grandpa!' Jonas dropped the snow he was holding and ran over to the car. 'We've been sledding and making a snowman and Uncle Adam was telling me all about him and my dad.'

His father glanced over at Adam, their eyes meeting in a moment of understanding, and Adam felt a shot of warmth injected into his cold body. His dad looked old – even older than his seventy years. A stark contrast to the vital, driven man Adam remembered from his youth.

'Did he now?' Francis stooped to cup Jonas's cheeks. 'I hope he told you all about the trouble they used to get up to when they were boys. They used to drive Annie crazy in their school vacations.'

'They used to build forts and go swimming in the lake and pretend to be pirates,' Jonas rabbited on. 'But now they don't like each other very much.'

Francis winced, pulling his thin lips tight. Adam couldn't help but see the expression of pain on his father's face. No parent liked to see their children fighting, Adam knew that, but he still couldn't find it in himself to forgive his brother.

'How was Mom?' Adam asked, in a vain attempt to change the subject.

'Comfortable. The hip's healing nicely. And they're managing the pain.'

Her broken hip was taking a long time to heal – to be expected, the doctor had told them, for a woman her age. Still, she was going crazy cooped up in that hospital bed.

'Did they say when she could come home?' Adam asked. The doctors had promised it would be before Christmas. She wouldn't be fully mobile by then, but at least she'd be able to recuperate at home.

'In the next few days. The doctor wants her to have an X-ray first. He doesn't want to cause any more issues with her hip in the ambulance home. That gives us enough time to arrange for a nurse and to get her room ready.' Francis smiled. 'She's going to need a special bed and a few other things.'

'I'll call up the agency,' Adam offered. 'They already have

nurses on standby, we just need to give them a date.' He'd spoken with them a few days earlier, when the doctor had first mentioned his mom coming home.

Francis nodded. 'Thank you, son. That would take a weight from my shoulders.'

With that, Francis shuffled the final few feet to the porch. As his grandfather left, Jonas pulled Adam's hand, pointing over to the snowman, and Adam allowed himself to be dragged back to their task.

It looked as though all the family would be home for Christmas. What a damn shame he couldn't feel happy at that thought.

9

The cat will mew and the dog will have its day
– Hamlet

Kitty glanced in the rear-view mirror. The glass was taken up with the view of Everett Klein still talking down the mouthpiece of his phone, his voice loud and brash, as though he was shouting all the way to California. Biting down a grimace, she tapped her fingers on the wheel, wishing she could turn the stereo on and drown out the noise.

He'd been on edge for the entire journey, as though he was living on his nerves, spending the first twenty minutes of the drive in an argument with Mia. And now his assistant was taking the brunt of his ire. Kitty would have felt sorry for him, but she was just thankful Everett wasn't shouting at her for once.

'Drake, I'm not asking you to perform fucking miracles,' Everett shouted. 'Just wake up the goddamned judge, get it notarised, then bring it straight back to the office.'

There was a pause, where Kitty imagined Drake was protesting against his fate. Waking a judge up at an early hour? What was Everett thinking of?

'Give him a freaking blow job for all I care, just get it done,' Everett thundered. 'I pay you the big bucks to make things happen. So get your sweet little behind out of bed and do what you're fucking paid for.'

Delightful.

Kitty tried to remember if Drake Montgomery had a sweet little behind, but she couldn't remember at all, even if her last memory of him was walking out of the interview.

'I don't give a flying rat's ass if it's only six o'clock in the morning, just wake the old bastard up. Hey, wait . . . *fuck*, you just missed the damned turning.'

It took a moment for Kitty to realise the last sentence was directed at her. Alarmed, she glanced at the satnav, only to see that she really had managed to ignore the right-hand turn. *Shit, bugger, bollocks*, that's the last thing she needed – just when she was about to hit a highway that didn't look like a scene out of *Misery*, she'd managed to botch the turn.

Her heart dropped as the I-66 disappeared into the distance in her wing mirror.

'Can't you read a map?' Everett asked her, clearly agitated. 'Jesus Christ, I should have driven myself. Or gotten somebody who knew how to drive a car.'

Kitty wondered where Jonas learned his manners, when his father clearly didn't have any.

'It's recalculating,' Kitty said quietly, nodding her head at the built-in satnav.

Everett let loose a series of sighs as the dark blue screen calmly told them it would take an extra twenty minutes to reach their destination.

'Drake, call the airport, tell them I'm going to be late. They're going to need to get another slot. And for my sake, arrange for a competent driver to pick me up. If I have to suffer another journey like this, I'll end up killing somebody.'

The man was a drama queen. She had to bite her lip to stop herself from saying anything.

'By the way,' Everett said, hanging up the call to Drake without bothering to say goodbye, 'Drake tells me you're looking for an internship. Is that right?'

The abrupt change in conversation made Kitty breathless. 'Yes it is.'

He nodded. 'Remind me when I get back from LA. I might be able to help you with that.'

She tried not to show how excited that made her, but it was hard to keep her expression neutral. 'That would be wonderful,' she finally said. 'Thank you.'

Everett said nothing for a moment, scrolling through the messages on his smartphone. Eventually he glanced up, meeting her eyes in the mirror. 'Yeah, well, you're doing a good job with Jonas. He seems happy. I'll make a few calls and we'll see what we can do.'

She tried to keep the smile on her face, even if it felt distasteful.

'I'm always appreciative of staff who work hard and keep their mouths shut. You'll find I'm a good person to have on your side. Remember that.'

The rest of the journey passed in relative peace. Kitty followed the satnav instructions, navigating them back to the I-66, while Everett made phone call after phone call from the back seat. They managed to reach Reagan Airport only twenty minutes after the original time. Pulling up to the charter terminal, she switched off the engine while Everett pulled his small case from the boot, still muttering down the phone, and stomped into the terminal without saying goodbye. He hadn't even bothered to close the boot. Sighing loudly, Kitty climbed out of the driver's seat and walked around to the back, pushing the boot closed with an angry bang. Good riddance to him. She might have needed his help, but she had a feeling that she'd be paying for it. And maybe the price was a little too high.

Her next stop was the freight terminal, where Mia had given her instructions to pick up Jonas's Christmas gifts. They'd been purchased at great expense by Arlo, Mia's personal shopper.

The man at the gate directed her to the parking lot, and she swung the Escalade around and into an empty spot. Then she walked into the small reception, dodging the mistletoe that was hanging from the doorway, and rang the bell at the desk for attention.

Ten minutes later, she was carrying a huge pile of boxes over to the Escalade. Two uniformed workers trailed behind her, each carrying their own towers of cardboard. Organising them into the boot was an act of precision, with the boxes filling practically all the available space.

She'd just closed the boot when a woman came running out of the depot. 'Wait up, there's another package you need to take.' Her dark hair flew behind her, revealing her harassed expression. 'We won't be sad to see the back of this one, I can tell you.'

A man walked out of the depot carrying a black furry puppy. Despite its cute face, it was snapping and snarling at him, and he held it at arm's length. His expression was full of distaste.

'What's that?' Kitty asked, her voice faint.

The man put the dog down, still holding its leash. The dog ran straight for Kitty, barking and dancing around her, causing the man to shoot forward.

'It's a Portuguese Water Dog. They're supposed to be friendly.' He looked down at the animal, his eyes wide. 'This one might be a little too friendly.'

'Am I really supposed to take it?' Kitty asked, though in her heart she already knew the answer. Most employers would have warned her in advance, perhaps suggested she got a cage or at least a bowl of water to keep him hydrated. Instead, all Kitty had was a full boot and a hyperactive puppy. The thought of driving all the way back to Cutler's Gap with a puppy in the back was making her queasy.

'I can't take him in the car,' she said. 'He'll jump all over me before I even get on the highway.'

'He's not so bad. He didn't like being sent in the hold of an airplane, is all. They drugged him up; he's just coming out of it now, and it's sending him crazy. The chances are he'll be asleep as soon as you turn the engine on, although you'll do well to put something down on the floor. This one suffers from travel sickness.'

For God's sake, this was all she needed. Kitty stared at the puppy who looked back at her, his gaze open and excited. Taking a deep breath, she leaned down, scooping the beast up into her arms, and to her surprise he stopped yapping and nuzzled into her.

Maybe he wasn't so bad after all.

But then he bared his teeth and nipped her arm hard enough to almost break her skin. Kitty yelped, dropping him on the floor. He made a bid for freedom, dodging past the dog handler who started chasing him around the parking lot. Then the receptionist joined in, both of them lunging for the puppy who merrily outflanked them, heading back inside the cabin and into the warmth.

Five minutes later they were loading him into the Escalade once again. The handler had a look of supreme relief on his face. Kitty put him on the back seat, sighing when he jumped across the centre console and into the driver's seat, putting his paws on the steering wheel as if he was going to drive.

One thing was for sure; it was going to be a long journey home.

Every time Kitty looked in the rear-view mirror, the dog was staring back at her. His dark brown eyes were watery and round, his head tipped to the side at a plaintive angle. The bouncing and yapping had changed into gentle whimpers as the effects of the car journey were taking their toll on his stomach. If a dog could cry, then this one would almost certainly be bawling right now.

Kitty felt like crying herself. Apart from her old neighbours' crazy mutt, she was totally inexperienced when it came to dogs. She had no idea what to do with the puppy, apart from to stop every hour or so to let him try to do his business and wipe any dog sick from the Escalade's leather back seats.

By the time she'd stopped for a third time – in a godforsaken truck stop somewhere east of the mountains – the puppy was literally digging his heels in the mud, growling every time she tried to scoop him into her arms.

'You're not going to win,' she told him through gritted teeth. 'Even if I have to go back to Cutler's Gap with a mangled arm, you're still getting in that bloody car.'

The puppy just sat stubbornly and stared, refusing to move. How could such a cute dog look so defiant?

'Come on, it's only another hour,' she coaxed. 'Just sixty minutes and you'll be out of the car for good. You can curl up in Annie's kitchen and yap at somebody else instead.'

Not that there would be anything for him to eat. Annie's stodgy food probably wouldn't do his delicate stomach any good, and knowing Mia's distractedness there was no way she would have arranged for puppy food to be delivered. If she had any reception she'd call Annie and warn her, but once again the tall trees were blocking out her signal. Ah, she'd have to worry about that when she got back to Mountain's Reach. That's if she made it in one piece.

Half an hour later she made it to the snow-covered mountains, marvelling at the way they looked as though someone had sieved icing sugar across the land. The cloudless sky was a cerulean blue, reflecting off the Blue Ridge peaks and leaving no doubt in Kitty's mind how they got their name. Unlike the rental she'd driven a few days earlier, the Escalade gripped the road with determination, its weight and powerful engine a good match for the icy roads as they made their ascent.

The roads were winding here, twisting and turning like a blacktop helter-skelter. With each swing of the car the dog growled loudly, before promptly emptying the contents of his belly over the footwell. The stench of dog vomit wafted across to the front seat, turning Kitty's stomach until she thought that she, too, might end up sick as a dog.

If there was any doubt before, it was obvious Kitty wasn't an animal person. Not a country girl, either. More than ever she longed for the reassuring pavements of the city, lined with shops instead of trees. They may not have the same natural beauty as the snow-topped mountains, but they were infinitely safer. Not to mention fairly dog free.

'Look, dog, you're not doing yourself any favours,' she told him. 'Last time I was on these roads I managed to kill a deer. Do you think I'll have any problems committing canine murder?'

If dogs were like humans, Kitty swore that he'd be laughing right about now.

She was about to pull over to try to clean up the mess when the screen on the front console lit up, indicating an incoming call on her Bluetoothed mobile phone. Seeing Mia Klein's name formed in green lettering, Kitty rolled her eyes, accepting the call with a flick of her finger.

'Hello?'

'Kitty? It's Mia, can you hear me?' She was shouting, her voice echoing around as if she was in a metal box. 'I'm in an elevator. Did you manage to pick up everything we need?'

'I've picked up the gifts,' Kitty told her. 'And the puppy. I've definitely got the puppy.'

'How is he?' Mia asked. 'Do you think Jonas will like him? I wanted to surprise him on Christmas morning, he has no idea about it at all. The puppy's related to Bo, the Obamas' gorgeous doggie. I took one look at him online and just knew Jonas had to have him.'

Kitty glanced back at the dog. He was standing upright on all fours, still glaring at her as if she was the source of all his woes. 'He's, um, a character all right. I'm sure Jonas will love him.' Even if nobody else did.

'Oh, thank goodness. Children are always so hard to buy for. I can't wait to see his face on Christmas morning; we must shoot lots of video. He's always wanted a little brother or sister.'

Kitty looked over at the dog who was now yawning on the back seat. The puppy had two speeds – crazy or fast asleep.

' … so you just need to hide him somewhere for a week,' Mia continued, interrupting Kitty's thoughts.

'What?'

'The puppy,' Mia said patiently. 'You need to keep him out

of Jonas's sight for a week. It's a big house, it shouldn't be that difficult. Hide him in the attic or something, nobody will find him there.'

It was the first time that Kitty began to feel sorry for the dog. He may have been irritable, and a disgusting vomit machine, but he was going to more than meet his match with the Kleins. If Mia thought it was appropriate to stash a living, breathing animal in an attic for a week, God only knew how she was going to treat the puppy once he was part of the family.

Maybe Kitty had more in common with him than she thought.

'I don't think we can hide him in the attic,' she said, weakly. 'I'll ask Annie for her ideas. Maybe there's an outhouse or something that we can put him in.' That's if she managed to finish this journey alive.

'Oh, would you? That would be wonderful. I don't think she likes me very much.'

The puppy barked loudly, making Kitty jump. It was the first time he'd done anything other than yap or whimper. Maybe he understood what she'd said and was making his distaste known. She couldn't blame him, really, it was cold enough to freeze the lake out there, and who would want to spend the next week hiding in an outhouse?

Who would want to spend a lifetime being holed up with the Kleins, come to think of it? Once again it seemed the two of them had a lot in common. At least she was getting something out of it after Christmas. The poor dog had no such luck.

'Well I'd better go. I've got an appointment and then some phone calls to make. Oh, they did tell you he's a vegan, right? You'll need to order him in some special dog food, there's somewhere on the internet that stocks it.'

Vegan. Of course. What dog would want to eat meat when it could have a bowl full of tofu mixed with some yummy, filling pulses? Kitty rolled her eyes and ended the call, wondering how the hell she was going to get the vegan dog food company to deliver in Cutler's Gap within the next twenty-four hours. And whether the puppy would ever forgive her for denying him meat-based protein.

From the expression on his face, she didn't think he would.

10

Sir, he's a good dog, and a fair dog
– The Merry Wives of Windsor

'What's that?' Annie asked, her nose wrinkling up as Kitty carried the puppy into the kitchen. Kitty presumed it was a rhetorical question. In spite of having lived in the middle of nowhere for more than forty years, she was certain Annie had laid eyes on a dog before.

Maybe not one like this puppy, though.

'It's Jonas's Christmas present,' Kitty whispered, gesturing at Annie to keep it down. 'Mia had him flown in from LA this morning. I don't think he's enjoying his trip.'

'He stinks.' Annie's distaste was written all over her face. 'What on earth *is* that smell?'

In an effort to keep the puppy hidden from Jonas, Kitty had kept him locked in the Escalade until bedtime. He clearly wasn't house-trained, nor had the effects of the winding road gone unnoticed by his bowels. As a result, the inside of the car now resembled a cesspit.

'You don't want to know,' Kitty told her. 'I've tried cleaning it off him as best I can, but without a hose I don't think I'm ever going to get the smell out.' She put the dog down and grabbed a bowl from the cupboard, filling it with water and placing it on the floor. The puppy approached it slowly, stilling his tail as if he was suspicious. Sniffing at the water, he shot a baleful look up at Kitty before dipping his tongue into the bowl and taking a drink.

'She bought him for Christmas?' Annie asked, still frowning. 'What's she planning to do, wrap him up with a bow?'

Kitty shrugged. 'She wants me to hide him somewhere for the next week. If Jonas finds him before Christmas morning she won't be happy.'

'She never is,' Annie grumbled. 'Fancy buying a puppy for Christmas, hasn't she heard all the warnings? What breed is it anyway?'

'A Portuguese Water Dog,' Kitty said. 'Oh, and he's a vegan, too,' she added.

'A what?'

Kitty tried to stifle her smile. 'A vegan. No meat, no fish, no dairy products. I'm supposed to order his food online.'

Annie gaped in horror, as if Kitty had told her that she needed to feed him with human remains. 'I've never heard such nonsense in my life. What kind of dog doesn't eat meat? What are you going to feed him while you wait for his special food to arrive? It's not as if you can starve the poor little mite.'

Kitty looked down at the puppy, who was still lapping at the water. She hadn't thought of that. It was going to take at least a day for his special food to be delivered. She couldn't refuse to feed him while they waited for the courier to arrive, could she?

'Kitty!' Jonas's plaintive cry filled the air. Suddenly the kitchen was full of action as Annie scooped the dog up and

Kitty searched in vain for somewhere to stash him. Her eyes lighted on the pantry door, and she turned to Annie with a questioning look, only to receive a severe shake of the head.

OK, then. Clearly the pantry was out.

'Get the dog away from here,' Annie hissed. 'I'll distract Jonas.'

That's how Kitty found herself stuck outside the kitchen window, trying to keep the puppy calm in spite of the inky-black night and the cold, wet ground. He kept dipping his paws in the snow then wiggling his nose, staring up at Kitty as if it were all her fault.

She squatted down, beneath the line of the window, trying to disguise herself from any prying eyes, aware of how stupid she must look.

It was a full five minutes before Annie showed her face, craning her head around the kitchen door in an attempt to locate the errant Kitty.

'You still there?' the housekeeper hissed.

'I'm here,' Kitty called back, her voice just as low. 'But I think he might have done a poop on the deck.'

'Well he can't stay here,' Annie told her.

Kitty knew that. She needed to find a hiding spot. At least until Christmas Day, when hopefully he was going to be some-body else's problem.

'Where should I hide him?'

Annie gave a deep sigh. 'There's nowhere that I can think of. Unless you shove him in the old icehouse, but I suspect he'd die of hypothermia within a few hours.'

Annie was right. There was nowhere outside that Kitty could hide the dog that wouldn't result in him getting frozen. Even the summerhouse at the edge of the treeline was covered in snow and icicles, its windows frozen opaque. The inside of it couldn't have been much warmer than the icehouse.

'We're going to have to tell Jonas,' Kitty whispered, sighing at the thought of his gift being spoiled.

That's when Annie stretched her head around the doorjamb again. 'You could take him down to the cabin.'

'Where?'

'To the cabin by the lake. It's got heat and it's got food, plus Adam has nothing better to do. Take the dog down there and I'm sure he'll help us out.'

Kitty was taken aback. The thought of taking the puppy down through the forest and over to the ramshackle wooden house was enough to make her stomach turn. The last thing she wanted to do was ask Adam for help after their previous encounters. He may have apologised, but she was in no doubt what he really thought of her. This would only make it worse.

'Surely there must be somewhere up here I can keep an eye on him,' she whispered back. 'A garage or something?'

A silence was followed by Annie's hollow laugh. 'If you can think of anywhere let me know. I've been looking for a bolthole for these last forty years.'

In the gloom of the evening, Kitty scanned the grey-coloured landscape, her eyes failing to take in anything but the snow-covered land. There was no good hiding place for a small dog.

It was the cabin by the lake or bust.

'Does Adam even like dogs?' Kitty hissed. 'Am I going to embarrass myself by turning up at his door?'

Annie walked through the doorway, her stout frame illuminated by the yellow kitchen light. It lent her an almost angel-like aura. 'If there's one thing I know about Adam, it's that he's a sucker for a sad story. All you have to do is spin him a line and he's bound to look after the dog.'

'I need to spin him a line?' Kitty repeated faintly. 'What kind of line?' She was rubbish at lying, couldn't tell a fib if she tried. A sense of impending doom came over her.

Annie huffed. 'Just tell him it's a rescue dog or something. Make up a story about how he managed to save a whole family from a fire before being burned himself. Anything to make Adam inclined to lend us a hand.'

'You want me to lie to him?' Please, no. Anything but that. She didn't need to make him any angrier than he already was.

'No!' Annie protested. 'I wouldn't dream of it. Just make it easy for him to say yes.'

Somehow, Kitty couldn't imagine a single situation where Adam would easily say yes. All she could think of was his irritated tone and his disapproving stare.

'OK, if you say so,' she agreed. 'But if he shouts at me, I'm blaming you.'

'Adam won't shout at you, he's a teddy bear,' Annie replied.

Kitty grimaced, pulling her bottom lip firmly between her teeth. If there was one thing she knew, it was that the angry man living down by the lake was nothing like a teddy bear. If it wasn't for the puppy and the fact that Jonas deserved a Christmas surprise, there was no way she'd be going down to the lake right now.

She couldn't help wondering how she'd managed to get in this position. Reliant upon the good grace of a man who had already proved himself graceless. More importantly, she wondered what the hell she had to do to get herself out of it.

*

With the puppy trotting alongside her, they cleared the final distance to the old cabin, leaving two parallel trails of footprints behind them. Behind the thick drapes, Kitty could make out that there was a light burning, and from the wispy grey smoke curling up out of the chimney, there was a fire burning in there, too. The sight of it made her shiver.

What wouldn't she give to warm up beside a roaring fire right now?

'Well, boy, here goes nothing,' she whispered, rapping on the wooden door with her knuckles. 'Try to behave, OK? If he refuses to take you then we're both out of luck.'

The door swung open, revealing Adam behind it, a look of surprise crossing his face when he saw Kitty and the dog standing there. His hair was wet – maybe he'd just come out of the shower – and he was wearing a plain black T-shirt along with soft, comfortable jeans. Once again she was hit by his attractiveness, so much clearer to her when he wasn't shouting. This time her heart pounding against her ribs had nothing to do with fear.

And everything to do with the way he looked.

Before she went to sleep last night, she'd spent an hour on her laptop, Googling him. All the pictures of him showed Adam as freshly shaven, his dark hair spilling over his forehead, his height eclipsing everybody around him. Even in those still images he had an aura that couldn't be denied. No wonder people opened up to him in his documentaries, with those wide brown eyes and warm smile, it was almost impossible not to crumble in front of him.

Her eyes slid down from his face, taking in the broad shoulders and the hard planes of his chest, barely disguised by his tight T-shirt. He had this aura of protection, as though he could just stand in front of you and shield you from a blast, like some kind of superhero in a comic.

'Are you OK?' His eyes scanned down from her face, to the excited puppy next to her. He frowned slightly, taking it all in. But he didn't seem angry. Not this time, thank goodness.

'I hope so,' Kitty said, following his gaze down to the black furry dog. 'I have a bit of a problem.' She inclined her head to the puppy. 'Can we come in?'

He licked his lips slowly, his eyes blinking faster than usual, lifting his hand up to rub his bearded jawline. Then he stepped aside, gesturing for her to come in, closing the door behind her. She scooped the dog into her arms, walking into his warm, welcoming living room.

'I'm not exactly prepared for company,' Adam told her. 'I can't offer you anything unless you like either coffee or beer.'

The thought of a beer after the day she'd had was like nectar to the soul. 'I'd love a beer,' she said, trying to hide just how desperate she was for it. 'And a bowl of water for the puppy would be great.'

'What's his name?' he asked, walking into the small kitchen at the end of the living area and pulling open the fridge.

'He hasn't got a name yet,' she said, wondering if she should have remedied that. How long could she go on calling him 'the puppy'?

'Where's he come from? Is he yours?' Grabbing two brown bottles of beer from the refrigerator, he popped the caps off and passed one to her, lifting the other to his lips and taking a mouthful.

Kitty took a long sip of her own beer, letting the liquid slide down her throat and warm her stomach. She couldn't remember the last time she'd had a bottle of honest-to-God beer. It tasted better than ice-cold water on a summer's day.

'You want to sit down?' Adam gestured at the old sofa and chairs that surrounded the roaring fire. The whole room looked cosy and rustic, with hand-carved furniture and lived-in uphol-stery. It made her want to curl up and relax.

He filled a bowl full of water and placed it down on the tiled floor. Seeing it, the puppy began to wriggle in Kitty's arms, until she placed him down. He ran straight over and lapped furiously. Adam's face softened as he watched the little bundle of fur drink from the old china bowl, and he squatted down, stroking the puppy's back. His hand was almost as big as the animal itself. The puppy stopped drinking and began to furi-ously lick at Adam's palm, causing a smile to break out on his face. It was crazy how good-looking the man was, especially when he was smiling. Kitty tried to remind herself that this same man had spent most of the week shouting at her.

Yeah, tell that to her racing heart.

Leaving the puppy by his bowl, the two of them walked over to the chairs beside the old inglenook fireplace. Unlike the rest of the cabin, the fireplace was clad with stone, with orange flames dancing in the cast-iron grate. Kitty was desperate to feel its warmth seeping into her bones. They sat silently for a moment, sipping at their drinks, and it felt somehow peaceful. For the first time that day, she felt herself starting to relax.

Funny how quickly things changed.

Though the chair was big, Adam's body dominated it, with his thick, rippled chest and long, lean legs. He took another sip of beer, regarding her silently. He didn't seem at all embar-rassed at his scrutiny of her, and didn't seem in a rush to end it, either. She could feel her cheeks flush, and not from the warmth of the fire. There was something about the way he was looking at her that made her feel exposed.

Clearing her throat, she glanced over at the dog. He was sitting patiently next to his bowl, his tail wagging. So much happier than when he'd been in the car. Maybe he really was just travel sick.

Finally, she broke their silence. 'Um, I need somewhere to hide the puppy, and Annie suggested that you might be able to help.'

Adam raised his eyebrows. 'Why on earth would you need to hide a puppy?' His voice was deep and smooth – the same voice she'd heard in the clip she'd watched on her laptop last night. The kind of voice you paid attention to.

'It's a Christmas present for Jonas, and we can't let him see it. Otherwise the surprise will be spoiled. So I need to find somewhere that we can hide him without Jonas finding him, and this was the only place we could think of.' Her words tumbled out of her mouth as if she couldn't stand their taste.

'So I'm the last resort,' Adam said drily.

'No! Not at all.' Kitty's tongue tripped over her words in an attempt to form them. 'It's just that there are no outhouses and if I put him in the attic Jonas is bound to get suspicious and go up there to investigate. And Annie said you liked animals. So . . .'

Adam leaned back in his chair. His long legs were sprawled out in front of him. Kitty couldn't help but admire the firmness of his thighs and the way they filled out the denim of his jeans. Out of his bulky coat and thick beanie – and most importantly without a furious look on his face – he seemed a different person.

She shook her head as if to get some sense into herself. This

96

was the man who'd shouted at her twice, and told her she was a terrible nanny. She needed to take hold of herself.

'Is he house-trained?'

Kitty side-eyed the puppy, remembering the steaming pile she'd had to clean out of the car. 'I think so.' It wasn't really a lie, was it?

'What does he eat?'

There was no way she was going to tell him the dog was a vegan, not when Adam seemed almost willing to helping her. 'Oh, anything. Beef, chicken, rice. Whatever you happen to have in your cupboards.'

He turned to stare at the dog again, his gaze steady as he took him in. 'What kind of breed is he anyway?'

'A Portuguese Water Dog. Like the Obamas' Bo.' She didn't know why she bothered to add this. It wasn't as if his similarity to the ex-president's dog was a selling point.

'I've never heard of them.'

'Oh, they're a lovely breed. Friendly, happy, really a man's best friend. You'll hardly notice he's here.' Suddenly she sounded like an infomercial for Portuguese Water Dogs. No wonder Adam was biting down a laugh.

'Why do I think you're full of shit?'

Because she was? 'Honestly, he's as good as gold. It's only for a little while, I promise he won't be any trouble.'

'If I take him, and I mean *if*, then you'll owe me.'

She nodded rapidly. 'Of course.'

'So I get to ask for something in return.' He didn't say it as a question. The tone of his voice – low and gravelly – sent shivers down her spine.

'You do?'

'Yeah,' he said slowly. 'I do.'

97

Her heart was beating annoyingly fast. When she finally found the words to reply, her voice was thick with anticipation. 'What do you want me to do?' Was it wrong that she had bad thoughts of her own?

Adam stared at her, the tip of his tongue running along his full lips. Kitty watched its progress, fascinated, trying to ignore the way he took her breath away. He didn't reply for at least a minute, preferring to look at her as if he was sizing her up, or maybe considering her fate. It was both tantalising and terrifying.

'I don't know yet, I need to think about it,' he said finally. 'I'll tell you when I've decided.'

Excited by the realisation she'd solved the puppy problem, yet shocked by his bargaining, Kitty found herself nodding, still unable to tear her eyes away from his. The thought of having to do whatever Adam asked of her was enough to send shivers of anticipation shooting down through her spine.

The puppy was curled up in the makeshift bed Adam had put together – a wooden box lined with blankets and pillows. He snored softly, his tiny body rising up and down with each breath, the occasional shudder interrupting the rhythm of his sleep. Adam stared out of the window, looking at the path Kitty had made in the snow as she walked back to the big house, wondering if he should have insisted on walking her back there, rather than letting her go alone.

Not that there were any dangers between here and the big house, unless you counted the lake. But she had a habit of attracting trouble – from a deer in the road, to a puppy in her arms – and he wouldn't put it past her to make heavy work of the journey back.

The puppy gave a little yap, then shuffled in the box, curling up like a cat. Adam glanced at him, still trying to take in the fact he'd actually agreed to look after the mutt. It wasn't like him to acquiesce quite so easily.

He was doing it for Jonas, he reminded himself. For his nephew. The poor kid deserved a surprise on Christmas Day, he had to put up with enough shit the rest of the year. It wasn't Kitty's pretty smile or big blue eyes that made him agree to this arrangement, no, it was his need to make his nephew happy.

So why was it that when he climbed into his soft, queen-size bed, pulling the blankets over his strong body, all he could think about was her? The way she'd smiled at him as he petted the dog, the way she'd drunk the beer as though she'd never tasted anything better. The way she'd thanked him softly before she left, leaning down to stroke the puppy one more time, her expression warm and open.

He closed his eyes, tossing and turning in the bed until the covers were all twisted on his body. From the living area he could still hear the dog – for such a small animal he knew how to make a lot of noise, even when he was asleep.

He'd been living here for too long, that was the problem. When there was nothing in your life except snow, running and the occasional bit of woodwork, a pretty girl arriving in town took on a meaning it never would have before. She was only here for a few weeks, he just had to get through them, and then everything would go back to normal.

Whatever the hell normal meant.

11

Thou knowest, winter tames man,
woman and beast

– The Taming of the Shrew

'Hey.' Adam gave her a nod as he opened the door. 'Sorry it took me a while, your dog's just crapped all over the cabin floor.'

It wasn't the welcome Kitty had expected. She was standing at the front door to the lodge, wrapped warmly in her Michelin-man ski jacket and insulated trousers, dusting the thin layer of snow from her hat. Before Adam had opened the front door she'd been staring at the lintel, thinking it would be perfect for a large bunch of mistletoe. The luscious green leaves and pale white berries would look beautiful against the dark wood of the building.

She could tell he wasn't exaggerating from the stench that hit her as soon as he pulled the door open. For a small puppy, that dog really knew how to make himself known.

'Oh goodness, I'm so sorry,' she said, grimacing at the pile of crap the puppy had deposited on Adam's gleaming tiles. 'Where's your cleaning stuff? I'll get rid of it now.' She quickly shed her outer layer of quilted warmth, revealing tight black leggings and a thick woollen sweater, hanging her coat on the hooks next to the door.

'The bleach is under the sink,' Adam told her, pointing at the kitchen. 'If you get rid of the shit, I'll mop the floor.' He gave her an enquiring look. 'I thought you said he was house-trained.'

Kitty tried not to look guilty. 'Maybe he's just not used to it here. Did you let him out this morning?'

'I let him out pretty much every two hours in the night. Every time he woke me up yapping.'

She felt terrible. She'd always assumed dogs slept through the night straight away, hadn't considered they might be more like babies than adults. 'That sounds awful. You must be exhausted.'

Now she looked at him, she could see the dark shadows beneath his pretty eyes.

'Yeah, well, next time you want to bring your dog round, maybe let me have a week's notice first. I'll stock up on sleep in advance.'

'It's not my dog. It's Jonas's dog, I'm just the sap who has to keep it hidden,' she pointed out.

Adam raised his eyebrows. 'I think you'll find I'm the sap around here. I don't see the stupid mutt crapping all over your floor.'

'Just give him the chance,' Kitty muttered.

The puppy was sitting happily on the slate tiles in the middle of the cabin, wagging his tail and staring up at Kitty with a satisfied expression. She grabbed a bag from the kitchen, scooping the mess up with the plastic, picking at the remainder with some kitchen towel.

Oh boy, did it stink. It must have been all that meat they'd given him yesterday. Clearly it didn't agree with his intestines. Luckily, Adam pulled a bucket full of bleached water over, mopping at the floor with easy movements, the clean smell of ammonia replacing the earlier stench.

Christmas really couldn't come soon enough. After that, the puppy wouldn't be her problem any more. Wouldn't be Adam's either. Strange how that thought didn't make her feel any better. Even stranger that even though the crap on the floor was absolutely disgusting, she was somehow enjoying herself.

'There, all done.' Adam took the bucket and mop and placed them outside on his porch. It was strange watching this man, the same man who was responsible for all those amazing documentaries, being so domesticated in his own cabin. Sexy, too.

Damn it, she needed to stop with that line of thought.

'Thank you for being so gracious about it,' Kitty said, scrubbing her hands in the sink. 'You didn't have to be.'

He gave a half-smile. 'It's fine. He's a dog, a little mess is to be expected. And anyway, it's helped me decide what I want from you.'

She blinked rapidly. 'What do you mean?'

'Remember last night? When I said you owed me for looking after the dog, and I needed to think about what you could do in return? Well I've decided. I want you to come down here every morning and help me with the dog. You can feed him, help me clean up. Maybe take him out for some exercise.'

There was a depth to his voice that sparked her interest. Not that it needed sparking. She was hyper-aware of his proximity, and his masculine presence. It surrounded her like a blanket.

'I can't,' she said, breathless. 'I have Jonas to look after. I have to get him up, make him breakfast. He'll wonder where I am.'

Adam shrugged. 'Annie can help you. So can Mia and Everett if they want you to keep the dog secret. Come over before he's up, if you want, I'm always awake before six anyway.'

'You are?' Her mouth felt as dry as the logs crackling in the fireplace. Her face felt as hot, too.

He nodded. 'Yeah. And I really could do with your help. I go running every day, I don't want the dog interfering with my routine.'

'But you're OK that he interferes with mine?' Damn, she really should just bite her tongue off and be done with it.

Why was it that every time Adam looked at her, she felt a jolt of pleasure rushing from her head to her toes? He was just a man. OK, so he was a very fine, very strong, very gorgeous man. But he was still just a man.

'If you don't want to help me, then say so,' Adam said. 'Maybe Annie can come down or something.'

'No, no, it's fine.' She nodded, as if to emphasise her words. 'Of course I'll help. After all, you're the one doing me a favour, or at least doing Jonas a favour.'

'OK then. If you can get down here by six thirty, that will give me enough time for my run before you need to get back to Jonas. And if there're any problems, I'm sure Annie will help.'

Kitty nodded, trying not to think of how early she'd have to get up in the morning. Early enough to make sure she'd done her make-up, brushed her hair, and wasn't looking like some hag-troll. 'I guess I'll see you tomorrow.'

This time his smile widened. 'I guess you will.' His gaze

locked on hers, and for a moment it felt as though all the air had been forced out of her chest.

The thought of seeing him every morning thrilled and frightened her in equal measure. She wasn't sure which feeling she liked more.

Adam stood on the porch, watching Kitty's path long after her shapely body disappeared into the forest. His cheeks were aching from smiling so hard. She'd turned out to be completely different from the girl he'd imagined her to be. If he was being honest, he'd expected her to baulk at the smell, and tell him she was above cleaning up dog shit from the floor. The fact she'd got down on her hands and knees and scrubbed his floor had intrigued him. He couldn't imagine Mia, or any of the other women he'd worked with in LA, agreeing to clean up after the pooch. What was it that made Kitty so different?

It had given him the opportunity to get another look at that body, too. Once she'd taken that ridiculous padded jacket off, revealing a pale pink sweater that moulded her curves, he'd found it hard to tear his eyes away. Maybe that's why he'd made that stupid request for her to come down to the cabin every day. God knew, he didn't really need any help with the puppy. The tiny ball of fur didn't do much more than eat, yap and crap everywhere.

He really needed to get out more. Maybe if he wasn't so isolated, he wouldn't find her nearly so attractive. Boredom, that was all it was, right?

The puppy yapped loudly, running out to the porch and sitting down at his heel. The steaming pile of crap aside, he really wasn't a bad mutt.

He gave another short, sharp bark.

'What is it, boy?' Adam dropped to his haunches and tickled the dog beneath his chin. In return he got a nuzzle, soft fur pressed against his arm, and he smiled again, somehow enjoying the companionship.

The dog's gaze was pointed up the mountain, following the trail of footsteps that led into the woods. 'You worried about Kitty?' Adam whispered. 'She'll be fine. Nobody would dare go up against her.'

Taking one last glance up the mountain, Adam shook his head and walked back into his cabin, pulling the door closed just as soon as the dog had followed him inside. Damned if he wasn't feeling as interested in her as the stupid mutt was.

He wasn't at all sure how he was supposed to feel about that.

Kitty arrived back at the big house to a scene of intense activity, with Annie running from room to room, her face flushed and shiny from her exertions. Kitty's face was red, too – more from her encounter with Adam than the short, frozen journey back from the cabin. She was still a little breathless at the memory.

The smell of cinnamon and allspice filled the air, along with a clean pine scent wafting from the huge tree propped up in the hallway.

'You're here!' Annie said, staring at Kitty with relief. 'Thank goodness, we've got a lot of work to do.'

Jonas's head popped up from beneath a huge pile of paper chains. 'We have exactly three hours to decorate the house for Christmas.'

Unlike Annie, Jonas looked as though he was thoroughly enjoying himself. A Santa hat was jauntily perched on top of his blond curls, and he had tinsel wrapped around his neck like a scarf. Music echoed out from the speakers in the living room; the perennial Christmas tunes that everybody knew. Stacked in the hallway were boxes full of old decorations, with beautifully painted glass baubles that looked like family heirlooms. Her heart warmed to see him so happy. He really was a good kid.

'What's the rush to decorate?' Kitty asked, as the oven timer bell began to chime, sending Annie bustling back to the kitchen. The old housekeeper grabbed a thick padded oven glove to pull a baking tray full of fragrant cookies from the hot stove. Kitty trailed behind, still trying to work out what was going on.

'Mrs Klein is coming home, we just got the call from the hospital. Mr Klein is arranging for her ambulance right now. He wants us to get this house shipshape and ready for Christmas, to cheer her up.'

The atmosphere here was a complete contrast to the relative calm of the cabin – the puppy's accident aside. She could feel her pulse start to speed with the tempo of Annie and Jonas's running around. It was impossible not to get caught up in the whirlwind.

Since she'd arrived, Kitty had wondered about the sort of woman Mary Klein was. Along with her husband, Mary had worked hard at the family business, building it up into a multimillion-dollar empire. When the boys were still small, the couple took the company public, retiring permanently to West Virginia with the proceeds. Beyond that she knew very little about the lady.

'Then we should make this the best Christmas ever,' Kitty said, scanning the kitchen for ideas. More than anybody she knew how important it was to be surrounded by family during the holidays. 'Let's decorate and bake, and then we can plan some nice things for Mrs Klein, something all the family can enjoy with her. What sort of things does she like?'

A smile pushed up Annie's plump cheeks. 'Oh, bless you, you're a good girl. You've never even met her and you're trying to cheer her up.' Her expression darkened. 'Which is more than I can say for *some* people.'

Kitty didn't ask who she meant; with Mia still in the city, and Everett stuck in meetings in LA, it was pretty obvious.

'Does Mrs Klein like Christmas movies?' Kitty asked.

'Oh yes, she loves them. Back when the boys were young they'd all sit together and watch *It's a Wonderful Life*. This family has always been crazy about the movies.'

'Then we should get a screen put into her room,' Kitty suggested. 'If she's up to the company we could all watch movies with her. There's something so heartwarming about watching festive films surrounded by the people you love.'

Both women were silent for a moment, lost in their thoughts. They had more in common than you'd first think by looking at them, Kitty thought. They were living far, far away from home, with families that weren't their own. Maybe that's why silly things such as holiday traditions seemed so important to them.

'She'd love that,' Annie said softly. 'I'll ask Adam to arrange for the big screen to be put in her bedroom. We can have a different movie each night – I know all her favourites – and we can introduce Jonas to some Klein family traditions. It's just a shame she won't be able to go to church. That's the other thing she likes to do every Christmas Eve, without fail. You never heard somebody with a voice as sweet as hers – she loves singing along with all the carols and hymns.'

Kitty frowned. There was no way they could transport Mrs Klein to church, not with her hip in such a fragile condition. Though they had plenty of Christmas music set up on the stereo system, it wasn't the same as hearing a choir of voices; it didn't come close at all.

Leaning her elbows on the kitchen counter, she propped her chin up with her hand. If Mrs Klein loved church services and carol singing, then that's what she would have. She didn't know how and she didn't know where, but somehow Mrs Klein would get her Christmas Eve service.

Even if it took all the creativity Kitty had left.

12

Kindness in women, not their beauteous
looks, shall win my love

– The Taming of the Shrew

'You're in charge of a dog?' Cesca asked, sounding as though she was trying to swallow down a laugh. 'But you hate dogs.'

'He's OK,' Kitty said, keeping her voice low as she leaned her head against the living room wall. Jonas was about ten yards away, attempting to arrange the nativity scene on the console table. Even with that distance, she didn't want him to hear and spoil the surprise. 'He's just a puppy.'

'How the hell do you get yourself into these situations?' Cesca asked. 'Only you would end up in the middle of nowhere with a bloody dog.'

'Unlike you,' Kitty pointed out, still whispering, 'who just ended up in the middle of nowhere with the man she hated most in the world.'

'Well now you put it like that, maybe we've got a lot in common.' This time Cesca let her laughter escape, chuckling loudly. 'But don't forget I ended up falling in love with that man. Don't tell me you're going to fall in love with the dog, too?'

Kitty rolled her eyes. 'That's lovely, Jonas,' she shouted as he looked at her for a reaction. 'They look great.' Bringing her attention back to her sister, she added, 'I don't think I'll be falling for any animals here. Or men, for that matter.' Why the heck did that make her think about Adam? Ugh, she needed to get him out of her brain. 'And anyway, the dog has been found a temporary home, far away from me. I only have to see him once a day.'

'Ooh, where?'

'He's staying with Jonas's uncle.'

'The famous Adam Klein? Mr Cornflakes?' Cesca asked, sounding surprised. 'Doesn't he hate your guts?'

'That's him.'

'Maybe he's not so bad after all,' Cesca said. 'How old did you say he was again?'

'Cess ... ' Kitty warned. 'Don't go there.'

'Where? I'm just asking how old he is, for sisterly reasons. You know, in case the two of you end up bonding over cornflakes or something.'

'Stop it.'

Cesca laughed. 'So how old is he? Tell me, or I'll Google him. And then I'll send you sexy photos of him every day.'

Kitty sighed. Once Cesca got the bit between her teeth she was impossible to evade. 'I don't know, thirty-something, I guess?'

'Ooh, a much older man. You floozy.'

'There's nothing going on!' Kitty protested. Annie walked into the living room and raised an eyebrow at her. 'I've got to go, I'm in the middle of decorating the house.'

'OK, but call me back later. I need to know everything.'

'There's nothing to know. And I'm busy later.'

'Doing what?' Cesca asked.

'Avoiding you. Now goodbye.' Kitty flicked her finger across the screen, ending the call, before walking over to help Jonas and Annie with the decorations.

Less than a minute later her phone buzzed in her pocket, telling her she had a text message. It was almost certainly from Cesca.

Yeah, she wouldn't be looking at that any time soon.

By the time Adam and his father returned to the house in the late afternoon, all the decorations were hanging and the tree was lit up with hundreds of tiny lights. They blinked on and off to the sound of the Christmas album, while Jonas and Kitty sang along.

Adam's expression of shock when he walked through the door made Kitty want to smile. He looked around, his eyes wide, as if full of childlike wonder. Mr Klein's eyes filled with tears, and he shook his head.

'Did you do this?' Adam asked Annie, his voice gruff.

'The three of us did. Though I have to admit with my knees being as bad as they are, Kitty did most of the hard work.'

'You should have seen her climb up the ladder to put the star at the top of the tree,' Jonas told him. 'She was so wobbly I thought she was going to fall off.'

'I'm not good with heights,' Kitty admitted, looking at the floor with embarrassment. 'I got a little dizzy up there.'

When she looked up again, her eyes met Adam's. Like earlier, when they were talking about the dog, he had a softness in his expression that almost took her breath away.

'Thank you,' he finally said. 'It means a lot.'

'Kitty had another idea as well. She suggested we move

111

the big screen TV up to Mrs Klein's room so we can all have movie nights together. You know how much Mary loves her Christmas films.'

'It was your idea, too,' Kitty protested. She felt uncomfortable in the spotlight of everybody's stares. 'You were the one who said she loved *It's a Wonderful Life*, so don't give me all the credit.'

Adam was still looking at her. Kitty had to admit there was something about his scrutiny that made her feel warm from the inside out. There was also something about seeing him up here in the house that confused her; surrounded by civilisation he looked less angry and feral than he did when she saw him down by the lake.

For the first time she saw a resemblance to Everett in him. As much as she disliked her boss, she had to admit he was a good-looking man. Not attractive, though. That took more than simple skin-deep beauty. To be attractive you had to have a beautiful soul. With his angry temperament and heated outbursts, Everett clearly didn't have that.

'I think it's a great idea,' Adam said, his voice still soft. 'I'll get the TV carried up to her room. Her ambulance should be here in an hour or so. It will be good to have her home for the holidays.'

Something about his expression tugged at Kitty's heartstrings. His eyes were clouded and distant, like a little boy lost.

Memories of her own mother popped into Kitty's mind. Faded photographs of a woman who always had the biggest smile, surrounded by four young girls and the chaos they brought with them. With her family around her, Milly Shakespeare always seemed in her element.

Maybe he noticed the tears springing to Kitty's eyes, or

perhaps he was just grateful for her suggestions. Whatever it was, Adam walked over and grabbed her hand, squeezing it tightly within his calloused palm. The unexpected shock of his touch made Kitty's heart stutter.

'Thank you,' Adam said again. 'It will mean everything to Mom.'

Her breath still caught in her throat, all Kitty could do was nod, biting her lip to stop the tears from forming. Adam let her hand go and turned away, walking out of the kitchen and into the hallway. She watched him intently, trying to work out exactly who he was. Angry deer-killer, gruff bearded man, kind uncle ... None of them quite described the man whose touch just set her on fire. He was multifaceted and complicated as hell, more difficult to work out than a quadratic equation.

Yet he was a puzzle she was desperate to solve.

Adam walked into the living room and over to the wide picture window, leaning against the wall in an effort to catch his breath. He had to leave the kitchen before he did something stupid ... like cry, or possibly hug the hell out of Jonas's English nanny. There was something about the way she was staring at him, her eyes wide and glassy, her expression full of emotion, that made him want to gather her in his arms and hold her tight.

It was just the excitement of the day playing tricks on his mind. Even when he was filming, and having to deal with the horrors of drug dealers or traffickers, he always managed to find succour in the warm arms of a willing woman. This need for Kitty Shakespeare was no different to that.

A distraction, that's all she was. Not an unwelcome one, either. But it took a lot for him to drag his mind away from the way she'd looked in that hallway, her blonde hair haloed by the flashing tree lights. A conflict raged inside him, and he tried to remind himself that she'd driven him crazy ever since she'd arrived on the mountain, from the moment he'd climbed out of his truck and seen her leaning over that dying deer.

But that wasn't all she was. He'd seen her play with Jonas until the kid was howling with laughter, take care of a puppy that she hadn't asked for, and now she'd decorated a house that didn't belong to her. She was kind, that much was obvious, but there was so much more to her than that. It was taking every ounce of strength he had not to want to find out what that was.

His father walked into the room and came to a stop on the rug in the centre of the wooden floor, looking all around at the festive decorations. He had an air of frailty that wasn't there before. His wife's accident had taken its toll on his father, too. The man Adam remembered from his childhood – that vibrant, alpha male who spent his daytime hours in the corporate rat race and yet still managed to find quality time for his sons – was long gone.

'Your mom's going to love this,' his dad said, finally resting his gaze on Adam. 'She always did like to go all-out for the holidays.'

Adam flashed his father a stiff smile. 'She will. Do you remember the Christmas I broke my arm? She still insisted I climb up the ladder and hang the decorations one-handed. She said that just because I was stupid enough to get caught on the football field, didn't mean I got excused from doing the hard work at home.'

Not that he'd minded. Adam was always too active a child to willingly sit on the sidelines.

'It's going to mean a lot to her, spending this Christmas surrounded by her family.' His father's look was pointed.

'It will,' Adam agreed.

'But there's something that would mean more to her, something that's been worrying at her for these past months.'

Discomfort wrapped its way around Adam like a heavy cloak. He knew exactly what his father was going to say, yet he didn't want to engage with that train of thought. Truth be told, he didn't want to have a conversation like that at all. He and his father usually stuck to easy topics, like sport and the Nasdaq, peppered with the occasional conversation about the news. As much as he loved his father, Adam had never shared an emotional vocabulary with him. The long, deep talks always happened with his mom.

But this was a discussion he was unwilling to have with either of them.

'Dad . . .'

'You know it's true, son. It's broken her heart seeing you and Ev at each other's throats. We thought when you came back from Colombia and went to stay in LA, that everything was going to be OK. What the hell happened to the two of you out there? Why won't you talk to him?'

Adam's heart dropped. As a kid, his role in the family had always been that of the peacemaker. To be the one causing pain for his parents made him ache inside. But still, there was no way he could forgive his brother.

It choked him up to be caught in the middle.

'I'll be civil to him,' Adam said. 'But I can't promise any more than that.'

'But why?'

The confusion on his father's face was killing him.

'You don't want to know.' Of that Adam was certain. Though he'd never been a parent, he knew enough to understand his folks loved him and Everett equally. It had been so hard on them when he'd come back from filming in Colombia, not only hurt, but suffering from flashbacks that made him sweat in the night. To tell them what happened in California would only break their hearts even more than he already had. He wasn't sure he could face that. Especially now his mom was coming home.

'Can't you give him a break? I know you're not having a good time right now, but nor's he. You can tell just by looking at him and Mia that things aren't right. They can hardly stand to be around each other.' His father shook his head slowly. 'I don't claim to understand what happened to make you hold a grudge, but I know your brother well enough to hazard a few guesses. Whatever it is, I can't believe it's worth losing a family member over.'

There was a part of Adam that wanted to spill the beans. To be that kid so long ago who trusted his parents with everything. But times had changed and now he bore the responsibility of his parents' happiness. He wasn't planning to make it any harder than it already was on them all.

So instead he shook his head, unable to say anything more. Mostly because there was nothing left to say.

The ambulance carrying his mother arrived a little over two hours later, accompanied by two private nurses and her personal physician. Money talked, and it mostly told people that they'd be well compensated if they worked for the Kleins. It took almost an hour to get her comfortably situated in her room, lying in the special bed they'd bought just for this purpose. She was hooked up to a drip – an intravenous pain relief that she could control herself. By early evening she seemed

116

comfortable enough for visitors, and Adam sat with her as he ate his dinner, joking about how much better Annie's stew was than the stuff she was getting through the tubes.

'You always did love her cooking,' his mom pointed out. 'You should come up and eat with us more often.'

Adam took another mouthful of lamb casserole. 'Yeah, well, I'm a big boy, I can look after myself.'

'I know you can, darling.' She patted his hand. 'But sometimes we miss you. It must be very lonely in that cabin down there.' She didn't ask him how long he intended to hide out there. Even if she did, Adam wouldn't have been able to answer her.

'Your father tells me you've got a puppy down there,' she said, changing the subject. 'That must be interesting.'

They carried on talking as he ate, Adam entertaining his mother with stories about Jonas. He was careful not to mention Kitty too much, even though her name seemed to try to force its way in to every sentence he spoke. He didn't want his mother asking him questions he wasn't ready to answer yet.

Like why the hell did he ask her to come down to the cabin each morning, when he was already finding it hard to get her out of his mind?

His mother dozed a little after dinner, while Annie sat with her and did her knitting. So Adam wandered back downstairs, rinsing his dinner plate under the faucet and sliding it into the dishwasher. Standing up, he felt prickles on his neck when he realised he was being watched.

Kitty shot him a wary glance when he turned around. 'How's your mum doing?'

For some reason, he liked the way she kept her pronunciations. 'Mum' was so very British. 'She's sleeping right now, but she should be rested in an hour or so. We can start the movie as soon as she wakes up.'

Kitty shook the small, square box she was holding. 'I was going to make some popcorn for Jonas. He's so excited at staying up late to watch the movie. If he doesn't scoff it all I was planning to show him how to thread it onto string. We can make popcorn chains.'

'To eat?' To his surprise, Adam found himself smiling at her. Did she know that her eyes always softened whenever she talked about Jonas? For some reason it warmed him. 'Or for decoration?'

'Knowing Jonas, for both. I can't see the popcorn lasting long. He's a monster when it comes to Orville Redenbacher.' She put the first package into the microwave, pressing buttons so fast it almost made his eyes water. Kitty Shakespeare was a demon with the popcorn. Maybe they taught that kind of thing at nanny school. He closed his eyes, imagining a crowd of young women, all dressed like Mary Poppins. Except younger, and sexier.

Damn, where did that come from?

When she handed him two big bowls almost overflowing with fluffy white kernels, Adam grinned at her again, wishing that she'd smile back. 'Sweet or salty?'

'Both, of course.' She rolled her eyes, as though his question had been stupid. Grabbing some cans of soda, she turned sharply on her heel and started to walk to the door. 'Which one's your favourite?'

'Guess.' He flashed her a grin. Was he flirting? It certainly seemed like it. A better question would be *why* was he flirting? And why couldn't he tear his eyes away from her pretty pink lips?

Kitty stared at him, her eyes narrowed. Her silent scrutiny was pain and pleasure in equal measure. 'Hmm, an amateur would immediately choose salty. After all, men like savoury things, and you come across as very manly ...'

He held his breath as she continued.

'But even though you're very bristly on the outside, I'd swear that somewhere deep within there's a little boy with a very sweet tooth.'

He swallowed hard. 'Have you been talking to my mother?'

She bit her lip, and it sent a shock straight to his gut. 'No,' she said, still rolling the plump pinkness between her teeth. 'Should I?'

'Oh no, not unless you want to hear stories about how I always used to wet the bed, and that my first words were cookie and sugar.'

Finally, Kitty smiled, and it felt as though he'd won a big victory. 'Your mum sounds like a very interesting lady.'

'Oh yeah, that she is.'

He could feel the blood rushing through his veins, his pulse audible in his ears. Had he really thought she was self-obsessed? Nearly every word that came out of her mouth was about somebody else: his mom, Jonas, Annie. He remembered her kindness earlier that evening when she'd decorated the hallway and dug out the old holiday DVDs his mom had stashed in the family room. Kitty was both sweet and sexy, a dangerous combination that made him want to know everything about her.

An hour later they carried the snacks up to his mom's bed-room, where Jonas had already taken residence on the easy chair next to her bed. His legs were curled beneath him, and he was sucking at the tip of his thumb, in that familiar way he did.

Adam laid the bowls on the table beside his mom's bed. 'We've brought snacks,' he told her.

His mom coughed loudly. 'Who's we?'

Adam flushed, realising nobody had bothered introducing Kitty to his mother. For some reason that bothered him, much more than it probably should. For a girl who only walked into his life a few days earlier, she'd made a big impression.

'Mom, this is Kitty. She's Jonas's nanny.' The explanation fell far short of what he wanted to say. He couldn't think of another way to describe her, though.

'Come here.' Mary Klein's words seemed more of a command than anything else. Kitty stepped forward, placing her hands in Mary's outstretched ones. He watched as his mother squeezed them, her grasp still surprisingly strong in spite of her condition. 'Jonas has told me a lot about you,' he heard her whisper. 'Thank you for taking such good care of him.'

His father and Annie joined them, carrying eggnog for the adults and a chocolate milk for Jonas. Adam cued up the movie, while Annie and his father made themselves at home on the small velvet couch in the corner of the room. With Jonas on the easy chair, that only left the floor, and Kitty sat down cross-legged at the left-hand side of the bed, placing her bowl of popcorn down on the plush floor before taking a sip of her drink. He switched the lights low, with only the glow of his mom's machines casting any illumination in the room until the TV came to life.

'You hogging the snacks?' he whispered, sitting down on the floor next to her. Unlike Kitty, sitting cross-legged wasn't a natural position for Adam. Instead he stretched his long legs in front of him, taking up much more floor space than she did. Without asking, he grabbed a handful of her popcorn, putting the salty sweet kernels into his mouth. She huffed indignantly and he tried not to grin.

'Get your own popcorn, you snack thief,' she whispered, batting his hand away when he went in for more. On his second attempt, she grabbed hold of his hand, and he automatically found himself circling his fingers around hers. Like the rest of their bodies, his hand dominated hers, and he watched with fascination as she tried without success to escape his grasp. There was something about the way her palm fitted so perfectly within his that meant he couldn't tear his eyes away.

Then the opening credits began and she used his distraction to pull away from his hold, swatting him softly on the wrist when he tried to grab her again. It was strange, but there was an emptiness in him, as if he'd already gotten used to the feeling of her hand. He wanted it back, that sweet feeling of contentment, of her soft, warm skin against his.

Like a teenage boy, he started to plot, working out how best he could maintain contact between them. Between the cloak of darkness, and the fact they were on the floor out of everybody's view, it was as though they were the only two people in the room.

Each time she reached for more popcorn, Adam did the same, using the opportunity to brush his hands against hers. Sometimes he'd grab the handful she was going for, forcing a sigh of aggravation from her lips that made him want to kiss them hard and long.

He was like a kid pulling braids. Annoying her seemed the only thing he could do, and if he was being honest, he was enjoying it immensely. So when she finally picked up the bowl and moved it to her other side, far away from his grasp, he happily used the opportunity to snake his arm around her waist and dip his hand into the bowl.

'What are you doing?' Her soft voice was a rush of warmth against his ear. He hadn't realised they were quite so close.

'I'm hungry,' he whispered back, unable to keep the smile from his face. 'You can't waft all that goodness in front of me and then take it away.'

'Get your own snack.'

'I like yours better.' He took another few kernels, using the opportunity to brush his hand against her back, causing her to shiver in a way that made him want more.

'You're so annoying.' Kitty dug her elbow into his waist. But she didn't sound annoyed at all. Instead she sounded a little breathless, and when he looked at her face, illuminated by the flickering screen, he could see her eyes were wide and her lips plump. If only there were more light he'd have sworn her cheeks were flushed, too.

She had no business being so goddamned pretty, but he was glad she was. Silhouetted against the opening scene of the movie, he could see her thick eyelashes flutter as she blinked, and the way her lips opened slightly when she breathed in. He felt the urge to touch them, to trace a finger along the swollen skin, to watch her eyes widen as he pushed a thumb into her mouth.

'Can we thread some popcorn now, Kitty?' Jonas threw himself down next to them. Adam hadn't noticed him getting up. Not that he had been paying any attention to anybody but Kitty. 'We can loop it around the tree like you said.'

The interruption should have relieved the tension that had been building up between them, but when Adam glanced over at her again, Kitty was staring right back at him. She had her bottom lip pulled between her teeth. He could see the reflection of the big screen in her shining eyes, as James Stewart threw a lasso around the moon, promising to bring it down for his sweetheart.

In the movie, George wanted to give the girl of his dreams anything she wanted.

Even if Adam had a rope long enough, he never could have done the same.

13

Beauty is bought by judgement of the eye
– Love's Labour's Lost

Kitty lay awake in her bed long after the rest of the family had gone to sleep. She'd listened to the sounds of the creaking house, hearing the clicking pipes, the groaning shingles, and a collection of other noises that formed the soul of the mansion. Each house she'd lived in had its own soundtrack, as distinctive as a fingerprint would be to a human, but this was the closest she'd ever heard to her childhood home. It could have been the age of the house, or the fact it was filled with people. Or perhaps it was simply a coincidence that the tap-tap of the water in the old pipes seemed to have the same rhythm as her father's London house.

There was another similarity, too. As a child she'd lived in the attic room, part of the house originally intended for servants. Now here she was again, nestled under the roof of another house, feeling thoughtful and alone. Unlike this one, though, her London bedroom had been cramped, with a low roof, but the magical feeling of being on top of the world grabbed a young Kitty every time she climbed the three flights of stairs to get up there. It was a refuge from her family, from her noisy, nosy sisters who could sometimes be too much. It was her haven from problems at school, and somewhere she could hide from her kind yet befuddled father, who when he was busy concentrating on his work would often mistake her for Cesca or Juliet.

Right now her bedroom was somewhere she could lie and think about what happened earlier, when Adam had kept grabbing her hand and stealing her popcorn, wearing a huge grin that stole her breath away. She'd called him annoying but he was anything but. Everything about him had been alluring.

Even when Jonas came and sat with them, she could still feel Adam's stare. It burned her skin and sped up her heartbeat, and she hadn't wanted it to end.

Of course it had, and he'd stood up to kiss his now-sleeping mother, telling Annie he had to leave because he had 'something waiting for him' back at the cabin. They'd all known he was talking about the dog, well, all of them save Jonas, yet Kitty couldn't help but feel disappointed at his departure. He'd shot her a final look, and mouthed that he'd see her in the morning, and her chest constricted all over again.

It was hard to understand how somebody so infuriating could also be so completely attractive. When they'd sat together watching that movie it was as though a chemical reaction was taking place between them. It left her breathless and aching, wondering if he was going to touch her every time he reached for more popcorn. And if she was honest, every cell in her body was hoping he would. He was like an addiction.

She spent the night tossing and turning with nervous anticipation, replaying the scenes of the evening in her mind into the early hours. Was it really only a few days since she'd

125

first met him? She'd been so afraid as he'd grabbed his gun and stalked towards her, his face grim even though his only concern had been for the suffering animal. Then so angry when he chewed her out by the lake, his mouth drawn into a tight, bleached line.

From the first moment they'd met, the two of them had clashed, like they were drawn together by a magnet. And now she didn't seem able to escape the attraction.

Maybe she didn't want to.

She slept through her alarm, not waking until it was gone six. Panic immediately gripped her chest as she realised the hour. In a tangle of fresh clothes and toiletries she somehow managed to make herself look decent, before running downstairs to find Jonas colouring at the old kitchen table. Crayons were scattered over the table, red, green and yellow scrawls across the paper. He was filling in the outline of a Christmas tree, drawing the baubles, making the star stand out. Why did he have to be up so early today of all days?

'There you are. We weren't expecting you so early.' Annie's smile was warm as she looked up from the table. 'We figured you deserved a lie-in after all your hard work.'

Kitty reached out to ruffle Jonas's hair. 'I should have been up earlier,' she said, then shot Annie a pointed look. 'I've got that errand to run, and things to do this morning.'

Annie beckoned Kitty over to the corner of the kitchen, pulling her into the pantry and closing the door so Jonas couldn't hear them. 'If you're going down to the cabin, I found a box of decorations we didn't use yesterday. Could you take them down and offer them to Adam?'

Annie knew all about the arrangement between Kitty and Adam, and the fact she was due to go down to the cabin each day. Though her eyebrows had risen up when Kitty recounted the story, it had seemed more in surprise than in judgement.

'Does he *want* to decorate his house?' Kitty couldn't disguise the disbelief in her voice.

Annie grinned. 'He may not realise he does, but with a little gentle persuasion ...'

Kitty's eyes widened. She'd heard all this before. What made Annie think she could make Adam do anything? 'He won't listen to me. The last time I went down there the dog had messed all over his floor.'

'You'd be surprised.' Annie was having none of it. 'You persuaded him to look after the dog, not to mention getting him to agree to a movie night with his mother. I'm thinking bringing a little festive cheer to his cabin is all in a morning's work for you.'

Were they talking about the same person here?

'You've got it wrong,' Kitty protested. 'He doesn't like me at all. Remember how he treated me when I totalled my car on the way here? He made me walk up the drive in the most useless pair of shoes.'

Annie shook her head. 'I saw how he looked at you last night. Believe me, there's nothing that can make Adam do something he doesn't want to. But when he was looking at you, oh boy, there were some serious pheromones flying through the air.'

Kitty spluttered with laughter. 'Pheromones?' She wasn't expecting that. Annie had a way of surprising her.

'Pah, you know what I mean. When that boy looks at you, it brings me in mind of the day Mr Drewer asked my daddy for my hand in marriage. And back then my parents had a party line, he had to send them a telegram to arrange a time. He had seven days to stew about that conversation with my father.'

Kitty couldn't help but smile at the sweetness of Annie's story. There was a timelessness to the old housekeeper that made it hard to believe she was once a young girl filled with romantic hopes and dreams. Yet hope was timeless, just like love. Kitty needed them both. Craved them, even. Not that she was sure she'd ever find them.

'OK, I'll take the decorations down with me,' she agreed. 'But if he shouts at me, it was your idea.'

Annie laughed. 'I can take that. Now shoo, it's not long until Christmas. You and I have a lot to do.'

It felt so lovely to be included in a plan that it brought tears to Kitty's eyes. The Kleins may not have been family – nor was Annie come to that – yet there was something about staying in this house that made her feel like she'd come home.

Right then, in an old mansion in the middle of the West Virginian mountains, covered with snow, icicles and a thousand twinkling lights, it felt as though she was starring in a holiday special all of her own.

Adam had been awake for most of the night. His inability to sleep reminded him of those times when he was filming in a foreign country, his mind full of questions, his body on high alert. Even in his downtime he hadn't allowed himself to wind down. Now, cooped up in his cabin in the middle of a West Virginia winter, he felt as though he was getting ready for battle.

Except this time, it was with himself.

There was no way he should have flirted with Kitty last night. It was as though somebody else had taken hold of him, let his guard down, until all that was left was the boy he'd once been. Hopeful, honest, vulnerable even. Not the world-weary man he'd become.

More than most he knew where vulnerability got him.

He'd been sitting in his running gear for hours, ready to leave just as soon as she walked through the door. He couldn't even spend ten minutes cooped up with her in here. Didn't trust himself to behave the way he knew he should. If he could put some distance between them, maybe he could control the attraction that kept drawing him toward her.

The puppy came padding over to him, sniffing at his hand. Adam had already washed the floor once that morning, grumbling at the dog as he did so, and was rewarded with a wagging tail and a hopeful nuzzle for his efforts.

Growing up, he'd never had a pet. His parents had been too busy when he was small, and when he was a teenager he'd been a boarder at school, only visiting home during vacations. That itinerant lifestyle was no place for a beloved dog. Then, of course, as an adult he'd been even worse, leaving the country at a moment's notice, his work taking him all over the world. These past few months had been the first time he'd settled down in one place for any amount of time, and only now was it dawning on him just how lonely a lifestyle he'd made for himself.

The puppy started panting, his tongue lolling as he came to a stop. Adam reached out to pet him, running a hand down his thick, curly fur, and the puppy breathed out a contented sigh. The next moment his back stiffened, his ears turning up as if on high alert. Running to the door, he barked loudly at the dark wood, his tail wagging.

It came as no surprise to Adam when there was a soft knock on the door. He tapped his fingers on the arm of his chair, pushed himself up to standing and then strode across the wooden floor. His heart was beating furiously by the time

129

he reached the entranceway, and he had to take a deep breath before reaching out to open the latch.

Centre himself, that's what he needed to do. She wasn't anybody special, just a pretty British girl who'd taken his fancy. He'd faced bigger demons than her before and still come out alive.

His mouth went dry as soon as he opened the door. Kitty was standing on his porch, her blonde hair half-hidden beneath a red woollen cap, and a matching scarf wrapped warmly around her neck. She was carrying a box full of what looked like tinsel and ornaments, but the thing he really noticed was the huge grin on her face.

She looked so pleased to see him. He couldn't remember the last time he'd been so disarmed. Half of him wanted to scoop her up in his arms and swing her around the room, while the other half wanted to run far, far away, where he wouldn't have to be entranced by her.

The second half won. He grabbed his running shoes, pulling them on while successfully avoiding her stare. Ignoring the gentleman inside him who wanted to take the box out of her hands and relieve her of her burden, he cleared his throat.

'You only just caught me. I'm off out for my run.' Did he sound nonchalant enough? Adam wasn't sure.

'Oh.'

Only a single syllable, yet he could hear every emotion contained within it. Disappointment, surprise, sadness. It made him feel even more of an asshole than he already did, but it also strengthened his resolve to avoid her. She didn't deserve his mood swings.

'Annie gave me this,' she said, still holding the box. 'She wants us to decorate the cabin.'

He felt even worse. 'You can do it while I'm out. You'll probably be gone before I get back, just be sure to slip the door on the latch and make certain the dog is inside. I don't want to have to search for him in the snow.'

He felt, rather than saw, her flinch.

'You're not staying? Annie sent down some hot chocolate, too.' Kitty pulled a flask from the box, lifting it in front of her like it was a prize. 'Knowing Annie it will taste fabulous.'

Could she make him feel any worse?

He could take off his shoes right now. He could lift the flask out of her hands, grab a couple of mugs and pour out the sweet liquid, giving her a smile as they clinked their cups together. They could pull out the decorations, sharing laughter as he recounted tales of his childhood holidays, telling her the provenance of the old baubles that were sticking out of the box.

If he was any kind of a man, that's exactly what he would do. But he wasn't that man, and as sure as ice would melt in springtime, he knew she deserved more than that.

'I'm not a big one for the holidays.' He couldn't look at her face. 'Decorate if you want, or don't bother. I won't tell Annie either way.'

With a shrug, he pulled open the door and turned to look at her one last time. Her expression of disappointment seared its way into his mind, imprinting itself like a brand.

Adam stepped out on the porch, closing the door behind him. He tried to wipe out the memory of her distress as he started to warm up his muscles. Jumping to the ground, not bothering to use the steps, he let the spikes in his shoes steady his gait. The run would do him good, make him forget about everything except the air in his lungs. He'd run faster, harder, further. Do whatever it took to erase her face from his memory.

To forget how she'd stared at him, her eyes wide, her pretty mouth open. The way her forehead creased as she still held tightly to the box was still so clear in his mind even when he'd crossed the wide-open space of the meadow and made it to the treeline.

He'd hurt her.

Without meaning to, without wanting to, he'd caused her pain anyway. And though he'd been trying to avoid doing exactly that, somehow he'd ended up acting like an asshole.

'Shit.' He slapped his palm against the rough bark of a pine tree. He'd stopped running, even though he hadn't yet even broken a sweat. His mind was consumed with thoughts of her, and nothing else really seemed to matter. Not his memories of that damn documentary in Colombia, or his breakdown in LA, not even the conflict that raged within him, telling him to keep the hell away from her.

'Damn it.' His hands balled into fists, the way they always did when he sensed danger. Without really thinking about his next move, he turned around and started to run back to the cabin, his eyes trained on the wooden building. It took him less than a minute to get there, his breathlessness more a factor of the anticipation coursing through him than any exertion it might have caused. Still he ran up the steps and yanked the door open, surprised to find her still standing right in front of it, the box cradled in her arms.

'You're back?' The creases in her forehead deepened. 'What happened?'

Adam didn't reply. Instead he took the box from her grasp, and dropped it to the floor. The dog trotted over and tried to sniff the decorations, and Adam had to swat him away. The look of surprise on Kitty's face – so much more welcome than the sadness of only a few moments before – made him want to laugh out loud. It sent a sensation of lightness through his being, as if he were floating in the sky. He wasn't sure of the last time he felt so good.

Her bottom lip dropped open, enough for him to see the tip of her tongue just inside, making the urge to kiss her come over him again. He wanted to taste her, to be tasted, to see exactly how she felt against him, but he didn't have a clue how to make this happen.

'I'm sorry.' It was the only thing he could think of to say. He wanted to convey so much in those two words, yet they fell far short of his needs.

'For what?'

He shook his head. 'I've no idea. For shooting that deer? For making you cry? For screaming at you by the lake?'

Kitty laughed then. A warm throaty chuckle that seemed out of place coming from her lips. Yet it touched him deep inside, enough to make him reach out and cup the side of her face with his palm. With his other he took her hat off, brushing the hair from her brow.

'You're so damned pretty.'

'I am?' She frowned. It only increased his estimation of her, a beautiful girl who didn't even know it, somebody who was lovely on the inside and out.

He nodded slowly. 'You are. With your glowing skin and your shiny eyes and your plump, kissable mouth. You're a sight for sore eyes.'

'Kissable?'

His heart stuttered when she smiled.

Still cradling her face, he dragged his thumb down until he was running it along her bottom lip. She stared up at him, wide-eyed, the open, trusting expression sending a shot of pure pleasure to his veins.

'Kissable,' he agreed. Dropping his head down, he touched his brow to hers. They were so close he could feel her lashes fluttering against him as she blinked, and the warm rush of her breath against his skin. Still they stared at each other, both silent, yet wanting to say everything, their eyes sharing a conversation that couldn't be had with words. Then Adam wrapped his hand around her neck, angling her face to his, before pressing his cool lips against her warm mouth.

It felt so good he almost lost his mind.

14

Then come kiss me, sweet and twenty

– Twelfth Night

Kitty had been kissed before. Her first was a stolen peck in the playground from Tom Jenkins, the seven-year-old Lothario who stole her tender heart in primary school. Since then she'd had chaste brushes and drunken snogs, duelled with tongues and sucked at necks. Oh yes, she'd been kissed …

But she'd never been kissed like this.

Adam held her close, one arm circling her waist, the other still cupping her neck. He kissed her as if he was a dying man seeking his final breath, stealing hers away as he plundered her mouth, taking and giving in equal measure. His lips were softer than she'd thought they would be, moving assuredly against hers, his tongue coaxing her open before he slid inside her sighing mouth. Her arms were snaked around his neck, clinging on as he dipped her backwards, still kissing her deeply as if he was fighting some kind of battle.

He smoothed the stray hair from her face, then curled his fist around the hair at the nape of her neck, pulling at it as if it were a rope. The motion moved her head back further.

135

Dragging his lips to the corner of her mouth, he kissed a trail to her neck, nipping and caressing the sensitive skin just below her ear.

The feel of his bristles against her skin made Kitty moan softly. With every movement of his body, Adam was dominating her. His arm tightened around her waist, pulling her firmly against him, until all she could feel were the hard planes of his muscles against her.

Her senses were full of him. The scent of warm pines filled her nose, while her skin shivered at the touch of his lips. She could hear his breath as he was kissing her neck, fast yet even, and though her eyes were tightly closed she swore she could still see his face behind her lids.

'You taste so good,' he murmured, pulling her sensitive earlobe between his teeth. Though it didn't hurt, she gasped at the feeling it created, sending pleasure shooting straight down to her toes. She pushed her fingers through the dark hair at the nape of his neck, her breath coming in short gasps as he continued to kiss at her throat. Beneath the layers of her coat and sweater, her nipples tightened, her body becoming desperate for more.

As if he sensed her need, Adam tugged at the zipper of her jacket, still kissing at her as he pushed the quilted fabric from her shoulders. Releasing her hair, he moved his hands to her waist and pushed up beneath the cotton fabric of her sweater. Feeling his rough hands pressed against her skin, Kitty opened her eyes, looking straight into his dark brown stare. She could see desire there, a need as great as hers. She swallowed hard, her mouth suddenly dry.

'Kiss me again.'

The second time he lowered his mouth onto hers was as

intoxicating as the first. With the added sensation of his palms stroking her sides, Kitty thought she might combust. His tongue slid against hers, soft yet firm, and she dragged her teeth against it. Her heart felt as though it was growing in her chest, pressing against her ribs until her whole torso ached for him. With every caress of his hand it felt as though she was coming home.

Then the world exploded above them with the sound of a thousand flapping wings. The lodge started to shake, pictures moving on the wall, fine china rattling in the cupboards. Adam wrenched his face from hers, a look of consternation on his face, eyes narrowed as he started to look around the room.

'What the hell?'

The noise increased, along with the tremors. For a moment Kitty wondered if it was an avalanche. Adam was still holding her tightly, though she could feel his agitation growing. Finally he pulled his hands away and ran to the window, gazing out to the meadow outside.

'Asshole,' he murmured, still staring out.

'What is it?' Kitty ran to his side, peering out through the misted glass. The tops of the trees were bending downwards, as if being blown by a great force. The snow that capped their peaks was blasted down to the ground in a sudden flurry.

'It's a helicopter.' Adam's voice was still low, though laced with anger. 'The fucker's going to land in the meadow.'

Even in her short stay in Cutler's Gap, Kitty knew the town wasn't exactly teeming with money. There weren't many people who could afford to land a helicopter in the middle of rural West Virginia.

Not unless they happened to be wealthy movie producers.

'Is it Everett?' she asked.

Adam's laugh was short and devoid of any humour. 'Of course it's Everett. Who else would be that insane?'

The helicopter landed in the middle of the meadow, its blades slowing as the engine cut off. A few moments later the door opened and two figures climbed out, running the length of the meadow until they emerged from the downdraught. The one in front – Everett, she presumed – was looking back and shouting. The other person was carrying a holdall and a briefcase, half sliding in the snow as if they didn't know how slippery it was. From his height, Kitty guessed it had to be a man, and as he came closer she could make out that he was wearing a tailored business suit, with no snow jacket to keep in the warmth. He was shivering, his leather brogues still stumbling in the snow, and as he came closer still she realised she recognised him.

'That's Drake,' she whispered. Adam's arms were still circling her waist, holding her against him.

'Who?' Adam's reply was sharp.

'Drake Montgomery, Everett's assistant,' she replied, staring at the two figures as they approached the cabin. 'What on earth is he doing here?'

'I've no idea. But I've a feeling we're about to find out.'

While they waited for Everett and Drake to clear the distance between the helicopter and the cabin, Kitty was aware of the atmosphere growing between her and Adam. It was almost tangible, like a dragon hissing and snapping in the air. Something almost impossible to ignore.

Adam was rubbing his lips with the rough tip of his index finger, his eyes narrow as he kept a watch on his brother's progress. Everett stumbled among the snowdrifts created by the helicopter's beating blades. Then they were at the door, rapping impatiently, and Adam sighed audibly before letting go of Kitty and heading to the entrance.

Wrenching it open, he did nothing to hide his irritation. 'Was that really necessary?'

Kitty hung back, hoping to stay invisible. She really didn't care to explain her presence at Everett's brother's cabin. The dog had no such qualms, barking loudly as he ran across the floor, stopping at Adam's heel as if he were his protector.

'Was what necessary?' Everett asked, motioning for Drake to follow him in.

'The helicopter landing. You could have just taken your dick out and shaken it everywhere. It would have had the same effect.'

Everett stared at his brother as if he was talking in a foreign language. 'I heard about Mom coming home and decided to get here the fastest way I could.'

Each time Everett opened his mouth the dog barked loudly, making Everett have to almost shout his words. Kitty remained in the shadows.

'She's not at death's door, you could have arrived normally.'

'What's normal?' Everett shrugged. 'Anyway, Drake and I have some work to do here, there's some locations I want to take a look at.'

'Hey, I recognise you. It's Kitty, isn't it? The girl who's named after a cat.' Drake's valley-boy accent cut through the lodge. He smiled, revealing an expensive set of white, perfectly even teeth. She opened her mouth to tell him that it was thanks to him she was here, and his passing her details on to Mia. She wasn't sure whether to be annoyed or grateful to him.

Maybe she was both.

Drake walked over to her, shaking her hand as if the last

time she saw him he hadn't been stalking out in the middle of her interview. He was staring at her cheeks – was her face as flushed as it felt? Her lips were stinging, the memory of Adam's kisses making her whole body tingle. Drake leaned closer to her, until his face was only inches from hers. 'What kind of hellhole is this, anyway? Tell me there's at least a Starbucks nearby.'

Kitty smirked, remembering how similar her own thoughts were when she arrived in Cutler's Gap. Funny how quickly she was able to change her mind. She was about to dash Drake's hopes when she looked up at Adam, who was staring angrily at them. Immediately she stepped back from Drake as a fresh flow of blood rushed to her cheeks.

'Are you staying here long?' she asked, as much to hide her embarrassment as anything else.

Drake gestured at the bags he'd placed on the scratched wooden floor. 'Everett had me bring the mobile office so we could be here for a while. I've packed enough to see me through to the 27th.'

Though she knew that Everett would be itching to get back to LA after Christmas, the 27th seemed so close. Too close. For some reason, knowing that the cosy little movie show of last night wouldn't be repeated made Kitty feel sad.

And yet in a strange way it was a relief to see Everett's assistant. Like her, he was an outsider to this family, and he clearly saw her as an ally right now. If her sisters were here, they'd tell her to work on him, see if he could help her find an internship, but right then her mind was too muddled to even think straight about that. Plus, when he wasn't dodging screaming phone calls from Mia, he actually seemed like he might be a nice guy.

'This isn't where we sleep, is it?' There was horror in

Drake's voice. 'This place looks like something out of a *Davy Crockett* episode. It's a tourist attraction, right?'

She felt her hackles rise. Drake might not have meant to criticise Adam's self-made home, but she still felt herself get defensive, wanting to protect the man who was standing only a few strides away. OK, maybe Drake wasn't *that* nice.

If she protested too much, would Everett notice? There was no way she wanted her boss to find out about her feelings for his brother. Not to mention the fact she'd just experienced the hottest, most sensual kiss of her life. So she laughed lightly. 'Don't be silly, there are no tourists here. Just us and a puppy.'

She was more than aware of Adam's disapproving gaze burning into her skin. Every cell inside her screamed, wanting her to turn and look at him, to shoot him a reassuring smile that would tell him she was only pretending. That she wasn't anywhere near as vapid as she was pretending to be. But she also felt Everett and Drake's eyes on her, and knew that any hint of a relationship between her and Adam would only complicate this situation even further. She was a child tiptoeing through cornflakes, trying not to make a noise.

'Well, it might just work . . . ' Drake's murmur trailed off as he stared around the room. 'This could be the hideout we're looking for, Everett. Just the sort of place a man would escape to.' He looked eager to please his boss.

Everett cleared his throat. 'Let's not talk business now. We should make our way up to the big house and get settled in.' He glanced at his brother before gesturing at Drake to gather their things. 'You and Kitty can take the luggage up, I'll join you in a few minutes.'

There was no reason she should feel embarrassment about being ordered around by Everett. He was her boss and paid her salary, after all. Yet Kitty's face reddened further, knowing that her status as a paid servant had just been confirmed in front of Adam. She had no option other than to follow Everett's command.

'Come on, I'll show you the way through the woods,' she told Drake. 'Though you may want to put on something warmer, it's quite a trek.'

'I haven't got anything warmer.' Drake's face fell as he glanced at the pile of luggage in the corner. 'I had no idea it was going to be so cold. Maybe I could borrow your scarf or something?'

Adam's loud sigh was impossible to ignore. 'A scarf isn't going to do anything to fend off hypothermia, you can borrow some clothes from me. And if you can wait for five minutes I'll get the snowmobile out. It will be faster than walking through the trail.'

'I'd really appreciate that.' He looked around him, eyes wide as he took in the landscape. 'I've never been anywhere with non-fake snow before.'

She would have found Drake's reaction funnier if she hadn't had a similar one herself when she'd first arrived in the mountains. Her clothes had been as inappropriate as Drake's and her response had been equally infuriating to Adam. But now she felt at home here, used to the cold weather and the warm clothes. She was even getting used to the family, learning their ways, becoming accustomed to them.

Had she become used to Adam, too? No, that wasn't right, it would be almost impossible to get used to him. But she was drawn to him, wanting to know him, to feel him, to taste him.

The only problem was, since Everett and Drake walked through the door, he hadn't once met her eyes.

15

I, that did never weep, now melt with woe, that
winter should cut off our spring-time so

– Henry VI, Part 3

If she wasn't feeling so confused, the ride back to the mansion would have been exhilarating. Adam handled the shiny blue snowmobile with calm assurance, breaking through the banks of snow with ease. He'd hooked up a trailer for the luggage, with the four of them perched on the seats behind him, a blanket around their legs to try and keep out the cold. It was almost like being in a boat, the smooth gliding sensation very similar to her friend's motorboat in Venice Beach. Yet the cold wind whipping around their faces left them in no doubt they were in the middle of a mountain winter, snow ploughing in front of them as if it were a wave parting in front of a boat.

'So, about that Starbucks.' Drake had to shout above the noise of the engine and the wind to be heard.

'What Starbucks?' Kitty replied. 'The closest you'll be getting to a venti mochaccino is Annie's gritty percolator, and that's if you manage to sweet talk her.'

'Who's Annie? Is she a barista?' He scrunched his nose up, as though something smelled really bad.

She tried to stifle her shocked laugh. 'No, Annie's the house-keeper. We're in the middle of nowhere. There aren't any coffee shops or restaurants. Apparently there's a store and a run-down bar and that's it.' She shot a glance at Adam's back, remember-ing his harsh words when he found her next to that dying deer on the road. There were no businesses in Cutler's Gap.

Was it really less than an hour ago that he was holding her in his arms, giving her the most sensual experience of her life? All the while that he prepared the snowmobile and loaded everything on board, Adam had continued to avoid her gaze. Now she was more baffled than ever. The man blew hot and cold so fast she wasn't sure if she was supposed to burn or freeze.

Every time she looked at him she could feel butterflies somersaulting in her stomach. That couldn't be good, could it?

'A bar?' Drake asked. 'Is it one of those authentic mountain bars with bearded old men and a pool table in the corner?' He turned to Everett. 'We should check that out. It would be perfect for the farewell scene . . .'

'Drake.' The tone of Everett's voice cut him off before he could finish. 'We can talk business later, OK?'

'Oh, of course. Do you play pool, Everett?' The rest of the ride to the big house carried on something like that. Drake and Everett managed to keep up an unending stream of conversa-tion that distracted her from her thoughts.

Adam pulled up just behind the house, shutting off the engine before climbing down from the driver's seat. Everett jumped out, with Drake following close behind, the younger man muttering his thanks before they rushed towards the warmth of Annie's kitchen. Adam held his hand up to Kitty, his head tilted to the side as he looked at her, and she grasped his gloved palm with hers, allowing him to lift her down from the seat.

Wrapping his arm around her waist, Adam squeezed her tightly as he set her feet down onto the snow-covered lawn. His hold lingered for a moment longer than necessary, sending shivers pulsing down Kitty's spine.

Damn those butterflies. They got everywhere.

'There you go,' he said, finally releasing his grasp. 'You should get inside before you catch the cold.'

Kitty looked up at him, trying to read his expression. Between the hair and the thick cap he was wearing, there wasn't very much she could read at all.

'Aren't you coming too?'

He shook his head. 'No, ma'am. Not while it's all so busy in there.'

'It's not that busy. Just a couple of extra warm bodies.'

They both knew it wasn't the number of people stopping him, it was who those people were. Curiosity washed over her. 'What is it between you and Everett anyway?'

She wanted to kick herself as soon as she'd asked. Adam frowned and kicked at the snow with his heavy boot, looking angry at her intrusion.

'It's a family thing.'

She couldn't equate the brooding man standing before her with the one who was so sensual less than an hour before. He looked the same, he even smelled the same, but it was as if the guy who kissed her had retreated inside his shell.

'I should think so, you're brothers after all. But it's the season of goodwill, peace to all men, isn't there any way you could try to reconcile? Especially with your mother's accident?'

Memories of her own mother came rushing back. Or rather

her lack of mother. Each Christmas it felt as though there was something missing, in spite of the efforts of her father and her sisters. A memory flashed into her brain, of a young Kitty curled up on the sofa, ramming sweets into her mouth as she watched some Hallmark Christmas movie.

Alone, as she so often was.

'Don't get caught up in something that doesn't concern you,' Adam said, his voice low. 'What happens between me and my brother is my business and I'll thank you to keep out of it.'

Stepping back as if he'd slapped her, Kitty stumbled in the thick snow. Her chest tightened in response to his vehemence, as she wondered what on earth she had done to deserve such a response.

'I'm sorry,' she said softly, blinking to disperse the tears. 'It's just that if my family was here I'd be delighted, not hiding away in a cabin by the lake.'

Something clouded his face, an emotion that she couldn't quite put her finger on. All the same, it was enough to soften his voice when he replied. 'Well in that case you're very lucky.' Pulling at his hat as if he was agitated, he quickly shrugged and then turned back to the snowmobile. 'I'll see you around.'

Those four words panicked her, as if she was losing something she wasn't willing to let go. 'Won't I see you in the morning?' she asked, still breathless. 'When I come down to see to the dog.'

Adam turned his head, finally meeting her gaze. But instead of saying a word, he switched the engine on, the roar of the motor drowning everything out. He backed the snowmobile up, then turned the giant machine around, until every part of him had his back to her.

That was the end of that, then. Sighing, she watched him

disappear back towards the cabin, snow shooting out from beneath the machine as he crossed the distance between the house and the trees.

Stupid, angry, sexy bastard. So what if he kissed better than anyone she'd ever met? As far as she was concerned he could disappear into the forest and never come back out.

Yeah. That's exactly how she felt.

Adam was driving too fast, yet the need to feel danger, and let exhilaration wash away the anger he'd been feeling, was too compelling to ignore. He kept his foot firmly pressed down, manoeuvring the snowmobile around the ridge of trees, refusing to look back at the big house behind him, and the wet-eyed girl he knew was still standing in front of it.

Damn them all. Why the hell did Everett have to spend Christmas in West Virginia, complicating things with his family and his staff who seemed set on driving him crazy? How the hell did he end up kissing Everett's nanny anyway? With her wide-eyed innocence and her perfectly pouty lips, she was everything he should be avoiding. She was . . .

His?

Adam sighed as he parked the snowmobile up in the shed at the back of the cabin. Of course she wasn't his. If she belonged to anyone, she was Everett's; after all, it was his brother who paid her wages. He was the one she owed her loyalty to. Once again a surge of irrational anger overtook him. Like a jealous kid, he wanted to steal Everett's toy, and keep it for himself.

What the hell was he thinking, kissing her? He of all people knew what living in LA did to people. Kitty was no different to the rest of them, with her bronzed skin and easy laugh, not to mention her inability to dress appropriately for the season.

Yet there was a part of him that knew it wasn't true. She might have flown in from LAX, but she didn't have the guile he'd seen in most people in his industry. He didn't feel that sense of appraisal when she looked at him; that wondering who he was and how good he'd be for their career and whether he could help them climb up another rung of that greasy, slippery ladder.

In that respect, Kitty was as far from Hollywood as he was. Adam could tell from the gentle way she dealt with Jonas, not to mention her supreme patience when she was handling the dog, that she wasn't working any angle while she was here. She was just being who she was supposed to be. Nanny, employee ... friend.

That brought him full circle to feeling like a shit of the highest order. What kind of man practically made love to a woman with his lips and then refused even to smile at her, let alone acknowledge the fire burning between them? Maybe he should admit that Kitty was better off without him. What on earth could a girl her age see in an asshole like him anyway? He was broken, a mere shadow of a man since he'd come back from Colombia and LA. He could barely venture out of his cabin, let alone be the sort of man Kitty deserved. She was young, pretty, and admittedly a little bit naive, but clearly didn't have a bad bone in her body.

That fact alone was exactly why he needed to keep away from her.

And precisely why it was impossible to do so.

Kitty and Jonas spent the afternoon in the kitchen with Annie, helping her with the holiday preparations and trying to keep her calm. The room was warm, the aroma of coffee filling the air, along with the jars of spices she had open.

'All these last-minute changes,' she huffed. 'And now they

tell me Mr Montgomery's a vegetarian. What on earth am I going to cook for Christmas Day? He won't eat turkey or ham. I'm going to have to get some of that tutu or something, otherwise he's going to starve.'

'You mean tofu.' Kitty tried to block the image of Drake wearing a ballerina skirt from her mind with only limited success. 'And I honestly wouldn't worry about Drake, I don't think he eats anything anyway.'

'Oh, he's one of those.' Annie poured another spoonful of cinnamon into the mixing bowl. 'All those people in Hollywood who never eat. I'm surprised there are many of them left. Of course, your mum's no better, Jonas.'

The boy nodded happily and grabbed a handful of chocolate chips. 'Yep, she hates food.'

Glancing down at her thighs, Kitty wished for a moment that she could hate food too. But then Annie pulled open the oven door, and the mouthwatering aroma of fresh cookies filled the kitchen. How could anybody hate food when it smelled so good?

Adam hadn't seemed to mind her curves when he was kissing the life out of her in his little cabin. Her cheeks flushed as she recalled the way his mouth had moved against hers, and the teasing sensation of his palms as he slid his hands beneath her sweater. She'd never been kissed like that before, with an animal ferocity that took her breath away. But then he'd practically dismissed her after the lift he gave them in the snowmobile, leaving her with a lingering feeling of distaste.

Sadly, even Annie's warm cookies couldn't remove the nasty flavour from her mouth.

Why was it that everything reminded her of Adam? It was so frustrating the way he invaded every thought. The memory of his kiss lingered like the taste of good wine on her lips, and it was all she could do not to touch them again and again. Kitty couldn't remember the last time she'd felt like this – if she ever had – so consumed by somebody she had nothing in common with, except the chemistry that kept growing between them.

Maybe she'd watched one too many movies. She'd always assumed that passion was an invention, made up by writers in order to put bottoms on seats in the cinema. Now she'd experienced it for herself, she wasn't so sure.

One thing she was certain of though, she needed to calm herself down. Whatever this thing between her and Adam was, it was sure to end in tears.

'Can you take some cookies through to the library?' Annie handed Kitty a china plate piled high with snickerdoodles. 'They've set up shop in there, though goodness knows what on earth they're doing so close to Christmas.'

Kitty slid the plate onto a tray and poured two steaming mugs of coffee out before balancing them all on the surface. Maybe a chat with Everett was just what she needed – it was the oral equivalent of a cold shower. 'Are you coming, Jonas?'

The seven-year-old shook his head. 'No way, Dad's in a stinky mood. I've already been told off for messing with the equipment. I think I'll just stay here with Annie.'

Annie gave Kitty a nod of agreement. 'I'll keep an eye on him.'

'In that case wish me luck,' Kitty said, making a dramatic face. 'And if I'm not back in ten minutes, send out a search party.'

Jonas grinned, grabbing another cookie, while Annie rolled her eyes. From the looks of them, neither would be in a hurry to save her from an ear-bashing if she managed to upset Everett or Drake. So much for loyalty.

When she walked into the library, Kitty saw exactly what

150

had enticed Jonas inside. It was as though the musty room filled with books had been transformed into a modern-day control centre. Laptops hummed, a Wi-Fi booster blinked and the desk was covered in paper. She looked a little closer. It looked like the pages of a printed script.

'Where should I put these?' Her voice sounded louder than usual, echoing around the tall-ceilinged room. Both men immediately stood up and swung around to face her, but it was Everett's angry expression she noticed first.

'You shouldn't be in here. It's strictly off limits. How many times do I have to tell you all? And stop looking at that script, it's top secret.'

Kitty hesitated, still balancing the drink and cookies in her hands. She looked around in vain for somewhere to place the tray, but it seemed as though every surface was filled with computer equipment and piles of papers. 'Annie asked me to bring some coffee in for you,' she stuttered. 'And there's cookies, too.' Part of her wanted to tell him where he could stick those damn cookies, and it wasn't going to be anywhere near his mouth. But he was her boss, and more than that, her key to an internship. For better or worse, she needed him.

'Are you deaf?' Everett asked her. 'Just get out. Now.'

Drake gave an uneasy laugh and walked over, taking the tray from her grasp. 'It's OK, Everett, it's not as though there's anything to see here. And she's signed a non-disclosure agreement, hasn't she?'

Non-disclosures were common for Hollywood staff, whether they were directly employed by the movie industry or not. The last thing a famous actor wanted was for his nanny to sell his dirty secrets to the newspapers. Pretty much everybody had to sign an NDA before taking up employment.

'It doesn't matter, if this gets out we could lose everything,' Everett growled. 'All it would take is the right word in the wrong ear and copycat movies will be showing up all over the place. I want this kept under wraps.'

He was being dramatic. Hollywood gossip always trumped secrecy, they both knew that. Whatever he was working on wouldn't be secret for long. So why was he so tetchy?

'Kitty won't say anything, will you?' Drake looked over at her, his eyebrows raised.

'Of course I won't. There's nothing to tell anyway, just a whole load of flashing equipment and a script flung everywhere.' It took everything she had not to roll her eyes. Any hint of excitement she'd felt during her first few weeks in Hollywood had long since passed. One thing was for sure, the movie business just wasn't that glamorous.

Everett turned back to his assistant. 'I want this room sealed off, you and I are the only ones allowed in here, and if it's empty we lock it with a key.'

'Sure, of course.' Drake placed the tray on top of a pile of papers then gestured at Kitty. 'I'll show you out,' he said, steering her towards the door.

Kitty didn't resist; she couldn't wait to get out of there. Everett was treating her as if she were a piece of dirt he'd found on the sole of his shoe. What with him, and his mercurial brother, she'd had about enough of the lot of them.

She couldn't care less about whatever movie it was that Everett was producing, as far as she was concerned he could be making box-office millions and it wouldn't concern her. She only wanted to look after Jonas for a few weeks, and then find an internship, with or without his help. Everett could keep his secrets to himself; she didn't want them.

16

Friendship is constant in all other things,
save in the office and affairs of love

– Much Ado About Nothing

'Are you OK?' Annie asked, as Kitty pulled a couple of cans of soda from the refrigerator. 'You seem kind of jumpy.'

'Do I?' Kitty stood straight, sliding the cans into her bag. 'I don't mean to be.'

'Maybe it's the way Mr Everett talked to you yesterday,' Annie said sympathetically. 'There's no call for him to speak to anyone like that.'

'He's just highly strung,' Kitty said, pulling the cupboard door open to grab some cookies. 'A lot of people in Hollywood are like that. I'm used to it. I used to work in a restaurant in downtown LA, and Everett isn't any worse than some of the customers I had there.'

'Hmm,' Annie murmured from her usual chair – the one closest to the stove. 'I noticed you didn't go down to help out with the puppy this morning either.'

'I didn't think I was needed.' She kept her voice light, even though her chest felt as constricted as hell. 'It's only a puppy, I think Adam can look after him. He doesn't need me interfering.'

She'd been on edge ever since the previous day. It had been a hell of a one, too – with that kiss from Adam and the telling-off from Everett, and now neither of them appeared to want to acknowledge her presence. Jonas was the only Klein male who even seemed to take any interest in her right now.

And that was how it should be, she reminded herself. He was the reason she was here, after all.

'Have you two had words too?' Annie asked, taking a sip of her coffee. 'I thought you were getting on well.'

If only she knew. 'We're fine,' Kitty said, her voice a little curter than she'd planned. 'I just want to spend some time with Jonas. And goodness knows that boy could do with a little attention.'

'Sit down and drink your coffee,' Annie said, pointing at the full mug on the table. 'You must have emptied half the cupboards into your bag. You're not going to need that much food, it's a parade, not a week-long camp out.'

Kitty sighed with resignation and pulled out the chair opposite Annie, sitting down heavily on it. 'Jonas likes to eat a lot,' she said.

'All those Klein boys do. That's how they grew so big and strong. Jonas will be the same,' Annie said. How did every conversation they had come back to Adam and his brother? Kitty wasn't sure whether she liked it or not.

'Let's hope that's the only way he resembles them,' she muttered.

'They're good boys. A little overenthusiastic sometimes, and definitely too quick to judge, but they're good nevertheless,' Annie said. 'And Adam has a heart of gold. The number of people he's helped after the cameras stop running. Do you know he paid for those girls from that documentary to go back to school?'

'The ones from the human traffic ring?' Kitty asked. 'No, I didn't know that.'

She wasn't exactly surprised, either. It sounded like Adam. He had a black and white sense of right and wrong. Of course he'd try to do anything he could to help the victims.

'He's got a big heart, that one. He loves his family, too. That's why what happened in LA was so awful.'

Kitty leaned closer, her interest piqued. 'What did happen in LA?' she asked.

Annie shook her head, stirring at her half-drunk coffee with the sugar spoon. 'I don't know all the details, haven't asked for them either. All I know is that the two of them had such a big fight Adam ended up getting arrested. He tore up Everett's home office, by all accounts. Left him with a black eye, too.'

'What did they fight about?'

'I've no idea.' Annie shrugged. 'But Mrs Klein told me the only way Adam could get the charges dropped was by agreeing to come home here and go into therapy for a few months. Mrs Klein, she wanted him to stay here in the big house, but he refused. She didn't have the heart to argue with him. So he moved down to the cabin, fixed it up within a week, and that's where he's been living since.'

'And he isn't working on anything?' Kitty asked. 'What about that documentary in Colombia I've heard about? The one about drug mules.'

'I've no idea. He hasn't said anything about that.'

Kitty rolled her bottom lip between her teeth, wondering what went on between those brothers in LA. How did they end up in a fight so bad that Adam had to flee the state?

None of it made sense.

'It's breaking Mrs Klein's heart, the same way that slippery step broke her hip,' Annie said. 'The problem is that hips can mend but hearts can't.'

'Can't they?' Kitty asked, frowning as she looked up at Annie. 'I think they can.'

Annie stared at her for a moment. 'You're right,' she said finally. 'I guess they can mend, but only if you let them.'

'Are we going soon?' Jonas asked, running into the kitchen with his coat already on. 'We want to make sure we get a good spot. Oma always says the best place is outside Rinky's Drugstore, that way you get a great view of the bandstand.'

He'd been talking about the parade non-stop all day, his voice growing more and more excited with each passing hour. Kitty was pretty sure that if they didn't leave for Harville soon, he'd be practically exploding.

She glanced at her watch. It was two o'clock. The parade was due to start at five, just as the darkness would begin to creep in. All the better for seeing the lit-up trucks and characters, as they made their way to the bandstand to begin the annual Harville Christmas concert.

'I guess we could go soon and have a walk around the town,' Kitty agreed. 'I don't think we can stand around for two hours, though. We'll freeze to death if we do.'

Jonas rolled his eyes. He had the gift of a speedy circulation, and hands that never felt cold no matter how long he spent making snowballs. Kitty wasn't quite that lucky.

'You grab that bag, and I'll go and get my coat and boots,' Kitty told him, knowing she wouldn't be able to restrain him for too much longer. 'Let's go watch us a parade.'

*

156

'You got a dog?' Martin stared at Adam enquiringly, trying to disguise the smile on his face. 'That's a turn-up for the books.'

'It's not my dog, I'm just looking after it for my nephew,' Adam told him. 'I nearly brought him with me, but then thought better of it.'

'I'm glad to hear it. I'm allergic to animals.'

Adam shrugged, thinking about the puppy's thick black coat. 'He's hypoallergenic,' he said. 'Doesn't moult, doesn't cause reactions. He's the perfect dog.' Or he would've been, if it wasn't for the crap in the kitchen every morning, which Adam had to clean up himself today. There had been no sign of Kitty, not that he blamed her. Christ, he really had messed everything up.

'Anything else changed since I last saw you?' Martin asked.

'I kissed a girl.'

'Hmmhmm.'

'You don't sound that surprised,' Adam said. 'I was kind of expecting a bigger reaction than that.' Was it wrong he was disappointed? Even the dog had more of an effect on Martin.

'It was Kitty, right?'

'How did you guess?'

Martin had the good grace to laugh. 'It's not much of a detective story. She's the only woman you've come into contact with in weeks, if you don't count your mother, her elderly housekeeper, or the sister-in-law you claim to hate.' He steepled his fingers beneath his chin, scrutinising Adam. 'So, how was it?'

Amazing? Glorious? There didn't seem to be a word to describe it that didn't end up in clusterfuck. 'It was good.' He shrugged, trying to look casual.

Martin didn't look convinced. 'OK, and then what happened?'

'My brother arrived in a helicopter and I spent the rest of the time ignoring her.'

Martin shook his head, clearly exasperated. 'So let's talk this through for a moment. The first time you met this girl, you shouted at her for crying over a deer. You proceeded to ignore her and then chew her out again for taking her eye off your nephew for a minute.' He stopped to take a breath, his eyes still on Adam. 'The last time we spoke you were going to apologise to her, which I assume you did, if you ended up kissing. Wait, this kiss, it was consensual, wasn't it?'

'Yes, it was consensual.' Adam felt the back of his neck heat up. 'It was as consensual as hell.' Jesus, just thinking about it made his heart race all over again. The way her lips were so soft and smooth, the way she'd looked at him as he'd slowly unzipped her jacket. Her eyes wide and trusting, full of wonder, as though the sun was shining right from him.

'OK, so you kissed, *consensually*, and then you ignored her. Is that it or have I missed anything?'

Adam wanted to hang his head at the description. 'When you put it like that I sound like an asshole.'

'Sound like?' Martin raised his eyebrows. 'If I wasn't your therapist and bound by confidentiality, I'd go out and warn the poor girl off you.'

'I'm doing a pretty good job of that all by myself,' Adam muttered.

'Except you're not, are you?' Martin pointed out. 'Because she clearly hasn't been put off by your attitude. You'd been your usual miserable, taciturn self, and she still wanted to kiss you.'

Adam swallowed, feeling an ache at the pit of his stomach. The sort of hunger that food could never sate. 'I really have fucked everything up, haven't I?' he said quietly. 'My life, my work, even this poor girl. I'm like Midas in reverse, everything I touch turns to shit.' Even with his eyes wide open, he could picture Kitty's face as he left her standing there in the snow. The shock that moulded her features as he stalked away from her.

'That's not true though, is it?' Martin said. 'It's just another example of negative thinking. If you reframe the events of the past few months, you'll see that you've made a positive difference in lots of people's lives. Take your nephew, for example. What would have happened if you hadn't been there when he fell into the lake? He could have died, but thanks to you he's perfectly fine.'

Adam shrugged. 'I guess.'

'And that boy in Colombia, what about him?'

'I don't want to talk about that.'

'OK, then let's talk about something else,' Martin said smoothly. 'You've spent your life looking for the truth, staked your personal reputation on it. So what do you think the truth really is here?'

'What do you mean?' Adam frowned. 'I just told you everything.'

'I want you to look inside yourself. Try to work out why you keep blowing so hot and cold with this girl.'

Adam blinked for a moment, trying to work out what Martin was getting at. 'I guess I blow hot because I'm attracted to her, and cold because I don't want to be.'

'Why don't you want to be?'

Adam's mind was blank. He blinked a couple of times, trying to work out why he couldn't order his thoughts. 'I don't know . . . ' Why didn't he want to get close to her? What was it that stopped him? Her youth? She wasn't that young. Her job?

She was Jonas's nanny, but that didn't seem to matter. The fact she lived so far away from Mountain's Reach? Surely that should be a plus.

'Maybe I think she's too good for me,' he postured. 'Maybe I don't want to hurt her.'

'Go deeper still,' Martin urged. 'What is it you feel when I mentioned you getting close to her?'

'Fear. I feel fear.'

Martin smiled encouragingly at him. 'What makes you feel afraid?'

'I'm scared . . . ' Adam blew out a mouthful of air. 'I'm afraid I'm going to get hurt again.'

He felt as though Martin had led him far into a forest, and he had no idea how to get out of it. The trees were looming in on him, the air around him thick and dark.

'It's normal to be afraid after what you've been through,' Martin said quietly. 'It's OK to admit to your fears. But once you acknowledge them, the next step is to do something about them.'

Adam glanced out of the office window, onto the square below. The finishing touches were being made to the parade route. In an hour it would be getting dark enough for the lit-up vehicles to be seen. He'd been so lost inside his head, he'd forgotten about the Christmas parade. 'What can I do?' he asked. 'If you're scared, you're scared.'

'Fear's a natural thing,' Martin told him. 'It can even be useful in the right circumstance. It's a healthy reminder of our limitations, and that sometimes we should step away from danger. But when it's taken to extremes, or twisted in some way by our brains, it can cause us to behave in irrational ways. Like those people who are so afraid of flying that they won't even step on an airplane.' Martin looked up at him, catching his eye. 'Fear becomes unhealthy when it stops us from leading a normal life.'

'You think my fear is irrational?'

'Is this girl a danger to you?' Martin asked.

'I guess not.' Adam shrugged. 'She's not crazy or anything.'

'Do you think she could hurt you?'

Yeah, he really thought she could. Not physically, of course – she could barely cope with hurting a deer, and that was an accident. But he'd been hurt before, betrayed by those who should have taken care of him. How could he let her inside if he wasn't willing to make himself vulnerable?

Not that she probably wanted anything to do with him after the way he'd treated her.

'I think anything has the potential to hurt us if we let it,' Adam said slowly. 'Paper cuts are fairly harmless, but enough of them and you'd bleed to death.'

'So how do we protect ourselves against all these threats to ourselves?' Martin asked. 'Do we wrap ourselves up and hide away from the world, and refuse to let anybody in, for fear they might be carrying germs? Or do we take a risk and step outside and see the beauty the world has to offer?'

The answer was obvious, Adam knew that. But it was one thing to feel it in your head, another thing to feel it in your heart. 'So, what, I should just go back to the house and throw myself at her?'

Martin laughed again, his eyes lighting up. Somewhere over the past few sessions, the two of them had somehow connected. Where Adam had felt resentful before at having to attend therapy on a regular basis, he now found himself enjoying it.

161

'You're full of extremes, do you know that? In a few months you've gone from being an explorer to a hermit. And now you want to go from zero to a hundred. Have you ever thought about moderation? Just letting yourself be a little looser, allow things to happen naturally. Enjoy the moment, spend some time with her, see if you actually have anything in common.' He paused to take a mouthful of water from the sparkling glass beside him. 'You know, be her friend.'

'Be her friend,' Adam repeated. He wasn't sure whether to laugh or roll his eyes. His therapist made things seem so simple when it was just the two of them, closeted away in his elegant office. Life was never as easy as people made it out to be.

But that wasn't any reason not to try, was it?

'It's starting!' Jonas was almost vibrating with excitement as the loud beat of the bass drum cut through the noise of the chattering crowd. They were at the front of the spectator area, Jonas's head only just reaching above the metal barrier. He clung onto the rail with his gloved hands, leaning his chin on the top of it. 'Can you hear it, Kitty?'

She nodded, letting his enthusiasm sink in to her own skin. She couldn't remember the last time she'd watched something like this – the best comparison she could think of in London was the annual carnival parades she'd seen. But those all happened in summer, when the weather allowed. She felt almost like a child again as she heard the brass instruments start up their tune, and the lit-up band marched in unison along Main Street, playing a orchestral arrangement of 'Winter Wonderland'.

Jonas curled his gloved hand around hers, his face pink with frozen excitement as he pointed out the decorated truck that followed the band. Festooned with lights, and complete with a nativity scene, she could see Mary and Joseph surrounded by angels and shepherds.

'Santa doesn't come until the end,' Jonas told her, as if she might be concerned where he'd got to. 'He always rides on the fire truck, and all the firemen are dressed up as elves. They throw out candy to everybody.' From the way his eyes lit up, it sounded as though that was his very favourite part.

There was a murmur behind her as a line of old vintage cars followed on from the nativity truck, their chassis festooned with lights and tinsel. She felt a few people shuffle, the crowd next to them parting, and then saw a tall man come to a stop next to her and Jonas.

It was the first time she'd seen Adam since yesterday. Even separated by a few inches of cold air, not to mention their padded jackets, she could still feel her body reacting to him.

'I didn't mark you down as the parade type,' she said, still looking straight ahead as the cars passed them by.

'I spent my childhood watching this,' Adam said. From the corner of her eye she could see a half-smile on his lips. 'It brings back old memories.'

'Good memories?' she asked. On her other side, Jonas was leaning forward, craning to see the final truck of the parade – the infamous Christmas fire truck. He hadn't even noticed Adam's arrival.

He shrugged, the movement making his black jacket rise up. 'Yeah. They were good days.' She saw him glance down at Jonas, who'd finally noticed his arrival. 'Hey, Jonas, enjoying it?'

Jonas's face lit up at his uncle's attention. 'You're here!' he said, beaming. 'I didn't think you were coming.'

'I wouldn't miss it for the world.' Adam's voice was thick.

163

'Do you see the fire truck?' Jonas asked him. 'Do they have lots of candy? You're much taller than me, I can't see a thing.'

'You want me to lift you up?'

Jonas nodded enthusiastically, and the next moment Adam was picking his nephew up and putting him on his shoulders. Kitty couldn't help but smile at Jonas's delighted expression, King of the Castle with the best view in town.

Adam noticed her smile, and cracked one of his own, the corners of his eyes wrinkling. Neither of them said anything for a moment, though their gazes were locked together. Her heart was beating loudly in her chest, matching the rhythm of the band. Why did she react like this to him every time?

'Can we talk after the parade?' Adam asked her quietly enough that Jonas couldn't hear.

Her glance slid up to the boy. 'Jonas is with me,' she reminded him. 'Maybe later?'

His reply was drowned out by the squeal of a hundred children as the fire truck finally joined the parade. Jonas wriggled until Adam put him down, and he ran back to his space by the barrier, the best spot to claim his candy. Kitty and Adam stepped back to allow the other children to join him, all of them jumping up and down as Santa waved at them from his spot on the top of the fire truck. The firemen walked alongside, their elves' outfits looking ridiculous on their muscled frames, but each one of them was enjoying himself, passing handfuls of candy to the kids.

She felt proud of Jonas when he took his portion of candy and stepped back, allowing other children to fill his space. She hadn't even had to remind him to take his turn, he'd done it naturally anyway.

'Can we go over to the bandstand?' Jonas asked her, already

ripping the wrapper off a chocolate bar. 'They let the kids sit at the front when the concert begins, I want to get a good spot there, too.'

She followed Jonas as he weaved through the crowd, clearly used to the running order of the parade. In previous years his grandmother had brought him, and by all accounts she'd enjoyed it as much as Jonas had. It was a real shame she couldn't make it this year.

Adam shadowed close behind her, and she liked the way that felt. Technically Adam and Jonas were family, and she was the interloper, but somehow Kitty didn't feel left out at all. It was as though for once she was the heroine of her own story, at the centre of things, and she liked it. Maybe a little too much.

As they made it to the town square, Jonas joined the other kids on the bleachers somebody had placed out in front of the bandstand. The white structure was lit up, decorated with wreaths of holly and icicle lights hanging down from the roof. Inside, the band had already set themselves up, wearing red Santa hats, their music stands edged with tinsel. As soon as the fire truck arrived at the end of the parade, Santa was helped down from his perch on the roof, and he walked over to the crowd of children gathered in the square, as the band struck up a jaunty arrangement of 'Santa Claus is Coming to Town'.

'You want a coffee?' Adam asked her, inclining his head over at the catering truck to the side of the square.

'Sounds good.'

Five minutes later, Adam was back, carrying two festive Styrofoam cups and a bag of cookies. He handed her a cup, then pulled a cookie out for her, and for a moment they drank and ate, listening to the music.

165

'You did a good thing bringing Jonas here,' Adam said, after chewing the last mouthful of his cookie. 'He always says it's the best part of Christmas.'

She smiled. 'Apart from opening gifts on Christmas morning, I bet.'

'Yeah, that too.' He took a sip from his still-steaming coffee cup. 'I'm glad I saw you two here, I wasn't sure I would.'

'I didn't expect you to come,' Kitty said. 'It doesn't really seem like your thing.'

He tipped his head to the side. 'What is my thing, do you think?'

She blinked a couple of times, thinking about his question. How well did she really know him? Oh, she knew the things she'd read online, and from all those encounters she'd had with him over the past week.

'I guess I don't really see you as a spectator,' she said, trying to work out where he did fit in. 'You seem more of a participant than anything else.'

'I make documentaries,' he said, his voice light. 'You don't think that's the ultimate in spectator sports?'

'No, I don't think so. I've seen some of your documentaries, you're on screen quite a lot. You're definitely part of the story.'

His face warmed up at her words. 'You've seen them?'

She found herself smiling again. 'Who hasn't?'

'I guess I didn't think you'd be that interested in them.'

'Why not?' she asked, her hands still wrapped around her Styrofoam cup. The band finished their song, and segued into a faster version of 'White Christmas'. Dancers came out onto the stage.

'I don't know,' Adam said. 'Maybe I should have asked you.

There's a lot I don't know about you.' He paused for a second. 'I'd like to know more.'

'You would?' It was her turn to be shocked. What happened to the guy who practically stalked off from her after giving her the best kiss of her life?

'Why do you look so surprised?' he asked.

'I guess I didn't think you'd be that interested in me.' She stole his words, trying, and failing, to hide her smile.

'What made you think that?' He shook his head. 'Was it the way I kissed you yesterday? Or the way I demanded you come and visit me in the cabin every morning? Or maybe it was the way I keep bumping into you accidentally. Yeah, I'm really not interested at all.'

She could feel her pulse drumming in her ears. This was completely unexpected. Welcome, though. 'But you always seem so angry at me.'

'It's not you I'm angry at, it's myself. I'm an idiot, and I'm an asshole, and I keep digging myself a hole I can't climb out of. I'd really like to make it up to you.'

'Make it up?' she questioned.

'Yeah, make up for being such an asshole. It was completely ungentlemanly of me to kiss you then ignore you. Especially after a kiss like that.' He looked almost embarrassed, and completely adorable.

'OK,' she agreed, still wondering what he was getting at.

He blinked, like he was surprised it was that simple. What did he expect? Every time he'd shown her the slightest interest, she'd lapped it up like a hungry cat. Did he not realise how she felt every time he came close to her?

'Will you come back to the cabin tomorrow morning?' he asked her, the hope lighting up his face.

She bit her lip, looking over at Jonas. She could just about see the top of his head as he watched the show unfold in front of him. 'I don't know ... there's Jonas to look after.'

'I'd say bring him down with you, but that would spoil the point of hiding the dog.'

'Where is the dog, anyway?' she asked him.

'I've left him with Annie. Dad'll take him back down to the cabin before you guys get back. The dog's exhausted anyway, I took him out for a long walk this morning.'

She grinned at the thought of Adam taking the tiny ball of fur out in the wintry landscape. Seeing the two of them together would be enough to break hearts. A man with a puppy was only one step down from a man with a baby when it came to looking adorable.

'I hope he's not causing you too much trouble,' Kitty said. 'I really do appreciate your help with him.'

'I'm kind of enjoying it,' Adam told her. 'I've been working on teaching him to sit and stay.'

'Really?' Kitty raised her eyebrows. 'I'd like to see that.'

'Come down to the cabin and I'll show you tomorrow,' Adam promised her. 'And I'll make you breakfast, too.'

There was a loud round of applause and whooping from the crowd as the dance recital came to an end. Jonas turned from his position on the bleachers and waved madly at Kitty. She waved back with her free hand. 'OK,' she said, her body tingling at the thought of spending alone time with Adam. 'I'll come and see you in the cabin in the morning.'

17

Love all, trust a few, do wrong to none
– All's Well That Ends Well

Later that evening the whole family, minus Adam, gathered around the polished mahogany table in the dining room for dinner. Mia had arrived home an hour earlier in a taxi, looking exhausted before she'd even walked through the door. Annie had slunk back into the kitchen as soon as she'd seen who it was, desperately trying to eke out the lentil casserole she'd made for Drake, while the rest of them would be satisfied with the beef stew she'd had simmering on the hob all day. 'No red meat,' she muttered to herself as she shuffled down the hallway. 'She might as well be one of those vegetarians too.'

Dinner was an awkward affair, with Everett and Drake talking shop as Jonas tried desperately to get his mother's attention. Though she'd listen to him, and smile in the right places, her attention never lasted for long.

'Mom, did you hear what I said?' Jonas asked her. 'I was telling you about the parade. There was candy and everything.'

'Of course she didn't hear you.' Everett glanced at his wife.

169

'She's far too busy for that. What's the problem, honey, was three days at the spa not enough for you?'

Mia shot him a nasty smile. 'It was a lovely break. Though it would have been nice if my husband had joined me like he'd promised to.'

'Your husband was too busy making money to pay for your damned vacations,' he growled.

Kitty glanced down at Jonas. 'The parade really was lovely, wasn't it?' she said, desperate to change the conversation. 'It made me feel really Christmassy. And the singing was good, too.'

Turning her back on her husband, Mia smiled at her son. 'Oh yes, tell me all about it, darling.'

Jonas answered his mother as Kitty sat back, relieved at having averted another confrontation.

Jonas's grandfather sat at the head of the table, pushing his stew around with a fork, gazing into the mid distance. He must have been missing his wife, still unable to make it down the stairs to join them for dinner. A couple of times Kitty attempted to engage him, asking questions about the house and its history. He looked grateful for the distraction.

Wisely, Annie had chosen to eat her own meal in the kitchen, mentioning that she needed to keep an eye on the oven and the food she was baking. Truffles and pies, plus the most delicious-smelling brioches had joined the piles of cookies she'd made earlier. Kitty couldn't help but think what a shame it was that she and Jonas appeared to be the only people in the house enjoying Annie's food.

The stew itself was delicious, the meat mouth-wateringly good. Kitty had practically cleared her plate before the others had barely eaten a mouthful. She'd noticed Mia try one tiny forkful of her lentil casserole then wrinkle her nose, pointedly putting her fork and knife down on her plate to indicate she was finished.

The doorbell chiming through the hallway brought a welcome distraction from the dinner party from hell, and Kitty checked her watch, realising it could finally be the delivery she was expecting. The vegan dog food she'd express-ordered from a pet boutique in Rodeo Drive.

'I'm sorry, that's probably for me.' Kitty stood up, scraping the legs of the chair along the floor. Everett looked over, giving her no more than a flicker of a gaze, before gesturing for her to go with his hand, not bothering to stop his conversation with Drake.

'Can I come?' Jonas jumped up too, his chair wobbling on two legs where he'd tipped it backwards. 'What can it be? More gifts?'

'You haven't finished your dinner,' Kitty pointed out.

'I can finish it later.'

'No, sir.' Kitty shook her head. 'You stay here, I won't be a moment.' There was no way she wanted him to see the dog food delivery, not after all the trouble she'd gone to in order to hide the damn dog at the cabin. There was only a week until Christmas; she'd made it this far, she wasn't planning to give the game away now.

'Oh shoot.' Jonas gave in, sitting back down with disgust written on his face. 'You have all the fun.'

It came to something when receiving a delivery was more fun than spending time with his family. Kitty walked over to the hallway, ruminating about his lack of attention, and wondering how on earth she could make this a fun few days for him while his grandmother was laid up, and his parents were more interested in scoring points off each other than actually engaging with her son.

'You need some help?' Drake asked, looking as keen to escape the dinner as she was.

Kitty found herself taking pity on him, even if he still wasn't her favourite person in the world. Like her, he was an outsider, surely they shouldn't have to put themselves through this.

'Yeah, that would be great. Follow me.'

'No fair,' Jonas said, but stayed seated anyway.

'There you are.' Annie turned to greet Kitty and Drake as they made it out to the hallway. 'He's just bringing the packages now.'

A tall man wearing a brown uniform was walking up the porch stairs, carrying three big brown sacks. He tipped them onto the floor, pulling a clipboard out and handing it to Kitty to sign. She scrawled her name across the line then handed it back, thanking him for making a late delivery.

'No problem.' The driver gave her an easy smile, which broadened as soon as she passed him five dollars. 'Merry Christmas to you both.'

As soon as he was gone, Kitty walked over to the bags of food. They were as large as potato sacks, just as heavy too when she tried to lift one. Affixed to the outside was a photograph of the contents; an unappetising picture of dried grey pellets, which made Kitty's stomach turn.

'Poor puppy,' she murmured. 'He's not going to be happy about that.'

Drake carried the dog-food sacks into the larder, huffing beneath the weight as he lifted them onto the bottom shelf. 'There, that's it.' For a guy who professed to spend half his life

172

in the gym, he was looking surprisingly red in the face. Kitty couldn't help but think about Adam, and those hard, thick muscles that rippled beneath his thin T-shirt when he ran. He'd lifted an entire deer without batting an eyelid . . .

Best not to think about that.

'Thanks for your help,' she told Drake, as the two of them walked out into the kitchen. Dinner had finished in their absence – she'd spotted Everett disappear into the library, while his father and Jonas climbed up the stairs to join the older Mrs Klein in her sick room. Annie had finished cooking for the evening, and Kitty helped her tidy up the dishes from dinner. The housekeeper sat down in her easy chair in the corner, watching the small television mounted on the wall.

'You must have been upset, having to change your holiday plans to come here,' she said to Drake, pouring them both out a glass of red wine. Though strictly speaking Kitty's duties weren't over yet – not until Jonas was asleep in bed – she thought they could both do with a drink.

Drake shrugged. 'Not really. I was planning on dinner with some friends and then straight back to work on the twenty-sixth. I haven't been home for Christmas in years, I prefer spending Thanksgiving with my folks.'

'I always find it weird that everybody goes back to work the day after Christmas,' Kitty said, taking a sip of wine. 'In England everything comes to a standstill between Christmas and New Year. We spend the whole week stuffing our faces with chocolate and seeing who can drink the most without being sick.'

Drake's cute nose wrinkled up. 'Ugh. You English and your alcohol. Whenever we have an actor from the UK in one of our movies I just know we're going to have problems. Hangovers and early morning shoots really don't mix.'

She wanted to protest, maybe say something about that being better than the uptight valley boys, but if she was really honest there was more than an ounce of truth in Drake's words. At the few Hollywood parties she'd been to, the biggest hell-raisers always seemed to hail from somewhere in the UK or Ireland.

Looking down, she realised she'd already drained her glass of wine. Normally she'd pour out another without a second thought, but now she was hyper-aware of her alcohol consumption.

Seeing her expression, Drake quickly changed the subject. 'So Everett tells me you're still looking for an internship?'

'I am,' she said. She really wanted that second glass of wine now. 'I haven't found anything yet.' She wondered whether she should mention the half-interview he'd given her, but somehow it didn't seem like the right time.

'If you keep on Everett's good side, he may be able to help you. He's pretty well connected in the business.'

No shit. She noticed he hadn't mentioned the one she'd actually applied for though. Clearly that ship had sailed. 'I guess I'll get back into the search after Christmas.' And maybe learn how not to panic as soon as she was asked a question. Yeah, that would be good, too.

'Maybe you should see if you can get something back home,' Drake suggested. 'The movie industry in London is pretty healthy. Have you ever thought about going back there?'

Was he trying to get rid of her? Her interview technique must really have sucked. 'I want to stay here,' she told him. 'Or in Hollywood anyway. If I can.'

'Don't you miss your family, though, living out here?' Drake asked.

'Yes, but none of them are living in London any more,' Kitty told him. 'One of my sisters lives in Maryland, and another is in Scotland.' And even Cesca wasn't spending that much time in London. 'We talk on Skype and email, so me living over here doesn't make that much difference.'

'Can you pour me another glass of wine, Kitty?' Annie called out from her chair across the room.

Oh sod it. Kitty poured herself another glass as well. After a day with the Kleins she needed it. If Drake wanted to judge her with his hyper-white smile and perma-tanned glow, then let him.

'Why was Everett so cagey about that script the other day?' she asked Drake, after passing Annie her glass. 'He got really worked up about it.'

'This project is important to him, it's something he's been working on for months. If anything goes wrong now I think he'll have a fit. He sees it as his magnum opus.'

She raised her eyes to meet Drake's. 'A vanity project?'

'No, not at all. It's an important movie, one that has a real story to tell.' He lowered his voice. 'I really shouldn't say any more. It's very delicate and you know how angry he got when you came in the library.'

Kitty decided to take advantage of the thaw that had melted the atmosphere between them. 'Are you sure you can't tell me any more about it?' She was desperate to know. Who wouldn't be? It wasn't often that a film student got to see a huge production being planned first-hand.

Not that she was seeing it. In Everett's mind she was only the nanny, not a want-to-be intern.

'I really can't say anything about it at the moment.' Drake looked almost regretful. 'I would if I could. All I can say is that it's big. That's why Everett insisted I join him here.'

'What made you arrive in a helicopter? Would a plane not do?' She frowned, remembering the cacophony as the two of them landed in the meadow. Then she started to recall exactly what Drake and Everett's arrival had interrupted, and a blush stole its way across her face.

Did she really have to wait until the morning to see Adam? Part of her wanted to run down there now, to see exactly what he wanted to talk to her about.

Drake laughed. 'It was the fastest way to get from the airport. What were you doing down in the cabin anyway?' He countered her question with another one.

For a moment she wondered if he could read her mind. 'I had to look after the puppy,' she squeaked, panicking. 'He's a present for Jonas and we're hiding him down there until Christmas morning. It was the only place I could think of. Luckily Adam agreed to help out.'

'You should stay away from that man,' Drake warned, making a face as soon as she mentioned Adam's name. 'He's crazy, and vicious as hell. Not somebody you want to be dealing with.'

Kitty's breath caught in her throat. 'What do you mean?'

'Everett did everything he could this summer, after his brother got back from that clusterfuck in Colombia. Then Adam threw it back in his face, practically ripping the pool house apart. He even managed to give Everett a black eye. He's an animal.'

'Why did he hit his brother?' Her mouth was dry. Part of her wanted to know more, to learn about the person Adam was, but the information she was getting made her want to shiver.

Drake shrugged. 'They said it was a reaction to what happened in Colombia, that's why the LAPD was so lenient with him. But I heard the arguments between him and Everett, and there was no excuse for the way he treated his brother.'

Kitty took another mouthful of wine, still trying without success to equate the Adam he was describing to the man she'd spent time with that afternoon. Nothing about him seemed as dangerous as Drake was suggesting.

'Life does strange things to people,' she said.

'Well it definitely messed him up. If you need company when you go down there, I'd be happy to help. To give you some protection from him, I mean.'

Kitty spluttered, spraying red wine across the surface of the workshop. After the conversation she'd had with Adam that afternoon, the only sort of protection she needed definitely didn't come in the form of a valley boy.

Though she hated to admit it, Drake's description of Adam had only heightened her interest in the dark, possibly violent, yet gorgeous man who lived in a cabin in the woods. One thing was for sure, when she went down tomorrow, there was no way she was taking Drake with her.

Even if she had to sneak out of the house without anybody noticing.

18

My love is as a fever, longing still

— Sonnet 147

Kitty watched the early morning sunshine creeping across her carpet. It was only six o'clock when she stumbled out of bed, her messy hair framing her face like an off-centre helmet. She stood under the lukewarm shower for a long ten minutes; her eyes squeezed shut as water poured down her face.

The house still hadn't stirred when she walked into the kitchen. The usual aroma of coffee was absent, so she poured heaped scoops of ground beans into the filter, filling up the reservoir and turning it on. Flicking the switch on the old radio that Annie kept plugged in near the stove, she curled up into the easy chair, cupping her hands around her warm mug.

Taking a sip of coffee, she wondered when she should head down to the cabin. Adam had been insistent she come, but hadn't said a time. Was it too early? she wondered. Would he still be out on that morning run? Even worse, would she wake him up, making him answer the door with his hair still mussed and his eyes all heavy?

Or what if he'd changed his mind altogether and asked her to turn around and go back to the house?

One thing was for sure; she'd drive herself crazy if she sat here too much longer.

Grabbing a large Tupperware box, she filled it with vegan dog food, trying not to wrinkle her nose as the thick, dried granules landed in the transparent plastic tub. It had a smell she couldn't quite place – leafy, earthy, and more than a little pungent – and it was hard to imagine anybody could find that appetising.

Even a puppy. The poor thing.

Wrapped warmly in her thick winter coat and scarf, she followed her usual path through the trees. She'd learned the way by heart – turning left at the half-dead pine, then right at the three fallen logs – her legs following the path without her really having to think about it. The same route Jonas had taken her on their first few days here, when the snow was new and sparkling, and she hadn't realised what lay on the other side of those trees.

Or *who* lay there.

Coming to the clearing at the top of the hill, she stopped for a moment, staring into the valley below. The lake was still, the winter sun reflecting in its mirror-like surface, the cloudless December sky lending it a blue tint. Last night before she'd gone to bed Annie had said something about another storm brewing, but the stillness of the air belied that thought. The sky was too clear, the air too static. There was no sign of a blizzard to be seen.

Set back from the lake, Adam's cabin stood proud within the clearing of the meadow. A plume of grey-blue smoke curled up from his chimney, the only sign of life in a scene otherwise dominated by nature.

Was he waiting for her? Kitty's breath sped up as she stared at the lodge, her heart banging against her chest. She wasn't sure when she started walking again, leaving a trail of footprints behind her, but before she'd begun to clear her thoughts, she'd already covered half the distance between herself and the building.

That's when she spotted him standing silently in the open doorway, his eyes trained on her as she walked. His scrutiny lent her an air of self-consciousness, making her stumble a couple of times before she reached his steps. Unlike the last time she was here, the wooden slats that enclosed the porch and held the roof up were decorated with boughs of pine and holly. Laced between the greenery were twinkling lights, lending a grotto-like air to a cabin which had previously been so plain.

It looked like something from a fairy tale.

There was a lump in her throat when she spoke. 'You decorated.' She recognised the lights from the box she'd brought down two days ago. Never in her wildest dreams had she thought he'd do anything with them.

Adam leaned against the doorway. Though the air was freezing, he was only wearing jeans and a thin black sweater, the wool doing nothing to hide the definition of his chest. His hair was still wet, brushed back from his face, his beard recently trimmed. She could almost smell the pine scent of his cologne – an aroma that already had the ability to make her weak at the knees. 'The box was in the way. I figured I better do something with it before the puppy decided to eat it for breakfast.'

Kitty was still overcome by the wild, primitive wonder of the scene. 'It's beautiful.'

His eyes didn't leave her face. 'Yes it is.'

All those fears and doubts that had been her companion since leaving the big house seemed to evaporate into the winter air. The way he was staring at her with dark, hungry eyes was enough to melt her inside.

'I wasn't sure you'd be back from your run.'

'I was out before six.' The smile he flashed her was brief. 'I don't sleep a whole lot. I've already got the logs in for the day, too.'

She reached the top of the steps. Adam hadn't moved, his large body still blocking the door. Kitty came to a halt a few feet from the entrance, her rapid pulse making her breathless.

'I'm glad you're here.' Her voice was soft.

'So am I.' For the first time he took a step towards her, sending every cell in her body into high alert. A shiver worked its way down her spine, leaving a trail of goose bumps behind it. Adam reached out and took the dog food from her hands.

'It's for the dog.' She was aware of how stupid she sounded. 'It's vegan. Organic, as well. Apparently he'll love it.' She looked over in the corner, where the puppy was curled up in his makeshift bed. He looked out for the count.

Adam didn't reply. Placing the box on the rustic bench just inside the front door, he reached out again, this time wrapping his hands around Kitty's waist.

It was as if a spotlight had been trained on the two of them, flooding the outside world with darkness. They were actors on a stage, with an audience of two, and every movement was a gesture meant for their private performance. She felt his hands tighten around her through the layer of her coat, as he lifted her easily into his house. Disappointment flooded her chest when he released his hold.

That sensation was short-lived, as he tugged at the zipper of her jacket and slipped it off her shoulders, letting it fall to the floor in a heap. Then his fingers were on her neck, unbuttoning her sweater, warming her skin as he pushed down inside.

She looked up, connecting with his hot stare. His face was flushed, his lips swollen, a mirror of her own arousal. He lifted her sweater over her head, revealing her cotton tank and bra, his hands sliding the straps from her shoulders until they were bare.

'I thought you wanted to talk to me.' She tried to inhale, her mouth dry. Fearing he might take that as a rejection, she quickly added, 'Not that it matters right now.'

Adam dipped his head, pressing his face into the curve between her neck and shoulder. She felt his lips move against her aroused skin, his voice little more than a whisper, its volume muffled by her body.

'We'll talk later.'

He hadn't meant to pounce on her the moment she'd walked into the house. He'd filled the coffee pot and whisked some eggs, intending to have everything on the table for her arrival. He'd spent most of the night thinking about her, about the questions he wanted to ask, the apologies he wanted to say. But then he'd spied her from the kitchen window, emerging from the forest and onto the hill. With her silhouette illuminated by the burgeoning sun, she'd looked like something otherworldly. The need to touch her had flickered back to life until it was an inferno burning inside his belly.

Adam had lingered in the doorway as she'd walked down the hill, his fingers grasping the wood in an effort not to run to her. What had Martin told him? That he could choose a middle ground, it didn't have to be all or nothing. He could just be her friend.

She didn't feel like a friend right now, though, as he brushed his lips up her neck, feeling her shiver at his kisses. Then he reached the corner of her mouth – could feel the warmth of her breath against his lips, and he paused for a moment, his eyes meeting hers to check it was OK.

He was half afraid she'd change her mind and walk away. Even more afraid that she wouldn't. His mouth was aching with the need to kiss her, to taste her, to consume her.

He didn't want to be her friend.

He wanted to be her lover. Fuck blowing hot and cold, the heat was all he needed.

'Is this OK?' He wasn't sure why he was asking now.

She blinked at him, her lips parting slightly as he continued to stare. She swallowed, as though she was tasting the moment as much as he was. 'Yes.' She nodded. 'It's more than OK.'

Slowly, torturously, he slid his mouth to hers. At first it was little more than the softest feather of lips against lips, as he reached up to cup her jaw, angling her face to his. Then he deepened the kiss, his need to taste her overwhelming every other sense. She moulded her body against his, soft chest against his hard planes, warm thighs against his. Christ, she was delicious.

It only took a moment of them kissing for him to get hard, his dick throbbing in the confines of his jeans. Her lips were so soft, her mouth wet and warm as he slid his tongue inside her.

Adam moved his hands down, sliding them from her chest to her waist. Her skin was warm, smooth, and so very tantalising, but nothing compared to the heat flooding through his body.

She'd said yes. *To him*. He wanted to shout it out to the world. In this godforsaken corner of a snow-covered mountain, a beautiful, funny girl who he'd spent the past week consumed by, had walked over to give herself to him.

It felt like little short of a miracle.

'Can I take you to the bedroom?' As hormone-ridden as they were, having her against the wall of his cabin wasn't what he had in mind. She had a body to savour, not rush. If he was going to make it good for her, a knee-trembling quickie wasn't going to cut it.

'Is it far?'

He let his head fall back as he laughed. 'No, baby, not far at all.' He lifted her up until her legs circled his hips. Their relative heights made her face level with his. Kitty cupped his jaw, angling her head until their brows touched.

'I can't believe I'm doing this. I swear I only came down for breakfast.' She didn't look too unhappy about it, though. Her smile lit up her face.

Adam flexed his muscles. 'I think you'll find I'm doing all of the work here. You're just coming along for the ride.'

Her laugh blinded him. 'I mean *this*. Going to bed with you. It's hardly even morning. I'm honestly not the sort of girl who throws herself at strangers.'

'We're not strangers.' They were anything but. Right then he felt connected to her on every level. It was as though his heart was in tune with his brain for once. 'But if you're having second thoughts, we can stop now. No hard feelings.'

'Don't you dare stop.'

That settled it. They made it to the bedroom. Adam laid her gently on his bed, standing back to admire her for a moment. Her hair fanned out across the patchwork quilt, her skin soft in the morning light. Her top half was bare save for the half-open bra she was wearing. From the waist down, on the other hand, she needed some work.

Adam bent down and pulled off her boots, then tugged at the woollen socks keeping her feet warm. Her toenails were painted a vivid orange, shiny and bright. Something about that made him want to kiss them, so he did. One by one he pressed his lips to her toes, holding them hard when she tried to pull them away. She started to giggle at the sensation.

'Can I take my jeans off?' she asked him.

'That's my job.' He didn't want to be hurried. Adam planned on savouring every moment of that morning, burning each touch and sensation into his memory. He wasn't sure what would happen after today. For now, he just wanted to live in the moment.

With her.

Maybe that's what Martin meant after all.

She started to wriggle on the bed, responding to his touch. With a grin on his face, Adam climbed onto the mattress, leaning over her as he stared into her eyes, his hands resting on either side of her head.

'Adam, I need you.'

'Say my name again.'

Her lips turned up. 'Adam. Adam, Adam. Do it to me, Adam.'

He laughed and shook his head.

Slowly he unbuttoned her jeans. They were tight against her skin, enough to make her have to lift up her body as he tugged the denim down, watching it slide along her legs until finally he brought them over her feet. That just left her underwear. No, not underwear – lingerie. It was delicate and white, the intricate design on her panties matching those on her bra. It made him hard as a rock to know she'd worn this just for him.

Kneeling over her, he leaned down and pressed a kiss to her stomach. Her body was warm and silky beneath his lips. As he slid his mouth to her breastbone, Kitty gasped, her chest rising with the effort.

'Take my bra off.'

The way she kept trying to boss him around amused him. She didn't realise that he was planning to do it anyway. But knowing how needy she was, he took his time, making her gasp and squirm as his fingers brushed against the underside of her breast.

She was panting by the time he unhooked her bra.

Man, her breasts were magnificent. Pale and full with pink-tipped nipples, he couldn't stop himself from staring at them. Imagining how they'd feel in his mouth, his tongue rolling around until her tips were stiff.

Kitty's hands fluttered to her chest, as if to cover them. Firmly he grabbed her wrists and put her arms by her sides. Right now her breasts were his. Every part of her was his. But what he planned to do was for Kitty alone.

'You're beautiful.' His voice cracked.

'Really?' She sounded surprised.

'Like you don't know it.' He placed the pad of his index finger in the dip beneath her neck, tracing a line that intersected her breasts. 'Look at you lying here, like some kind of goddess. You must hear this shit all the time.'

'I don't.'

'Then you should. Every fucking day.'

He couldn't wait any longer. The need to taste her, to give

186

her pleasure, was too strong to ignore. He brought his head to her breast, stopping half an inch away from her nipple. Close enough to make her pucker with his warm breath. Pausing, he tasted the anticipation before wrapping his lips around her nipple.

She groaned loudly, making him pulse in his jeans. It was taking everything he had not to grind himself into her, to ease that throbbing ache between his thighs. To distract himself he reached out for her other breast, rolling her nipple between his thumb and forefinger.

Kitty's gasps told him how much she liked it. So did the way she was circling her hips, dancing to a rhythm as old as time.

'Touch me. Please touch me.'

'Soon,' he promised, caressing her breast again. 'When you're ready.'

'I *am* ready.' She pouted. Fuck, he wanted to kiss her again.

He had to bury his head to hide his smirk. 'Yeah, you're probably right about that.'

She reached down to tug at his sweater. 'You're not though. You've still got all your clothes on.'

'I can solve that problem in about thirty seconds.'

Kitty tried to sit up, but the cage of his arms prevented her. 'What if I want to solve it?'

He couldn't help but grin. 'You want to strip me?'

She swallowed visibly. 'Um, yeah? Is that OK?'

There was something about her reticence that pulled at him. 'Have at it. I have to warn you, though, it's a lot harder undressing a man than a woman.'

'You've undressed a man before?' she asked playfully.

Adam grinned. 'Only myself. And maybe Ev when he was too drunk to do it himself.'

187

'Can we not talk about your brother when I'm about to take your clothes off.'

'Fair point.'

She took it slow, inching the hem of his sweater up, trailing her fingers over his undershirt. It was his turn to get impatient, putting his arms up to encourage her to take it all the way up. When she did, beginning the torture all over again with his undershirt, Adam thought about taking over himself.

But then he saw the intense expression on her face as she slowly revealed his stomach. The way she stared, licking her dry lips, was enough compensation for the torture.

'You like what you see?'

She breathed in sharply. 'It's OK.'

Adam shook his head. 'I don't do OK. That's something you'll find out about me. It's shit or bust all the way.'

Maybe it had been too much bust lately. He'd tried hard for so long and eventually given up. Hiding in this cabin had seemed his only option, the way he could disappear from the world. He wasn't hiding now, though. He was becoming exposed, and not just physically. With every inch that Kitty pulled up the fabric of his undershirt, she was also opening up something deep inside him. Something he'd hidden for so long.

He wasn't sure he was ready for that. It felt too raw.

Refusing to think about anything but her body and his, Adam tugged at the buckle of his belt, pulling his jeans down and kicking them onto the floor. That left them both in their underwear – she in her panties, he in his shorts. When he climbed back up over her, his legs between her thighs, he lowered himself until they were grinding against each other.

Adam was done for. Like a kid, he wanted to keep moving until they were both gasping out loud, until they exploded into a blinding light. But he wasn't a kid, he was a man. If the years had taught him anything, it was that prolonging a moment was everything. Things tasted so much more delicious if you had to wait for them.

Kitty placed her hands on his behind, using the movement to create friction between them. He dipped his head to kiss her again. Their mouths were heated and desperate, their tongues touching and sliding against each other in an effort to consume. She started to rock against him in a steady rhythm, her gasps quicker, faster, harder. She was close to coming, that much he could tell, and he realised he didn't want to feel it against his body.

He wanted to feel it against his mouth.

Kitty cried out when he pulled back. Her hands dropped to her sides, her eyes glistening with disappointment. That turned to wide-eyed astonishment as he scooted down, hooking his fingers around the elastic of her panties to pull them down her thighs.

Throwing the scrap of fabric behind him, he reached out to grab her legs, spreading them wide so she was open and exposed. Her hands were grasping the bed covers, her head flung back with her eyes closed. He wanted to imprint that image for ever.

Softly, he scraped his beard along her inner leg, taking his time when he got to the soft, plump skin at the top of her thighs. Kitty moaned louder, one of her hands releasing the covers so she could bury her fingers in his hair.

'Please . . .'

'Please what?' he growled.

'Adam, stop teasing.'

But he wanted to tease. He wanted to drive her so crazy

189

she'd never leave. He wanted to blow her mind so hard that she'd have to stay with him in the cabin for ever.

'You want me to touch you?'

'Yes!' She tugged at his hair, trying to move his face closer. 'Please.'

'Since you asked so nicely . . .' He blew, parting the scant hair that covered her. Kitty shivered beneath his touch, her hips bucking.

He touched the most sensitive part of her with the soft tip of his tongue. Kitty rocked beneath him, crying out as he licked her again. She tasted good, enough to make him want more. Enough to encourage him to slide his tongue over and over again until her cries became screams. His body throbbed with every lick, the need to pull off his shorts and take her becoming almost feral. Ignoring the ache, he slid his fingers up, pushing them inside her until her body began to convulse around him.

She continued to buck as he crawled up and over her, pressing his warm, slick lips against hers. Swallowing her cries, he let her wrap her legs around his hips, her body seeking friction as she rode the final wave.

When Kitty finally opened her eyes, they were heavy and dark. She stared up at him, her lips parted. 'Wow. That was amazing.'

Hearing how good he'd made her feel was like winning an Olympic medal. He smiled, finally allowing himself to grind between her thighs.

'Babe, that was just the beginning. The best is yet to come.'

19

God hath given you one face and
you make yourself another

– Hamlet

Kitty didn't want to leave. She was lying in the circle of Adam's arms, feeling his breath fanning against her back. His body was curled against hers, his chest to her spine, his legs tucked behind her. She felt warm, protected, and a little bit horny, which was crazy after everything they'd done that morning. Every muscle in her body ached.

From the kitchen, she could hear the gentle snoring of the puppy. Strange how her world had taken a one-eighty turn, all while the dog stayed asleep.

The feeling of Adam cradling her, his body moving into hers, had been overwhelming. Every touch of his skin against Kitty's was like a song playing inside her. He'd filled her up, physically and emotionally, until it felt as though she couldn't take any more. Being with him had felt like a strange combination of newness and coming home. As though she'd slotted right into place.

The clock beside the bed told her it was almost nine thirty.

Everyone at the big house would be up by now. Jonas would be scooping cereal into his mouth, Mia would be drinking mug after mug of steaming black coffee. Everett would be holed up in the library, avoiding everybody. Kitty really should be up there too, doing what she was paid to do.

'I need to go.' She tried to wriggle out of Adam's arms.

'Not yet.' He tightened his hold, pulling her closer still. His voice was heavy with sleep. 'Stay with me.'

From her spot on the bed Kitty could see soft snowflakes falling past the bedroom window. It felt as though the two of them were bubbled up inside a snow globe. Untouchable. Beautiful. Fragile.

'I can't stay for long.'

'We haven't had a chance to talk yet,' Adam pointed out.

She bit down a smile. 'We were too busy.'

'Well we're not busy now. Not for the next five minutes, at least.'

She twisted in his arms, turning to look at him. 'What do you want to talk about?'

He pressed his lips against her shoulder. 'Tell me about England.'

Kitty frowned. 'Well, it's a country across the Atlantic—'

His laughter cut through the air. 'Not about the country. Tell me about you. What were you like as a little girl?'

This wasn't the usual post one-night stand conversation. Not that this was the usual one-night stand, either. It happened in the morning for a start. Kitty closed her eyes, savouring the sensation of Adam's body pressed to hers. She really needed to stop overthinking this.

She turned to him, a quizzical look on her face. 'Why do you want to know?'

He looked almost childlike in his embarrassment. 'I made a list of the things I wanted to ask you.' He coughed hard. 'My therapist suggested it.'

She tried to swallow down the laugh that tried to escape from her chest. 'He did? Why?'

'I told him I liked you. He suggested I try to be your friend. As you can see, that's working out really well right now.'

This time her laughter exploded, and he joined in, pulling her against him to feel his chuckles. 'Jesus, what a mess,' he said, finally getting back under control.

'But a beautiful mess, though.' She ran her palm over his jaw, as if to emphasise the point. 'OK, let's start again. What do you want to know?'

'Let's start with your family. Tell me about them.'

For a moment he reminded her of the man he was on the big screen. The documentary maker, not the sexy guy lying in bed with her. His interest was genuine, his scrutiny warm.

'I'm the youngest of four sisters. We were brought up in a big house near Hampstead Heath – that's in the north-west of London. At first it was the six of us, my mum, my dad and my sisters, but when I was ten my mum died in an accident.'

Adam kissed her shoulder again, his hand stroking softly on her stomach. 'I'm sorry.'

She swallowed hard. 'I really think it's possible to miss somebody you can't remember that well. I know I missed her dreadfully as a teenager, or the concept of her at least. My sisters were wonderful, they did all they could, but there's no love like a mother's.'

Her mouth felt dry from the words. Memories of that day fourteen years ago were still just below the surface – the merest rummage and they flew back up again. She'd been at a friend's house when the accident happened, could still remember her mother's best friend, Hugh, coming to pick her up, his face solemn. She hadn't realised her world was about to fall apart when he took her hand and led her down the steps. That her life would be divided into two – before and after Mum. She'd gone from being the much-loved baby of the family, to a loose thread, even if her sisters did their best to take care of her.

Adam squeezed her hand gently, as though he was giving her strength. He didn't seem to mind that she was baring her soul to him – maybe because he was used to it. Not that he usually filmed documentaries in bed, did he?

For a moment she wondered who else he'd had in his bed, but the thought made her stomach lurch.

She took a deep breath, shaking off her melancholy. 'But we were lucky. Before she died we had the perfect life. We laughed, we lived, we did a lot as children. We skated and we played and we argued a lot.'

'You said there were four of you?'

'That's right. I'm the youngest.'

'Four sisters. Wow, I can't even imagine . . . '

'My poor dad never really knew what to do with us. Sometimes we'd be shouting at each other and he'd open his study door, peer around then scurry back inside. We wouldn't see him for the rest of the day. I don't think he ever imagined he'd be bringing us all up without a wife by his side. Plus he was as upset at her absence as the rest of us.'

'He loved her.'

'He did,' Kitty agreed. 'Theirs was a true romance. He was a stuffy professor; she was an actress who caught his eye. The two of them were like chalk and cheese and yet somehow they worked. They brought out the best in each other.' Her sister had written a play about it, casting their parents as star-crossed lovers. Except the crossed star in this case happened to be an old uninsured white van, that her mum's car ploughed into.

She wasn't sure whether he wanted to hear all this, but she was telling him anyway. It felt good to talk about her family for a change. In LA nobody seemed interested in where you came from – it was where you were going to that counted. Nostalgia was for wimps.

'Are your sisters still in London?'

'Cesca is for some of the time. She's the second youngest. But she travels a lot with her boyfriend, he's in the business too.'

She didn't need to clarify what business. Anybody who worked in Hollywood knew what she was talking about.

'What about the others?'

'Well Lucy, that's the eldest, she lives in Scotland. And Juliet lives in Maryland.'

'She lives over here?' Adam asked. 'Maryland's not that far away.'

Kitty frowned. She hadn't really thought about how close Cutler's Gap was to her sister. She was so used to living on different coasts that it didn't even seem as though they were in the same country sometimes. The fact was, Juliet was almost as close in miles to England as she was to California. America really was that big.

'It's not exactly walking distance.' A 600-mile round-trip was hardly a hop, skip and jump. 'Anyway, she's busy with her own family. She has a little girl.'

'She's got a kid? How old is she?' Adam sounded surprised.

'A few years older than me. But she got married young. Poppy's five now.'

'That's a pretty name.'

Kitty smiled. Poppy's birth had been the best thing that happened to the family for years. Though they were scattered around the globe, somehow the tiny baby had brought them back together.

Adam's palm was still pressed against her stomach. 'You must miss them.'

'I guess I do. But we try to get together when we can, even if it's only on Skype. We're planning to all talk on Christmas Day if we can agree a time.' She placed her hand over his. 'It's a weird thing being sisters. We can go for months without speaking, and then it's as if we've never been apart. When the four of us – five now, I guess, if you include my niece, Poppy – are in the same room it can be pretty overwhelming.'

'I bet it can.' She felt him smiling against her shoulder. 'It explains how you're able to manage my family, though. We must seem almost normal to you.'

She squeezed his hand. 'No, you're all totally crazy. There's no hope for any of you.'

Adam growled loudly, flipping her over onto her back, hooking his leg over hers. She could feel him grow hard against her thigh as he ran his fingers down her side, nuzzling his head into her breasts.

'You think there's no hope?' His teeth grazed her nipple. 'I guess we'll just have to go out in a blaze of glory then.'

Kitty lay back, submitting her body to his touch, enjoying the sensations created by his lips and his fingers.

'A blaze of glory sounds good.' Her voice was strained. He must know he was setting her on fire every time he touched her.

Not that she cared – she planned to enjoy every single moment of it.

It was late when Kitty walked back into the kitchen, pulling off her boots and placing them on the drying mat. The room was empty save for Annie, who was folding laundry and putting it into piles on the kitchen table.

'Everything OK down there?' Was that a twinkle in Annie's eye? Kitty tried to ignore it, feigning an air of nonchalance.

'The puppy's still alive, if that's what you meant.'

Annie's smirk was totally out of place. Kitty's eyes narrowed as she stared at her.

'I didn't mean anything at all,' Annie said. 'Unless there's something you think I meant?'

A change of subject was probably for the best, thought Kitty. 'Where is everybody?'

'Everett and Mr Montgomery are in the library. Mr Klein is sitting with Mary. And Mia and Jonas have gone sledging.'

Kitty stopped dead. 'Sledging? Where?'

She didn't know what to think about first: the fact that Mia was actually paying her son some attention, or whether Kitty could actually trust her with Jonas's safety.

Oh God, listen to her. Mia was Jonas's mother; of course she had his best interests at heart. There's no way she would put him in danger. Kitty walked over to help Annie with the folding, trying to ignore the nagging feeling in her stomach.

Adam's cabin! That's where the best sled run was. Had she passed Mia and Jonas on her way and not noticed? She'd been so deep in thought she probably could have passed half the population of Cutler's Gap and not even bothered to look up.

'They only left a few minutes ago. I'm not sure where they were headed.'

It was hard not to worry about Jonas, even though Kitty knew it wasn't her place to fret. If Mia wanted to spend some time with her son what concern was it of Kitty's? After all, Kitty had only been looking after him for a little while, he'd been Mia's son for seven years. *And* she was his mother.

Not to mention the fact Jonas was desperate for her attention, bless him.

'Maybe I should go after them …' Kitty mused. 'In case they need something. It's always good to have two adults around.'

Annie looked up. 'You're becoming attached to that boy, aren't you?'

Her question made Kitty's throat tighten. 'He's a good kid. It's hard not to.'

'That's true,' Annie said. 'I've been tied to the Kleins for these past forty years. Good years they've been, too. I've seen those boys grow up into young men, and watched Mary and Francis become grandparents. It's been a joy to behold.' She looked up. 'But they're not my family, are they? I love them and I care for them, but at the end of the day I get paid to do that. And if I needed to, I could walk away. That's the difference between a job and a family.'

Kitty wasn't sure what Annie was trying to say.

'I know there's a difference.'

'Your head knows that. Your heart can't always be so logical. You care about that boy, and I know you'd do anything for him. But he has his own family.'

For a moment Kitty wondered if it was really Jonas they were talking about. The same words could apply to Adam. But

Annie didn't know what they'd been up to at the cabin, not unless she had some kind of CCTV.

No, she was definitely talking about Jonas.

'It's true I'm only the nanny for a few weeks,' Kitty said, her voice hoarse. 'But I worry about him and it's my job to make sure he's safe. That's all I'm trying to do.'

She wasn't sure why Annie's words were making her feel so raw. Maybe it was the effects of her morning, or perhaps they'd really hit a nerve. Either way, Kitty couldn't stop thinking about them as she helped Annie tidy up the kitchen.

They weren't her family. But they could end up breaking her heart anyway.

Adam was still half asleep when he heard the rap at the door. Jumping out of bed, he ran to the entranceway, pulling the door open for Kitty. A smile formed on his mouth.

'You didn't make it very far ...' His words trailed off as he realised his mistake. Mia Klein stood in the doorway, her eyes wide as she took in his unkempt state. Adam hadn't bothered getting dressed when Kitty left – heck, he hadn't even stepped into the shower. He was too busy enjoying the after-effects of a morning with Kitty Shakespeare to worry about anything as mundane as personal hygiene.

If he was truly honest, he was enjoying having her aroma still on him. A reminder of everything they'd done together. He wasn't sure he wanted to shower it away.

He was certain he wanted to now, though. Mia's nose wrinkled as she took him in, her eyes scanning him from head to toe. He was under no illusions she was sizing him up, he was so not her type for that. She liked her men suave, sophisticated with a bank full of dollars. Though he could fulfil her final requirement a few times over, the rest made him a big fail.

'What do you want?' It was impossible to keep the contempt from his voice.

When she stepped to the left he saw Jonas standing behind her. Adam immediately regretted his harsh tone. It was one thing to disrespect the mother, but he didn't want his nephew to see it.

Damn, he really was an asshole at heart.

'Can I come in? I need to talk to you.' She peered over his shoulder.

'What about?' Adam folded his arms across his chest.

She glanced beside her, looking down at Jonas. 'It's adult talk,' she said. 'Probably best if I come inside.' She reached out, stroking Jonas's face with her gloved hand. 'Can you wait out here for a minute, honey?'

From the corner of his eye Adam could see the puppy stretching in his basket. Any minute now and he'd be padding over to sit next to Adam's feet – his favourite spot to be. He was seconds away from Jonas discovering the big secret.

'Jonas, you stay on the porch, OK?' Adam nodded at the wooden deck that circled the cabin. 'You'd better come in,' he said to Mia, stepping aside so she could squeeze past him.

Jonas shrugged and started walking down the side of the porch, running his hand along the rail to collect up snow.

'Hey, Jonas,' Adam called out. 'We can go sledding afterwards if you like.'

Jonas turned around, his expression suddenly bright. 'Really?' His eyes slid to his mother. 'Can we, Mom?'

'Yes, of course, darling.'

Five minutes later Adam was pulling on some clothes,

having taken a cursory shower, enough to wash off the evidence of that morning's liaison. When he walked back into the living area, Mia was sitting on a chair by the fire, scooted as far forward as she could, as if afraid she might catch something.

'You want a coffee?'

She shot a glance at the kitchen, where the breakfast dishes were neatly piled next to the sink. 'I'm fine, thank you.'

Adam poured himself out a cup, adding some milk before joining her over by the fire. What was it about Mia and Everett that always put him on edge? Maybe it had something to do with the fact they were always walking in when he was half naked. That was enough to put anybody off.

Remembering the reason for his dishevelment, a surreptitious grin split his face. Mia glanced over at him, a question shaping her features.

'What are you so happy about?'

Her question made him want to laugh out loud. Adam imagined telling her exactly why he was smiling. That he'd spent most of the last two hours making love to her nanny. But that little slice of heaven wasn't something he wanted to share, and he planned to do whatever it took to protect it.

'I was just wondering why you're here.' He tried to bite down his amusement.

'You don't waste any time on the niceties, do you?' She sighed, leaning back on the chair. 'I just wanted to talk to you about Everett.'

'What about him?' Adam asked, uneasy. If there was one thing he liked less than talking *to* Everett, it was talking *about* him. Especially with his wife.

'He's having a hard time,' she told him. 'After everything that happened with the two of you. Can't you just make up with him? It's eating away at him, and making everybody's lives a misery.'

He took a big mouthful of the coffee. It scalded his tongue before slipping down his throat. 'I don't know what you mean. What happened between Everett and me has nothing to do with anybody else. How does it affect you?'

'Because he's biting all our heads off. He's upsetting Jonas, he's barely spending any time with your parents, and, well, he's not exactly being nice to me, either.' She wrinkled her nose up. 'Maybe if the two of you made up, he'd be a bit easier to live with.'

'Seriously?' Adam asked. 'You want me to make up with Everett because it's inconveniencing you?' He wanted to laugh at her gall.

'I want you to forgive each other because you're ruining Christmas. There's an atmosphere in that house so thick I could cut it with a knife. He's angry and bitter, and he's being hateful to everybody.' She lowered her voice. 'Even your mom's noticed.'

'Maybe he should have thought of that before he called the police.'

She looked down, suddenly entranced by her fingers. 'Yeah, about that. He didn't call them, I did.'

Adam frowned. 'You did? Why?'

Finally she looked up. 'Because you were a madman. You destroyed his office, and I was scared you were going to hurt him. Did you see that black eye you gave him?'

'No.' Adam shook his head. 'Because by the time it came up, I was on a plane to DC.' He sighed, running his hand through his hair. 'Look, I don't know what you want me to do here. I did everything that was asked of me. I moved back here, I complied with the agreement we all made. You're the ones who decided to come and stay here. It's not my fault if it's causing problems with you and Everett.'

'We didn't ask you to live in this shack.' She glared at him with disapproval. 'Why on earth aren't you staying at the big house? You're behaving like a madman, some kind of hermit. You're not living, you're making a point.'

He dug his nails into his palm to stop him from blowing up at her. 'This is my home. I'd like you to show it some respect.'

'You know, I'm not about to tell you how to live your life. I simply wanted to tell you that Everett is having a hard time. He's tried to apologise to you, and you threw it back in his face.'

'There's nothing else to say.'

Mia threw her hands up with frustration. 'It was just business. Why should he apologise for doing what he does? You're making this all so difficult for us. Why can't you just get over it?'

Adam wanted to laugh – but not out of humour. No, it was bitterness that made his chest hitch up and his tongue start to rise. *Just get over it.* Was she being serious? After everything that happened, he was supposed to just forgive and move on.

He kept his voice low and even when he replied. 'That's not going to happen.'

'So what are you going to do? Stay here for ever? Waste away in this godforsaken hut while your brother beats himself up?' She shook her head, her nose wrinkling up. 'Is that it? Have you just given up?'

'Do you care?'

'Not about you. But I care about my husband, and you're making his life miserable. He's your big brother, he cares about you. People keep asking us questions. Where's Adam? What's happening to his documentary? When's Adam coming back to LA? How do you think it makes us feel when we have to shake our heads and say we don't know?'

'I'm devastated for you.' He threw another log on the fire. 'Now is that it?'

Outside, Jonas was making patterns in the snow with his gloved fingers. He looked bored as hell out there. Poor kid.

'Can you let bygones be bygones for just one day?' she asked him. 'Join us for Christmas lunch at least. Your parents would be happy, and so would Jonas.'

'What about you and Everett?'

She licked her painted red lips. 'We can live with it if you can.'

He hadn't thought about Christmas Day, or the fact that if he wanted to avoid his brother he'd be spending it all alone in the cabin. For a moment, he imagined having Kitty here, the two of them lying naked in a blanket in front of the fire, holding a glass of wine as they toasted the season. Now that would have been a hell of a way to celebrate the day.

And it was never going to happen. She'd be up there with the rest of them.

'I'll think about it.'

Mia looked shocked at his response. 'You will?'

He shrugged. 'It's only for one day, isn't it? It doesn't mean anything. And as you said, it will make the old folks happy.' He stood up, making it obvious it was time for her to leave. 'Now there's a kid out there that wants to go sledding. I suggest we don't leave him standing alone in the cold any longer.'

20

In winter with warm tears I'll ... keep
eternal spring-time on thy face

– Titus Andronicus

'What made you decide to become a nanny?' Adam asked her the following day. He was at the top of the slope, holding Jonas's sled, as the boy scooped snow out of his hood from his last descent.

'I'm not really a nanny,' she said, watching as Adam pushed Jonas off, away from the direction of the lake. Though Jonas had protested – claiming this run down the hill was too lame – Adam had insisted, promising they'd do the more dangerous run together.

'You're not?'

'Well I am right now, obviously. And I've been a nanny before. But I'm a film student, I just took this job for the winter break.'

'You're a student?' Suddenly, his face turned as pale as the snow. 'You are legal, right?'

She burst out laughing at his expression. For a moment she considered messing with his mind. No, that wouldn't be fair.

'Of course I am. I'm twenty-four. I guess you'd call me a mature student, not that I like that term.'

'Thank Christ for that. I knew you were young, but not that young. So how did you end up working for Ev?'

It was strange hearing Adam refer to his brother by that name. As though there was still something between them other than hostility and hatred. 'It's a weird story,' she told him, watching as Jonas came to the bottom of the side hill and began the long trudge back up to them. 'I applied for an internship at Everett's production company, and ended up being interviewed by Drake.' She screwed her nose up. 'He walked out mid interview after getting an angry phone call from Mia, and I thought that was it. But then a few days later I got a call from Mia offering me the nanny job. I'm guessing Drake must have told her about my resumé.'

'So you still don't have an internship?'

She shook her head slowly. 'No. And if I let myself, I'd be all worked up and worried about that, but I'm not going to think about it until after the holidays.' She smiled at him. 'Anyway, maybe if I impress your brother enough he'll give me a job.'

Adam didn't like the sound of that at all. Didn't like the sound of Drake Montgomery interviewing her, either. 'I could help,' he offered. 'With the internship, I mean. I know a few people.'

Her smile wavered. 'That's really nice of you, but ...' She grimaced, trying to find the right words. 'I don't want to sleep my way to the top.'

'That's not why I offered.' He shook his head vehemently. 'I just wanted to help you out. A friend helping a friend.'

'Is that what we are?' she asked him, her head angled to the side. She looked at him, smiling. His dark hair reflected the light of the sun, framed by the snow-capped trees. He really was gorgeous. She wanted to pinch herself that he actually wanted to spend time with her.

'Friends? Yeah, I think we are.' His smile widened as Jonas finally reached the top. 'Good run, Jonas, I think that was your fastest yet.'

'Can we do the lake run now?' Jonas asked. 'I've been waiting for ages.'

'You want me to go with you, or do you want Kitty?'

Kitty took a step back, holding up her hands. 'Oh no, this is all on you, Klein.'

The corner of his lip twitched, and he reached out to ruffle Jonas's hair. 'What do you say, shall we do it?'

'Yeah, but I want Kitty to go next.'

Wonderful.

'Sure.' Adam nodded sagely.

'And I want her to go with you. You make it go the fastest.'

A slow smile spread across Adam's face. Jonas was right, Adam's weight really did make the sled fly down the hill, and Kitty felt weak just thinking about it. With the two of them on there, it would go faster still. 'It's OK, I'm happy up here.'

'No way, you're going next, Shakespeare. Don't wimp out on us now.'

She watched as the two of them flew down the hill, the sled barely touching the snow as they went. They stopped just short of the lake, with Adam tumbling out to the side, Jonas laughing like crazy as he clambered over his uncle. Her heart clenched to watch them. Isn't this what every kid wanted – adults who paid attention to you, who wanted to spend time having fun? Why was it that Jonas had everything that money could buy, except his parents' attention?

As the two of them climbed back up the hill, Adam pulling the sledge behind him, she felt the anticipation building in her stomach. Not just at the fear of the ride ahead of her, but at the thought of squeezing onto that sledge with Adam, his legs tight on her hips. She'd been bad enough before the two of them had sex, her body always reacting to his closeness. Now she knew what he could do with it, she could feel herself blushing all over again.

'Your turn,' Adam said, bringing the sled to a stop beside her. 'You want to get in first?'

She nodded, still feeling the hot burning spots on her cheeks. 'Jonas, you don't move an inch, OK? Don't come near the lake or you'll be in trouble.'

'OK,' Jonas agreed, wiping a dusting of snow from an old tree stump. 'I'll just sit here and wait. Then it's my turn again, right?'

'Right.'

She sat down on the sled, stretching her legs out in front of her, and Adam climbed in behind her, his long legs either side of her waist. His chest was pressed against her back, and he leaned forward to grab the rope that was lying tangled between her legs. She felt completely caged by him – his chest and limbs pinning her to the sled. His mouth was close to her ear, his breath tickling the sensitive skin just below. 'I'm going to have to wriggle to get this thing going,' he whispered. 'Try not to get too excited.'

'In your dreams,' she scoffed, even though her heart was racing.

'You were in them last night.'

The next moment they were sliding down the crest of the hill, the sled picking up speed as it careered down towards the lake. She felt Adam circle his arm around her waist, pulling her tightly against him, his other hand holding tightly to the rope. She opened her mouth to shout – partly in fear, partly in exhilaration, but the rush of cold air took her breath away.

'When I yell "go" you need to jump to the right,' Adam shouted, his voice barely audible above the howl of the wind. 'Don't stay on the sled whatever you do.'

'Why not?'

'Because of the lake,' he shouted louder. 'Now go.'

She tipped her whole body to the side, feeling Adam do the same, their movement causing the sled to flip over. Then they were tumbling into the deep virgin snow, their bodies sinking into it as they came to a stop.

She was breathless, her heart pounding like a racing horse, her whole body shaking at the sudden stop. By the time she'd managed to scramble up to her knees, her hair was soaked by the snow, wet tendrils hanging down her back.

'Are you OK?' Adam jumped onto his feet, offering her a hand to pull her up.

'I'm, I'm ...' She shook her head, not knowing what the hell she was. 'That was the second most irresponsible thing I've ever done.'

She started to laugh, not sure whether she was hysterical or not. Her heart was still racing like a thoroughbred. 'I can't believe you made me do that.'

'If that was the second most irresponsible thing you've ever done, then what was the first?' he asked, forever the interviewer.

'You. Definitely you.'

*

'Do you like Christmas?' Adam asked, feeding a spoonful of eggs into her mouth. They were sitting by the fire, a warm woollen blanket covering their post-coital bodies. For the past few days she'd got into the habit of getting up earlier and earlier, sneaking down to the cabin when it was barely light, only to find Adam at the door waiting for her, ready to lift her up and swing her inside, where the fire was roaring in the grate.

They were precious, stolen hours. Ones that only seemed to exist for them. She wanted to protect them the way you'd protect a faltering flame, cupping her hands to block out the wind.

'I like the idea of Christmas more than the reality,' she mused, swallowing down the eggs. 'This is really delicious, by the way. How did you learn to cook so well?'

'Amazing what you have to do to get by in strange locations. Sometimes there's nothing like the great American breakfast, even if you're filming in the wilds of Colombia.' He picked up a forkful of bacon. 'What do you mean by you like the idea more than the reality?'

She bit her lip, staring out of the steamed up window to the wintry wonderland beyond. 'It can never live up to the hype everybody creates, can it?' She wiped a speck of egg from the corner of his lips, brushing the now-clean spot with her own lips. 'We all grew up thinking the only proper Christmas was a white Christmas, even though statistically the chances of that are pretty much nil, unless you live somewhere like this. And we grew up thinking that we're nothing unless we're surrounded by family, one of us playing the piano while the rest of us stand around and sing festive songs together. Christmas has somehow been hijacked by big business and Hollywood, and there's no way to live up to the perfection they project.'

'You don't believe you can have perfection?'

She smiled. 'Not for very long. Reality always wins out, and reality is messy. You must know that.'

'You're very cynical for one so young,' he told her, brushing his lips against the shell of her ear.

'You can talk, Mr Grumpy. You're the one who films the dregs of humanity, and brings them back for us all to see. That must have knocked any romanticism out of you pretty quickly.'

He winced for a moment. She had no idea how close to the mark her words were. But he didn't want to think about that right now. 'I can be romantic,' he told her. 'The two aren't mutually exclusive. Just because I know how low people can go, that doesn't mean I don't think we can fly, too.'

She looked intrigued. 'Is that so?'

He shrugged. 'There's nothing wrong with a little romance. There's nothing wrong with hoping for the fantasy either. Just as long as you don't let it blind you to the dark side. All the best fairy tales have bad guys, after all. Romance isn't about pretending they don't exist, it's about defeating them.'

A slow smile spread across her face. 'That may be the most romantic thing I ever heard.'

'I've got more where that came from.' He was feeling cocky now. A combination of the way she was looking at him, and the way his body felt, having had her beneath him, followed by a satisfying breakfast. It really didn't get much better than that.

'I bet you have,' she said. 'I'm almost afraid to ask.'

He grinned. 'Let's try this one. It's almost eight o'clock, so I've got about half an hour to fuck your brains out one more time before you need to get back to the big house.'

'Oh, Mr Klein, you know how to woo a girl. I'm almost overcome.' She did a mock swoon, falling onto the blanket.

'That's right, stay right there.' He put the half-eaten plate of breakfast to the side.

He climbed between her legs, feeling himself harden as soon as she wrapped her thighs around his hips. Her blonde hair had fallen in her eyes so he reached out to brush it away. She licked her lips as she stared up at him, her eyes wide and warm. Was it wrong that he loved the way she stared at him? As though the world was a little brighter whenever he was around.

When he moved his lips to hers, she wrapped her hand around his neck, her fingers digging into his flesh. Their tongues were warm, soft, sliding and caressing as they kissed. She shifted beneath him, until the tip of his cock was sliding against her, slick and velvety and oh-so-inviting.

As he slowly pushed his way inside, he opened his eyes to see her staring straight at him, an expression of wonder on her face. Then she smiled, reaching out to caress his bearded cheek.

It wasn't just about sex. It wasn't just about the way she made him feel. It was about her, and the way she lit up his cabin just by walking inside. His own walking, talking, loving, secret-Santa gift.

He moved his hips, sliding ever deeper, until they were both breathless and panting, until she was tight and tense and ready to explode.

If this was a fairy tale, then he wanted to believe. He wanted her to believe, too. The alternative was unthinkable.

21

There was a star danced, and
under that was I born

– Much Ado About Nothing

The closer it was getting to Christmas, the harder it was getting Jonas to sleep. Even as his eyelids drooped, his body was still buzzing with excitement, as he talked about Santa and stockings, and presents and snow. Kitty, on the other hand, was exhausted. The combination of getting up at the crack of dawn, and the vigorous workout she got before the winter sun had barely settled in the sky no doubt the culprit.

Not that she was complaining, she already lived for those precious moments with Adam in his cabin. When she closed her eyes at night, it was him she saw, looking back at her with those dark eyes, framed with long, sweeping lashes. She could almost feel the way he cradled her, his biceps taut as he wrapped his arms around her waist; could feel the sensation of his beard against her face, as he stole kiss after kiss before she reluctantly left him every morning.

And now Christmas was only three days away; a thought that filled her with a mixture of excitement and dread.

'Will you read one more story?' Jonas asked, his eyes still open though his voice was sleepy.

'You've already had three stories,' Kitty told him. 'You need to get to sleep. We don't want you all tired on the big day.'

He sat straight up in his bed. 'I won't be tired. I really won't. I'm wide awake, see?'

She bit down her smile. 'But you have to get through the next three days first. And nobody can stay awake for three days without sleeping. Not even little boys who are overexcited for Christmas.'

'I'm not little.' He folded his arms across his chest.

'No you're not,' she agreed. 'And like the grown-up you are, you must know you need sleep. So lie down and close your eyes. If you keep them closed for ten minutes, I'll read you another book.'

It was a calculated risk, but it was worth a try. Surely he'd be asleep way before ten minutes passed.

'OK.' He lay back down, squeezing his eyes shut. He was silent for a moment, his brow creased as though he was thinking deeply. Then, with his eyes still closed, he asked her, 'How long is ten minutes anyway?'

'About as long as it takes to walk down to your uncle's cabin.'

'Oh, that's really long.'

Sometimes it was and sometimes it wasn't. On her way there, it couldn't pass fast enough. On her way back it always felt like the blink of an eye.

'Kitty?'

'Yes?' she said patiently.

'Does Santa know you're here?'

'What do you mean?' Her lips curled up in a confused smile.

'I mean, will he bring your gifts here on Christmas Eve, or will he take them to your parents' house? How does he know where you are?'

It was a surprisingly perceptive question for a seven-year-old boy. She had to think on it before answering. 'I think he knows I'm here,' she finally said. 'But I'm an adult, and Santa only visits children, so he won't be bringing me any gifts.'

'None at all?'

She shook her head, even though Jonas's eyes were still closed. 'No.'

'That really sucks. I'd hate to be an adult.'

'It's not so bad,' she told him. 'There are advantages, too.'

'Like what?'

'Like you get to eat what you like, do what you like. There's nobody telling you what to do all the time.' She thought of the other things she liked – the ones that involved a certain bearded relation of his. Best not to share anything about that.

'I'd rather have presents.'

'I bet you would.'

According to her watch, it took seven minutes for him to finally drift off. She sat on his bed for a minute more, to make sure he was sinking deeper, before leaving his room and flicking on the night light he always liked.

As she walked along the corridor towards the stairs, she looked out of the window, and at the evergreen forest beyond. For a moment she tried to picture Adam's cabin, and she wondered what he was doing right now. Eating a late dinner? Playing with the dog? She knew so much and so little about him. The big stuff was clear – it was plastered all over the internet for anybody interested enough to find it – but the tiny things that made him who he was were still a little fuzzy in her mind.

215

He was strong, he was kind, and he was even a bit of a closet romantic. That much he'd made clear. But she still couldn't work out what he was doing down there in that cabin, and whether he had any plans to leave it.

And where did that leave her? She thought of that plane ticket lying on the dresser in her bedroom, a one-way flight to LA leaving after the holidays. Her time here was finite, everything she did came with a sell-by date. Before long she'd be back in her old apartment, in her old life. And like a favourite dress she'd grown out of, she wasn't sure that old life would fit her any more.

Shaking her head at her own maudlin thoughts, she walked down the staircase and into the hallway. In the kitchen she could hear Annie's radio playing another round of festive songs, the familiar melodies making her feel wistful as they conjured up scenes of Christmas past.

'You hear back from the embassy?' Drake's voice cut through the silent hallway. For some reason the door to the library was open. Kitty looked over with alarm, but his back was to her – he was talking to Everett.

'It's a no go. We'll need to film in the studio and in California. We can simulate the mountains easily enough.'

'You think we can make it look authentic? Colombia isn't a whole lot like LA.'

She could almost hear Everett's shrug. 'Unless we get that cash injection we haven't got a choice.'

Drake lowered his voice, but it wasn't enough to disguise his words. 'Will your brother come on board? It's gonna make marketing it so much easier if he agrees to do the publicity.'

'He'll come round. It's a year or two before we're at that

216

stage anyway. I'm just concerned with the casting and locations right now. Not to mention the financing.'

Their voices drifted off as they walked to the other side of the library. Kitty let out a lungful of air. The last thing she needed was to be accused of snooping again, even if that's what she'd ended up doing.

Why did they mention Adam though? That was the thing she didn't understand. Everything she'd learned about his family led her to believe he wanted nothing to do with Everett or his work. She wondered if she should ask him, find out if Adam intended to move to LA and work with his brother. Just the thought of it was enough to make her heart hammer against her chest.

But then she'd already had it in the ear from Everett, and the last thing she needed to do was stir things up any more. Not when she needed that internship, and to stay in LA. The alternative didn't bear thinking about.

No, she wouldn't mention it to Adam. But she might keep her ear to the ground and try to find out some more information. It couldn't hurt, could it?

After helping Annie with her food preparations in the kitchen, Kitty climbed back up the stairs to her bedroom just after ten. She was more than ready to hit the hay – her body aching as though she'd spent the evening in a boxing ring, rather than kneading dough and icing cupcakes.

It was almost half an hour later when she finally started to drift off, her breath evening out as her eyelids began to get heavy. Soon they were more closed than open, her body feeling as though it were in some kind of suspension, spanning the distance between the waking world and the sleeping one.

And then ... *bang!*

Her eyes flew open. She frowned, looking around, trying to locate the source of the noise.

Another crash. This time she was more alert, enough to hear the sound of something hitting the window glass. She waited to see if it would go away. Maybe it was some heavy snow or the beak of a particularly annoying bird. A night bird – an owl, perhaps.

The third bang got her out of bed. She ran across the carpeted floor on her bare feet, pulling at her pyjama top to ensure she was fully covered. Just as she used to back in London, she pulled back the bottom corner of the curtain, trying to take a peek out of the window without being seen.

This time whatever was hitting the window was right in front of her face. The loud thud made her jump back, pulling the curtain with her. She fell to the floor, pulling half the curtain with her.

Oh shit.

Scrambling to her feet, she looked out of the window to the snowy lawn below. A figure stood in the shadows of the house, a hood pulled up over its head. Kitty stared, squinting to try and make out a face.

That's when he looked up, his face illuminated by the pale glow of the moon, the radiance of his skin contrasting against his dark beard. Her hand flew to her chest, feeling her heart pounding beneath her ribcage.

Fumbling with the latch, she pushed the window open, feeling the cold pinch of the wind as it blew through the gap. She had to stand on tiptoes to lean through it, her skin prickling beneath her pyjama top.

'What do you want?' She was half whispering, half shouting, but she couldn't hide the smile on her lips.

'You.'

His single-word response made her heart stutter.

'Why don't you come into the house like a normal person?'

She could see his grin from two storeys up. 'I think we'd both agree I'm not a normal person.'

'You're not wrong there.' Kitty took a deep breath. 'So what do you want from me?'

'You,' he said again.

'You're being very annoying.'

Adam lifted his woollen cap off, raking his hands through his hair. 'Come down here and I'll show you how annoying I can be.'

'I'm in my pyjamas.'

'I don't mind.'

Of course he didn't. Kitty looked down at her fleecy bottoms and top, smiling at the white sheep nestled into the pink flannel. Adam was probably imagining satin and lingerie, not a fairy-tale delight.

'And then?' she questioned.

'What do you mean?'

'What are we going to do then?' She was starting to worry somebody was going to discover them. It was still only the evening, after all. Everett or Drake could be taking a walk around the grounds and discover Adam shouting up at her window.

'You want me to spell it out?'

'I don't know. How many letters?'

His laughter boomed through the night air. 'Kitty, get your sweet ass down here and come see me. Then we can play Scrabble all night if you want to.'

Scrabble wasn't really what Kitty had in mind. She didn't think it was at the top of Adam's list, either.

'Give me a minute to get dressed.'

'Nah, come down like that, just put a coat and some boots on. We'll take the Skidoo. Hurry up, princess.'

Jesus, was there a snow-related vehicle the Kleins didn't have? 'Is there something wrong with princesses?'

'As long as they don't expect me to be Prince Charming, there's nothing wrong at all.'

She had to cover her mouth to deaden the laugh. 'You don't want to be my knight on a white Skidoo?'

'I'll be anything you want me to be if you'll just get your ass down here.'

Sensing his impatience, Kitty slammed the window shut and pulled on her socks and boots. She checked herself out in the mirror; pink sheep pyjamas, black insulated boots and a face devoid of make-up. She wasn't exactly dressed to kill. Doing the best she could, she fluffed her hair up and pinched her cheeks. Hopefully his cabin would be dark, lit only by the licking flames of the fire, and she'd be able to carry off that just-got-out-of-bed look.

Who was she trying to kid? It was more likely to be a just-got-into-bed look she was going to be wearing. She knew a booty call when she saw one.

When she wrenched open the kitchen door, Adam was standing on the step, his cap pulled firmly over his brow. His face split into a grin and he pulled her close, his coat freezing against her overheated face.

Of course, her traitorous nipples hardened straight away. When she pulled back, his eyes zeroed right in on them.

'That's from the cold, not because I'm insanely attracted to you.'

His lips twitched. 'Of course.'

'So maybe you could fire up your stupid Skidoo and get me down to your cabin before the rest of my body freezes up.'

'Put your coat on.' He gestured at the thick padded jacket in her hand. 'We're taking a detour.'

She threaded her arms through the coat, zipping it up tightly. Adam took his scarf and wrapped it around her neck, kissing the tip of her nose with his soft lips. 'Nice pyjamas, by the way.'

'I thought you'd like them,' she said, grinning.

'I'd like them even better on my floor.'

This time she laughed. 'Oh, you know how to charm a girl with your sweet words. Now are we going or what?'

'Your wish is my command.' Without another word he grabbed her hand and pulled her over to the waiting Skidoo. Unlike the snowmobile it was smaller and sleeker; more like a motorbike than anything else. Wrapping a blanket around her shoulders, Kitty slung her leg over the seat, nestling into Adam's broad back.

He reached back and squeezed her thigh. 'You ready?'

Kitty shrugged. 'Of course.' She didn't know why he was asking. The next moment it all became clear. He pulled the cord and the engine came to life, the whole machine humming between her thighs. Adam leaned forward, Kitty still clinging to his back, and then the Skidoo rushed forward, ploughing the snow into its wake.

If she'd thought about it she would have known he was a speed demon. In spite of his hermit-like habits, Adam was a man of the world, and had spent his adult years skirting on the edge of danger. So when the Skidoo sped across the snow, lifting and falling with the drifts, she held on tightly and prayed he knew what he was doing.

It was scary and shocking, yet so damned exhilarating to

221

be racing through the night forest. She clung to him hard, her hands almost connected across his muscled abdomen, refusing to let go lest she fly off the seat. He gripped on to the handles, manoeuvring the machine around the path through the trees, twisting and turning as if he knew the route well. The light on the front of the Skidoo illuminated their way, casting a glow across the winter wonderland before them. There was something magical about the landscape that made Kitty's eyes water. A haunting beauty that brought tears to her eyes.

'You OK?' His shout carried back in the wind.

She squeezed him in response, the squall swallowing her reply.

Just before they reached the clearing that led to his cabin, he took a sharp left, pulling them deeper into the forest. Kitty frowned, still clinging on for dear life. 'Where are we going?' Her voice barely audible over the hum of the engine and the noise of the wind.

'You'll see.'

Five minutes passed before he cranked down the gears, coming to a stop with a skid that made her almost fall off. She tightened her arms around him, feeling his body shake with laughter. Arsehole.

She was about to tear him a new one when she looked up, and the scene before her took her breath away. They'd stopped just short of a small clearing, a circle of treeless ground that somebody had boarded over. A pergola rose up over the decking, the wooden beams twisted with sparkling lights. It was like a fairy-tale grotto in the middle of the forest. Beautiful and unexpected.

'What is this place?' she asked him as he climbed off then offered his hand to her.

'It's been here for years,' he told her. 'Long before we ever bought the house. I never could work out why somebody would build something like this in the middle of the forest.' His eyes warmed as he helped her off the Skidoo, then pulled her close to him. 'But maybe I do now.'

'Did you put the lights up?' she asked.

'Yeah, they're battery powered, so they should last about five minutes longer,' he told her, raising an eyebrow. 'But that should be long enough.'

'Long enough for what?'

'To prove to you that I can be romantic.'

Her mouth felt dry. He'd done this for her? That was … Jesus, it was amazing. 'Wow,' was all she could say.

'Go stand up on the deck,' he told her, then grabbed his phone from his pocket, pulling his gloves off to fiddle with it. The next moment music was streaming out, as Adam placed his phone on the wooden balustrade, and walked over to where she was standing.

Above them a thousand tiny lights sparkled, and higher still she could see the stars shining through the clear night sky. The air was cold but still as he took her hand in his, placing his other hand on the small of her back.

'What's this music?' she murmured, listening to the deep voice crooning through the night air.

'It's Marvin Gaye,' he told her. 'It's called "I Want to Come Home for Christmas". A classic.' With the gentlest of pressure on her back, he pulled her to him, leading the dance as his feet moved across the boards with ease. A slow, sensual waltz that took them across the deck, as she melted into him like a candle with a burning flame.

'Marvin knows how to seduce,' she said softly. So did Adam.

She couldn't help but feel full of emotion as they continued to dance, their bodies swaying together. Nobody had ever done anything like this for her before. It was like being in a movie, except there were no cameras or directors, no booms or lighting. Just the two of them, and the night, and Marvin Gaye's sweet, soulful voice. 'I feel like I should be wearing a yellow gown, and maybe a singing teapot should be jumping up and down in the corner.'

Adam laughed. 'Does that make me the beast?'

She looked up, stroking his dark beard. 'It makes you the nicest, kindest man I've ever met.' How did she not see it before? When they'd first met she'd thought him gruff and angry, but looking back he'd been anything but. His first thought when he saw that deer had been to put it out of its misery.

And he'd done all this for her.

'He might have been a beast,' she said, as he twirled her towards the edge of the deck, 'but I bet he and Beauty had great sex. All that testosterone.'

Adam grinned. 'I'm trying to be romantic, and you're all dirty and talking about bestiality. What am I going to do with you?'

She looked up into his deep eyes, warmth flooding through her body, in spite of the frozen temperatures. 'Take me home and show me just how romantic you can be.'

'Are you using romance as a euphemism for sex?' he asked her.

'Yep.'

'In that case, what are we waiting for?'

22

*Love is begun by time and ... time
qualifies the spark and fire of it*

– Hamlet

Adam dropped back onto the mattress, his heart speeding in his chest like a freight train. Kitty curled up beside him, her soft body pressing against his side, and her head nestling into the crook of his arm. She was breathing as loudly as he was, their bodies covered with a soft sheen of perspiration in spite of the cold weather outside. Tonight's sex had been just as frantic as it had been that morning. Needy. Desperate.

Perfection.

Damn, he needed to kiss her again. He dipped his head, capturing her lips with his own. Her breath warmed his mouth as he slid his tongue inside, sweeping it gently against the soft skin inside her lips.

Kitty put her hand on his hard, flat stomach, running her palm along his flesh.

'You OK?' His voice was low.

'Mmhmm.'

'You want anything? Water, food? We can take a shower if you like.'

'Later,' she mumbled. 'I want to just lie here for now.'

That's exactly what Adam wanted, too. He wasn't ready to leave the bed yet. The feeling of her sweet body pressed against his was too delicious to let go.

He closed his eyes, breathing in the aroma of Kitty and sex. It was the ultimate aphrodisiac. If he hadn't spent most of the night worshipping at her feet, no doubt he'd be getting hard again. As it was, he was counting the minutes before he could muster up the energy for another round.

Sex with Kitty Shakespeare was like a drug, and he was getting addicted.

'Adam?'

'Yeah?'

'Is it my turn to ask questions?'

'What sort of questions?' Adam's voice was guarded.

'The sort of questions you asked me.'

He licked his dry lips, wondering why it felt so uncomfortable to be put in the spotlight. It was the same sensation he felt at therapy, as though all his tools were being used on him. 'I guess . . .'

'Tell me about your childhood.'

His stomach clenched. She was heading straight for the personal questions. No small talk for Kitty Shakespeare. Maybe that's why he liked her so much.

'Not much to tell. I was a rich kid. Spoiled. Sent away to school. I did what I was told and made good grades.'

She snuggled closer into him. 'That's it? No tales of rebellion or childhood neglect? No sob story designed to soften my heart?'

Adam smiled in spite of himself. 'It was normal, at least it was to me. I didn't know any better at the time.'

'And now?'

'Now . . .' His voice trailed off, as he tried to find the right words. 'Now I realise how privileged we were. And how much I took for granted.'

'What did you take for granted?' The way her fingers stroked his skin was distracting. And hot.

Down, boy.

'I don't know.' His voice was a shrug. 'The money, the vacations. For years I thought Annie was just some aunt, always ready to look after us. I didn't believe it when Everett told me she was paid to clean and cook.'

Kitty smiled. 'Sometimes I wonder if Jonas thinks that about me.'

'Jonas is much cleverer than I was.'

'Can I ask another question?' Her breath feathered his skin. It made his nipples go hard.

'Maybe.'

'Why are you here?'

He turned to look at her, a questioning expression on his face. 'With you?'

'No. I mean why are you living here in this cabin? Are you planning on making any more documentaries? How long have you been here? How long are you planning to stay?'

'That's four different questions.' And each one of them made him want to squirm.

'OK, then let's start with the first. Why are you living here?'

'I got into a bit of trouble when I was in LA. My attorney made a plea bargain to get me out of the charges. I agreed

227

to come back here to my parents' place and get anger-management therapy.'

She opened her mouth as if to ask another question, then closed it again, nodding encouragingly for him to continue.

'I really didn't want to live with my parents. I haven't done for the past fifteen years, so I moved in here and fixed it up a bit.'

'You fixed it up by yourself?'

'Mostly. Called in a few favours here and there. It's not exactly the Hilton, but it will do.'

She bit her lip, as though she was considering the next one. 'When did you move in here?'

'A couple of months ago. I pretty much moved down here as soon as the roof was watertight. Figured I could do the rest while I was in here.'

'And how long do you plan to stay for?'

'I don't know,' he said honestly. 'The mandated therapy is only for another month. After that I'm free to do what I want.' But what did he want? That was the question.

'But you'll make more documentaries, right?' she asked him. 'What about that one in Colombia, are you planning to finish it?'

His mouth went dry at the mention of Colombia. He really didn't want to think about that at all. He pulled her closer, until her chest was melded into his. 'That's a story for another day.'

'Oh yeah?'

He trailed a finger down her spine, making her body squirm beneath his touch. 'Yeah. I think I'm about done talking for now.'

Kitty didn't protest as he pulled her fully on top of him,

cupping her warm buttocks inside his palms. Sliding his hand up, he pressed his hand to the back of her head, pulling her down until their lips were inches away from each other.

'You feel good,' he said, growing hard as her body moved against him. Her touch was enough to make him forget everything, all the fears, the anger, the incessant reminders.

'So do you.' She dipped her head lower, until her mouth was on Adam's. They moved together, kissing each other slowly, as if they had all the time in the world.

'You taste good, too.'

'Mmhmm.'

Then he lifted her off him and onto the mattress, moving down the bed until his lips were pressed against her stomach. He didn't want to talk any more, but it didn't mean he couldn't use his mouth if he wanted to.

By the sound of her sighs, she wanted pretty much the same thing.

The cabin was surprisingly warm for a building made of little more than timber and sheer grit. Kitty nestled into the pillows, their softness undulating beneath her cheek, as Adam whispered something in his sleep before reaching out for her.

He'd held her all night. By early morning she was burning up, enough to make her wriggle out of his grasp. Lying there in the darkness, she'd tucked her hand under her cheek and closed her eyes, trying to remember every line of his face.

She was falling for him. Not in the way she'd been attracted to men before, in that chemical sizzle of lust and excitement. No, this was more soul shaking than that. A connection of hearts and minds that seemed to hum inside her. A need to protect as much as be protected.

It was too early to feel that way, and yet she couldn't help herself. The way he'd decorated that hollow in the woods, just for her, had been enough to crack open whatever remained of her defences. Not that she'd had that many to begin with.

Somehow she needed to guard her freshly exposed heart. An impossible task when he'd already stolen it clean from her chest. The way he'd looked last night with that little-boy-lost stare as he'd told her his story, was enough to make her want to give it to him all over again.

Damn, she was so bad at this. All the Shakespeare sisters were. Not one of them was able to separate their hearts from their minds. A need for love seemed to run through their veins along with their warm, English blood.

'Come here.' Adam wrapped his arms around her, until Kitty's head was tucked into his chest. They were still naked from their night-time exertions, and she could feel his muscles flexing beneath her cheek. She could hear his heartbeat, too. Strong and steady, it beat out a tattoo that emulated her own. A rhythm as reassuring as a maternal pulse, it made her eyes heavy and her breath slow.

Two hours later she awoke with a start. This time the cabin was bathed in the half light, the West Virginian sun slowly making its morning appearance. Kitty sat up, disoriented, having to blink a few times before the room came into focus. That's when she realised she wasn't asleep in the attic room. And that the big house was more than a few footsteps away.

She'd spent her first night with Adam, and it had been pretty much perfect. Why did it have to end?

'I need to get back.' She wasn't sure if she was talking to Adam or herself. 'Jonas will be waking up.'

'It's still early, there's plenty of time. Lie down, let me hold you.'

There was something so tempting about his offer that she nearly took him up on it. Spending a morning lying in his arms would have been a pretty good way to while away the hours. But she had things to do, a job to perform, not to mention a walk of shame to navigate. The last thing she needed was for her arrival back at the big house to have an audience.

No, best to leave right now before the house stirred. When they woke up they wouldn't even realise she'd left. She could simply run up to the attic bedroom and pretend she'd been in there all night. A shower and some clothes and it would be a morning like any other.

'I can't stay,' she whispered. 'They'll notice I've gone.'

'You come down here every day. You can tell them you just got here a little early.'

She felt torn between her need for him and her natural dedication to her job. 'I can't,' she repeated. 'It's so close to Christmas, we can't let them suspect anything.'

'You're right.' Adam sat up, the covers falling to his waist. His bare chest seemed to glisten in the morning light. He really was a good-looking guy. 'Give me ten minutes, I'll get the Skidoo out.'

She shook her head. 'They'll hear the engine. It might even wake them up. I'm better off walking.'

Kitty noticed he didn't protest about that. Maybe he was as afraid as she was about being discovered.

Of course he wouldn't want his family finding out. Why would he? It would only complicate things.

'I'll walk you, then.'

She put her arm on his bicep, feeling the warmth of his skin

231

leaching into hers. 'It's OK, I know the way. If anybody's up in the house it'll be easier to explain if I arrive alone.'

He stared at her intently, as if he was looking for something behind her words. 'I can stop at the treeline. Nobody will see me there.'

Kitty rolled her lip between her teeth, considering his offer. Part of her wanted to stretch their time together for as long as possible. She wanted to stay with him in this little bubble, in the protection of his arms. She was afraid that when she walked away the spell would break.

The other part, though, needed the space to think things through. As soon as she was back in the big house she'd be drawn into the mayhem of the day. Getting Jonas ready, helping Annie with breakfast, not to mention the last-minute preparations for Christmas. With less than twenty-four hours until Christmas Eve they really were running out of time.

She needed to think before she got in too deep. Before she let herself get carried away by romance and hopes and happily-ever-after. A cold, brisk walk up through the forest was exactly what she needed, even if her heart didn't want the reality check.

'It's OK, I'll be fine. You get on with your day, no doubt you've got lots to do.' She smiled, though it took some effort.

This time he didn't protest. Instead, he pulled on his pyjama bottoms and sat on the end of the bed, watching closely as she put on her clothes. The fluffy sheep pyjamas seemed stupid – not cute the way she'd thought they were last night. So unsophisticated and mundane.

Her boots were still by the door. She pulled them on, looking around for her jacket, but Adam already had it in his hands. 'You sure you don't want a ride?'

'I'll be fine.' She slipped her arms into the proffered coat. Adam lifted it onto her shoulders, his hands lingering there for a moment. She luxuriated in his touch, in his closeness, in the amazing way he smelled.

It was good. Too good.

She reached out for the door, turning the handle to let in the brisk morning air. When she turned back he was still staring at her, his expression unreadable. She wanted to say something to him, maybe ask him how he felt. Tell him she was going to miss him, even though he was only a trek through the forest away.

'I guess I'll see you later.'

He nodded. 'That you will.'

Was he angry at her? She wanted him to plead with her to stay again. To tell her he liked her as much as she liked him. But she was too shy to voice her needs.

When he remained silent, Kitty rolled onto her tiptoes, pressing her lips against his warm, bearded cheek. 'Goodbye, Adam.'

She hurried down the cabin steps and onto the snowy ground. The crash of wood against wood told her he'd closed the door, and it felt as though something inside her snapped. She turned back to check, and the porch was deserted, with only the decorations and fairy lights to be seen.

So that was that, then, the end of a perfect night. Time to turn and face the bright reality of the day. She squared her shoulders as she approached the snow-topped trees, trying to ignore the ache already forming in her chest.

She'd be OK. She always was.

Life was never supposed to be a fairy tale, she didn't know why she'd let herself believe it could be.

23

What's done cannot be undone

– Macbeth

Somehow Kitty managed to make it into her attic bedroom without being spotted. She'd been certain the sound of the stairs creaking, along with her noisy breathing, would have roused the whole house. Yet here she was, pulling off her coat and lying back on her bed, trying to regain her equilibrium after the long walk through the forest.

According to her watch she had around half an hour before Jonas was up. He'd taken to setting an alarm clock, afraid he was going to miss the day's festivities. Not that Kitty could blame him; she remembered as a child the run-up to Christmas was almost better than the real thing. The anticipation, the bonhomie, the endless hours of playing Go Fish and Beggar my Neighbour. She used to love everything about the final few days, from the last-minute dashes to buy a forgotten present to the aroma of turkey gravy wafting through the house.

Now, though, her mind was too full of Adam to think of much else. That was why it took her so long to notice her mobile flashing on the bedside table. Buried deep inside her memories, the green light barely made an impression until its incessant pulses finally made it through her fugue.

She reached out to grab it, the delicious ache of her muscles reminding her once again of the night before. Swiping the screen she saw she'd somehow managed to miss two calls and a message – all from her sister Juliet.

Frowning, Kitty pressed the message icon. There were a few brief lines, reminding Kitty how busy her sister always seemed to be. The result of being the wife of a prominent businessman, as well as a doting mother and starting up her own business. Out of the four sisters, Juliet was certainly the most outwardly successful. Kitty knew from her sister's confidences that appearances weren't always as they seemed.

Was just thinking of you, are you OK? Give me a call to tell me how things are going. Love you, xx

It was still early but Kitty knew her sister would be up. Even during school vacations her niece, Poppy, was awake with the larks, dragging her mum out of bed to keep her company.

'Hey, sweetie, I had the strangest feeling about you. Are you OK?' Juliet said, as soon as she picked up. It wasn't unusual for the sisters to react that way. Cesca had told Lucy and Kitty that Juliet was in labour hours before she called to say she'd given birth to a child. Maybe that's what came from growing up in such close proximity to each other. They felt everything.

'I'm fine,' Kitty said, two lines forming between her brows. 'What sort of strange feeling?'

'I don't know, it's stupid. I just felt you needed us. Maybe it's having you so far away at Christmas.'

'I'm closer to you than I have been for years,' Kitty pointed out. 'We're only a few hundred miles apart for once.'

'But it's your first Christmas away from London. I worry about you.' Juliet let out a soft sigh. 'Are you sure nothing's happened?'

Everything had changed, but how to explain that to Juliet?

'I'm fine, honestly. I'm going to miss being home for the big day, but it's OK. Maybe we'll all be able to be together next year.' Kitty tried to keep her voice light.

'Maybe . . .'

'Are *you* OK?' Kitty asked. 'You sound a little weird.'

Another sigh from Juliet, this one longer and deeper than the first. Kitty found herself starting to worry about her older sister. 'Thomas and I have been having some . . . problems.'

Kitty knew how hard it was for her sister to admit that. In her perfect world Juliet didn't allow problems to get in the way. To acknowledge them was a defeat in itself. If she was actually saying the words out loud, then things really were bad.

'What kind of problems?'

Juliet sighed. 'He's not happy with me,' she told her. 'Thinks I'm neglecting things at home because of setting up the flower shop. It seems like he spends more time at his parents' place than he does with us. As you can imagine, they're delighted. Their house must be full of I-told-you-sos and talk of my unsuitability. They never liked me.'

That was an understatement. Kitty recalled the wedding – a hastily planned occasion, as Juliet was almost six months pregnant by that point. Joan Marshall – Thomas's mother – had looked as though she was sucking a lemon throughout the whole church service.

'That sounds horrible,' Kitty commiserated. 'Especially so close to Christmas. How's Poppy holding out?'

'She's confused, she's sad, but then she's all excited about Christmas. I wish I could make it all better for her, you know. I wanted her to have the perfect childhood, and I can't make it happen.'

They all wanted that for Poppy. Strange how you hoped to give the younger generation a better life than you had.

'She's a good kid, she'll be OK. Maybe there's more to it than that. Is everything OK at Thomas's work?'

'The amount of time he spends there, I'd hope so. Do you know he told me I should always be a stay-at-home mom for the sake of his career? As you can imagine I told him where to shove his career.'

Kitty burst out laughing. In spite of the seriousness of the situation, she couldn't help but feel proud of her sister.

'Honestly, Kitty, never fall in love. It ruins everything.'

It was a little too late for that. 'I'll take that into consideration,' she said lightly, knowing she wouldn't listen at all.

'Talking of annoying men, how's it going with that shit who pissed in your cornflakes?' Juliet asked, reminding Kitty that the last time they spoke she'd been at loggerheads with Adam.

'Oh that? It was all a bit of a misunderstanding. We sorted it out, and everything's just fine now.'

'He sounded like a real piece of work,' Juliet said. 'What is it with guys thinking they know everything? Seriously, you should tell that wanker where to get off.'

'He's not like that,' Kitty protested. 'I got it all wrong.'

Juliet paused for a moment. Kitty could hear her soft breathing on the other end of the phone line. 'He isn't? So what is he like?'

Beautiful, wonderful, charming? They didn't seem the right words to sum him up. She wondered if there were any words that could perform that job. If the Eskimos had a hundred words for snow, Kitty could have a thousand and she still couldn't describe Adam.

'He's everything.'

'Kitty! What's going on? Oh my God . . . ' Juliet trailed off, no doubt shaking her head at Kitty's sudden confession. 'You need to fill me in right now.'

For the next ten minutes, Kitty filled her sister in on everything that had happened between her and the stubborn, funny, beautiful man who lived in a cabin by the lake. And even then, the words didn't do him justice.

'Are you certain?' Jonas screwed up his nose. 'Uncle Adam definitely told me they were washing their socks.'

The mention of Adam's name was enough to make her heart skip a beat. *Stop it*, she chastised herself. When she was being a nanny, Adam was the one person who shouldn't be on her mind. She was here to look after Jonas, and she was determined to do just that. Starting with practising Christmas carols with him so he'd be ready to sing them to his grandmother on Christmas Eve.

'No, they definitely weren't washing their socks. They were watching their flocks. As in flocks of sheep. They were shepherds, you see.'

Jonas gave her a look that screamed *'duh'*.

'I know that. It's in the first line. But even shepherds need to wash their socks, otherwise they'd get cheesy feet. Uncle Adam said a person's feet are the most important part of their body. If you don't look after them you're in trouble.'

'Sometimes your uncle makes things up for fun,' she pointed out patiently. 'You're singing about shepherds. And they were watching their sheep as the angel of the Lord came down.'

He screwed his face up in confusion. 'I don't want to get it wrong. What if everybody laughs at me? I want to make Oma proud.'

'You will.' She pulled him to her, wrapping her arms around his shoulders. 'Remember what Annie said? Your Oma used to love going to midnight mass, but this year she can't make it to church. So we'll bring the songs to her instead.'

'Will you sing with me?' Jonas gave her a beseeching smile.

Kitty made a wide-eyed face. 'Oh no, not unless we want to burst her eardrums. I may have many qualities, but a good singing voice isn't one of them. Honestly, she's going to love it. So will everybody else. You have a beautiful voice.'

His singing was pure and true, enough to bring a tear to her eye. Kitty started the music again, mouthing the words as he came in at the right time, remembering to sing about flocks instead of socks.

It was typical that the one afternoon she was trying to do anything but think about his uncle, Jonas would bring him up in every other sentence. For the past hour the room had been full of 'Adam said this' and 'Adam said that' until Kitty's mind was full of nothing but him.

Because he was all she wanted to talk about, too.

'How was that?' Jonas interrupted her thoughts. 'Did I get the words right?'

'You were perfect.' She flashed him a smile. 'Why don't we take a break? We could reward your throat with some milk and cookies.'

'The chocolate chip ones with the icing?' His eyes were as round as saucers. 'Oh boy, those are to die for.'

His words made her want to laugh. Kitty wondered if he'd heard his mother using the expression. It sounded so grown up for a seven-year-old boy. 'Well let's go and see if there's any left. I'll let you have two if you promise not to keel over afterwards.'

Jonas frowned. 'Keel over?'

'You said the cookies were to die for. I don't want you going that far.'

He laughed. 'OK, if I promise not to die for them, can I still eat 'em?'

'Sure.' Kitty hugged him, smiling.

Together they walked into the kitchen where Annie already had a pot of coffee brewing, and a saucepan of milk warming on the stove. If there was one thing Kitty was going to miss when she went back to LA it would be this kitchen. Stepping into it was like stepping onto the set of a TV programme, the visual equivalent of a warm, cosy hug.

Annie passed Jonas a mug of sweet chocolate and slid a plate with two cookies in front of him. Returning to the stove she poured out two mugs of coffee, turning to Kitty with a sheepish look on her face.

'Could you take these through to the library? Mr Everett asked for them.'

Kitty shook her head. 'No way, not after last time. He told me never to darken the library door again.'

Annie gave her a placatory smile. 'But he asked for these ones. I'd go myself but my knees are playing up. It's a long walk to the library.'

Kitty narrowed her eyes. Annie hadn't shown any sign of pain when they'd walked into the kitchen. Plus the library wasn't exactly miles away. If Kitty didn't know any better, Annie was as scared of walking into Everett Klein's operations hub as she was.

'Maybe Jonas could ...' Kitty looked around to see Jonas sitting at the table, his legs swinging as he took a mouthful of hot chocolate. He shot her a grin, his lips framed by a brown moustache, and Kitty didn't have the heart to send him into the fray.

'OK,' she said, sighing. 'I'll do it.'

'God bless you. The black mug is for Everett; he likes his coffee dark and sweet. The white mug's for Mr Montgomery.'

'Got it.' Kitty picked up the mugs and carried them the short distance out of the kitchen and into the hallway. As usual the library door was closed, and she had to bang on the dark mahogany wood with her elbow, both her hands occupied with the mugs. A moment later Drake pulled the door open, his face erupting into a smile when he saw her standing there. He ushered her in, and Kitty took her first step into the forbidden room.

'I've got your coffee.'

'Put it on the table in the corner, please.' Everett was sat at his desk, staring intently at one of the three screens there. 'Hey, Drake, take a look at this.'

Ignoring them both, Kitty walked across the room to the large oak table, stepping over leads and avoiding boxes. Lying spread out on the table was a script, the first page opened for her to see.

Her eyes widened when she looked at it. She glanced back at Drake and Everett, who were still distracted by the computer in front of them.

One little read wouldn't hurt. Right?

FADE IN

Extreme close-up of a pair of eyes shifting from left to right. Pan out slightly to reveal a bead of sweat running down their face.

Move camera up to reveal an old 3 blade fan, circling incessantly though clearly having no effect on the heat in the room.

Camera pans out to reveal a documentary being filmed. Pared down equipment including a camera, boom, lights and other paraphernalia.

Adam (to be renamed) taps a pen to his lips. His expression is set, his eyes narrow.

                    ADAM
I have evidence that you regularly use children under the age of ten to traffic drugs.

                   GARCIA
Who have you been talking to?

                    ADAM
I never reveal my sources, you know that.

Shouts come from just outside the windowless room. The door opens and a big burly thug drags in a teenage boy, who's kicking and screaming. A glance between the boy and Adam alerts the viewer that the two of them are already acquainted.

Garcia pulls a gun from the holster on his leg.

She stared at the black print for a moment, blinking to let the words sink in. Was his brother making a movie about Adam? It couldn't just be a coincidence that he was using that name. She reached out, wanting to turn to the next page, desperate to see what happened. Her hand hovered for a moment, unsure.

'What are you looking at?' Everett asked. Kitty glanced up to find him glaring at her, his muscles drawn into a frown.

She put the mugs on the table, feeling guilty. 'Nothing.'

'Everything in here is confidential, remember?'

She nodded. 'I remember.'

Drake stood up, ushering her out yet again. If he wasn't so into himself, she might describe him as a knight in shining Armani. 'And as we said before, she's signed an NDA. She can't tell anybody about the things she's seen in here, otherwise she'll be in breach of that. You're just interested in the way we make movies, right, Kitty?'

'Right,' she replied, still not quite clear in her mind about what she saw. 'What's your project about?'

'Please, Kitty.' Everett sighed, rubbing his face with the heel of his hand. 'Stop asking so many questions.'

He sounded almost defeated, as though he was carrying the weight of the world on his shoulders. She nodded quickly and hurried out, but not before taking one last glance at the script lying on the table across the room.

It was about Adam, that much was clear. What she didn't know was why, and whether Adam had any idea his brother was making a movie about him.

243

24

All made of passion and all made of wishes

– As You Like It

'You look different.'

Adam smiled indulgently at his mother. 'I've only just walked into the room. How different can I look?'

'Oh, you'd be surprised. A mother can sense things. When you were a child I knew as soon as you walked through the door if you'd had a good day or a bad day. Right now I'd say your day's been going pretty well.'

His chest tightened. He'd spent the morning playing with the dog before going for a run to end all runs. Anything he could do to stop himself from stalking up to the big house and hunting Kitty down. He had the urge to grab her and spirit her back to his cabin, back to where they'd lain together happy and sated. Back to where he'd got to know every inch of her body.

Even intense physical exercise hadn't been enough to eliminate the urge altogether. It barely made a dent on his need to see her. That was why he found himself walking up to the house later in the afternoon, letting the wind whip his face as he crunched through the forest.

Annie had raised her eyebrows as he walked into her kitchen, and he'd muttered something about needing to spend some time with his mom. To his disappointment Kitty was nowhere to be seen, and he couldn't exactly ask Annie where she was, could he?

Instead he'd made the trek upstairs to the master bedroom, where his mother lay on the bed, exhausted after an hour spent with her physiotherapist.

'It's Christmas, isn't everybody supposed to be happy?' Adam dragged a chair to her bedside. ''Tis the season, after all.'

'Speaking of which, I hear you're going to join us for Christmas lunch.' She squeezed his hand. 'I'm so pleased to hear that.'

'I'll suffer anything for you, Mom.'

She rolled her eyes. 'Don't pretend to be a Grinch. You walk in here with your eyes bright and your beard trimmed and you think I'm not going to notice?'

Adam ran his palm across his chin. His beard had needed grooming, and today had seemed as good a time as any; it wasn't anything more serious than that. Though he had, for one long minute, considered shaving all the hair off, in the end he'd opted for a neaten-up.

'As I said, it's Christmas. I don't want to come to dinner looking like a vagabond.'

'When's that ever stopped you before?' his mom teased. Then, turning serious she added, 'You really do look different. Alive. I can't tell you how much it warms my heart to see it.'

Adam suppressed a grin. He wasn't about to confess he hadn't felt this alive in years. Nor that it was the gorgeous blonde who happened to be taking care of his nephew who'd caused such a big change in such a short time. That was his secret to keep – his and Kitty's – and he wasn't about to dilute it by sharing it with anybody else.

'Maybe it's the puppy I've been looking after.'

'Jonas's puppy?' Her eyes twinkled. 'I heard about that. Annie told me you agreed to look after him until Christmas, that was very kind of you.'

'Kind? I was press-ganged into it. Saying no wasn't an option.'

'Oh stop it. You can pretend to be grumpy and gruff with everybody else, but you forget I'm your mother. I know you inside and out. You may be tough on the outside, but inside you're about as hard as a marshmallow.'

'A marshmallow?' Adam replied, raising a single eyebrow. 'I guess it beats being a teddy bear.'

Mary reached out to squeeze his hand. 'You're one of those, too. But don't worry, your secret's safe with me.'

He shot her a rueful smile. 'Who are you going to tell? Everett would never believe you. And Dad always said we were both as tough as steel.'

'Your father's soft as cotton, too.' Her expression turned sad. 'That's why he'll be so happy to have his family all together under one roof for Christmas. It means a lot to us both.'

He nodded slightly. He knew his feud with Everett had broken both of their hearts, and he hated that it did. He just didn't know how to get over it, how to forgive a brother who'd all but crushed his heart, too.

'Yeah, well don't get any ideas. This thaw is for Christmas, not for life.'

'I wouldn't dream of it.' She winked, but Adam knew that she definitely dreamed of it.

If he was any kind of son, he'd find a way to make those dreams come true.

He was deep in thought when he reached the first floor, walking right into Kitty as he reached the bottom step. She stumbled back, flinging her arms out in an attempt to steady herself. As quick as lightning he grabbed her around the waist, stopping her from falling to the floor.

'I didn't see you there. You OK?' He frowned, looking over her body, trying to find evidence of any injury.

Kitty was breathless. 'I didn't see you either.'

He was still holding her. His hands were moulded around her waist as if she was made for him. Her sweater was so thin he could feel the warmth of her body through it. In spite of the fact he was in his parents' house, only yards away from where his brother was working, he felt his own body responding.

When he looked again, Kitty was smiling at him. The way her lips curled, making her cheeks plump up, caused his heart to stutter. In all the excitement some hairs had escaped from her ponytail, so he reached out and tucked the strands behind her ear.

'I've been thinking about you all day,' he whispered.

'I've been thinking about you, too.'

That was all he needed to hear. Grabbing her hand, he pulled her into the living room, his eyes sweeping left and right to make sure they were alone. He kicked the door shut then pressed her against the wall, his body held against hers as he lowered his head.

'I've been thinking about this, too.' Adam kissed her hungrily. Her lips welcomed him, soft and warm.

She curled her arms around his neck as he put his hand in

247

the small of her back, pulling her closer still. Every sense was full of her, and of the need to have more.

Christ, he couldn't get enough. He slid his hands beneath the waistband of her jeans, fingers caressing her soft skin. She arched her back, pushing into him and he was immediately hard.

He stepped back, his heart racing. 'I'm sorry.'

Kitty touched her mouth with her index finger, brows knitted in a frown. 'Why are you sorry?'

'For dragging you in here and taking advantage of you, without even so much as a hello.'

She smiled coquettishly. 'What if I wanted you to take advantage of me?'

Adam shook his head, taking in a deep breath. Somehow he needed to get control of his body. 'You shouldn't say things like that,' he told her, his voice low.

Kitty took a step towards him, leaning her head back so she could look him in the eyes. 'There're a lot of things I shouldn't do. The problem is, I *want* to do them.'

His mouth was dry. It was hard to think straight when she was so close. His body was overriding every sensible thought he could muster. 'Kitty . . .'

'Hush.' She pressed her lips to his again. This time she took the lead, kissing him softly, her mouth enticing. Her palms cupped his face, her fingers brushing against his beard. When he opened his eyes she was staring right at him, hot and needy, and it took every ounce of self-control he had not to pick her up and carry her to her bedroom.

'Come down to the cabin tonight,' he said when they finally parted. 'Let me cook you dinner.'

'Oh!' She pressed her hand against her chest. 'Are you sure?'

She was so damned cute he wanted to kiss her again. 'I'm sure I want to cook you dinner,' he said. 'But are you sure you want to come?'

She tipped her head to the side. 'That sounds remarkably like a date.'

'That's because it *is* a date. I wasn't inviting you because you look hungry.' Although she did. She looked as hungry as he felt.

'I'd have to come down later, after Jonas is in bed. Would that be too late?' Her eyes sparkled as she asked him, reflecting the Christmas lights festooned around the fireplace.

'That would be fine.' He pulled her into an embrace. 'It'll give me enough time to work out what the hell I should cook for you.'

'Better make it good, if you want to top last night's romantic gesture.'

'I'm always good, you know that.' He kissed the tip of her nose, ruffling her hair with his palm. 'I'll see you this evening.'

Adam was still smiling when he walked into the kitchen, planning to steal some food from Annie for their date. Everett was leaning against the worktop, holding a mug of coffee in one hand and his phone in the other, pressing it against his cheek as he barked orders into the mouthpiece. On seeing his brother, he ended the call, shoving his phone into his pocket as he stared at him. He drained his coffee before he said anything, putting his empty mug onto the countertop.

'How are you?' Everett finally asked.

Adam's good mood immediately disappeared. 'Do you care?'

'What kind of question is that? I'm your brother, of course I care.'

Adam stared at him, trying to work out his angle. If there was one thing he'd learned about Everett since LA, it was that there was always an angle.

'In that case, I'm fine.'

There was a pause as Everett took another mouthful of coffee. Swallowing it down, he stared at Adam, an expectant look on his face.

'What?' Adam couldn't stand the silence.

'Aren't you going to ask me how I am?'

'Wasn't planning on it.' Adam couldn't even look him in the eye. He turned his back on him, walking into the food cupboard to grab what he needed. As far as he was concerned, the sooner he was out of the house and on his way back down to the cabin the better.

'Can't we put this behind us?' Everett's voice made him jump. He'd followed Adam across the kitchen and was standing in the doorway. 'Let bygones be bygones. It's Christmas, the season of goodwill. What else do you need, a visit from a freaking angel?'

Adam narrowed his eyes. 'This isn't a movie, Everett. You don't get to act like an asshole and then do a one-eighty in the last ten minutes. I'll come for Christmas dinner to please our parents, but that's all.'

His brother's face hardened. 'So there's nothing I can say ...'

'Nothing I'm going to listen to. Save your breath, and I'll save mine. While you're here I'll tolerate you, but we're not going to skip off into the sunset.'

'Well, you won't have to tolerate us for long.' Everett let out a frustrated sigh. 'We'll be gone by next week.'

Adam's jaw twitched. He should be glad to hear that. He

should be happy his brother was planning to leave as soon as possible. But if Everett left, so would Jonas, and that would mean Kitty leaving, too.

He'd only just found her. They were only just getting to know each other. And before he'd even had a chance to truly have her, he knew it was all going to be for nothing.

She'd leave, he'd stay here in his cabin, and everything would go back to the way it had always been. Maybe he shouldn't get involved, or risk getting his heart hurt yet again.

But even as he entertained that thought, he dismissed it without hesitation. He was going to spend as much time as he could with Kitty Shakespeare, and he wasn't going to regret a single thing about it.

25

'Tis an ill cook that cannot lick his own fingers

– Romeo and Juliet

Kitty raised her eyebrows as she looked at the stove. 'No meat? You surprise me, I put you down as a caveman type of eater.'

Adam turned, still stirring the pasta sauce, and shot her a grin. 'No beef, no chicken and definitely no deer.' He winked at her, reminding her of the day they met. 'Just mushrooms in an Alfredo sauce. Unless you have a thing against mushrooms.'

'I have nothing against mushrooms.' She took a sip of the wine he'd poured for them both. 'As long as you didn't shoot them with a rifle.'

'Even mushrooms deserve to be put out of their misery.'

'Mushrooms don't have misery,' she pointed out. 'They don't have feelings at all. They're fungi.'

'Fun guys. Just like me.' He winked.

'Mmhmm, just like you.' She rolled her eyes at his lame joke. Leaning towards him, she brushed her cheek with his, stealing a carrot from the salad he'd made. Adam tried to grab it back, mock-fighting with her until they were both laughing and the carrot dropped onto the floor.

'Stop playing with the food,' she chastised, as Adam grabbed the wine bottle to fill her glass. 'It's like cooking with a child.'

'Are you calling me a kid?' He tipped his head to the side.

'If the cap fits ...'.

'I think you'll find I'm all man.' He leaned down and kissed her, his lips warm and inviting. 'Only a man would kiss you like this,' he whispered.

'Mmm.' She wrapped her arms around his neck, kissing him back.

They'd been like this ever since she'd arrived at the cabin an hour earlier. Playful then heated, and oh-so-easy with each other. She'd been on dates before, but never ones that made her feel so at home and yet completely out of her comfort zone at the same time. They were walking a high wire, hand in hand.

Adam ran his lips down the side of her face, lingering at her jaw.

She gasped as he nipped the sensitive skin of her neck.

He left a lingering kiss on her lips and turned back to the stove. Leaning back on the work surface she swirled the wine in her glass, watching as it sloshed up the sides. She'd headed down to the cabin shortly after Jonas went to bed, claiming she had a headache and wanted to sleep it off. Though she'd felt a pang of discomfort at having to lie to Annie, she consoled herself that it was her night off, and if she wanted to go out on a date she could.

After dinner Adam built up the fire in the living area, hunkering down and placing the logs in a criss-cross pattern, fanning the flames until they began to lick up the chimney. Kitty sat back on the threadbare easy chair and watched the muscles flex beneath his flannel shirt, admiring the way his thighs thickened as he squatted down. There was a quietness to his strength that enticed her. He was at ease with his body, using it as another tool to make things work. She couldn't help but wish he was as comfortable with his soul. Because as beautiful as his body was, that wasn't the only thing that attracted her. Not the main thing, even. It was the way he smiled, that crooked half-curl that made her heart pound. It was how he answered her questions, thoughtfully and meaningfully, that caused her to lose her breath.

He'd cooked for her, cleaned up, and was making sure she was warm and comfortable. It made a change from all those evenings out at fancy LA restaurants with pretty-boy metro-sexuals who used their iPhone calculator to split the bill. She smiled, imagining Adam's furious response if she offered to go Dutch.

Maybe she'd have to try it some time. There was something delicious about the flashes of fury she sometimes saw behind his eyes.

The only problem was, there weren't going to be any dates. There weren't going to be any visits to restaurants or evenings at the movies. This was all they had. A few nights holed up in a cabin before they went their separate ways.

The thought made her chest hurt.

'Would you like some more wine?' Adam gestured at her empty glass. Kitty smiled, trying to swallow down her sadness, and held it out for him to top up. Filling his own, too, Adam lifted her, sitting in the chair and pulling her onto his lap.

He put his arm around her waist, and Kitty leaned her head back against his chest. They watched the fire dancing in the grate as they sipped the warm Merlot, and Kitty wondered if this was what happiness tasted like. It was simple, really. She didn't want fancy restaurants or smart clubs, as much as she'd liked them before. Sitting there with Adam's arm around her, the smell of the fire filling their senses, she couldn't think of any place she'd rather be.

'Will you stay with me tonight?' He ran a finger along her thigh.

'I don't know ...' She wanted to, but she was afraid. Not of getting caught – though that would be bad enough – but of getting hurt. Every cell in her body was becoming addicted to his touch.

'Stay,' he murmured, wrapping his hand around her leg. 'Just until morning. Let me make love to you and hold you all night.'

His suggestion set her on fire. There was nothing more she wanted than to be enveloped in his arms, letting him love her until they both cried out with pleasure.

Kitty closed her eyes, surrendering to the sensations assaulting her body. The sensuousness of his touch, the warm, smoky smell of the fire, and the taste of wine that lingered on her tongue. Was it possible to just live in the moment, let herself be free enough to enjoy what was left of her time with Adam and not worry about the future?

She wasn't sure, but the alternative – to leave now – felt too hard to contemplate. It struck her that the feeling she'd been searching for all her life was filling her up to the brim. Strange that she could discover it here, in this desolate snowy cabin, when she'd always thought she'd find it in LA.

'I'll stay,' she whispered.

She would have said more, but Adam's lips stole the words right out of her mouth.

*

Watching Kitty sleep was becoming his favourite pastime. Adam lay on his side, cheek resting on his palm, taking in her relaxed posture. She had a habit of frowning when she slept, in response to a dream, he imagined, and he wanted nothing more than to smooth the lines away. She was the one good thing that had happened to him in a long while, and he wasn't sure he was ready to let her slip away.

The thought made him want to hit something. Anything.

'Hey.' Kitty cracked open half an eye. 'What time is it?'

'Still night-time. Go back to sleep.' He stole a soft kiss. 'I'll wake you up when it's morning.'

She snuggled into him, looping her arms around his neck. Her lips pressed against the soft dip at the bottom of his throat. 'You should sleep, too.'

'I can't.' He pressed his face to her head, her hair muffling his voice. 'But that doesn't mean we both need to suffer.'

Kitty's voice was deep and slow, like a child waking up from an anaesthetic. 'Why can't you sleep?'

'Never can. I manage four hours most night, five hours at a push.' Adam glanced at the clock – it was nearly five a.m.

She stretched her arms above her head, her mouth opening into a yawn. 'I can't survive on less than seven, not on a regular basis.' She wrinkled her nose. 'Though recently I've been missing some sleep.'

He laughed softly. 'I noticed.'

It was strange watching Kitty wake up. Her body switched on a little at a time; eyes opening, arms stretching, legs unfurling and flexing. So different from the way Adam transitioned, his whole body flipping to alert as soon as sleep disappeared. Some of it came from his experiences abroad – sleeping in strange places, often having to avoid people who really didn't want him making a documentary about them. But he'd always woken quickly, even as a child. Kitty's cat-like stretches were an enticing difference.

'Can I ask you something?' she asked.

He blinked, staring at her. 'Sure.'

'What happened when you came back to LA this summer?'

His shields immediately went up. 'What do you mean?'

Something in his tone must have alerted her to his discomfort. 'I was just being nosy. Ignore me.'

He didn't like the way she shrank back from his harshness. It was enough to make his stomach curl. 'I'm sorry, I sounded wary. I just … it wasn't a good time for me.'

She said nothing. Maybe she was afraid to put him on the defensive again. Either way Adam knew it was up to him to clear the way. To try and regain the gentle ease they'd had only moments before.

'It's old news,' he told her. 'I fell out with Everett over something, and we came to blows. The next thing I knew the blue lights arrived and I was being arrested for assault and battery.'

'Didn't Everett get arrested, too?'

Adam licked his lips They were dry as a bone. 'He's not quite as good at fighting as me. He definitely came off worse.'

'What was the fight about?' she asked him, her palm flat on his chest, over where his heart was beating. She looked up at him through those pretty blue eyes, her expression soft.

Adam thought back to that day, when he'd discovered everything Everett had done. The deceit, the backstabbing, the payments he'd made. It was as though a veil of red mist had descended, colouring everything he looked at. He hadn't even planned to hit him the first time, but before he knew it, Everett was on the floor.

257

Christ, what a tangled web they'd both weaved.

'He double-crossed me on something.'

She moved her hand in a circle on his skin, her fingers sliding tantalisingly close to his nipples. Weird how he could feel so on edge and so turned on at the same time. Only she could make him feel this way.

More alive than he'd ever felt, and completely afraid he'd never feel this way again.

'We don't have to talk about it if you don't want to.'

'It's not that I don't want to,' he told her. 'It's more that I'm trying to forget it. At least for the next few days. I promised my folks I'd come to Christmas lunch and let bygones be bygones. If I keep talking about this shit I'll get all riled up again, and I don't want that.'

'Are you scared you'd hit him again?'

Adam shook his head. 'I'm getting better at controlling my anger. That's what my therapy's been about.' Or at least it was, until it had been hijacked by his feelings for Kitty. 'It's more that I want to be as genuine as possible. My folks have had a bad year, and part of it's my fault. They deserve to have their family around them at Christmas, and I want to give it to them.'

'And after Christmas?' Kitty asked. 'What will you do then? Will it be like that one-day armistice in the First World War when the soldiers all played football together, and then resumed fighting the next day?'

'Honestly?' Adam said. 'I have no idea. I guess things will go back to the way they were. Everett will go back to LA, and I'll stay here and finish up my therapy.'

'And I'll go back too . . .'

'But you're here now.' Adam's voice was thick. 'And that's what counts, right?' He placed his hand over hers, moving her

258

palm until it was brushing against his nipple. The sensation made him harder than hell. She could do that to him, arouse him at the simplest touch, until his body ached and needed her more than it needed air.

How the hell was he going to survive without her?

The morning light was streaming through the cabin shutters, making lines of white on the planked bedroom floor. Kitty stared at them, watching as they slowly moved towards the bed, playing a game of What's the Time, Mr Wolf with them. It was almost seven, time to get up, to feed the puppy, to hurry back to the house before her absence was noted.

It was hard to shake off the feeling of anxiety that had lain on her ever since she'd seen that script in the library. Of knowing something Adam didn't, of trying to find a way to tell him that didn't make things worse. Of opening a Pandora's box that threatened to engulf them all.

When she'd asked him about LA, she'd hoped somehow the conversation would lead to Everett, and she'd naturally be able to slip in questions about the script. But Adam had stonewalled her, using his body to make her forget anything that lingered in her mind, until all she could think about was him and what he did to her.

But what was her excuse now? Truthfully, she was afraid. No, it was worse than that, she was as frightened as hell that this little titbit of half-truth she was hiding from him could be the one piece of information to bring the whole house tumbling down.

Even worse, it was Christmas Eve, the day Jonas had been so looking forward to. What if she told Adam right now, and he stomped up to the house to have it out with Everett? Both of them could end up in the local police station, leaving Jonas and Adam's parents devastated. Could she do that to them, today of all days?

No, she couldn't. But she couldn't hide this from him either. Not after everything they'd been through. Even if she left next week, and never saw him again, she owed Adam her loyalty and the gift of the truth.

From the living room, she could hear the dog padding around, snuffling at the bedroom door. Another moment or two and he'd be barking for them to let him out to do his business, and the day would begin.

Adam said he wanted to forget about it all until after Christmas was over. Maybe Kitty could do the same. They could get through the day, make Jonas happy by spending it all together, and then when it was all over she'd tell Adam about that script she'd found.

Right on cue, the barking started and the puppy pawed at the bedroom door, knowing they were inside. Adam sat straight up at the noise, blinking the sleep from his eyes, smiling when he saw her lying beside him.

'Good morning.' He gave her the biggest, brightest smile.

Yes, so much better to keep everything quiet for now.

26

We two alone will sing like birds i' th' cage

— King Lear

The day was blessed with a squally storm that whipped up the snowdrifts and made them dance like butterflies. Old flakes mingled with new, enough to cause a whiteout. Kitty and Annie spent Christmas Eve morning lighting fires and stirring hot chocolate, singing with Jonas while he practised his carols for his evening's performance. By lunchtime the aroma of ham and pumpkin filled the kitchen, making Kitty's nose twitch with olfactory memories of her childhood.

Not that they'd eaten pumpkin pie when she was a child. Her holidays had been traditionally British, with spice-filled Christmas puddings and warm mince pies. Their meat of choice had been turkey, but there was always a ham, too. First her mum, and then Lucy, would cook so much the leftovers would stretch into January. Turkey curry, ham pies, all those things tasted like home.

She missed them.

'How long to go?' Jonas asked, pulling at her arm. 'Is it nearly time?'

Kitty ruffled his hair. 'There's nine hours to get through yet, so let's try not to wish it away, OK?'

For one night only, Jonas was allowed to stay up until late. They'd decided midnight was *too* late, even if his singing was supposed to be a replacement for midnight mass, but staying up until nine might just mean he slept in on Christmas Day. That would be a gift for everybody.

'That's such a long time.' He slumped down in the kitchen chair, pushing his empty mug away.

Mia and Everett had left earlier to travel to Washington, DC, for a meeting followed by a cocktail reception. Neither of them looked particularly happy about it, snapping at each other like angry dogs before they left. Mia had given Jonas an extra big hug, promising she'd be there before Santa arrived on his sleigh.

To make up for their absence, Kitty was determined to fill Jonas's day with delight.

'How about we watch a movie?' she suggested. 'I've downloaded a few. We've got *The Polar Express*, or *Elf*. I think there's *The Santa Clause*, too.'

His face lit up. 'Can we watch it with Oma?'

Kitty shook her head. 'She's resting today so she can be awake this evening. She doesn't want to miss your concert.'

'Can we have popcorn instead, then?' Jonas shot her a grin.

'Why not?' The kid was without his parents, stuck in a desolate house far away from his friends, with only his nanny, a cook and elderly grandparents for company. If he wanted popcorn, he was damn well going to get it.

'Yay!' He scooted into the living room to set up the TV while Kitty gathered their food and drinks. They spent the afternoon snuggled on the sofa beneath an Afghan rug, watching movie after movie and stuffing their faces. As the light of the day was slowly defeated by the onset of dusk, Jonas fell asleep against her, his slight body curled into hers.

There was something so comforting about having him dozing in her arms. Like having a favourite dog curled up on her lap. She felt protective and peaceful. At that moment contentedness was spilling out of her, and it was warming her up from the inside. She was going to miss him when she was back in LA. Hell, there was a lot she was going to miss.

'Is he asleep?' Annie popped her head around the door.

'He is.' Kitty smiled. 'I'd wake him up but as he's going to be staying up tonight I thought I'd let him rest.'

'Well if you can leave him for a moment, there's someone here to see you.'

'Who?' Kitty frowned.

'It's Adam. He wants to know when to bring the dog over. For Jonas's surprise.'

Kitty only had to hear his name for her heart to start racing. It was shameful the way he made her feel. Exciting too, in that schoolgirl crush kind of way. Just four simple letters and her body was in a full rush.

Gently, she extricated herself from Jonas, slipping a cushion under his head and tucking the blanket firmly around him. He murmured in his sleep, then turned over, twisting the blanket around him. With his golden hair and bright red cheeks he seemed more cherub than child.

The warm feelings followed her into the kitchen, where Adam was leaning on the counter, his brown eyes following her entrance. He didn't have to say a word. His expression said it all.

His intensity took her breath away.

'Hey.' She felt suddenly coy. Lingering by the table, a few feet away from him, she found herself twisting at her fingers. 'Everything OK?'

'It's fine.' His voice was thick. 'I just wanted to see you.'

'You did?' Kitty glanced behind, seeking out Annie, but the housekeeper was nowhere to be seen. Maybe she was being discreet, giving them some space. Kitty had long since suspected Annie knew exactly what was going on.

When Adam swallowed, his Adam's apple pushed out. 'I missed you.' A smile tugged at the corner of his mouth. 'I can't even make it through a day without seeing you.'

His words made her heart want to sing. He was echoing her thoughts, underlining the aching need they both seemed to have.

Maybe that's what made her bold enough to step forward and take his hands in hers. Rolling onto her toes, she lifted herself up, pressing her lips to his. The contact of his soft, warm mouth, framed by the sharp bristles of his beard was delicious.

A moment later he was scooping her up, kissing her hard and fast. His hands were everywhere, in her hair, down her sides, cupping her behind. Getting his fix while he could.

She was getting hers, too.

When she finally pulled away, her face was flushed. Adam's eyes were dark, searching, seeking answers she wasn't sure she could give. She wanted to try anyway.

'You came about the puppy?'

Adam shook his head. 'An excuse, I came about you. No, I came *for* you. If I had my way I'd steal you right now and hide you back at the cabin.'

'That sounds good.' A lie; it sounded perfect. There was nothing she'd rather do. But there was Jonas and there were complications, and there was that damn movie Adam didn't know was being made. Secrets and lies, all waiting to spill out. Was it wrong that she wanted to hide away from them all? To pretend it was just her and Adam and nobody else in the world? She couldn't remember a time she was happier than when she was lying in his arms.

'But I guess that's out of the question?' He tipped his head, his smile inviting. She wanted to follow him out of the door, to leave everything behind. For them to stay in their bubble for a few hours longer.

'I can't ...' It hurt her heart to say it. 'There's Jonas, his concert, it's Christmas Eve. I can't leave him alone.'

'Where are Everett and Mia?'

'They're out in DC. They won't be back until late this evening.' She tried to hide the bitterness in her voice, but it was impossible. 'They won't even be here to hear him sing to his grandmother.'

A flash of anger lit Adam's eyes. 'They won't?'

'No, and he's been practising for days, poor kid. He's so excited about it. Sometimes I want to shake them, make them realise what they're missing out on. It's one thing to be dedicated to your career, another to forget your child at the most important time of year.'

'Doesn't matter what time of year it is. The kid should always come first.'

Kitty nodded in agreement. Another reason why she felt so connected to Adam – he was on her wavelength. How often did you meet someone who seemed to echo your own beliefs so completely?

'Will you come to his concert?' she asked him.

'I wouldn't miss it for the world.'

'Thank you,' she said softly, squeezing his hand. 'You're going to make his day.'

Mary Klein's bedroom smelled of rosewater and soap. At some point that week, Annie had made it look festive – with a tree in the corner and garlands on the wall. Even the patient herself was looking better, any residual pain seemed to have gone, bringing the pinkness back to her cheeks.

Maybe it was the fact she'd be coming downstairs for the first time tomorrow that made her eyes sparkle. Or maybe it was Jonas's concert that made her look so alive. Either way, it was nice to see her looking so awake and happy.

Next to her in the cosy chair was her husband, and Annie had taken the chair on the other side. Adam was perched on the end of the bed, while Kitty was standing closer to Jonas, to give him the support he needed. Even Drake was there, lingering in the doorway. It was a fine crowd for Jonas's debut.

'OK?' she whispered to him.

Jonas nodded, and took another mouthful of water, nervously swallowing it down.

Kitty gave him a squeeze. 'Knock 'em out. You're going to be great.' She could see his hands trembling as he walked into the middle of the room, all eyes following him. A burst of pride shot through her. He was overcoming his fears, and she knew she'd had a lot to do with that.

The room fell silent as Jonas took a deep breath, then sang the first note, his pure voice cutting through the cloying air. Though his eyes were open, he was focused on something far away, his face taking on a wistful look. 'O Little Town of Bethlehem' was the first carol. His grandmother's favourite,

266

Annie had told them. And as he continued through the verses there wasn't a dry eye in the room.

Kitty stole a look at Mary Klein, who was mouthing the words along with Jonas, staring at her grandson with adoration. One papery hand was folded in her husband's, the other tightly clutching at her bedcovers. Francis and Annie's eyes were trained on him, too. And in the front was Adam, *her Adam*, staring at his nephew with the ghost of a smile on his lips.

Within moments Adam had caught her gaze. Like always, he made her chest tighten. It was as though there was a physical connection between them, fizzing and hissing like an electrical fault, and it made her feel jittery and high.

When Jonas began the next song, Kitty's pulse was racing. For the rest of her life, she knew she'd always think of this moment whenever she heard a Christmas carol. It would be impossible to forget the way Jonas sounded so heartbreakingly wholesome, or the way the flickering candles created shadows on the white walls. Most of all she'd remember the way she felt, like a ball of fire was rolling inside her, and the person stoking it was Adam Klein. The knowledge of him lifted her like a spiritual awakening. He filled her body, her mind, her soul. Every part of her ached to touch him, for him to hold her close and never let go. She wanted nothing more than to disappear into his skin.

Was this love? She didn't know. But whatever it was that she felt, it was too powerful to ignore. He was a rumble of thunder through the dark night, a storm coming ever closer, with no building or tree to shield her. He was going to strike her down, and she wanted it. Craved it, even. Their connection – whatever it was – had taken on a life of its own, and neither of them seemed able to control it.

Jonas came to his final song, and Kitty tore her eyes from Adam's. Her body was reacting in ways she'd never felt before, like a bear awakening from hibernation. She wanted to stretch her body, let him invade her like a fresh breath of air.

When Jonas hit the final note, Mary Klein gestured him over and he sat on her bed, burying his head in her arms. The cocktail of emotions stirring through Kitty's blood paralysed her, her heart hammering against her chest while she stared at the tableau of people in front of her. A family connected on Christmas Eve.

Maybe that should have made her sad. Caused her to miss her own family. But right then, right there, she couldn't think of a single place she'd rather be. Home wasn't where your blood was. It wasn't even where your heart was. Home was where you felt accepted, love, at peace.

Home felt strangely like Adam Klein.

Jonas gave a huge yawn, stretching his arms above his head in an almost parodic way. His mouth was opened so wide she could practically see his tonsils.

'OK, buddy, time for bed,' Kitty told him, shooting a glance at his grandmother to make sure it was OK. She still felt strange, as though she was having some kind of out-of-body experience.

'She's right,' Mary said. 'If you don't get to sleep, Santa won't come. You don't want to miss out on your gifts tomorrow.'

And boy, what presents they would be. Kitty wondered if the puppy would be a welcome addition.

'What are we waiting for?' Jonas jumped off the bed. 'C'mon, Kitty, it's bedtime.' With that he was out of the room and racing down the stairs to the second floor, heading for the bathroom. Kitty glanced over her shoulder before following him. Adam was still standing in the corner, his gaze warm. She wanted to say something to him, to tell him goodbye. To ask when she'd see him again. But she couldn't, not now. Not when everybody was here.

She hated that their secret meant she had to remain silent.

She hated secrets, full stop.

She gave him a half-smile, then turned, still feeling the heat of his stare on her back as she left the room.

Along with an emptiness she couldn't quite put her finger on.

Adam watched Kitty leave, her blonde hair swinging behind her as she whipped around and walked out of his mother's bedroom, her sheepskin slippers padding softly on the polished wood floor. He'd been staring at her all night. He couldn't help it. She was just too damned beautiful.

They couldn't go on like this. At first the secrecy had been part of the fun. A big f-you to his brother; an adrenalin-fuelled high. But now it was killing him.

His thoughts stole back to that morning, when Kitty was curled up in his arms. He didn't feel like hiding when she was around. He wanted to shout about her from the rooftops.

'Adam, did you hear me?' His mom's voice cut through his thoughts. He looked over at her, his smile warm.

'Sorry, I was miles away.'

'I can see that.' Her face held an expression of mischief. 'I was asking you when you were planning to bring the dog over.'

He shrugged. 'I guess I'll bring him over after breakfast, when we open the tree gifts.'

She gave him a beaming smile. 'You're coming to open the gifts too?'

269

'Of course. Who doesn't like gifts?' His eyes twinkled.

Mary lay back, closing her eyes. 'Who are you and what have you done with my son?'

Adam laughed. 'I tied him up and left him in the cabin.'

'That's good, because I like you much better.'

He walked over to the side of her bed. His father was still sitting on the other side, watching them fondly. Adam leaned down and pressed his lips to his mom's forehead, kissing her gently. 'You should get some rest.'

'She should,' his father agreed. 'It's been a long day.'

'But a good day.' She reached out and grabbed his hand. 'And it's been wonderful to have you here with us. After this summer, I never thought I'd see the day . . .'

Adam swallowed, a lump forming in his throat. 'I wouldn't want to be anywhere else.'

It was true. Kitty was the catalyst to opening his heart, but it was his family that made it feel full. His parents, Annie, Jonas, all of them were the reasons he felt so comfortable, the reason this felt like home.

Leaning down, he kissed her one last time. 'Merry Christmas, Mom.'

She squeezed his hand then released it, her eyelids starting to flutter with exhaustion. Her voice was quiet enough that he had to strain to hear her.

'Merry Christmas, son.'

27

For she had eyes and chose me
– Othello

Jonas had gone to bed without a fuss. The threat of Santa not coming was enough to get the naughtiest of children to crawl beneath their bed covers, and Jonas was no exception. He'd cleaned his teeth, climbed into his snowman pyjamas and then hung his stocking on the end of his bed before hopping onto his mattress and closing his eyes. He'd even waved off Kitty's offer of a book. *The Night Before Christmas* was no match for his impatient mind.

She'd waited for an hour before sneaking back in and filling his stocking. An assortment of gifts, brightly wrapped, spilling over the top in a satisfying way. Mia and Everett may have lacked many things, but generosity wasn't one of them.

It was almost midnight by the time she finally climbed the stairs to the loft room. Mia and Everett still hadn't arrived home. Snow had started to fall again, the flakes sticking to the windowpane and swirling in the beam of the out-side lights. She hoped they'd be home soon, that the snow wouldn't hold them back. That Jonas wouldn't awaken on

Christmas Day to find his parents had no choice but to spend it in Washington, DC.

Walking into her bedroom, she reached out to switch on the light. A figure was sitting on her bed. She jumped, clutching her chest with her palm, her eyes almost popping out of her head.

Adam. It was Adam.

Breathe, Kitty.

'What are you doing here?' she whispered. 'You gave me the shock of my life.'

'Who were you expecting, Santa Claus?' He gave her a lop-sided grin. 'You took for ever, by the way. I almost fell asleep.'

'I was busy,' she told him. 'I had to make sure Jonas was asleep before I could put his gifts in his stocking. He still believes in Father Christmas, you know.'

Adam winked. 'You're one hell of a sexy Santa. Maybe next time you can wear the suit.'

She raised an eyebrow, liking this playful Adam. 'Do you have a thing for fat old men?'

He grabbed her, pulling her onto the bed with him. Hooking his leg around her hip, he held her down. 'I've got a thing for you, baby.' He ran his nose along her jaw, pressing his lips to her throat. 'Fat, old, I don't care. I just want to hold you.'

She slid her fingers into his hair, holding him close. 'That might be the nicest thing anybody's said to me.'

Adam's lips moved against her neck. 'Then you're talking to the wrong people, sweetheart.'

It felt as though any time she was talking to somebody but him was wrong. They were in a snow globe, the two of them – hell, the whole family, if you wanted – just them and their winter wonderland, protected from the world outside. Maybe

272

there was something in Adam's need to retreat. Something concentrated and precious. She couldn't help but think she wanted this bubble to last for ever.

'Are you staying the night?' It was wrong, she knew, but the thought of him leaving her felt worse.

His lips had reached her clavicle. Kissing, nipping, licking, he made her flesh his own. 'I can't leave the dog on his own.'

Damn, she'd forgotten about the puppy. It would be nice to think he wouldn't be her problem after tomorrow, but that would be one hell of a lie. It was only just beginning.

'So you just stopped by to say hi?'

'Something like that.' He'd reached the swell of her breast. Unbuttoning her blouse, he moved his lips down until he met the lacy edge of her bra. 'I needed to see you.'

Her breath caught as he edged the cup down, until her breast was exposed. 'That's nice.'

He traced a line of fire with his tongue. Down her breast, around her areola. She could feel her skin pucker and tighten.

'It *is* nice,' he agreed, the tip of his tongue barely glancing her nipple. 'Very nice.' His lips closed around her, sucking her in, and any words she could think of escaped her mind.

When he took her other nipple between his thumb and forefinger, his exquisite pinching made her arch her back off the bed. Every touch sent pleasure shooting down her. Every bite made her moan softly.

'I want to make you come like this,' he whispered.

'I'm not sure I can ...'

'I want to try. A Christmas gift for me.' He smiled against her breast. 'A gift that keeps on giving.'

But she wasn't giving, she was taking. Pulling pleasure from him inch by inch, until her body felt as though it was floating.

Her body was vibrating, her cells singing a silent song, as he kissed and loved her until she was nothing but sensation.

An orgasm ripped through her like a tornado, leaving devastation in its wake. For a minute her body was a storm, then she was falling. Down, down, and into his waiting arms.

He held her tight, his lips soft against hers. Tasting her pleasure, giving it back. Her muscles loosened, exhausted, her eyelids heavy as she curled into his embrace.

28

*My tongue will tell the anger of my heart, or else
my heart concealing it will break*

– The Taming of the Shrew

Adam slipped out some time before dawn, leaving Kitty to grab a couple of hours of sleep. By the time Jonas roused her just after six a.m. her whole body was aching. Her mind ached too, full of thoughts of Adam.

She had fallen for him, she could admit that much. But she was afraid of Everett, damn, she was afraid of everything right then. It was all such a mess. She couldn't wait for Christmas to be over – at least then she could come clean.

She hated secrets.

'Santa's been. Can I open my gifts?' Jonas bounced on her bed excitedly. 'There's so many of them!'

'Not yet.' She stroked his hair. 'You need to wait for the family to get up.'

Mia and Everett must have come home some time in the night, because the car was parked on the gravelled drive. Maybe she'd been asleep, or maybe she'd been too absorbed by Adam. Whatever it was, she had no idea when they'd returned.

275

'But that's not fair. Mom takes for ever to get up.' A stubborn expression washed over his face. 'How about just one?'

Kitty reached under the bed. 'Maybe you could open one of my presents for you?' She passed him a box covered with Disney wrapping paper, depicting Mickey Mouse wearing a Santa outfit.

Even that reminded her of Adam.

'What is it?' He grabbed it impatiently. 'What did you get me?'

'Open it and see.'

He slid his fingers beneath the tape, ripping at the edges of the paper. Each tear revealed a little more of the package, until the remaining paper fell down and onto the floor. 'You got me a magic box? Awesome!' He pulled at the lid, opening it up and searching through the contents. 'I've always wanted one of these.'

She smiled. 'I know, you told me, remember?'

'When can I do some tricks?' He lifted out the cups and ball. 'Maybe I can put on a show.'

'Definitely. After you've had a chance to practise ...'

'I'm going to practise all day. Until I'm the best magician ever.'

'I'm not sure you're going to have much of a chance today. Maybe tomorrow?'

Tomorrow, ah tomorrow.

His face dropped. 'But that's ages away.'

'It will fly by. Today you'll have more presents to open and a family to spend time with. There's plenty of time to learn magic tricks afterwards.'

'I suppose ...' He pulled the rest of the tricks out, examining them one by one. 'I guess I can wait.'

'Good boy.'

After getting dressed they made their way downstairs. Everett and Mia were already down there, sipping coffee as Annie dressed the turkey. Jonas's grandfather, Francis, was watching her work, passing the dressing when she asked for it.

'Merry Christmas, darling!' Mia held her arms out for Jonas, who ran into them. 'Did Santa bring you any presents?'

'So many, Mom. Kitty said I couldn't open them until you were up. Can I get them now?'

Looking over his head she nodded at Kitty, as if to thank her. 'Of course, sweetheart. Bring them down. I can't wait to see what Santa's brought you!' She wiggled her eyebrows as if they were sharing a joke. But of course it was an adult one, not understood by Jonas. As far as he was concerned, Santa was a living, breathing, gift-giver.

Jonas ran out of the room and thundered up the stairs. Mia sat back down, looking relieved, taking another sip of coffee. 'What have you done with the dog?' she whispered.

'Adam's bringing him up later, when we open the tree presents. I said I'd meet him outside so we can surprise Jonas. Maybe you'd like to join us?'

Mia wrinkled her nose, looking out at the snow still falling onto the white ground. 'Maybe you can bring him in here instead.'

When ten o'clock arrived, Mia was busy drinking a mimosa and gossiping with Drake, leaving Kitty to shrug on her coat and pull on her snow boots and trudge around the house to where Adam was hiding. The puppy was standing quietly on a leash, good as gold, not straining or fighting to get away. Adam had fixed a bright red bow to his collar, much to the puppy's disgust. He tried to bite it off, but was having trouble getting the right angle.

'You gift-wrapped him.' She couldn't disguise her delight.

'Ah, I figured that if we're going to do this thing, we should go all-out for kitsch.'

'So how should we do it?' she asked. 'Just take him in and shout surprise? Bring Jonas out? What do you think?'

'Let's have a bit of fun.' His grin was infectious. 'We'll hide him in the closet and then let him loose. Create some mayhem.'

Kitty's eyes widened. 'I'm not sure we should do that. What if he makes a mess in there?'

'It won't be for long, and we've trained him anyway.' His expression was full of mischief. 'Come on, let's liven things up in there. It's Christmas, for goodness sake.'

'If you're sure.' Kitty hesitated. 'I don't want to cause any problems.'

'Look, who is Christmas for?' He stepped forward, cupping her face with his cold palm.

'The children?' she ventured.

'That's right. Now what will make Jonas's day?'

She shrugged. 'Chasing a dog around a house until it makes his mother scream loudly?'

'Exactly. So let's go and have some fun, OK?'

True to his word, Adam sneaked the dog into the closet, barely chastising the mutt when he started to eat Everett's dress shoes. Jonas was handing out presents to the family gathered around the tree. The piles grew big; even Drake and Kitty – the relative outsiders – had a fair haul.

'There's one more present in the closet, buddy,' Adam told him.

'Really? Who's it from?' Jonas stood up, excitement lighting up his eyes. Before any of them could answer he was in the hallway, heading for the closet. Kitty jumped up and followed him, Adam close behind, neither of them remembering to close the door. The next moment Jonas opened the closet, and was all but bowled over by an overexcited, frightened dog.

The puppy started barking and running, darting this way and that, not knowing where he was in this strange place. Every time one of them tried to catch him, he slipped out of their grasp, as elusive as the Scarlet Pimpernel. First he ran into the living room, then seeing all the people there, came straight out, heading for the kitchen. His excited growls echoed through the hallway, and he dodged around Adam's legs, slipping his way across the tiled floor. The aroma of turkey drove him crazy, as he careered straight for the stove in the corner, skidding to a halt just before he hit the glass door.

'Get that mutt out of here,' Annie hollered. 'I'm trying to cook.' Jonas chased after him, laughing loudly, closely followed by Adam and Kitty. Getting bored with the game, the dog then headed for the hall once again, this time making his way to the door at the far end.

He reached the library before any of them could stop him, nudging his wet nose into the gap where the door wasn't fully shut. Then he was in the room, racing around in circles, knocking over furniture as the three of them chased after him.

Jonas was still giggling, shouting at the dog to slow down, while Kitty followed him, trying to block his exit. She couldn't help but snigger at the spectacle of a puppy outwitting the three of them, and turned to Adam to see his expression.

'He loves it,' she told him, her voice breathless. 'I haven't seen him so excited in ages.' Jonas was still darting around the library, going this way and that. Then the puppy jumped up on the oak table, his paws skidding on all the papers fanned out there. He reached the edge of the table, peering down with wide, brown eyes, just as Jonas caught up with him.

'Got him!' he announced joyfully. 'Now come here, you bad boy.' He lifted the puppy easily, laughing as his tail wagged like crazy.

Adam reached out to rub the puppy's head. 'I'm going to miss that old mutt,' he said quietly. Kitty smiled and reached out to squeeze his hand. She wanted to do more, but was aware of Jonas watching them.

Why did it feel as though everybody was watching them today?

The next two hours flew by, as Jonas spent hours trying to teach the puppy to fetch. All his other toys were ignored as he patiently spoke to the tiny animal, rolling a ball back and forth until he finally got it.

It took a lot of persuasion for him to leave the puppy tethered up in the hallway so they could all eat dinner in the dining room together. He was still protesting as Kitty helped him onto his seat, tucking his napkin into his smart blue shirt. Then the rest of the family arrived, the room filled with the noise of people talking, Kitty helping Annie bring the pots of food in, laying them out down the middle of the table.

She was helping Jonas fill his plate with turkey when he turned to his father to ask a question. 'Dad, are you friends with Uncle Adam now?'

Kitty passed the plate of turkey meat to Drake, who was sitting next to her. She couldn't quite bring herself to look at any of the Klein men. A feeling of awkwardness descended over the table.

'Well, ah, sort of, I guess.'

But that wasn't good enough for Jonas. He had the bit between his teeth now. 'Uncle Adam, do you like my daddy?'

Next to her, Drake shifted uncomfortably in his seat.

Mia cleared her throat. 'Maybe we should say grace,' she suggested, shooting an awkward glance at Jonas.

'Why don't you ask them later,' Kitty whispered to him. 'After we've had dinner?'

'But they're making a movie together, so they must be friends,' Jonas told her.

Drake cleared his throat, and Kitty turned to look at him. He was deliberately staring down at his meal. She couldn't bring herself to look at Adam, not at Everett either, not when she knew exactly what Jonas was talking about.

'We should hold hands,' Mia said, her voice higher than usual. 'For the grace.'

Kitty felt frozen to the spot. It was as though everything in the room was suspended in time. Nobody was moving, nobody was eating.

'We're not making a movie together,' Adam said, his voice rough. Looking down, Kitty could see her hands starting to shake.

'Yes you are. I saw Daddy's script. It had your name on it.'

'Jonas, you need to be quiet now.' Everett's voice boomed out. 'Your mother's right, we should say grace.'

'What script?' Adam's voice was dangerously low.

'Jonas,' Mia pleaded. 'Hold Kitty's hand now.'

Jonas slid his small hand in hers. His lip was trembling. He knew he'd said something wrong, but the poor kid had no idea why.

'What script?' Adam asked again. Jonas's grip on her hand tightened.

Mia took a deep breath. 'Dear Lord, we thank you for this day—'

'What. Fucking. Script?' Adam pushed himself up to

281

standing, his sudden movement making all the dishes on the table rattle. Kitty looked at Everett, who had stood up, too, watching the two brothers as they stared angrily at each other.

'Sit down,' Everett barked. 'We'll discuss this after dinner.'

'No.' Adam shook his head. 'You need to tell me about this script with my name on, before I shake the truth out of you.'

'Adam,' his father barked out. 'Your mother's here. Take this outside please.' Mary Klein was watching her two sons, her hand covering her mouth.

'Are you still making that movie?' Adam asked Everett, ignoring his father completely. She'd never seen him look so angry before.

'It's only in pre-production,' Everett protested. 'I tried to tell you about it. We're taking it in a whole new direc—'

The next moment Adam's fist was flying into his brother's face, and Everett staggered back, his head recoiling at the sudden punch. He lifted his hand to his nose, where a line of blood was already forming. He opened his mouth to say something, but then Adam was in front of him again, his hand curled into a fist.

'Adam!' Kitty cried out, scraping her chair as she jumped up. 'Stop it!' Jonas started to sob, throwing himself against Kitty. She wrapped her arms around him, stroking his soft hair.

Adam's hand froze in mid-air as he turned to look at her and Jonas. His eyes widened but the next moment, Everett lurched towards him, tackling his brother around the chest. The movement brought them both down, and as they fell, Everett reached out, trying, and failing, to steady himself on the tablecloth. The cloth slid across the polished table, pulling the dishes and the silverware with it, half of them landing on the floor with a resounding crash.

Kitty's heart was pounding. She turned to Drake, her

expression panicked. 'Can you take Jonas out of here?' she asked him. The kid shouldn't have to see this.

Drake nodded rapidly, looking as though he couldn't wait to escape. 'Sure, of course.'

As they left the room, Kitty ran towards the two brothers. Their father reached them at the same time, trying to pull them apart. 'Adam, please, stop this,' she begged. 'It's not worth it.' She grabbed his arm, holding tightly onto his bicep. 'Whatever happened between you, whatever happened in Colombia, it isn't worth it.'

Adam turned to look at her, the fury still on his face. 'Did you know about this movie too?'

She felt as though all the breath had been knocked out of her. Everett took advantage of Adam's inattention to slide out from under him, running to the back wall and putting space between them. Slowly, she released Adam's arm, allowing him to stand. She opened her mouth to say something.

But the words didn't come out.

'I was going to tell you,' she finally said. 'Tomorrow, I was going to tell you tomorrow.'

He looked disgusted. 'How long have you known?'

She bit her lip to swallow her sob. 'Not long. A few days. I'm so sorry.'

A mixture of confusion and anger formed on Adam's face. 'Did you know about this when you were at the cabin the other night?' he asked her. 'Did you know about it when you were in my bed? Did you know about it when I held you in my arms?'

'You're fucking my brother?' Everett asked. 'Jesus Christ, what the hell's going on around here?'

Everything was still for a moment. Nobody said a word. Kitty could hear the whistle of her blood as it rushed past her ears, her pulse beating a rapid tune. Everybody was looking at her. Adam, Everett, their parents. Even Mia. She turned to see Annie standing in the doorway, her mouth dropped open.

Adam shook his head, still staring at her with a furious look. Then he pushed his way past her, his shoulder moving her out of the way, stalking past Annie and into the hallway without saying a word.

'Adam!' Kitty shouted, turning on her heel to follow him out. By the time she made it to the hallway he was halfway out the door. She ran after him in her sweater and her slippers, out of the door and onto the porch, down the stairs and onto the snow-covered lawn. 'Adam, wait.'

'Leave me alone.' His strides were long and determined. 'I don't want to talk to you.'

'Adam, please, let me explain. I'm so sorry.' She had to run to catch up with him. The snow was gathering inside her slippers, the chill air wrapping its wintry fingers around her skin. It only took a moment for the shivers to wrack her body. She reached out for his arm, trying to slow him down, but he shrugged her off.

'Get off,' he told her. 'Go back to the house, I don't want you here.'

She stopped running, her feet sinking into the snow as she stood, watching him walk away. She wrapped her arms around her waist, trying to stop herself from shaking, but it was futile. As he walked to the treeline, she saw him become smaller and smaller, until his distant figure was swallowed up by the forest. And then she was alone, all alone, in a stranger's backyard, in a strange land, wondering what the hell she should do next.

29

If you have tears, prepare to shed them now

– Julius Caesar

Kitty walked through the open front door, her whole body shaking. Silently, she wiped away the tears falling down her cheeks. Everett and Mia were standing in the hallway, staring at her as she walked inside. Her feet were like ice, her sheepskin slippers sodden and cold. Even kicking them off did nothing to warm her skin.

'I should find Jonas,' she said, not able to meet their eyes.

'No you don't.' Everett put a hand on her shoulder, halting her escape. 'My parents have taken him upstairs. We need to talk.'

What a terrible thing for a child to witness, especially on Christmas Day. She wanted to talk to Jonas, tell him it wasn't his fault. That his uncle was angry, but he didn't mean it.

None of them did.

'We think you should leave, Kitty. I've asked Drake to pack your things. He should be down in a few minutes.' Mia was wringing her hands together, her eyes downcast.

'What?' Kitty was incredulous. 'You want me to leave now? But it's Christmas Day. Where will I go?'

'Drake will drive you to the airport. There's a flight back to LA today. You should just about make it.'

She opened her mouth to protest, but really, what was there to protest about? She messed everything up. She'd failed Adam, she'd failed Jonas, and she'd failed her boss. Nobody wanted her here, that much was clear.

'Can I at least say goodbye to Jonas?' she asked. Her voice felt as rough as sandpaper.

'I don't think that's wise. He's upset enough as it is, you don't want to make things worse.' Everett shook his head.

She thought of Adam, stalking back to his cabin, all alone. 'What about your brother? Who's going to tell him?'

'Adam's a big boy, he can look after himself. I'm more worried about Jonas,' Mia said. 'We trusted you, and you betrayed us.'

'I'm sorry . . .'

Everett sighed. 'If you're really sorry, you'll leave quietly and without a fuss.'

He was right, she knew he was. She might not have caused this, but her presence had somehow made it ten times worse. And upstairs a little boy was sobbing, because his Christmas was completely ruined.

His wasn't the only heart that was breaking, either.

'OK,' she agreed, 'I'll go. But please tell Jonas I said goodbye.'

'Very well.' Everett nodded his head. She had no idea if he would, or if he was just humouring her.

Drake came walking down the stairs, carrying her suitcases in either hand. 'Shall I take these straight out to the car?' He was asking Everett, not her.

Kitty felt her face heat up at the thought of Drake packing

286

her things. A mixture of embarrassment and indignation washed through her. She opened her mouth to say something and closed it again. She was already standing on precarious ground, she didn't dare make things worse.

'Yes, take the Escalade,' Everett agreed. 'You need to get a move on, the plane's due to leave in a few hours.'

Kitty followed Drake wordlessly out of the house, not bothering to look back or say anything. There really wasn't anything left to say, and even if there was, Everett didn't want to hear it. She was alone again, and on her way back to an empty apartment in a city without mercy.

Without the man who had filled her soul with hope.

She cried all the way to the highway. Drake drove stoically, trying to ignore her distress, but she could tell by his expression how uncomfortable he was. So she kept as quiet as she could, save for the occasional sob, which she covered with her hand. Her eyes were trained out of the window, at the slush-filled ditches to the side of the road. Covered with a layer of black exhaust soot, they were a testament to the supremacy of man over nature.

It took almost two hours to get within reach of Dulles Airport. Even on Christmas Day it was a hive of activity, cars screeching across lanes, red lights flashing on and off. Impatient, angry people forgetting that this was the day of goodwill to all men.

Kitty's phone rang as Drake steered right into the departures lane, and he glanced at her for the first time, his face a picture of pity. Was that what she had become? Somebody to be pitied?

Lucy's name flashed across the screen, and Kitty tried to

287

bite down the disappointment. There was only one name she really wanted to see, and as she didn't even have his phone number, and certainly never gave him hers, it was unlikely it would ever be Adam calling.

'Hello?'

'Happy Christmas, honey. Why aren't you on Skype? We were all waiting for you?'

In the midst of the craziness she'd forgotten about her family and their planned Christmas Skype. 'I can't call you right now.' She started to cry again. 'I'm in a mess.'

'What's happened?' Lucy sounded alarmed. 'Are you ill? Has someone hurt you?'

From the corner of her eye she could see Drake staring straight ahead, desperately trying not to listen to her call, but it was impossible for him not to hear every word she said.

'I've been fired.'

'What? On Christmas Day? What kind of arseholes would do that?'

'The kind of arseholes I work for.' She sobbed again, tears rolling down her cheeks and onto the phone. 'I'm on my way to Dulles airport.'

'Why are you going there?' Lucy sounded confused.

'I'm flying back home to LA.'

'*On Christmas Day?*' Lucy's bemusement was replaced by incredulity.

It sounded ridiculous, Kitty knew. Like some kind of gothic melodrama. What a mess.

'It looks that way.'

'But you'll be all alone for the holidays. That's awful.'

Kitty sniffed. 'I need to be alone,' she told her sister. 'I don't really want to talk to anybody right now.'

'What happened?' Lucy asked. 'Why did they fire you?'

'Can I tell you later?' Kitty asked. 'I'm in a car right now. I just want to go home, have a shower, and pour myself a big glass of wine.'

She really, really didn't want to talk to anybody right now, and she definitely didn't want to share the whole sordid story in front of Drake, no matter how interested he seemed at her conversation with her sister.

'OK,' Lucy agreed softly, her voice full of concern. 'But make sure you call me when you can. I'm worried about you.'

'You don't need to be.'

'I'm your big sister, of course I need to be.'

'I'll call you soon. Goodbye, Lucy.'

'Goodbye, sweetie, take care of yourself.'

Kitty slid her thumb across the screen to end the call, and rested her head on the cold glass window beside her as Drake pulled the car into the drop-off lane.

So that was that then, the end of her time here, the end of Christmas, and the end of her and Adam.

If only she could end the pain squeezing around her broken heart.

30

Give sorrow words: the grief that does not speak
whispers the o'er-fraught heart, and bids it break

– Macbeth

Everywhere he looked there were reminders of her. The box by the fireplace where they'd first put the puppy, a cardigan she'd left behind on the back of a dining chair. A glass, still lipstick-stained, that he couldn't even bring himself to touch. He was afraid he'd squeeze it hard enough to break it.

The way his own heart had shattered.

He couldn't even face going into his bedroom. He'd tried, but the door only opened a crack before he could smell her fragrance – a sweet floral scent that made his stomach clench – and he'd slammed the door firmly shut.

Jesus, what was he supposed to do with himself? He paced up and down the small room, his body as tense as a caged animal, his hands fisted tight. He stopped by the fireplace again, closing his eyes for a moment, remembering the way she'd looked at him as he'd told her he didn't want her. Her eyes were watery, reflecting the green of the forest behind him, and her lip trembled until she stilled it with her teeth.

And then he got to thinking about the meal. The way everybody knew apart from him. The way they all hid the truth from him as though he didn't matter. The way she'd sided with his brother when he needed her the most.

He was going to be sick. He ran to the bathroom, kneeling in front of the toilet, but nothing came out. Just a dry retch that made his guts ache the same way his heart did. He lay there for a while, his cheek pressed against the cool floor tiles, before he finally stood and cleaned his mouth and his face. His reflection stared back at him – dark eyes rimmed with red, mouth twisted into a scowl – and he barely recognised himself.

Every now and again he'd look out of the window, his eyes scanning the treeline to see if anybody was coming. Did he want her to come? Hell no. Was he disappointed she didn't? Damn right he was.

He wanted to give her another piece of his mind. Tell her that her lies had cut him like a knife, only he didn't think these wounds would heal. No, that was wrong. He wanted to show her that she didn't affect him at all. That she was just a convenient piece of ass, almost hand delivered to him for Christmas.

If only that were true.

Later, after a run that did nothing to calm his brain, he collapsed in front of the fireplace, ignoring the way even the rug smelled of her. He closed his eyes for a moment, breathing only through his mouth, and before he knew it, he'd drifted into a restless sleep. One that made him sweat like crazy and yet still wake up freezing. One that gave him no peace at all.

He wasn't sure he'd ever find it again.

It was as though the whole of LA had decided to shut up shop for Christmas. As the taxi made its way through the city streets, past the lit-up houses and the closed-up shops, she was surprised at how empty the normally blocked roads were. For the first time ever, her journey from the airport to her home took less than half an hour. Just when she'd be happy for the distraction to continue, the cab pulled up at her Melrose apartment.

She paid the driver and pulled her cases up to the front door, tapping her electronic key against the pad to let herself in. She checked their small metal mailbox before calling for the elevator – taking out the pile of mail that had accumulated during their absence.

Her room-mates had gone home for the holidays. When she let herself inside, the place smelled a little stale, as though the air had stayed still for too long.

Flicking on a light, she dragged her cases into the living area – a small space only just big enough to fit a single sofa inside. Taking the pile of letters in her hand she sat down heavily on the cushions, letting her head fall back onto the sofa for a moment.

What a day. No, what a month. The last time she'd been in here was just before she left for West Virginia, her mind full of showreels and assignments, not to mention that internship she still hadn't got. Speaking of which, a quick sort through the letters revealed another two rejection notes. Way to make her day even worse than it already was.

Not that it could really get much worse. In the history of bad Christmases, this had quickly found its way to the top, eclipsing even the first Christmas Day after her mother had died. At least then she'd been surrounded by family – celebrating the day with her sisters and their father.

Today she was completely and absolutely alone.

And it hurt like hell.

She couldn't let herself think about him. If she did, she

knew the tears would start to fall, and if they started, she wasn't sure they'd ever stop. She only had to remember the way he'd looked at her just before he turned and made his way back towards the forest to want to cry all over again. He'd stared at her as though she'd stabbed him through the heart with the sharpest of knives.

Maybe she had.

She couldn't blame him for walking away. She'd betrayed him in the worst kind of way. She'd told herself she was lying to him for his own good, that she'd give him the gift of Christmas Day with his family before telling him about the movie script she'd seen.

But the fact was, it was herself she was protecting. In the end it had taken a seven-year-old boy to do what she couldn't – to tell Adam the truth about Everett's plans.

She was so ashamed.

Later, when it felt as though the rest of the world must be sound asleep, Kitty found herself firing up her laptop and typing in his name. So much for not thinking about him. She watched as the search results filled the page, clicking on a link to a video interview with him.

And there he was, in full, glorious detail, the man she'd fallen for, the man she'd hurt. He looked so very different, and yet familiar. In the frozen frame he was beardless, his hair styled in an easy mop, his eyes crinkled the way they did when he smiled.

Damn, she missed his smile.

Even though she knew it was masochistic, she moved the cursor with her mouse, clicking play on the video. It came on to full screen, with Adam sitting cross-legged in a chair, answering the questions posed to him by the interviewer.

'Did you always want to make documentaries?'

Adam smiled. 'No, it was something I fell into. I started off studying to become a director. My brother and I had this plan that we were going to be some kind of major force in the film world, with him producing movies and me directing them. But I guess the Coen brothers have nothing to be worried about any more.' He gave an easy laugh.

From the notes on the video, this interview was at least two years old. She couldn't tell how old he was here. But his reference to his brother told her that it was made when the two of them were still at least on good terms with each other.

'So you decided not to become a film director. How did that come about?'

'I was given an assignment at school. We had to make a ten-minute documentary on a controversial figure. I ended up choosing to interview Lance Beckford – who was on death row at the time. A few months later his appeal came up and he won. There was no direct link between the documentary and his appeal, but somehow I got a taste for the form.'

'Lance Beckford the LA Bomber?'

'Except he turned out not to be.' Adam winked. 'And from the moment I interviewed him I knew something was really wrong. He seemed innocent to me.'

'Is that what appealed to you about documentaries?' the interviewer asked. 'The ability to right wrongs.'

Adam shook his head. 'No, it was more elemental than that. I love the way the form gives you the ability to find the pure unadulterated truth. In a world full of lies, it's important to be able to cut through the bullshit. That's what appealed to me about it.'

Kitty clicked on the pause button, closing her eyes before

the tears started to fall. It hurt way too much to watch him any more. Even hearing his voice made her heart ache.

In a world full of lies, it's important to be able to cut through the bullshit. He'd certainly managed to cut through hers today. He must hate her for not telling him the truth straight away. For persuading herself that a family Christmas was more important than telling him what she'd found.

God knew, she was starting to hate herself.

31

The fool doth think he is wise, but the wise man
knows himself to be a fool

– As You Like It

'So I guess I shouldn't bother asking if you had a good Christmas then?' Martin gave him a wry look.

Adam's smile died on his lips before it even made it out of the gate. Even after two days it was impossible to find anything funny about it. 'Yeah. Don't bother.'

Martin looked him over, a worried expression forming on his face. 'I'm glad you called.'

'I wasn't sure if you'd answer,' Adam said. He didn't bother telling Martin he'd been his last hope. Two days of pacing and running and trying not to pull his cabin apart were testament to that. But that wasn't the worst part. It was the ache in his chest that refused to go away. The desperation he felt every time he smelled her scent. The way he kept looking up at the big house whenever he ran past, somehow hoping she'd see him.

And still not having the balls to go in to see her.

'And is your brother pressing charges this time?' Martin asked, referring to Adam's fight with Everett. He hadn't looked

296

best pleased as Adam had described their confrontation – not that his reaction was very surprising. They'd been working on controlling Adam's anger for months, and the first time he was riled, he'd given in to it again.

'Not as far as I know. The police haven't been down to see me.'

'So that's that then?' Martin asked. 'It's all over, and everything's back to normal?'

'I guess.' Adam's stomach lurched. If this was normal, he hated it. Hated the silence in his cabin. Hated the way everything felt so empty. He felt constantly on edge without her.

Jesus Christ, he missed everything about her. And it didn't seem to be getting any better.

'Why haven't you gone back to the house yet?'

Adam's mouth tasted of regret. 'I can't face them,' he said. 'I ruined everything. I messed Christmas up.' He couldn't help but think of Jonas's expression, his mother's tears, the way his father had been so disappointed. 'They don't want me there.'

'How do you know?'

'Because they haven't come down to see me.' Adam started to pull at a loose thread on the chair arm.

'Maybe they're giving you some space. You're the one who walked out and told them to leave you alone,' Martin pointed out. 'Perhaps they're feeling exactly the way you are. The fact Everett hasn't called the cops seems like a good thing, doesn't it?'

Adam shrugged. 'Maybe.'

Martin was silent for a moment, though he continued to look at Adam. There was a soft wind outside, rattling the office windows. 'Do you miss them?' he finally asked.

Adam closed his eyes, feeling his chest ache again. It was becoming so familiar to him. 'Yeah, I do.' Well some of them anyway. Especially the girl who lit the cabin up whenever she walked into it. He missed her so much it was painful.

'Maybe you should go see them.'

'Maybe.'

Sensing a dead end to the conversation, Martin changed tack. 'Are you going to involve your lawyers this time?' he asked. 'To stop the movie?'

Adam waited for the familiar anger to take hold of him at the mention of Everett's plans. But there was nothing. 'I couldn't give a shit about the movie.' Not quite true, but compared to everything else that had happened it had paled into insignificance.

Compared to her.

'And have you heard from the girl?' Martin asked. Could he read Adam's mind on top of everything else?

'From Kitty? Not a peep. Not that I expected to.'

Martin crossed his legs, tapping his pen against his lip. 'Why not?'

'Why would she want to hear from me?' Adam was perplexed. 'She saw me lose it in front of all my family. She saw what I was capable of.' He couldn't forget the expression on her face when she saw Everett's nose bleeding. She looked disgusted.

'And yet she still followed you out of the house, and tried to talk to you. Does that sound like the act of somebody who didn't want to talk to you?'

'I think she felt guilty,' Adam admitted. 'That it was her fault I went crazy. She was just trying to make amends.' And he'd shaken her off like an annoying animal, never looking back at her as he almost ran back to the sanctuary of his cabin.

'Why would she think it was her fault?'

'Because she knew all about the movie.' Adam's stomach contracted just thinking about it. He took a mouthful of ice-cold water, but it did nothing to quell the ache in his gut.

'She knew about it?' Martin finally looked surprised. 'Was she in on it like Lisa was?'

Placing the glass back down on the table beside him, Adam blew out a long mouthful of air. He hadn't thought about Lisa for weeks. She'd been his assistant in Colombia, a friend with benefits, no more than that. And yet when she'd agreed to work on the movie with Everett it had felt like a betrayal.

But compared to Kitty, it was nothing. Absolutely nothing.

'I've no idea,' Adam said. But he couldn't really believe it, in spite of the things he'd shouted. She was too kind, too open for that kind of subterfuge.

'You didn't ask her?'

Adam shook his head, trying to remember everything they said. The scene in the dining room felt like a half-forgotten dream. He could remember small sequences of events, but nothing quite clicked together. His head was doing a pretty damn good job of suppressing the bad memories. 'She said something about knowing for a few days, but that was it. I didn't let her say anything else, I was too furious with her.'

'It sounds as though you may be more angry at her than you are at Everett,' Martin reflected. 'Why do you think that is?'

'I'm not angry with her. I'm more angry at myself.'

'Then what is it you're feeling?'

If it didn't hurt so much, Adam would have laughed at the question. What was he feeling? It was almost impossible to explain. It was as though his body had been pumped full of

299

so many emotions he wasn't sure which was which any more. Anger morphed into sadness, which quickly gave way to a sense of futility. And the pain, God the pain, it was almost too much to think about.

'Hurt,' he finally said, his voice quiet. 'I feel so hurt. And I miss her.' Christ, he really did.

'You hurt because you miss her?' Martin tried to clarify.

Adam leaned forward, his expression intent. 'No, not just because I miss her. I hurt because I hurt her, too. Because I pushed her away, I didn't give her a chance to tell me anything. I hurt because I'm not just the victim here, I'm the villain, too. And I hate myself for it.'

'Isn't that what we all are?' Martin asked, his voice sympathetic. 'The victims and villains of our own lives? We have to come to terms with the good and bad inside of us, accept that we'll never be all one or the other. And if we acknowledge we have a bit of Beast as well as Beauty in there, maybe we can find a way for them both to live together.'

Adam frowned. 'Did you just use a fairy-tale analogy on me?' His lip twitched. He wanted to laugh but it seemed so damned inappropriate.

'I might have.'

'Jesus, you know how to hit a man when he's down.'

This time Martin was the one to laugh. 'I'm trying to make an important point here. The fact is we have to learn to live with the good and bad parts of ourselves, and that brings a certain peace to our lives. The panic and the anger and the destructiveness comes from when we try to fight against ourselves, where we try to cling on to a modicum of control when there really isn't any there. Acceptance, it's the key to everything.'

Adam listened to his words, absorbed them, even saw the

sense in them. 'So what should I do about Kitty? Do you think I should call her, apologise?'

Martin grinned. 'I'm an anger-management therapist, not your girlfriend. This one's all yours to figure out, my friend.'

When Adam pulled his truck into the driveway at the big house, Jonas was sitting on the doorstep, throwing a ball for the puppy. Every time the dog brought the ball back, Jonas petted him, making a fuss of him before throwing it again. Adam climbed out of the cab and stood back for a while, watching his nephew, taking in the dejected slant of his shoulders.

'Hey.' He sat on the step next to Jonas. 'Did you give the dog a name?'

Jonas shrugged morosely. 'Does it matter?'

Adam gently nudged him, shoulder to shoulder. 'Of course it matters. Would you like to have no name? Names mean somebody loves you, that you belong. That when somebody calls you they want you.'

'Clarence. That's his name.'

The dog's ears perked up.

'After the angel? The one in *It's a Wonderful Life*?' Adam asked.

Jonas nodded, then threw the ball again.

'That's a great name.' Adam clapped his hand on his nephew's shoulder. 'Clarence. A strong name, it's perfect.'

The dog trotted over, the ball still in his mouth. As soon as he reached Jonas he let go of it, waiting expectantly until the boy picked it up and threw it again. Adam's heart ached when he saw how half-hearted his nephew's movements were.

'It's been a bad few days, huh?' he said.

Another shrug. 'I guess.'

301

'Well I'm sorry for my part in it. I shouldn't have shouted and I certainly shouldn't have hurt your dad the way I did. I'd like to make it up to you if I can.'

'How?'

Adam tipped his head to the side, looking at the boy. 'Any way you like, you name the price. We can go sledding, we can go out somewhere on the Skidoo. I'll watch any movie you want. What do you say?'

For some reason the kid's face fell. 'Oh.'

'What is it?' Adam leaned in closer. He may not have been the most intuitive man in the world, but there was something bugging Jonas so bad he could barely meet his eye. 'Was it something I said?'

Jonas shook his head. 'I thought you might bring her back.'

Adam was confused. 'Who?'

'Kitty.'

His stomach did a flip-flop. 'What do you mean, bring her back? She's here, isn't she?'

For some reason Adam's hands started to shake. Of course she was inside, where else would she be? Even if he couldn't face talking to her right then, part of him still wanted to know she was OK.

'She's not here,' Jonas said quietly. 'She left two days ago. Dad said she was going home.'

'To LA?'

'I guess. Drake drove her to the airport. They didn't let me say goodbye.'

Adam stood up abruptly, his mouth suddenly dry.

'Is your dad in the house?'

Jonas's eyes went wide. 'In the library, I think. Are you going to hit him again?'

302

Adam shook his head. 'I shouldn't have done that, and no, I'm not going to do it again. I just want to talk to him. To say sorry.'

He almost surprised himself. He was going to apologise? What else was going on in the bottom of his mind?

'Will you ask him to bring Kitty back?' Jonas suddenly looked hopeful.

'I can't do that.' He hated disappointing his nephew. 'But she's going to be OK, and so are you.'

He ruffled his nephew's hair and walked up the steps to the front door, pushing it open and walking inside. The house was silent, making the sound of his boots against the wooden floor seem louder than ever. He looked around the hallway, taking in the decorations hanging desolately from the staircase, the tree lights not even turned on. Shaking his head, he headed for the library, rapping lightly on the door to alert them to his presence. Drake opened it, his eyes wide as he took Adam in. 'Oh, it's you.'

'Who is it?' That was Everett, his voice as loud as ever.

'Ah, it's your brother,' Drake said, looking behind him.

The next moment Everett was wrenching the door wide open. 'You can leave us for a minute,' he said to Drake. The assistant almost ran up the hall to the kitchen, as though afraid he was going to get caught up in the violence.

'You want to come in?' Everett asked.

'Sure.' Adam followed his brother into the library, closing the door behind him. In the corner, on the main table, he could see pages of a script. His stomach lurched at the sight.

'Where's Mia?' he asked, as much to fill the silence as anything else.

'She's gone to DC again.' Everett looked down at his hands.

'We've been having a few problems. She has a therapist there.' Finally he looked up again. 'She wants us to get a divorce.'

It was like being slapped around the face with a plank. 'The therapist?' Adam asked.

'No, Mia.'

'Jesus, I'm sorry.' He really was. In spite of everything he still loved his brother. Even if that emotion was buried very deep, beneath all the bullshit he'd caused.

'Yeah, well, things haven't been great for a while. I just worry about Jonas, you know?'

Adam nodded. 'Yeah, that poor kid's been through enough.'

'We both knew this trip was going to be kill or cure. I guess I was hoping to give him a final Christmas with all his family. One he could remember for the rest of his life.' Everett's laugh was humourless. 'We all managed to mess that one up, too.'

'There are more Christmases,' Adam said, not certain why he felt the need to reassure him. 'And family is what you make it.'

He leaned against the chair, rubbing his face with the heel of his hand. When he pulled it away, it took a moment to regain his focus. 'Look, I'm sorry for hitting you. Especially in front of your son. It was wrong and I shouldn't have done it.'

Everett's mouth fell open. Whatever he was expecting, an apology wasn't it. 'You're sorry?'

'Yeah.' Adam could feel his back stiffen. It wasn't quite giving him the relief he'd expected.

'OK.' Everett slowly nodded his head. 'OK. I kind of understand why you did it.'

'You do?' It was Adam's turn to be surprised.

'I'm not happy you did it. God knows I tried to talk to you so many times over the past couple of weeks. To explain what was going on. But every time I opened my mouth you shot me down.'

'Because you betrayed me,' Adam pointed out, trying to swallow down the anger. 'Because you wanted to tell my story and put people in danger on the way. Not to mention the fact you called the cops on me.'

Everett sighed, scratching the back of his neck. 'Look, will you let me explain?' He pointed to the easy chairs by the window. 'Sit down, let's talk. Finally.'

Adam stared at the chairs for a moment, weighing up the options. Was he ready to listen to his brother without resorting to his fists once again? Yeah, he thought he probably was. And maybe if he listened, he might find out more about Kitty, why she left, where she was, if she ever wanted to see him again.

'OK,' he said, clearing the distance to the chairs, as Everett picked the script up from the library table. 'Let's talk.'

'Happy New Year, darling.' Cesca engulfed Kitty in a hug. Her voice was loud enough to silence the coffee drinkers around them. 'How are you doing?' she asked, releasing her. 'I bought us both a latte, I hope that's OK. You haven't gone all vegan or anything on me again, have you?'

'Nope, milk is all good.' Kitty sat down opposite her sister, lifting the cup to her lips, not bothering to point out it was already January. 'I swear you'll never let me forget that year I became a vegetarian.'

'How could we let you forget?' Cesca teased. 'I came down to the kitchen at midnight and saw you stuffing five chipolatas into your mouth. Some vegetarian you turned out to be.'

'It was your fault for leaving them out there,' Kitty

protested. 'It was cruel, like leaving an open bottle of vodka in front of an alcoholic.'

'Well I'm glad that particular phase only lasted a few months.' Cesca looked her up and down. 'Not that you look like you've been eating much of anything for a bit. How much weight have you lost?'

Kitty shrugged. 'I don't know. I'm not on a diet or anything.' As if to emphasise her point, she took another sip of her full-fat latte. 'I'm just not very hungry.'

'No wonder, after everything you've been through. You should have seen us all on Christmas Day, we were fuming. Lucy and I spent most of the night trying to dream up ways of getting even with that horrible family. I can't believe they sent you away, the bastards.'

Kitty sniffed. 'It was my fault,' she said quietly. 'I got involved in things I shouldn't have.'

'You mean you got involved with a guy you shouldn't have?' Cesca corrected, rolling her eyes. 'I've made Sam promise never to make a movie with any of those arsehole Kleins. I don't know who they think they are, treating you like that.'

Kitty opened her mouth to protest that Adam wasn't an arsehole, but really, what was the point? It didn't matter if he was an arsehole or an angel, he wasn't here and he didn't want her.

'I wish you'd flown back to London instead of coming here on Christmas Day,' Cesca continued. 'We tried Skypeing you and you didn't answer. Lucy was all for flying over and dragging you back home.'

Kitty shook her head, her mouth feeling dry in spite of the coffee. 'I wanted to be alone. So much had been going on, I needed a bit of silence to get my head straight.'

Cesca leaned her head to the side. 'And is it straight now?'

'Not really,' Kitty confessed. 'But it's a little straighter than it was. I even managed to get a couple of assignments finished.'

When she wasn't watching YouTube clips of Adam over and over again, she'd been holed up in the Young Research Library, or in the editing suite at school. Her enforced solitude may have been bad in some respects, but academically, it had been a huge step forward.

'And what are your plans now?' Cesca asked. They were both aware that Kitty's future depended on an internship with a production company. And she'd all but shot that hope out of the water.

'I've absolutely no idea,' Kitty admitted. She hadn't let herself think about that too much. She'd been too focused on getting through the day to consider the future. 'I guess if I don't get anything I'll have to go home to London.' She shook her head at that thought. It felt like defeat, having to fly back to a city she'd left behind with such high hopes. To return with her tail between her legs, and not much more than she left with – unless you counted a post-grad degree that had cost her more money than she cared to think about.

The door to the café opened up, letting in a fresh draught of warm air. The room went suddenly silent. Cesca turned around to see who it was, her face lighting up with recognition. 'Sam, we're over here.'

He walked over, pointedly ignoring the chattering girls and phone-camera-pointing women who were all following his progress. And no wonder, with his dark, Italian good looks, and movie-star presence, he drew eyes wherever he went. Kitty felt herself get embarrassed for Sam – she knew how much he hated the constant attention. If it was her, she'd probably

307

become a hermit, hide away from it all. She had to give him credit for braving the inside of the café.

'Happy New Year.' He leaned down to give Kitty a kiss on the cheek, before kissing Cesca's lips and ruffling her hair. 'Have I missed anything?'

'Not really, unless you're keen on tales of woe,' Kitty told him.

'I love tales of woe, especially when I'm not involved in them.' Sam shot her a smile. 'So what gives? Have you heard from this douchebag or what?'

'Sam!' Cesca tapped him on the arm. 'You can't call the man she loves a douchebag.'

'Hey, who said anything about a man I love,' Kitty protested. 'I didn't say I loved him.'

'Well, you're certainly not indifferent to him,' Cesca told her. 'You've lost, what, eight or nine pounds in a week. You're moping around as though the world's about to end. And you've started to talk about moving back to London when we all know you've always dreamed of living here in LA.'

'Sounds like somebody else I know,' Sam said. 'Didn't you fly back to London and mope after we fell out?'

'Yeah, but I had every right to,' Cesca said, her voice playful. 'You really were an asshole.'

'An asshole you were in love with,' Sam corrected.

'Yeah, and that just proves my point.' Cesca looked back at Kitty. 'You don't react this way about someone who just sparks a bit of interest. I should know. Remember how I told you it was all over and he meant nothing to me?'

'Lies, all lies.' Sam smiled, a dimple forming in his cheek. 'We all know it was love at first sight for you, babe.'

'I don't think so. More like hate at first sight.'

He slung his arm casually across the back of Cesca's chair. Everybody was still staring at him. 'There's a thin line between hate and love.'

'Yep,' Cesca agreed. 'And I think Kitty and Adam crossed it a long time ago.' She caught Sam's gaze, the two of them smiling at each other. The warmth between them made Kitty's heart ache.

'I am here, by the way,' Kitty said, 'before you two go all lovey-dovey and forget about me.'

'We wouldn't forget about you.' Cesca turned to look at her. 'Now let's get back to this internship. Are you still waiting on any replies?'

Kitty thought back to the ever-growing pile of rejection letters. She'd added another two this morning. 'A couple,' she said, 'but I'm not holding my hopes up.'

'Then you'll have to let Sam help you.'

Sam nodded encouragingly. He was pretty much at the height of his fame – a word in the right ear could secure her a position in a second.

But no. She didn't want that at all.

'I want to make it on my own merit,' Kitty told them. 'Not because Sam puts in a good word, or knows somebody who knows somebody. I want to be employed because I'm good enough.'

'You *are* good enough,' Cesca said gently. 'But sometimes you need a helping hand.'

Kitty looked at them both for a moment, taking them in. Her beautiful, talented sister, and the gorgeous man she was in love with. They were like a fairy-tale couple, no wonder they were constantly followed by the paparazzi. A photograph of the two of them together was a sure-fire seller for the gossip rags.

'You're both very lovely,' she began, screwing her face up to find the right words, 'and it's wonderful to know that you've got my back. But this is my mess and it's my life, and I want to be the one to clear it up. I'll go and see my supervisor on Monday and ask him for his help in finding an internship. OK?'

'Are you sure?' Cesca asked. She looked desperate to help.

Kitty nodded, feeling more resolute than she had in a long time. 'I'm sure,' she told her, a tentative smile creeping across her face. 'Try not to worry about me. I've got this.'

And maybe if she said it enough, she might even start to believe it.

32

True hope is swift, and flies with swallow's wings

– Richard III

'This is good. Really good.' Her supervisor paused the video and turned around in his swivel chair to look at her. 'The edits made a huge difference – did you document what you did in the project report?'

Kitty lifted the file that was sitting on her lap. 'It's all in here.' It had been drummed into them from the beginning that the report was as important as the reel itself. They had to journal every part of the process – from turning the idea into a script, to finalising the finished product. 'I finished writing it all up on Friday,' she told him. 'It's ready to go now.'

'You didn't take much of a break over the holidays,' he pointed out. 'Did you stay in LA?'

'For some of the time,' she said, not wanting to get into things with him. She'd played the past weeks over in her head again and again. It was as familiar to her as her showreel. Scenes of her running in the snow to Adam's house, of her reading the script with his name on. Sometimes, when she was feeling particularly down, she'd try to change the ending. Imaginary

Kitty would tell imaginary Adam about Everett's plans straight away. But after that, there was always a blankness. She had no idea how that would have turned out.

'Did you hear back from any of your interviews?' he asked her, looking up from the desk. 'You had that one at Klein Productions, right?'

Damn, she'd forgotten she'd told him about that. Every time she heard that name, it made her heart pound like a bass drum. 'Yeah, that's a no go,' she said. 'I heard back last week.'

It wasn't a lie, she told herself.

'Damn.' He shook his head then gave a sigh. 'I was sure you'd get an internship by now. You're one of my best students. Maybe we should take a look at your resumé again, make sure it's hitting the right buttons. Or should we work on your interview technique? What are your thoughts?'

Kitty licked her dry lips. It all felt like too little too late, but what other choice did she have? She'd tried the sitting-in-her-apartment-crying option, and look how that worked out for her.

'That would be good.' She nodded. 'But just in case, I'm thinking of applying to some production companies in London,' she told him. 'I might have more luck over there.'

He frowned. 'I thought you wanted to stay in LA? I remember when you first arrived you were so excited to be in Hollywood. What's changed?'

There was a noise from outside the door as a group of students walked past, talking loudly about something. Her supervisor checked his watch for the time.

'I'm just trying to be realistic,' Kitty said. 'Maybe I'm not meant to work over here. Maybe my skills are better served in London.'

'No, that's not true. You're trying to settle, and that sucks.

Don't stop dreaming, Kitty, and don't give up. This isn't over until you decide it is.'

The problem was, she'd already made her decision.

'Just sit on it for a while,' he suggested. 'There are a couple of people I want to talk to before you give up completely. I think you could do really well over here.' He checked his watch again, muttering under his breath. 'Damn, we need to get to the lecture theatre. I'm supposed to introduce our guest speaker.' He got up from his chair, closing his laptop and sliding it in his desk drawer. 'We'll talk about this later, OK?'

'Sure.'

The lecture theatre was almost full by the time she arrived – surprising for the first week back at school. She said hello to a few people as she walked up the stairs, heading for her preferred seat at the back of the room, sliding into a chair next to a small brunette she knew from a post-production class she'd taken earlier in the year. She'd barely pulled her notepad out and put it on the desk when the lights above them dimmed, leaving the only illumination on the podium at the front of the room.

'Happy New Year, everybody, and thanks for arriving so promptly.'

Kitty couldn't help smiling at the irony of her supervisor's words.

'Today we've a small change in our lecture schedule. Rather than the advertised lecture on changes to the distribution network, we're going to be discussing documentary production, and how to find the truth in lies.'

Oh great, just what she needed. School was supposed to be the one place she could come and not think about Adam – and now they were going to be discussing his niche subject. Well played, UCLA.

'And though our guest speaker needs no introduction, I'm going to give him one anyway. He's an alumnus of this film school, and since graduation has gone on to make reflective and insightful documentaries showing the human side of issues such as domestic terrorism, the modern slave trade, and more recently, drug trafficking. His documentaries have twice been nominated for the Academy Award for Best Documentary Feature, and in 2013 he won the Critics Choice Award for the documentary *Truth in Lies – Looking for the Real Michael Davies*. So please join with me to give a big welcome to Adam Klein.'

She was frozen to her chair as she watched him appear on the podium, his gait strong and easy as he walked up and shook hands with her supervisor. Even from this distance he looked so different than she remembered. Instead of the jeans and checked shirt she was used to seeing him in, he was wearing tailored trousers and a white cotton shirt, open at the neck to reveal his freshly shaven skin. The beard had gone completely, so had the messy, overgrown hair, and for a moment she found herself bereft at their absence.

It felt as though somebody had taken her Adam away, and replaced him with a doppelganger.

But then he began to speak.

'Good morning, everybody. I'm going to keep this as short as I can, so I don't send any of you back to sleep.' Laughter erupted around the theatre. 'I'm really pleased to be here today to be able to share a little about the documentary-making process, and to give you a few ideas of why I believe it's the truest, purest form of the film-making arts.'

He took a breath and pressed a clicker to bring the screen above him to life. 'Errol Morris – a friend of mine – once said that what interested him about documentary was the fact that at the onset we never know how the story ends. That's what makes it different to filming a scripted story. But for me it isn't the ending that matters, it's the process, it's finding the truth piece by piece, by pulling back the layers until the facts are finally exposed.'

The room around her was quiet, save for the soft breaths of a couple of hundred students. They stared raptly as Adam continued.

'The real focus of any documentary I make is the search for humanity. Not just in those who are affected, but by those who do the affecting, too. The one thing I've learned from my years in the medium is that criminals are humans, too. And they're fascinating, because they started out the same as you and me. They were born as little screaming, eating, shitting humans, who like the rest of us at that point in their lives, didn't understand right from wrong.'

His eyes scanned the crowd. Though Kitty couldn't see them, she could picture them in her memories. Deep and warm as melted chocolate. The sort of eyes she could drown in.

'It's easy to paint anybody as purely evil, but it's harder to look beyond that shell they've become to what made them that way. To say that maybe we, as a society, have a role to play in creating the beast that lives inside us all.' He scanned the audience again. Was he looking for her? What was he doing here? Her whole body felt as though it was buzzing, a few seconds away from detonation. Her pen was shaking in her hand.

'Anyway, enough of this talking. Let me show you a few clips to try and demonstrate what I'm trying to say.' He turned to the big screen behind him, clicking the remote in his hand to start up the stream of video.

For the next twenty-five minutes, Adam showed them clip after clip, talking through the background to the story, and the interviewee, showing how he delved deeper into their psyche to try to find reasons for their actions. It was mesmerising watching him on screen, but not as mesmerising as it was having him so close to her. He was less than fifty feet away, so close she could almost smell his warm, pine scent. She could almost feel the way he used to touch her, his hands strong yet soft, his eyes warm as she responded to him.

But why was he here?

He had to know she would be at this lecture. He knew she was a film student at UCLA, after all, what were the chances that this was a coincidence? And yet he was talking in front of all these students as if it was the easiest thing in the world. Laid-back, sure of himself, and as confident as hell.

The complete opposite of the way Kitty felt. She was so confused – trying to classify the emotions as they rushed through her veins, and failing miserably. Did he still hate her? Had he travelled all this way to make her pay for what she'd done to him? He didn't look angry though, he looked completely calm.

The minutes felt as though they stretched halfway into the next day, each second so thinly pulled it seemed to resonate throughout the room. Adam continued to talk, to point out the parts of his documentaries he was most proud of, and she couldn't help but find herself entranced by him.

Not that she was the only one. The girl next to her was practically drooling. Damn her.

Finally they made it to the question and answer part of the lecture. By this point Kitty wasn't sure if she was pleased it was almost over or not. Because what came next? Would he seek her out, ask to speak to her? Or – horror of horrors – would he leave without even acknowledging her existence?

A student in the front row asked the first question, nervously running his hands through his hair as he spoke into the microphone. 'Ah, in your talk you said something about needing to understand the beast in all of us to make documentaries. What did you mean by that?'

Adam smiled, leaning into the lectern at the front of the podium. 'I guess I meant that making documentaries has a lot in common with psychotherapy. And if you all stay in LA for much longer, you'll probably all discover that.'

Cue the laughter.

'For those of you lucky enough to avoid psychotherapy so far, I'll try to explain it. A lot of therapy is about accepting the good and bad in all of us. In understanding that nobody is a hero or a villain, but a mixture of both. What rises to the surface at any given time can depend on a variety of things – the circumstances surrounding us, our upbringing, how we react to certain triggers and stimuli. When I make a documentary I don't want you all to go away thinking what a bad man that guy was. I want you to go away wondering if you'd have done the same thing in his situation, if it's possible that this person who has caused death and destruction isn't that different to you and me.'

Finally his eyes stopped on her. She felt their warmth before she even caught his gaze, her cheeks pinking up at his scrutiny. She stared back at him, her face expressionless, waiting for him to respond.

But then somebody asked a question and the moment was broken. Adam answered them all easily, his smile casual as he talked about his experiences and the knowledge he'd gained

317

from them. She could tell from the quiet appreciation of her fellow students that they were impressed by him.

God knew, she was, too. She'd been impressed enough when he'd been Adam, the bearded guy who lived in the cabin by the lake. But now he was Adam Klein, the award-winning documentary maker, he took her breath away.

After a few more minutes of questions, the lecture finally came to an end, and the room was filled with the sound of students standing and gathering their things, and the music of their conversation. Kitty stayed in her seat for a moment, watching as the others filed out down the stairs and to the exit. She wondered if she should join them, maybe hide in the crowd. Would he even be looking for her?

Closing her eyes for a moment, she took in a deep lungful of air, trying to steel herself for what happened next. Then she opened them and slid her pen and notepad into her bag, slinging it on her shoulder as she stood to join the end of the line.

The progress was slow, as people stopped to talk to Adam, causing a back-up in those trying to leave the theatre. Finally she made it to the bottom step, and she was less than ten feet away from him, though those ten feet were filled with students trying to catch a moment with him.

It took him a moment to notice her. He was talking to a blonde girl who kept flipping her hair over her shoulder in a way that made Kitty want to cut it all off.

But then he lifted his gaze to hers, and everybody around them was forgotten. The noise surrounding her was drowned out by the sound of her pulse, drumming in her ears. He stared at her without embarrassment, his gaze softening. Her lips parted so she could take in a breathful of air, and his eyes lowered to look at her mouth.

Was he remembering the way he'd kissed her? His lips soft yet demanding, his hand cupping the side of her face? She ached to feel him touching her again.

She only realised she'd stopped moving when somebody jostled into her from behind, trying to push their way past to the exit. The movement launched her forward, until she was closer still to Adam, the two of them only separated by a few stragglers now.

She glanced around her, wondering what she should do next. Wait until they'd all left? Or go quietly, in case he really didn't want to see her again? But then he was walking towards her, and her feet were glued to the ground, impossible to move even if she wanted to. But she didn't. The last thing she wanted to do was run away from him, not when he'd been on her mind every day since the moment she'd left Mountain's Reach.

'Hi.' He stopped a few feet short of her, as if to give her space. A couple of students were staring at them with interest.

'Hi.' She attempted a smile. 'You shaved off your beard.' She had to clench her hands into fists to stop herself from reaching out and touching his cheek. She wondered how different it would feel, to have soft smooth skin brushing against her palm, rather than the rough hair she was so used to.

As if he could read her mind, he reached up to touch his own cheek. 'Yeah, I figured it was time to cut the barriers away and face the real world.'

'It suits you.' She rolled her bottom lip between her teeth. 'Though I kind of miss the rough look.'

'Do you two know each other?' Her supervisor joined them, oblivious to the heat flowing between their eyes. 'Adam, this is the student I was telling you about, the one who's still looking for an internship.'

Adam nodded, still looking at her. She didn't want him to stop. 'Sure,' he said. 'Maybe the two of us can discuss it over coffee?' he suggested to Kitty. She nodded, her eyes wide, still not able to form any useful words on her tongue.

'I can't join you, I'm afraid,' her supervisor told them. 'I have another lesson in a moment. But if you need any references, I'd happily supply one.'

Adam nodded, finally pulling his gaze from Kitty's. 'I'll let you know.' Then he turned back to her. 'Are you free now?' he asked her. 'Shall we grab a drink in the library café?'

'Sounds good.' Her voice, when it finally came out, was as rough as sandpaper. Holding her bag closely against her chest, her fingers holding tightly onto the leather, she followed him out of the lecture theatre.

33

Hear my soul speak: the very instant that I saw
you did my heart fly to your service

– The Tempest

If LA had different seasons, Adam would have sworn that spring was almost in the air. The weather was warm, even for the start of January, and the campus was full of students wearing jeans and T-shirts, with only the occasional jacket to be seen. The trees that lined their route to the library were verdant and leafy, casting dappled shadows on the footpath as the soft breeze made them dance.

There was a silence between them that didn't feel at all awkward. She was walking close enough for him to reach out and place his hand in the gentle dip of her back, his fingers spread out to feel the warmth of her beneath her T-shirt.

She didn't protest at this. He took it as a good sign.

It was strange being back on campus again. Hell, it was strange being back in LA again. His attorney had spoken to the LAPD to allow him back into the state, evidencing his regular attendance at therapy to show his commitment to change. And he had changed. He didn't feel like that angry guy any more. Didn't recognise the man who had trashed an office, didn't even recognise the guy who had hit his brother on Christmas Day. Maybe because then he didn't know what he had to lose.

The café was half empty when they walked inside. They bought their drinks – latte for Kitty and an Americano with room for him – and wandered over to a table in the corner, where Adam slid the tray onto the white plastic-coated table.

'You sure you don't want anything to eat?' he asked Kitty.

She shook her head. 'I'm not hungry.'

No, he wasn't either. Hadn't been for days. Strange how the body worked – the nutrition it so desperately needed had tasted like ashes in his mouth.

Then they were sitting opposite each other, and there was no more action to stand in the way of them talking. Adam stared at her for a moment. Here in LA she looked so much younger – she fitted in with the students that surrounded her in the lecture theatre. And yet there was a depth to her eyes that reminded him of who she was – and why he'd missed her so much. She wasn't the unopened notebook, her pages had already been written on.

'I'm so sorry,' she blurted out, her hands cupped around the Styrofoam mug. 'I should never have lied to you, and I know that's what it was. A lie. I thought I was protecting you, but really I was protecting myself.'

His mouth was dry. He licked his lips to be able to form the words. 'It wasn't you, it was me.' He wanted to laugh at the cliché, even though he saw little humour there. 'I was a dick. I didn't let you explain, I didn't let you even talk. I just assumed the worst and ran away.'

She lifted the cup to her mouth, her lips forming an 'o' as

she sipped from the hole in the lid. Her blue eyes gazed at him as she swallowed, as though she was thinking on his words.

'I don't blame you for reacting like that,' she said, putting the cup back on the table. 'I would have, too. You must have thought everybody was lying to you.' She frowned, pulling her gaze from his. 'I'm sorry that you're hurting.'

But she was hurting, too. He could see that. And not because of some script that really meant nothing right then, but because of the way he'd treated her. As though she was expendable.

'I want to tell you a little bit about Colombia. Is that OK?' He'd gone through this in his mind a hundred times, when he tried to imagine how he'd explain himself to her. In the end it seemed simple – start at the beginning. Documentary-making 101, right?

She looked up, her eyes wide. 'Really?' Then she nodded quickly, as though afraid he would change his mind. 'Of course, I'd be honoured to hear about it.'

He let out a mouthful of air. His chest felt tight, but not suffocatingly so. More of a reminder of a feeling he used to have. 'I'm not sure how much you know about the documentary I was making over there. I'd been researching it for years. I wanted to show the human side of drug trafficking, concentrating on the kids that are used every day to smuggle drugs into the US. Some of them younger than ten. That's how I started investigating the Garcia gang. It took a few months for us to find somebody who was ready to talk, but when we did, we knew we had a story.'

Kitty leaned her elbows on the table, resting her face in her palms. She was listening avidly, as though every word was pulling her in. 'Who did you talk to?'

'His name was Mat. Matias Hernandez.' Adam shook his head. 'He told us he was fifteen years old, though from the start he looked a little young for his age. It turned out he was actually twelve.'

Kitty looked shocked. 'Twelve?' she repeated.

He couldn't help but share her distaste. 'I didn't know, but I should have. Looking back, I was so pleased to finally find somebody who would talk that I didn't think about anything else. Didn't think about the fact he was a kid, didn't think about the fact talking to me would have repercussions. I was too busy looking for the truth to see the train wreck waiting to happen.'

She stirred her spoon in the empty cup. 'And it did happen?' she asked. 'The train wreck, I mean.'

Adam slowly nodded his head. His stomach was clenching like a fist, tight then loose. 'It was inevitable. Over there, if you squeal you get dealt with. The only things Mat had on his side was the fact he was a kid, and that his mom was related to Garcia. If it wasn't for that he would be dead by now.'

Kitty leaned in closer still. 'So he's not dead?'

Adam sighed, closing his eyes to the light streaming through the windows. But behind his lids all he could see was that day. The windowless room lit only by the makeshift lamps he and his assistant had rigged up. The camera rolling. Garcia's smug smile. 'He's OK.' Adam's voice was gruff. 'But no thanks to me.'

Kitty slid her hand across the table, grabbing his. He could feel the warmth as she threaded her fingers between his. 'What happened, Adam? What happened out there?'

He squeezed her hand as though nothing was more important than the connection between them. A few more words from him and she might pull away altogether. And who could blame her? After what he'd done, he could hardly bear to look at himself.

'Garcia agreed to meet with us. I should have known right then that something was up. But I had protection over there, a couple of guys with guns who weren't afraid to use them. I thought we were safe. So we arrived at this warehouse in the mountains and set up inside. Then Garcia arrived with his caravan of security, and sat down opposite me and told me to roll the camera.' Adam swallowed the last of his coffee. 'From the start, he was in charge. When I tried to ask my first question he told me to wait, that he had a gift for me. That's when two of his guys dragged Mat inside, and made him come and stand next to me.'

'He pulled a gun,' Kitty whispered.

'What?'

'He pulled a gun on you. I saw it in the script.' She was still holding his hand, her thumb resting on his palm. Somehow it felt as though she was grounding him.

'Yeah, except it wasn't me he pulled the gun on. It was Mat. He pulled out his pistol and shot Mat in both knees, then stood up and left the room. The kid was screaming – God only knew how painful it was. I was trying to stem the blood loss, shouting out for help, and in the end one of Garcia's doctors came in and took Matty away. Then they made us leave – and confiscated all our equipment – telling us that if we carried on with the documentary then they'd make sure we'd all pay. Including Mat.'

'They shot a twelve-year-old kid in the knees?' She looked horrified. 'Jesus, that's awful. What happened to him after that?'

'He recovered from the gunshot wounds, but he has a

325

permanent limp. He spent the last few months hiding with his family somewhere near Bogota.'

'You've seen him?'

Adam shrugged, though he still looked conflicted. 'He's here in LA.'

'He is?' She couldn't hide her surprise. 'What's he doing here?'

Adam shrugged. 'He's been having some meetings with the doctors at County General, to see if there's anything they can do to help.'

'That's good.' Her voice was soft. 'That he's here, that is. It must be a weight off your mind.'

He nodded, but said no more. She frowned, as though a thousand questions rushed into her mind, but she couldn't find a way to ask any of them. Slowly, she licked her lips. He watched as her tongue trailed along, his eyes following its progress.

He wondered if she understood. If she knew how he still had nightmares of Mat screaming as he held his bleeding legs. 'It was the least I could do.' He looked down, at their intertwined fingers. Hers were long, elegant, and his just big and strong.

There was silence for a moment, more awkward than the last one. She opened her mouth a couple of times to say something, then silenced herself. Adam wondered what she was thinking. He was desperate to know.

'And Everett?' she finally asked. 'How did he get involved in this?'

'With the movie?'

She nodded. 'Yeah, that. I'm guessing that's what led to your bust-up in LA.' She squeezed his fingers.

He swallowed, his mouth drier than ever. 'I discovered he'd had a script written. He gave it to me, asked me to be a consultant on the movie. I went crazy. At that time Mat was still missing, somewhere in Colombia. If Garcia had found out about it, there could have been huge repercussions.'

Kitty squeezed her eyes tight. 'And now? Is he still making that movie? I saw the script at Christmas, didn't I? Has he learned nothing?'

Adam licked his lips. The way she was looking at him made his chest feel tight as hell. It hurt and it soothed him. 'We've talked about that.' He knew she'd hate the way he sounded so guarded. 'It's under control.'

She raised her eyebrows. 'I guess that's your way of saying you don't want to talk about it.'

He didn't like the way her voice sounded. As though he'd wounded her again. 'I can't,' he told her. 'Not right now.'

'I suppose I should go, then. I have classes this afternoon.'

He found himself tightening his grasp on her hand, as though to stop her. 'We need to talk about that internship,' he told her, finally catching her eye.

'Oh, I thought that was just an excuse to talk,' she said, frowning. 'Honestly, you don't need to help me. You don't owe me anything.'

He wanted to laugh at her innocence. She thought he owed her nothing? Jesus, he owed her everything. He'd been a shell of a man when she met him, it was thanks to her that somehow he was coming back to life.

'I saw your showreel,' he told her. 'Your supervisor sent me a copy. It's damned good. You have talent, you know that, right?'

Her breath caught in her throat. All that time she'd been watching those YouTube videos, he'd been watching her work, too. She wondered if he'd been as obsessive as she was, if he'd watched it over and over again.

'You really liked it?'

He nodded. 'I did.' His voice was soft. 'It was unique, I could tell you were the one who made it.'

She licked her lips. They were suddenly dry, in spite of the coffee. 'Well thank you. That means a lot.'

'It means you deserve to get an internship. Let me help you.'

'You can't. Every time I have an interview I freeze. I might look good on celluloid, but in person I mess it up.'

His smile was sympathetic. 'Then let your work speak for itself. Let me help you. There's this project I know about, you'd be perfect for it.'

She shook her head. 'I couldn't work for you, it wouldn't feel right.'

He tried not to show how much of a kick in the gut that was. 'You wouldn't be working with me. I wouldn't ask that of you.'

'Then who?'

'Are you free tomorrow morning?' he asked. 'I'll bring you over to meet him. He's got a project ready to go. You'd be perfect for it.'

'Are you sure it's not you?' She looked suspicious.

'Would it be so terrible if it was?'

It was her turn to look down at their hands. When she looked back up at him she seemed confused. Her eyes were full of questions. 'I can't work for somebody who doesn't trust me.'

Was she only talking about work? Adam wasn't sure. 'I trust you.' His voice was resolute. 'I don't think there's a single person in the world I trust more than you.'

She blinked, as though the light was blinding her eyes. 'You do?' She bit her bottom lip.

'Yes, I do. So will you do me a favour and meet me tomorrow?' Reluctantly, he released her hand and grabbed a card from his pocket, scribbling an address on there. 'I'll be here at eleven o'clock.' He looked up at her. 'I hope you will too.'

He slid the card across to her, and she scooped it up, lifting it to her eyes. She frowned again, reading his words. 'But this is—'

'I know.' He stood up. 'I'll see you tomorrow, I hope.'

And if she didn't turn up, what then?

His heart ached as he watched her retreating back. He'd let her walk away from him once before. He wasn't planning on making that same mistake twice.

34

Who ever loved that loved not at first sight?
– As You Like It

When she walked through the door to her apartment later that evening, the place was in chaos. She'd barely kicked her shoes off before Sorcha barrelled past her, mumbling about being late for her job at a nightclub in downtown LA. Anais was running between the bathroom and her bedroom like a pinball, shouting out that she couldn't find her earrings, her purse, her credit card. That left Sia, who was sitting quietly in the living room, already dressed for wherever she was planning to go that night.

'You're late,' Sia observed, looking up at Kitty. 'Are you back to working at the restaurant again?'

'No, I was hanging out at the library.'

Sia grinned. 'You know how to live life on the edge.'

'Why's Anais so crazy tonight?' Kitty asked, as the girl started screaming about her heel being scuffed. Not that Anais was ever completely calm. Kitty had become used to the dramatics, living with three wannabe actresses. It wasn't completely different to living with her three sisters.

'There's a party tonight. Rumour is that a few big names

are going to be there. Anais's boyfriend reckons he can get us on the guest list. You should come.'

Kitty wrinkled her nose. The last thing she wanted to do was go to some bullshit evening and make small talk for hours with people who preferred staring at themselves in the mirrored glass walls than actually look at you while you spoke. 'I think I'll just stay here.'

'It could be good for you,' Sia pointed out. 'There're bound to be producers there, you could ask them about that internship.'

It was on the tip of Kitty's tongue to tell her she had an interview for one tomorrow. But that would only lead to more questions. It was hard enough fending off her sisters' interest, she couldn't face having to do the same in her own home.

After the three of them left – Sorcha climbing into her car and heading for the club, while Anais and Sia were picked up by Anais's boyfriend – Kitty collapsed on the sofa, pushing a pile of rejected dresses to the side. From the looks of them they had to be Anais's, but the girls all borrowed each other's clothes. Who knew their origins really? She'd never been part of their crowd. They were kind, but while she spent all day on campus, they were bonding over failed auditions and budding relationships. Even here Kitty was the odd one out. The story of her life.

It was barely eight. The evening stretched in front of her like an unwanted interval – a long, lonely gap that she didn't really know how to fill. She shoved a ready-meal in the microwave and then pushed it around with a fork for a while, before scraping the contents down the waste disposal and turning it on with a satisfying crunch. She managed to fill another twenty minutes by sorting out her portfolio ready for tomorrow, in case she decided to actually go to the place. Then she looked at the card again, at the address Adam had scribbled on it.

Who was she fooling? Of course she was going to go. Even if it was just to make a fool out of herself.

She even thought about killing time with a bath, but one look at the devastation Anais had left in her wake made her think again. She could barely get in the bathroom to clean her teeth and wash her face. Her shower would have to wait until morning.

When she looked at her watch it wasn't even nine o'clock. Without anything to take her mind off things, she found her thoughts drifting to Adam. *Again.* Analysing everything he said, every movement he made, remembering the way he'd pressed his hand into the small of her back as they walked across campus to the library. What had he meant by that? She wanted to call one of her sisters to dissect that afternoon's events, but she was afraid.

Afraid they'd tell her she was reading too much into it. It was as if a tiny flame of hope had been relit inside her, buffeted on all sides by a wind that she couldn't stop. The best she could do was protect it, cup her hands around it, and hope that somehow the flame wouldn't be extinguished.

After pacing around the apartment for ten minutes, she stripped her clothes off and climbed into her pyjamas, determined to get an early night. At least if she was asleep she wouldn't be obsessing over every word he'd said in the lecture theatre, or the way his face had looked when he'd told her about his experiences in Colombia.

But even in bed she was way too jittery to relax. She jumped out and grabbed her laptop, climbing back on the mattress to balance it on her knee. Then she called up the old familiar page – the one that would have been worn out by now if it wasn't virtual – and pressed play on the video she'd already watched too many times.

There he was, in full screen glory. His hair styled, his face freshly shaven, looking exactly like the man who'd stood at the front of the lecture theatre and engaged two hundred students with little more than a good story and a lot of charm.

The same way he'd engaged her in West Virginia. Except back then he'd been less than charming, and definitely not clean-shaven. And yet beneath it all he was one and the same. A man who saw a child being shot in front of him, and carried the blame like a heavy weight. A man who had been hurt by those who were supposed to love him. A man who had somehow found his way into her heart.

She pushed the laptop screen down, leaning back against the padded headrest, her eyes squeezed shut. For a moment she allowed herself to indulge in all those questions that had been shooting around her mind ever since he'd walked into the lecture theatre. Why was he there? What did it mean? Was he simply trying to make amends for the way he'd treated her, or did he want something more?

Was it normal for a guy to fly all this way just to say sorry? Was he planning to leave after the meeting tomorrow?

She clenched her fists, feeling the frustration washing over her. She couldn't just lie here wondering what the hell was going on. She needed to talk to him.

And she wouldn't take no for an answer.

Sliding the laptop onto her bedside table, she climbed out of bed and walked into the living room, grabbing her phone and the business card he'd left for her. It had his number on – something she'd never thought of asking for back when they'd been holed up in his cabin. She hadn't needed it, all she'd had to do to talk to him was follow that winding, snowy path through the forest. And when she'd left under that dark, dismal cloud, the last thing she'd thought to ask was if she could call him.

She could feel the anxiety build in her chest as she pressed the numbers into her phone, sliding her eyes between the card and her screen to make sure she had the right ones.

Just as she pressed to call, there was a buzz from the intercom. *Damn.* She hung up, rolling her eyes at the interruption, and walked over to the speaker. 'Hello?'

'It's Adam.'

She froze for a moment. Then when she tried to form a word her mouth opened and closed like a mute fish. Finally, she found enough breath to force it out. 'Hi.' Yep, that was one for the history books. Way to go, Kitty.

'Are you there?'

Shit, she'd forgotten to press the button. 'Yeah, I'm still here.'

'I thought you'd run out on me again.' The warmth in his voice made her heart pound.

'No, I'm still here,' she repeated. She sounded about as exciting as Dory right then.

'Can you buzz me in? I just wanted to talk to you about something.'

Alarmed, Kitty looked down at her pyjamas. Not the fluffy sheep ones she'd worn in West Virginia, but equally stupid. There were a joke gift from Cesca – red and white love-heart shorts, with a top that said 'Gangsta Napper'. Not exactly the cool, sophisticated look she would have liked.

'I'm in my pyjamas,' she told him.

'At nine o'clock?'

She could just imagine the perplexed expression on his face. 'That's how I roll.'

'Well it's nothing I haven't seen before.' Was he smiling? She hoped he was. 'But I promise not to drag you out on a Skidoo this time.'

Was it wrong to feel disappointed at that? 'OK, come on up. We're the last door on the third floor.' She pressed the button to release the front door. Then as she turned from the intercom, a sense of horror washed over her as she saw what a mess the apartment was. Clothes everywhere, a pile of underwear on the kitchen counter – clean she hoped – and dishes stacked in the sink that had been ignored for days. And the bathroom was even worse, it looked as though a bomb had hit it. The only room in the whole apartment that wasn't in a state of complete disarray was her bedroom.

No, that wasn't happening. Definitely not.

How long did it take to walk up the three flights of stairs to their level? Not enough time, with Adam's sure, long strides. Damn him and his muscles. There was no possible way of tidying all this away before—

There was a knock. Strong, sure. Just like him. She could feel her heart start to pound again, like it was banging on her ribcage to be let out. Swallowing down her nerves, she walked in her bare feet over to the door and slowly opened it.

There he was, in full-size glory. The man she'd been obsessing about ever since she'd arrived back in LA. He was more casual than he had been earlier – wearing jeans and a black cotton Henley that emphasised the planes of his chest. As she dragged her eyes up to look at his face – damn that gorgeous face – she could see he was checking out her clothes, too.

335

'Gangster Napper?' he questioned, raising one eyebrow. 'It suits you.' Then his eyes slid down to her shorts and her long, thankfully waxed, legs, and she wondered what emotion she could see flashing behind his eyes.

'Come in,' she said, stepping aside to let him past. 'You'll have to excuse the mess. My room-mates don't understand the concept of tidy as you go.'

Every time he stood in front of her, she found herself surprised by his height, by his strength, by the way he commanded a room. He was looking around, no doubt taking in the cramped living room, the threadbare sofas, the clothes that seemed to be everywhere. His lip quirked up when he saw the pile of underwear by the kitchen.

'They're not mine,' she told him hastily. 'None of this is my mess.'

His smile got wider.

Hastily she changed the subject. 'Would you like a drink?'

'I'm good.' He was still smiling. He looked so different without a beard covering his face.

'I'm still getting used to you being clean-shaven,' she told him, as much to fill the silence as anything.

'Don't you like it?' He rubbed his thumb along his jaw.

'It's not that I don't like it,' she told him, watching as his thumb slid smoothly along his skin. 'It's more that you look so different than the Adam I got to know.' She licked her lips, still staring at his face. 'Can I touch it?'

Was it possible to feel any more embarrassed? Why the hell did she ask that?

'Sure, go ahead.'

She took a deep breath, the air rushing into her dry mouth as she lifted her shaking hand until her fingers were almost touching his jaw. Adam closed his eyes, his lips pursing together as she brushed the pads of her fingers on his soft, smooth skin, blowing out a mouthful of air as she stroked him, her fingers moving further up, past his lips, his cheek, his eyes. Then her hand was in his hair, feeling the cropped strands tickle her palm. His eyelids flew open and he was staring at her, his gaze hot and intense.

'Please don't play with me,' he said, his voice rough.

'I'm not playing,' she whispered.

He covered her hand with his, pressing her palm hard against him, closing his eyes once again. 'Do you know how often I've dreamed of this?' he asked her. 'Of you touching me, holding me, looking at me the way you are right now?'

She knew because she'd been dreaming of it, too. Half of her felt as though she might be dreaming still.

Then he was cupping her jaw with his hand, the warmth of his palm searing her skin. 'Did I mess everything up that day?' he asked urgently. 'Did I put you off ever wanting to be with me?'

His eyes were searching hers, looking for answers. Her chest felt constricted as he caressed her face with his thumb, softly stroking as he waited for her reply.

'You didn't mess anything up,' she whispered. 'I managed to do it all by myself.' As usual. He was silent, his lips slightly parted as he took in short breaths. 'And even if you did, you could never put me off. You're all I've been thinking about. I've watched every damn interview I could find with you on YouTube. I've been watching your documentaries over and over again just so I don't feel alone.'

A slow smile broke out on his face. 'You've been watching me?'

'Apart from my school work, I haven't been doing much else.'

'Why didn't you call me?' he asked her.

'Why didn't you call me?' She tipped her head to the side, pushing against his palm.

'Because I'm a fool,' he said, his voice soft. 'Because I was afraid you wouldn't want me. I needed to make things right first, be the man I need to be. One worthy of you.'

'Is that what this is about?' she asked, touching his jaw again. 'Is that why you shaved?'

'Partly,' he said. 'And partly because I was sick of looking like a hermit. I wallowed for way too long. After you left I took a long damn look at myself in the mirror, and I didn't like what I saw.'

'You're being too hard on yourself. I always liked what I saw.'

His smile widened. 'There's other things too,' he told her. 'Like finishing my therapy, and asking to be allowed back into LA. They were all big steps, and I wouldn't have taken them if it wasn't for you.'

She couldn't tear her eyes away from his. There was too much emotion in there, pulling her in. She stared at him for a long moment, her breath caught in her throat. 'You didn't say any of this earlier at the library,' she told him. 'I didn't know how you felt.'

'I was trying to play it cool,' he admitted. 'Take it slow. Look how that turned out.'

She burst out laughing, and he joined her, the skin around his eyes crinkling as he continued to gaze at her. Then the smile slid from his lips and he moved closer, until his face was only inches from hers.

'You're so beautiful,' he whispered, tilting her head with his hand. She stared at him, still breathless. Waiting, wanting, needing.

'So are you,' she said, her voice as soft as his. 'Inside and out.'

This time his smile was brilliant. He leaned closer, until his nose brushed against hers. She could feel the warmth of his breath against her skin, the planes of his chest as he pressed his body against her.

Then he was kissing her, claiming her, consuming her, his mouth moving against hers as he slid his hands down her back. He pulled her closer still, his tongue sliding against her lips, then inside until it brushed against her tongue. She moaned softly, her hands wrapped around his neck, as though clinging on for dear life. His skin was warm, smooth, such a contrast to before, and she found herself liking the way he felt.

Liking it way too much.

Her whole body was responding to his kiss, her legs trembling, her hands shaking. Her nipples hardened beneath her pyjama top as he pushed his hands inside, sliding his palms up her back.

When he pulled back, both of them gasping for air, she found herself wanting more. 'Shall we take this somewhere more ...' She trailed off, trying to find the words.

'More tidy?' he prompted.

She laughed. 'I was going to say more intimate, but tidy works too.'

He grinned, stroking her hair back from her face. 'I like intimate,' he confessed.

'So do I.'

'And I like you, Kitty Shakespeare. Way too much for your

own good.' He kissed her again, and she delighted in the sensation, her eyes squeezing shut and her toes curling with delight. And when he lifted her up and asked her to point him in the direction of her room, she found herself enjoying his brute force a little too much.

He might have shaved his beard off, and replaced the checked shirts with designer clothes, but inside he was still the same man. Her beast with a heart, the one who tried to scare her off but only managed to pull her in. The man who tried to destroy himself, but only emerged stronger.

It wasn't quite a fairy tale, at least not like the ones she'd grown up reading. It was darker and more real than that. And yet as he held her in his arms and carried her to her bedroom, she found herself liking this one so much more.

35

We know what we are, but not what we may be

– Hamlet

She arrived at the address a few minutes before eleven, parking her car in the multi-level lot opposite the huge office building. As she crossed the road she looked up at the shiny glass tower, the winter sun reflected from the windows. It felt familiar yet strange as she walked inside, giving her details to the security guard operating the desk. Just like last time, she clipped her ID to her jeans, then took the elevator to the top floor.

When had she last been here? Was it only six weeks ago? She screwed her face up, trying to work through the dates. It felt like a lifetime since she last walked out of the elevator and onto the carpeted floor, making her way through the glass doors that led to Klein Productions.

She'd been a different person back then. More afraid, more alone. Now she didn't feel frightened at all. Didn't feel desperate either. A calmness had descended over her since the previous night, when Adam had held her in his arms.

'Can I help you?' the receptionist asked when Kitty arrived at her desk.

'My name's Kitty Shakespeare. I have a meeting with—' Damn, who was her meeting with? Should she ask for Everett or Drake or somebody else? She had no idea.

The receptionist looked back at her questioningly.

Kitty gave a nervous laugh. 'Adam Klein asked me to join him for a meeting,' she explained. 'But I've no idea who with.'

'Let me take a look for you.' The receptionist typed into her computer, then looked up with a smile. 'Yes, you're in the boardroom. Just through the door behind me and to the left. The boardroom is at the end of the corridor.'

She followed the receptionist's directions, coming to the boardroom within a minute of walking. She hesitated, wondering whether to just walk in or to knock first. In the end, politeness got the better of her and she found herself rapping on the door with her knuckles.

It was Drake Montgomery who opened the door. He grinned at her and pulled the door wider. 'Come in, we're just about to start.'

'We', as it turned out, was a room full of people. She recognised Everett, of course, and Drake, plus the beautiful Lola, who interviewed her last time she was here, though Kitty still had no idea what job she did here at Klein Productions. Then she saw Adam, sitting in the corner, smiling at her. So that's where he disappeared to so early this morning. He'd left her sated and sleepy at stupid o'clock, telling he would call her later.

Next to Adam was a teenage boy, and somebody who looked like his mother from the way she kept fussing over him. On her other side was a younger boy, maybe twelve or thirteen. Then there were three suited men – lawyers or businessmen of some kind.

If this was an interview it was the strangest one she'd ever been in. She looked around again, surprised.

Everett gave her a nod. 'Please sit down, Miss Shakespeare. Maybe we can start by making some introductions. Obviously you know me.'

Yep, she certainly did. 'Hello.'

'And I believe you've met Lola before. And Drake, of course.'

'Hi.' She smiled at both of them.

'And you know my brother, Adam.'

This time she blushed. 'Hi, Adam.'

He looked at her knowingly. 'Hi, Kitty.'

'And this is Matias Hernandez, his mother Ana, and his brother Tomas.'

Kitty recognised the name straight away. She found herself looking at the boy who'd been so brutally kneecapped, searching for evidence of his pain. But he sat there quietly, nodding over at her as Everett made the introductions, not displaying any emotion at all. 'It's good to meet you,' she told them.

'And in the corner is David Madsen, my lawyer, plus his two assistants.'

'Good morning, Miss Shakespeare,' David said, his voice low. 'As a precaution we'd like you to sign this NDA, agreeing that the discussions in this room remain private.'

The request didn't faze her – NDAs were handed out like candy in LA. She read the two-page document quickly – there was nothing in there that worried her. Taking David's pen she scrawled her name across the signature line and passed the document back to him.

'OK, well we're here today to discuss a project that starts

filming in April,' Everett told her. 'I believe you've seen some of the script before.' His voice was pointed.

'You're still filming Adam's story?' Her eyes were wide. 'Seriously?' She looked over at Adam. He looked strangely calm. What the hell was going on?

'No, I'm filming Matias's story.' Everett slid the script across the table to her. 'We've been working with Matias for months on his account of what happened to him in Colombia.'

She turned to Matias. He looked as calm as Adam. 'Are you OK with that?' she asked him.

'I'm very happy,' Matias said, his English perfect. 'It means my family and I can afford to live here in the US.'

Her gaze slid to Adam again. He looked relaxed, his long legs crossed as he leaned back in his chair. 'What about you?' she asked him.

He shrugged. 'It's Mat's story, he can tell it any way he wants to. I'm glad it means he can move over here and to safety.'

'What about your family?' she asked Mat. 'Are you worried about reprisals?'

'Mama and Tomas are moving here with me,' Mat said. 'We're going to be fine.'

She was silent for a moment, trying to take it all in. The script – it had never been about Adam after all. 'Why didn't you tell the truth about it at Christmas?' she asked Everett. 'Why didn't you tell Adam about Mat and his story?'

'I was planning to, after Christmas, once everything had calmed down. But I knew he wouldn't be happy that I went behind his back.'

'I'm still not happy.' For the first time emotion crossed Adam's face. 'I'm resigned to it. For Mat's sake.'

344

'So why am I here?' she asked, not sure who to look at for answers. 'What's this got to do with me?'

'Ask Adam.' Everett shrugged. 'It was his idea.'

Adam raised an eyebrow at his brother. It was clear there was still animosity between them, no matter how laid-back Adam tried to look.

'I agreed not to block this if I had somebody on the inside,' Adam told her. 'Somebody I could trust. And there's only one person in the world I trust enough to do this for me.'

It was her turn to raise her eyebrows. 'Me? You want me to work on the production.'

'You're free in April, aren't you?' Drake said. 'And you're still looking for an internship?'

'Yes.' Her answer was short. She kept looking over at Adam, who remained impassive. He gazed back at her, his brown eyes warm yet unfathomable. 'But I don't know if I can do this.'

'We're happy to negotiate your salary,' Everett said. 'You can talk with Drake about that afterwards. And we know you can do this,' he added. 'Adam showed us your showreel. It was good.'

'What if I say no?' she asked, still looking at Adam.

He smiled at her question. 'Nobody's forcing you to do it,' he told her. 'But the way I see it you're looking for a job, and I'm looking for some help. We might just be able to support each other on this.'

'And we really are flexible on the salary,' Drake piped in. 'You'll be pleasantly surprised, I'm sure.'

She looked over at Matias, next to his mother and brother, and then to Everett who was staring at her as intently as his brother. She couldn't work out whether he was the devil or just a run-of-the-mill arse.

'We're happy to give you a couple of days to think about it,' Everett said, 'but we need an answer fairly soon.'

All eyes in the room were on her. Adam's soft gaze, Matias's interested stare, Everett's anticipatory study. She could feel her cheeks pink up at their scrutiny.

'I'd like to talk to Adam first,' she said. 'Is there somewhere we can go?'

A moment later the two of them were walking into the same small meeting room she'd been interviewed in. The walls were still bare, the room still sparse. But this time she was sitting on the edge of the table while Adam stopped next to her, reaching out to stroke the back of her head.

'Are you OK?' he asked.

'No, not really. You could have warned me. I felt blindsided in there. Why didn't you tell me about this?'

He grinned. 'You know that NDA you signed? I signed one too. This was the only way.'

'But why did you sign it?' she asked him, confused. 'Why did you agree to any of this? After everything Everett did to you, why are you letting him do all this now?'

She was almost frustrated at his calmness. Was this really the same man who'd hit his brother at the mention of a movie?

'If Mat wants to tell his story, knowing everything he does, then I can't stop him. He's the one who wants to work with Everett.'

'But he got hurt last time, what's to stop that happening again?'

'Money and geography,' Adam said. 'What happened in Colombia won't happen here, thanks to the rule of law. And Mat and his family are being paid handsomely for his story. Enough to pay for any protection if they need it.' He sat down

346

next to her, taking her hand in his. 'Seriously, this is happening whether I like it or not. And either I go all crazy about it again and cause more unhappiness to all of us, or I accept it, and try to have a positive influence on the movie.' He nodded at her. 'You're the positive influence, by the way.'

'You trust me to do that?' she asked him.

'I trust you completely,' he said, leaning closer to her. 'I wasn't lying in there, you're the person I trust most in the world.'

'But I'd have to work with Everett.' Her mouth screwed up. 'After everything that's happened, I'm not sure I can.'

'Give him a chance,' Adam urged. 'He's still an asshole, but he's a bit more mellow than he was. He's split up with Mia, and the separation has been good for him. For both of them, really.'

'It has?' Her eyes widened. 'But what about Jonas? Is he OK?'

Adam smiled. 'I love the way you worry so much about everybody. It's one of the things I love most about you. But you don't have to worry about Jonas, he's doing fine. Getting more attention from his parents now they're apart than he ever did when they were together.'

The way he was looking at her took her breath away. As though she was something precious yet strong. She loved the way she looked, reflected in his eyes. Loved the way he couldn't stop touching her.

And he loved her, too, didn't he? Wasn't that what he'd just said? Her heart pounded in her chest at the thought of it.

'What about you?' she asked him. 'What are your plans?'

He tipped his head to the side. 'I thought I might hang around LA for a while. Maybe finish up a few projects, hang out with some friends. And there's this girl, I thought I might try to make something work with her, too. If she'll have me, that is.'

'You're going to stay?' she asked him, a little breathless.

'That's the plan.'

'What about the cabin?'

'It will still be there,' he told her. 'Mom and Dad aren't going anywhere, after all. And maybe if we get a free weekend we can fly over there. It's damn beautiful in spring, plus the perfect place for a dirty weekend.'

She laughed. 'Sounds like my kind of place.'

'That's because you're my kind of girl.' He wove his fingers into her blonde hair.

'In that case, the answer's yes.' She felt a wave of warmth wash over her. Of excitement, too. As though a door had just opened, and the sun was shining brightly through it, waiting for her to step inside.

'Yes?' he asked. 'To which question?'

'To both,' she told him. 'Yes I'll take the job, and yes I'll take you, too.'

This time his smile was dazzling. It still curled his lips as he inclined his head, brushing his mouth against hers. 'OK then,' he said, when he pulled away. 'Shall we go tell them your answer?'

She smiled at him. 'Lead on, Macduff,' she said, threading her fingers through his. 'Let's go make a movie.'

Epilogue

I would not wish any companion
in the world but you

– The Tempest

'Why are we stopping here?' Kitty looked over at Adam as he steered the car onto a gravelled driveway, then parked in front of a set of steps leading up to a cream stucco bungalow with a red tiled roof. Beyond the house she could see the cerulean blue of the Pacific Ocean, the waves crashing onto a beach that must lie just beyond the back of the building. There were palm trees, too, lining the pathway to the bungalow, and a wraparound deck that was filled with potted plants and cosy chairs.

Adam shrugged, holding his hand out to her as she climbed out of the passenger side. 'I just wanted to show it to you.'

'Aren't we going to be late?' she asked, glancing at her watch. It was almost eight. The sun was starting to make its descent into the ocean, flooding the sky with an orange-pink glow. The silhouettes of the palm trees looked beautiful, and the sound of the waves against the shore made it feel all the more peaceful.

'It's only ten minutes away,' Adam reassured her. 'You won't be late, I wouldn't let you be. This is your big moment.'

'Hardly. It's a wrap party, but the work for me is only just beginning. We have all the post-production stuff to do. I have to be in the editing suite first thing tomorrow.'

It had been a long few months. Though the majority of the production had taken place on the studio lot, Kitty had spent some time in Mexico with the cast, supervising as the filming took place. It had been too risky for Mat to travel south of the border, so she'd been the one to make sure the story stayed true to his recollection. The two of them had spent hours poring over rushes together.

And now it was coming to an end. It was a strange feeling. Like so many employees in the movie industry, she had no idea what project she'd be working on next. It felt both freeing and anxiety-inducing at the same time.

But she couldn't hide the fact she was delighted to be finally spending some quality time with Adam. She couldn't wait to wake up with him in the morning without having to rush out to a dawn shoot, or make phone calls over breakfast to locate an errant cast member.

'You want to come inside?' he asked her, pulling at her hand as she followed him up the steps to the front door. She frowned as he pulled out a key, sliding it into the lock and pushing the door open to reveal an open-plan living area. It was cosy, with warm wooden floors and white painted walls, filled with furniture that looked lived-in. So different to some of the places she'd been in during her time in LA, where the houses looked more like museum pieces than places to live.

'Who owns it?' She looked over to the other side of the room, where floor-to-ceiling glass doors revealed a large wooden deck. Beyond it was the beach – pale sand that stretched out for a good thirty feet to the ocean. It was so beautiful it took her breath away.

'We do.' He stopped in front of her, looking down at her with those deep, warm eyes. The clouds behind them had long gone. They were as clear as the evening sky. 'Well, we will if you agree to it. They've provisionally accepted my offer.' He bit down a smile, shaking his head. 'I'm doing this all wrong, aren't I? What I'm trying to ask is if you'll move in with me.' He took her hand, sandwiching it between his. She could feel his warmth, his strength, his roughness. All things that made her feel weak at the knees. 'Should I be dropping to my knees?' he asked her. 'I can do that.'

Kitty thought of her apartment in Melrose – of the bathroom she could hardly get into. Of the rooms covered in whatever mess her room-mates had left. The whole place was smaller than the living area here, and so much more claustrophobic. Two different worlds separated by only a few miles.

Not that she'd been spending too much time there in the past months. Whenever she had a free night she'd inevitably spend it at Adam's rented apartment, only a few hundred yards down the road. But it was still home, still hers.

Was she ready to leave it?

'Are you renting it?' she asked him. He was still staring down at her. She could feel warmth blooming in her face, in her chest, all over her body. The way she always reacted to him.

He slowly shook his head, his eyes still on hers. 'No, buying. I wanted something permanent.'

The way he said it made her wonder if he was talking about the bungalow or their relationship. 'It's beautiful,' she said. 'I can see why you like it. But it's out of my league, I can't afford anything like this.'

'We can,' he said. 'It's not about you or me. It's about us. And we can afford it. If you'll have it.'

She felt tears stinging at her eyes. Not just at the beauty of the place – or the beauty of his words – but at the thought of the future. She could picture Adam in the kitchen, cooking up his usual pasta, or him sitting on the deck with his laptop, working on his plans for the next documentary.

She could picture herself here, too. In her shorts, with her legs folded underneath her, looking out at the ocean as she drank a glass of ice-cold white wine. Being chased by Adam on the beach as they both laughed so hard they couldn't run any more.

Leaning down to talk to a small child – their child – in the kitchen, as she taught him how to bake cupcakes.

Christ, where the hell did that come from?

Though it was thousands of miles – and a lifetime away – the beach house somehow reminded her of the cabin. Maybe because they'd made that place theirs, too. Built a relationship inside those four walls, one that lasted beyond Christmas, beyond a brief fling, into something so big neither of them could stop it even if they wanted to.

But she didn't want to. Not ever.

'It's beautiful,' she told him, taking a step towards him. They were both in their finest tonight – Adam in a pair of tailored grey trousers and a white shirt, unbuttoned at the collar, revealing the shadow that always seemed to cover his face by the end of the day. It wasn't quite a beard, but it was sexy enough anyway. She was in a short cream dress – fitted at the bodice, flaring out to her thighs below the waist, with spaghetti straps that crisscrossed her back. Her skin was tanned from all her months here in LA, her blonde hair flowing in waves down her back. When Adam had arrived at her apartment to take them both to the party, he'd pushed her back inside again, his eyes flashing at the sight of her bare thighs, her smooth shoulders, and the way her dress clung in all the right places. He'd practically dragged her to her bedroom, leaving her in no doubt about how much he liked that dress.

She reached up, running her fingers along his stubbled jaw. 'I love it here,' she told him. 'It's perfect.'

'Will you move in here with me?' he asked her.

She nodded, her heart too full to speak.

'I want us to do this properly,' he told her. 'If we move in together, then it means something. It's a commitment from both of us. That we want to be together. That we want more.' He leaned down, brushing his lips against her cheek. 'This is where I want to propose to you, in front of the beach and the palm trees and the waves. And this is where I want us to bring up our kids, where the sun always shines and the sand's always warm.'

It was strange how in-sync they were, and yet perfectly normal, too. They were both thinking about the future – about their future – and it didn't frighten either one of them at all.

It made perfect sense, because they made perfect sense. Together, they were so much more than the sum of their parts.

'I want that too,' she said, her voice hoarse with emotion. 'So much.'

His lips crashed down on hers, and he wrapped his arms around her waist, pulling her into his warm embrace. She hooked her arms around his neck, rolling on to her tiptoes to kiss him harder, her fingers stroking his closely cropped hair.

When they pulled apart they were both breathless. Her chest rose and fell rapidly as she tried to calm her rushing pulse. He was still holding her, his arms loosely circled around her waist, his palms pressed into her spine.

'I can't wait to wake up to this view every morning,' he told her.

'You're not even looking at the beach,' she pointed out.

'That's not the view I'm talking about.' He leaned forward to kiss the tip of her nose. 'It's you I want to wake up with. Whether it's here in Malibu, or in a snowy cabin in West Virginia, you'll always be the most beautiful thing I've ever seen.'

'You always know the right things to say.'

'That's because I love you.' He slid his hands up her back, cupping her neck with his hands. 'I love you and I want you, and now I've got you I'll never let you go.'

'I love you too,' she told him, a huge smile breaking out on her face. 'But you may need to rethink the letting go bit. We're already late for the party.'

He lifted his hand from her neck, checking the silver watch on his wrist. 'Shit, you're right. OK, I'll let you go for long enough to drive us over to Everett's place. After that all bets are off.'

Sliding her hand into his, she let him lead her back out to the front of the bungalow, watching as he locked the house up before they walked back down to his car. As he pulled away, she found herself turning around, craning her head to look back at the house. Taking in the location, the beauty, the feeling of home.

It was the first step in their for ever, but it wouldn't be their last. That thought made her happier than she ever thought she could be.

*

'Uncle Adam!' Jonas called out from his spot beside his father. Adam turned to look at him, a glass of champagne in his hand. Kitty had wandered off to talk to some friends from the costume department, leaving him to order drinks from the bar.

He raised his hand to his nephew, who beckoned him with an impatient hand. Smiling, Adam walked over to him, giving his brother a curt nod when Everett turned to see him.

'How's it going?' Adam asked Jonas, ruffling his hair. 'School OK?'

Jonas grinned, nodding rapidly. 'I got a gold star today for my reading. And Angela Merritt told Kirsty Evans that she likes me.'

Everett looked down at his son. 'That's high praise indeed.' There was no trace of irony in his voice. In the past few months the producer had mellowed out even more. Ever since Mia had left him, shortly after Christmas, he'd started spending more time with his son. According to their parents, Everett was a changed man.

Adam wasn't rushing to judgement, but even he'd seen the way Ev had bonded with Jonas. That counted for a lot, in his book. The two of them might never be as close as they had been, but the hatchet had been buried, and neither one of them was planning on digging it up again.

'Is Kitty here?' Jonas asked. In spending more time with his father, he'd also been hanging out a lot on the production sets. Whenever he was there he'd singled out Kitty, shadowing her like his puppy shadowed him. Not that Kitty minded – she'd fallen in love with Jonas the way she'd fallen for Adam. He'd joked with her that maybe she just had a thing for Klein men.

Then she'd pointed out Everett was a Klein man, and that was the end of that conversation.

'She's inside somewhere,' Adam said. 'She'll be out here in a while – I bet she'd love to see you.'

'Can I go find her, Dad?' Jonas asked, pulling at Everett's hand.

'Sure, just make sure you come back in twenty minutes. I want you with me when I make my speech.'

As Jonas pushed his way through the crowds that lined his house, Adam found himself turning to Everett. 'He seems happy.'

'He is. We both are.' Everett cleared his throat. 'Mia and I have agreed on joint custody. Fifty-fifty down the middle. It works for me.'

'That's good to hear.' Adam found the corner of his lip turning up. Was he smiling at his brother?

'And you?' Everett asked him. 'Are you happy?'

Adam took a mouthful of his champagne, feeling the sparkling liquid tickle his throat as he swallowed. He thought of Kitty and the way she'd smiled up at him at the ocean bungalow. Of the image he'd had of her playing on the beach with their future kids. Of the way the setting sun had turned the sky orange, illuminating the side of her cheek, highlighting her beautiful face.

Blinking, he turned his eyes back to his brother, who was looking at him expectantly. 'Happy?' Adam asked, then nodded slowly. 'Yeah, I'm fucking ecstatic.'

'Congratulations.' Cesca squeezed her tightly around the waist. 'Your first movie. How do you feel?'

Kitty looked around Everett's oversized living room, filled with the great and the good of Hollywood. The party spilled out into the yard, people thronging around the poolside bar.

Occasionally there was a splash as an unsuspecting – and drunk – reveller managed to fall in.

'Ask me when we've finished post-production,' Kitty said, hugging her sister back. 'I'm so glad you could make it.'

'I wouldn't have missed it for the world.'

'Nor would I.' Lucy passed them both a glass of champagne she'd managed to grab from a passing waiter. 'I'm so proud of you, Kitty. I feel like a parent whose kids have finally grown up.'

'You always were our makeshift mum.' Kitty squeezed Lucy's hand, the one that wasn't holding a champagne glass. 'You should be proud. We're who we are today because of you.'

'Stop it.' Lucy couldn't hide the tears in her eyes, even though she was obviously trying her best. 'You guys should be proud of yourselves. Look at you – a best-selling playwright and an up-and-coming producer. I wish Dad could be here to see this.'

'Well at least the four of us are here.' Juliet walked over to join them, her daughter Poppy clinging to her hand. 'Well, five of us, I guess. How often do we all get to be in the same place?'

Kitty reached for Poppy, giving her niece a huge hug, then turned to Juliet to embrace her, too. 'I can't remember the last time we were all on the same continent, let alone in the same room. It makes me so happy to have you all here.' She couldn't help but feel warm inside, surrounded by her family.

'You're glowing,' Juliet said. 'You look fabulous.'

'That's because she's in love,' Cesca said. 'And you guys thought Sam and I were bad. These two put us in the shade.'

'Stop it,' Kitty said, rolling her eyes. 'At least our PDAs don't make it onto TMZ.'

'Maybe you could both tone it down,' Lucy said, looking amused. 'Take it easy on those of us who are single.'

357

Sensing the opportunity to take the spotlight from herself, Kitty grinned at her eldest sister. 'When are you going to find a nice man and settle down, anyway?' she asked her. 'I'm sure Sam and Adam might have some friends you'd be interested in.'

'If I want to get set up by my sisters, I'll tell you,' Lucy said. 'But I think I can take care of my own sex life, thank you.'

'What sex life?' Cesca asked. 'Inquiring minds want to know.'

'Um, there are children here,' Juliet pointed out, putting her hands over Poppy's ears. 'And by the way, if it's anything like mine, it's non-existent,' she whispered, before releasing Poppy from her grasp.

Kitty sensed it was time for a change in the conversation. Licking her lips, she steeled herself to tell them her news. 'Um, Adam and I have something to tell you.'

That got their attention. All three of her sisters turned around to stare at her. She noticed Cesca take a surreptitious glance at her left hand, as though to check if she'd got engaged.

Adam walked up behind her, sliding his arms around her waist. She rested the back of her head on his chest. Sam was with him – in the past few months they'd spent a lot of time together whenever Cesca and Sam were in LA. The four of them got on so well, it made Kitty's heart swell.

'Are you making an announcement without me?' Adam whispered in her ear. He didn't sound the least bit upset with her.

'I'm not doing anything without you.' Kitty smiled, tilting her head back to look up at him. 'We're a team, you know that.'

'So what's the big announcement then?' Lucy asked. 'Don't leave us all in suspense.'

'What suspense?' Jonas walked over to them, grabbing at

Kitty's hand. She smiled down at him, squeezing his palm in her own.

'Hey, Jonas.' Her niece, Poppy, gave the boy an excited smile. There were two years between them, but Poppy had latched on to him as soon as she arrived at the party. Thankfully, Jonas was as patient with the little girl as he was with everybody else.

Adam reached down to ruffle Jonas's hair. Another good thing about him being back in LA was that he got to spend a lot of time with his nephew. It wasn't unusual for Kitty to find the two of them together, their heads almost touching as they bent down and made surreptitious plans. It gave her a glimpse into the kind of father Adam would be one day. 'Kitty and I have a secret we want to tell you,' Adam told him. 'We want to tell everybody.'

'Then it won't be a secret.' Jonas looked confused.

Adam laughed. 'That's true, buddy, but we're OK with it not being a secret any more.'

Lucy was staring at Kitty's stomach. Was she looking for a baby bump? Kitty tried to bite down a smile. 'I think we should tell them before the wild speculation starts,' Kitty told him. 'Before you know it they'll have us married off with five babies.'

He squeezed her tighter. 'That sounds kind of awesome to me.'

It did to her, too. One day. Once she'd managed to establish her career. But the fact that it was 'when' and not 'if' felt like a warm sun beating down on her. Was it possible to feel any happier?

'So what's the news then?' Lucy prompted.

Adam kissed the sensitive skin below her ear. 'I asked this beautiful woman to move in with me.'

She twisted in his arms to brush her lips against his. 'And I said yes.'

His eyes flashed as he looked down at her. He gave her a smile, *that* smile, the one that promised they'd celebrate later, when it was just the two of them. When they were naked and tangled up together in bed.

The room echoed with congratulations from her family, but Kitty was too busy staring at Adam to take much in, too busy grinning at him, and seeing him grin in return.

As a child she'd dreamed of finding her happy-ever-after. Now he was here, it was more wonderful than she'd ever imagined, and so much sweeter than she'd ever believed it could be.

It really didn't get much better than that.

Acknowledgments

Grateful thanks to my editor, Anna Boatman, for all your encouragement and support. My thanks also to all of the team at Piatkus – I feel very lucky to be one of your authors. To my agent Meire Dias, and to Flavia Viotti at the Bookcase Agency, thank you for always believing in me. You both work so hard on my behalf, and I really appreciate it.

All my love to Ashley, my husband – thank you for being by my side. Let's run away to a cabin in the snow together. As long as it has WiFi and a laptop. Plus a fridge full of beer. You can chop the wood and I'll sit there and look impressed.

To my beautiful children, Ella and Oliver, I feel very blessed to be your mum. Watching you both grow up to be the funny, clever and sometimes challenging young adults you are today has been a pleasure, and I love you both so much. I hope you both achieve everything you dream of – but remember that sometimes (as in my case) it can take a lot longer than you think! The trick is always to enjoy the ride.

I have such a supportive family and so many lovely friends – both in real life and online – that to name you all would be a new story in itself. Just know that you're loved and I'm so pleased to have you in my life. Let's get together very soon.